THE
ART
OF
BREAKING
THINGS

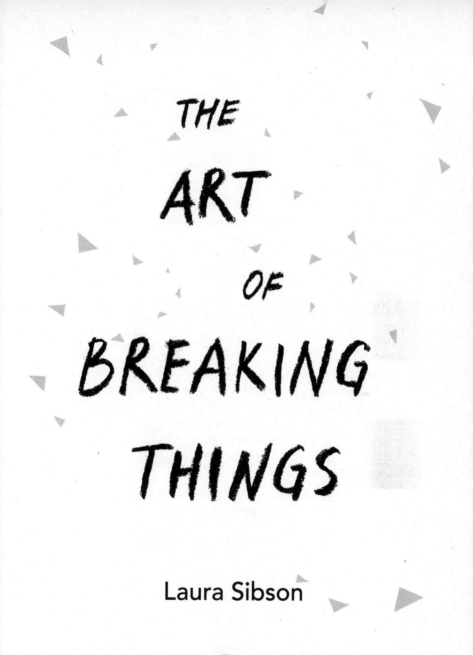

THE ART OF BREAKING THINGS

Laura Sibson

VIKING

VIKING

An imprint of Penguin Random House LLC,

New York

First published in the United States of America by Viking,

an imprint of Penguin Random House LLC, 2019

Visit us online at penguinrandomhouse.com

Library of Congress Cataloging-in-Publication Data is available.

ISBN 9780451481115

Printed in the United States of America

1   3   5   7   9   10   8   6   4   2

To all the girls who
haven't been heard yet

1

This Is How I Deal

WITH MY SKETCHBOOK and charcoal, I'd capture Ben lying on the couch as *Figure Reclining in Smoky Haze*. I could disappear into that sketch, consumed by getting his curls just right and the way his hands rest on his stomach like they're just hands, not like they can pull magic from a guitar. I'd change the setting to be a little more exotic, a little less wood-paneled basement. But I don't have my sketchbook or my charcoal. All I have is this half-empty bottle of tequila and some weed.

Dan was at my house. The truth that I've been avoiding all night weasels into my mind. Mom was sitting at the kitchen table with Dan. After all these years. I'd like to think that he needed legal advice. But . . . Mom is only a paralegal. Or maybe she was asking for information on writing essays. Truth is, I knew that neither of those possibilities made sense. I just didn't want to believe the other possibility: they might be thinking about reuniting.

"Want a shot?" I say. I knock one back and grit my teeth as the fire snakes into my belly.

Ben shakes his head and holds a joint out to me. "How about a hit?" His voice is tight from holding in the smoke.

I lean way out of my recliner to take the joint from Ben's fingers. My lungs pull the smoke in deep, and I hold it there as long as I can. Ben never teases when I cough, but I try not to anyway.

"Is Luisa going to be pissed that you left?" Ben asks.

Luisa. Shit. I'd been so focused on trying not to obsess about Mom and Dan talking again that I'd forgotten about Luisa. I pull my phone from my jeans pocket and text her. I pause in my typing to ask, "How long have we been here?"

Ben purses his lips and stares at the ceiling. "Forty-five minutes?" he says. "Or maybe a couple of hours."

"You are exactly no help."

"I whisked you away from that lame-ass party," he says.

"Whisked? Really?" I type a bunch of *I'm sorries* with a string of emojis that I hope will make Luisa forgive me.

"Did I just say *whisked*? Who says that?" Ben says. "Whisk. Whisk. Whisk." Ben takes a hit, sits the joint in an ashtray on the card table, turns off the music, and grabs his acoustic guitar, one of several instruments in the room. He strums experimentally and then settles on a folksy chord while singing *whisk* over and over.

The giggles explode out of me. Ben starts laughing too and we know it isn't that funny, but we can't stop. I snatch some paper and markers from the card table—left over from Ben working on a song or a new art project, probably—and start sketching.

"Play this," I say, holding up a piece of paper on which two girls hold hands and skip down a sidewalk.

"That? Child's play," Ben declares, strumming a playful sunshiny rhythm. We haven't played this game in a while and I'd forgotten how much fun it is. Ben and I have been in the same schools forever, growing up in a small town and all, but I didn't *know him* know him until sophomore year, when we landed in the same art class at the same table. While Mr. Mozowski spent the first day boring us about the obligatory course goals and planned assessments, Ben opened his sketchbook and began drawing. I watched the way his hand moved without hesitation across the page as an elephant appeared.

After a few moments, he turned the sketchbook to me and offered his felt-tip marker. His bold confidence inspired me, and though I was usually slow and careful with my drawings, I accepted his challenge. I created a dance floor around the elephant and drew a glass for her to hold in her upraised trunk. We traded the drawing back and forth until our disco elephant became so ridiculous that we both busted out laughing. Mr. M gave us The Look, and even though he's my favorite teacher of all time, his disapproval only served to seal our bond. I still have trouble diving into my drawing without thinking too hard about it, except when I play this game with Ben. He is the only guy I hang with who seems to actually see *me,* not just a pair of boobs or whatever else guys see when they look at me.

But sometimes, like tonight, I sort of would like to know if he thinks of me the way that he thinks of the girls he flirts with at his shows.

I sketch like mad. "Okay, this." The paper shows cars on a road at night. He nails it, playing in a way that absolutely pushes your mind to road trips and highways, dimly lit dashboards, and falling asleep with your head against the window. While he plays, I sketch again. My hand pauses as I see the scene unfolding beneath the marker. Two people kissing. I crumple the paper.

"Come on. No tossaways. Let me see."

"Nah," I say, not looking up. "That one was too easy." I draw something safer. A butterfly on a flower beside a pond. A bright sun. Some grass. "This?"

Ben raises his eyebrows and slows the tempo of his playing to something easy and quiet. "That was a gimme," he says. "I thought you were going to draw something hard."

I smile and fall back on the recliner. "Guess I don't have the touch tonight." I think of the two figures kissing in my balled-up drawing; the guy has the same curly hair as Ben. Luisa texts back asking who I'm hooking up with. I respond that the only hooking up I'm doing is with this bottle of tequila, as if typing will hold me to my word.

After setting the guitar in its holder, Ben turns the music back on. He lights a cone of incense and retrieves the tiny joint from the ashtray. "You want to come sit?" he says, patting the couch cushion next to him.

"No, I'm good over here." Sitting close to him right now would make it hard to ignore that we're a boy and a girl alone in a house at night.

"Well, in that case," he says, lying down again across the length of the couch. He holds the joint in one hand and with the other, taps his fingers on his stomach to the beat of the music pouring from his speakers.

I thought Mom was finished with Dan for good. But what if she isn't? I doodle thick, choking vines on my jeans with the marker.

"I'm glad we left," Ben says.

"Yeah, thanks for that." When I walked up to my front door after my Saturday night shift at the diner, through the windowpane I could see Dan sitting at the kitchen table. I hadn't even stepped inside. I'd gone straight to Luisa's and begged her to drive because I wanted to get royally messed up. But once we got to Jeremy's, even though the house was packed with people I know, I felt like an island. The party eddied around me, no one approaching me or giving a shit about the confusion swirling inside. Until Ben, who'd found me sitting on the steps, nursing a lukewarm beer in a red Solo cup. When he asked if I wanted to hang at his house, I'd thought others were coming, so I was surprised when it was just us.

"Seemed like you needed cheering up and Jeremy's wasn't doing it," Ben says now from his spot on the couch. His voice offers relief from the noise in my head.

"Jeremy's definitely wasn't," I agree. My phone buzzes again.

"Did it work?" A smile is laced through his words.

"Did what work?" I've lost the thread of the conversation.

"Are you all cheered up?"

"I *am* cheered," I say, trying my best to sound cheered.

"Hmm, not sure I believe you."

Luisa's text warns me not to eat the worm in the tequila bottle and teases that Ben would be yummier. I respond with a stream of laughing/crying emojis. Luisa thinks that Ben and I would make the perfect couple. If there is such a thing as a perfect couple.

"What could cheer me up more than getting baked in your basement?" I say.

Ben raises his head from the couch, cocks half a grin at me. "*Get baked in Ben's basement.* Has a nice alliterative ring, don't you think?"

His grin sends a flutter deep in my belly that I chase away with another shot. "You should get T-shirts made."

"Somehow I don't think Susan would approve," he says.

"Since when do you call your mom Susan?"

"Let's not bring my mother into this."

That sends us into another round of giggles, like bubbles rising from a bottle, and when they stop, the room is quiet except for the music. The smoke from the cone of incense drifts on an invisible current, wreathing us until it disappears into the air we both breathe. Ben drops his head back on the cushion, and when he closes his eyes, mine are drawn to him. There's no harm in looking. His jeans ride low on his lean body. Bare feet angle up from the end of the couch because he's too tall to fit. With eyes still closed, he pushes his T-shirt up to scratch his stomach and I see the dark hair tracing its way down from his belly button and disappearing into his jeans. My mind whispers that there are other ways to nail down this moment besides a sketchbook or some charcoal. My mind is a traitor and I'm worried that my body is not far behind. I've got to get out of here before I do what I'll regret.

"I think I should go." I sit the bottle of tequila on the small table and rise from the recliner, weaving a bit on my feet. Last time I stood up, the floor didn't tilt like this. Just how much tequila did I drink?

Ben raises his head from the couch to peer at me. The gesture tightens his abs. "You're not going anywhere."

I clear my throat, look away from his exposed stomach at anything, the wall plastered with giant band posters, the rickety card table, the smoke circling our heads, twining us together. I'm losing the fight. I'm going to jump him, and we'll have sex, and then our friendship will be just another broken thing that I push into the shadows. "Emma might need me," I say, reaching for an excuse, one he'll believe.

"You said she's sleeping over at a friend's house," Ben says.

He's looking at me again, meeting my eyes, and I'm getting a vibe that maybe I'm not the only one thinking about us as more than friends. But this is Ben. My best guy friend. Nothing more.

"And you and I have a promise." His fingers pick the beat of the music again, as if the topic is settled.

The promise. That we wouldn't drive if we were messed up.

"Man, hear everything going on in this tune? If I could create songs like Kevin Parker, the band would have a recording contract tomorrow."

The promise forces me to sink back into the stinky recliner. I pull the lever to raise my feet; if I'm staying, I might as well be sure that I'm going to remain in my own chair.

"You *do* create awesome songs, and Arthouse Scream Machine *will* have a recording contract," I say. "I totally and one hundred percent believe!"

I expect Ben to laugh at my superlatives, but he's quiet, fiddling with the string bracelet around his wrist. I'd made a bunch of them last summer, and Ben had hinted strongly about how much he needed one. That was around the same time they were naming the band. Ben had found a group of guys who were as serious about music as he was and they wanted to go beyond playing for fun. While the band smoked weed and debated over whether they should call themselves 21st Century Avocado Death Spiral or Arthouse Scream Machine, I'd woven Ben's favorite colors, orange and green, into the slim bracelet and given it to him on the Fourth of July when we were on the way to a party at Keith's. After they decided on Arthouse Scream Machine, Ben put on the bracelet and said it would be his good luck charm. But I'm not sure a few square knots are all that strong.

"You really think we're that good?" he says, his eyes trained on the bracelet.

"You are absolutely that amazing." I smile, pulling a grin from him.

"Let's drink to that!" he says.

I raise my bottle. "To being awesome!"

"To being awesome," Ben says, tipping his beer in my direction. He sets the beer on the table and swings his legs around to sit up. He rests his elbows on his knees and looks at me. "Skye?"

"Hmm?" My eyes drift closed, and my recliner becomes a tiny boat on a rocking sea. I push the lever back down and set one foot firmly on the floor. Seeing out of one eye focuses everything—pretty much. "What were you saying?"

"Oh, MICA!" he says like he's found something. "When's your interview?"

The butterflies in my belly wake up at the mention of my art school: Maryland Institute College of Art. I can call it mine because I've been admitted. I just need to make the scholarship committee fall in love with me so I have money to attend. "Thursday."

"Thursday," he says, leaning back on the couch. "A perfect day for a visit."

"Why's Thursday perfect?"

"I don't know exactly." He blows out a stream of smoke. "Just sounds perfect, doesn't it? Thursday."

"Thursday!" I join in, singing it out to the room.

"What are you taking?"

"Myself!" I start laughing, and Ben does too.

"I meant what pieces? Of art?"

"Oh, right! Definitely the Whomping Willow landscape and the still life of Emma's stuff that you and I decided on. But Mr. M still needs to weigh in on some others."

"No self-portrait?"

We have to complete one for Art 4. "You know I haven't started mine," I say.

I look in the corner where Ben's self-portrait sits, almost

complete. It's a multimedia piece: his face in pastels surrounded by bits of sheet music, guitar strings, and picks.

"Why haven't you?" His voice is not judgmental, just curious.

I shake my head so that my hair falls over my eyes and I cross my arms over my chest. The idea of staring at my own face for hours makes me want more tequila. "I just haven't figured out the right medium yet," I say.

"That's okay. Those other pieces are awesome. The committee will love you."

Ben's just spoken my dream. That my portfolio review and interview with the scholarship committee will go well, that they'll give me the money I need, and that this time next year, I'll be pursuing my art and not living anywhere near home. Even though Mom considers an art major completely impractical. "As long as I don't screw up the interview," I say.

"Let's drink to nailing the interview," Ben says.

I raise my bottle once more in Ben's general direction.

"You're too far away," he calls to me, as if I were on another continent. "Come closer."

He has no idea how much I'd like that. I lean over from the chair, keeping myself at a safe distance.

"Still too far," he says, shaking his head like he's disappointed in my lack of effort. He doesn't realize my level of restraint.

"Is it that important?"

"It's of the utmost importance that we toast your upcoming

interview. It's like a good luck charm. If we don't toast, bad things may ensue."

"Well," I say, "I need all the luck I can get." If the committee doesn't give me the scholarship, it won't matter that MICA has let me in, because I won't be able to afford to go. By invoking the potential for bad juju, Ben draws me to him, despite my fight to stay away. In three short steps, I'm standing next to Ben's couch. I lean toward him to clink his can with my bottle. Ben grabs my wrist and I fall on him. He chuckles as beer gurgles from his can. "I so got you." His voice is low.

He has no idea. I push up so that I'm sitting next to him on the edge of the couch. I feel the solidness of his chest beneath my hands. It would be too easy to lean down, skim his lips with my mine. Nibble his earlobe. I want this. I want it so bad. His hands encircle my wrists on his chest. My heart starts going double-time and I feel my breath speeding to match. Ben's thumb rubs my inner wrist, and a tingle zips through my body. I feel myself leaning toward him even as my mind is screaming at me to stop, not to mess with this friendship, not to ruin this perfect thing. I lean closer still. So close that our breath mingles and his eyes, red from smoking, hold mine. My head swims with tequila, but I'm sure that no boy has ever looked at me in the way that Ben looks at me now. He wants this too. He wants it as much as I do.

2

What Happens After

POUNDING ON THE door shocks us away from each other. I jump up and look away, finding my way back to the recliner. My heart is still stuttering. I touch my lips. They almost betrayed me. But they didn't, I remind myself. Nothing happened.

"Party's here!" a deep male voice booms through the door along with the pounding.

Ben sits up, runs a hand through his hair, and glances at me, but my eyes skitter away.

"Sounds like Keith," I say to my lap. Keith's personality is even bigger than he is, and that says a lot. He can be obnoxious, but he's a great football player, he always has beer, and he's awesome with cars. These things go a long way in our circle of friends.

"Which means Ashton too." Ben looks at me again, but I don't know what his eyes are saying to me. I adjust my top as if I have something to hide. But nothing happened, I say again in my mind.

"Open sesame, man!" Keith yells.

"Door's open, dumbass!" Ben calls back.

Keith pushes his way in with Ashton right behind. They own the room when they enter it. I shrink, and Ben doesn't feel just a few footsteps away; he's a world away.

"Yo, what's going on?" Keith slams two six-packs on the card table, sending the bong wobbling. Ashton stands closer to the door. I feel his eyes on me.

"Good timing," Ben says, holding his hand up for a beer. "Skye here just spilled my last one." He's so casual, like he didn't just pull me down on top of him. But nothing happened, I keep saying to myself. He was joking around. I want to adjust my shirt again, but I force my hands to remain still. My heart refuses to slow down because it's half-thrilled that maybe Ben sees me that way and half-bummed that maybe Ben sees me that way. Even if he does, it's only tonight. Because we're messed up. It means nothing.

"Ditch us at Jeremy's, but you'll drink my beer." Keith loosens a can from the plastic ring and tosses it to Ben, who catches it in one hand.

"Jeremy's sucked," Ben says. He taps the top of the can before cracking it open to keep the bubbles down.

"Yeah, but you could've told us you were bouncing," Keith says.

I glance at Ben, waiting to see if he'll protest, saying that he texted those guys to come over, but he says nothing.

"You want one, Chicken Little?" Keith says to me. Everyone

thought he was hilarious the first time he said it—the night I fell down after one too many tequila shots.

"Don't call me that and yeah to the beer," I say, not because I need a beer, but because if you're going to hang with the guys, you've got to party like the guys.

Keith tosses the can, which of course I fumble. Now I won't be able to open it for a while. I set the can upright on the small table next to the recliner.

"You guys hooking up or what?" Keith says, looking from me to Ben.

"No!" I feel my face running through all the reds of the color palette from peach to crimson with some vermilion thrown in too.

"I just figured because you didn't ask us to come along . . ." Keith presses.

"Just partying," Ben says. "Like always." He says this last part quietly.

Ashton looks from me to Ben like he's evaluating a football play. He and I had a thing in the summer after junior year, but he's been with Ellen most of our senior year. I'm not about to touch that. Ellen Kim and I were friends in middle school, but in high school she decided I wasn't good for her reputation. Since then, she's worked her way to class president and captain of the Spirit Squad.

On the card table, the incense has burned down to a blackened smudge and the musky-smelling smoke, so thick and curling moments ago, is nothing more than a weak, thin stream.

"Who wants to hit the bong?" Ben says, a little loudly, like maybe he's changing the subject. Sometimes I can't tell if Ben actually likes Keith and Ashton or if they're all friends simply because they've always been friends and in a small town, there aren't many to choose from.

"I'm in," Ashton says. He digs in the front pocket of his jeans and flips a quarter in the air, catching it in his palm. "And then maybe Quarters?"

"Quarters sounds good," Ben says. "There're some chairs over there." Ben points to the folding chairs leaning against the wall.

Ashton slips the quarter back into his pocket, and his hazel eyes, so striking against his darker skin, stray to me, making me hyperaware of the way my tank top clings and just how skinny my skinny jeans are. My body auto-responds to male attention, which might explain my reputation. I kick the footrest down and sit up, leaning my elbows on my knees to watch Ben while he packs the bong. Ashton grabs a folding chair and sets it up between my recliner and the card table.

Keith lands heavily on the couch next to Ben and cracks open his beer. If I were going to draw these guys, it would be called *Same, but Different* on account of how they all come from this town and they're similar in small ways, but unique in big ones. Starting with pencil, I'd nail down their different heights. I'd work on Ashton's muscled build versus Ben's lean one. Then I'd draw Keith's slightly shorter, but much bulkier body, and I'd work on his wiry black fade next to Ashton's twists and Ben's dark curls hanging into his eyes.

Moving to pastels, I could use the burnt sienna that has a touch of red in it for Keith's skin and probably an ocher on the yellow side with a light smidge of terra-cotta for Ashton's and a sandy beige for Ben's. But it would take more than a few minutes to capture Ashton's cocky assuredness compared to Keith's who-gives-a-shit attitude and Ben's alt-rocker vibe.

"Man, you got any *good* music?" Keith says.

The Strokes is blasting from the speakers, all big guitar and gritty voiced.

"Don't be a hater," Ben says. "The Strokes single-handedly brought back garage rock and made the guitar important again."

"Whatever, man. You got anything from *this* year?" Keith says.

Ben hands Keith the bong and picks up his phone. "I've got everything from all the years," he says. He scrolls and clicks, changing the tunes to the latest by Chance the Rapper. Even I like Chance, and I don't listen to that much rap.

"Aw, yeah. Much better," Keith says.

Ashton sits in that wide-legged way that some boys do. His knee presses into mine. He catches my eye, quirking an eyebrow and offering half of his Hollywood grin.

"Where's Ellen tonight?" I ask, to dim the sparkle.

"She's babysitting," Ashton says to me, scooting his chair a little closer. "And I've got something to celebrate."

I move slightly away from Ashton so that I don't feel his leg against mine. I'm combustible right now and I can't let Ashton be the spark.

"Oh, yeah? What's that?" I ask, trying not to look at his

full lips or remember what they feel like on my skin.

He inclines his chin toward me. "Just heard that I got that scholarship."

"That's awesome!" I say, and I mean it. I'm all for people getting out of this town.

He nods. "Yeah, it is."

"For football?"

Ashton laughs. "Well, it's not for academics."

He leans down and flips the recliner footrest up, popping me backward with it.

"What are you doing?" I protest.

Ashton grins. "I need somewhere to put my feet." He stretches his long legs over mine.

"Your legs are heavy!" I move mine on top of his. Funny how he'd rather celebrate with us instead of with his girlfriend. Then again, babysitting isn't much of a celebration.

"What've you guys been up to?" Keith says to Ben.

"Smoking. Drinking. Skye has been trying to reach the all-time record in tequila shots."

Nothing about how he had tugged me down on top of him. Not that he would admit to that. Ashton swivels my chair back and forth with his foot. A thought slips into my wasted mind. If I don't want to mess up my friendship with Ben, and Ashton's showing me attention . . . I push the thought away. Ashton belongs to Ellen.

"Any more tequila?" Keith says, handing the bong past me to Ashton.

"It's half-empty," I say, holding up the bottle and shaking it.

"Man, that was my tequila," Keith says, grabbing the bottle from me. "I left it here last week for safekeeping."

"I was wondering where that came from," Ben says, taking the bong from Ashton.

Ashton's phone buzzes. He stares at the face while he exhales a long stream of smoke. His thumbs compose a quick text before he clicks the silent button and slides the phone back into his pocket. Probably Ellen. Ashton and Ellen are an excellent example of why I think relationships mostly suck. An even better example would be my mother and Dan, unless good relationships are supposed to feature yelling, crying, and a general tug-of-war.

I've got to pee. Really bad. I pull myself from the chair and focus on reaching the bathroom without looking desperate.

I crack one eye open. Gray morning light penetrates the haze of Ben's basement. Morning? But I don't remember . . . I peer into the dim light. I'm lying on Ben's couch. The afghan his grandmother made for him is draped over me. How'd I . . . ? I push the blanket off of me. My jeans are unbuttoned and unzipped. My bra is . . . not on my body. My head is cracking in half and it tastes like something has died in my mouth.

Dan was at the house. Last night with Mom. And Emma? Emma's at her friend's house. It's Sunday morning. I'm supposed to pick her up. What time is it? And my car. My car. Where's my car?

It's at Luisa's. I feel around the dirty floor for my boots. Dan is back.

Flashes of memories from last night strobe through my mind as I button my jeans. Ben and I partying. Ashton and Keith showing up. Quarters with the boys. I shrug into my jacket, hoping it hides my lack of a bra. Something almost happened with Ben. But it didn't. Or did it? Ben's bedroom door is closed. Before there's a chance of facing him, I grab my phone and keys from the dish on the table and slip out like last night's smoke.

Emma has already texted me five times and called twice. I text her back that I'll be there in ten minutes. Then I call Luisa and hope that I can make good on my promise to my little sister. When she answers, I brace myself for questions.

"So . . . your car is here, but you're not. What happened? I didn't hear from you again after we texted."

I squish my eyes shut and pull in a deep breath through my nose. I let the breath out. "Not sure."

"Seriously? You don't remember?"

I reach into the tatters of my memory for what happened after the guys showed up. A dim impression of Ashton and me in the laundry room by the bathroom. Whispering in my ear. Hazy after that. "Not so much."

"You ate the worm, didn't you?"

"Ew, no! At least I don't think I did."

"You may as well have if you don't remember."

"What about you?" I ask.

"There maybe was a little something with Matt." I can hear the smile in her voice.

She's been lusting quietly after one of the guys in our group for a while now, determined to have a boyfriend before we graduate.

"Really?" My tone asks for more info.

"We just talked. Let's see what happens," she says.

"He's a decent guy. I would approve that match."

"Like I need your approval."

"True. You don't. But I get a vote, don't I?"

"I'll allow you a vote."

"Okay," I say, then after a pause. "Lu, can you come get my sorry ass?"

"I figured. Give me five, okay?"

"You're the best."

"I know. You're at Ben's?"

I look back at his house. I'm not sure what I'm expecting, Ben standing barefoot in his jeans, with that smile alongside a plate of waffles? Or Ben standing with arms across his chest, shaking his head at what a loser I am? I start walking. "I'll be at the corner. You know, at Meadowbrook?"

"Got it."

I trudge the two blocks to Meadowbrook, clutching my jean jacket against the February chill and against my bra-less chest, hoping that none of the neighbors see me in my post-party morning glory.

Luisa shows up as promised. "You look like shit."

"Thanks for that boost to my self-esteem."

"You got it." Luisa smiles at me, dark eyes flashing. Her thick black hair is still straightened from last night and she's pulled it into a ponytail. If I drew her I'd call it *Day and Night*. Yeah, she's a model student at school, but she also tears it up on the weekend.

I buckle in and Luisa points the car back toward her house. We drive through Ben's neighborhood of two-story houses with garages and into Luisa's area of tiny ranchers and split-levels. I'd use graphite pencil to capture this area and *Suburban Clones* is what I'd call it. Some houses have more shrubs, and some have a bay window instead of a regular window. Some have abandoned toys on the front lawn. One has a rusted truck up on cinder blocks, and a couple have sofas on the front porch. But essentially, they are all the same. Pennswood is made up of little neighborhoods like this one. At least Luisa has a single home, unlike me in my tiny town house.

"Was it only you and Ben last night?" she asks.

"Yeah. For a while."

"I'm telling you, Skye. He likes you."

"Ben and I are friends." I don't state the obvious: if we hooked up, the friendship would be over because who wants to be friends with the girl he just screwed?

"Well, if no one was there . . ." Luisa's moving toward the obvious conclusion, but she doesn't have all of the information.

"Why do you assume that I hooked up with someone?"

Luisa gives me a look that reads *that's what you do*.

I turn my face to the window. "Ashton and Keith showed up."

Luisa is quiet, like she's turning over this information in her mind. "Do you think Ashton?" she asks.

I cringe. "I don't know. We've got history, so maybe? I hate that I might have hooked up with him."

"But you were wasted."

"Why does that matter?" I hide my face in my hands.

I get enough blowback just for hooking up with random guys, but to be with someone's boyfriend? I never thought I'd be *that* girl.

"Let's hope Ellen doesn't find out."

"Yeah, that." I lean toward her and kiss her on the cheek. "Thanks for the ride. Give Miguel a hug for me." I try to say it with the accent that Luisa taught me.

"You know he wouldn't tolerate a hug." Luisa's brother has autism and doesn't like too much touching. "Take some gum. You stink." She holds out a pack.

"Give him a fist bump then." I pop the gum in my mouth. "Talk later?"

Luisa nods. As I'm shutting the passenger door, she rolls down the window and calls to me. I turn back and lean in the window.

"You never told me why you were so hell-bent on getting messed up last night," she says.

In my mind I see Mom and Dan sitting at the dining room table together. "Do you remember Dan?"

Luisa's eyebrows pull together in thought. "Of course. Your mom's ex-boyfriend. The one you didn't like."

"He was at the house last night."

"It's been, what? Three or four years?"

"More like five."

"Do you want to talk?" she says, concern wrinkling her brow.

I shake my head.

Luisa and I have been friends for a long time, bonding over having single moms and younger siblings we take care of. We've shared most everything with each other—our dreams and our fears, our firsts and our heartbreaks—but there was one thing that I never shared. It was so confusing and scary at the time, and since then, I'd just shoved it in a corner of my mind and kept it locked far away from my heart.

"I've got to get Emma," I say.

"Sounds like we need a good *Gilmore Girls* binge," she says.

"Yes," I say back, though not even *Gilmore Girls* can get rid of the memories pushing their way back into my mind after all these years.

She beeps her car twice as she pulls away. I wave and dig in my pocket for keys to Lucy, my 1988 Jeep Cherokee. When I had finally saved up enough to buy her, Ben and I had a naming ceremony, figuring that any car that was older than we were deserved a name. Ben had thought "Lucy" was a bit uninspired, but as soon as I saw her, I knew she was a Lucy. On the short drive to get Emma, I think about Dan and Mom sitting at the dining room table and what that may have meant.

3

BEFORE: I am ten.
Summer before fifth grade

"SEE THIS?" DAN says, holding the small, orange blossom with care between two fingers. "It's called jewelweed. Come here, watch."

I edge closer as he lifts the leaves of the plant to reveal seeds smaller than a pea. He presses a seed between his thumb and forefinger and lets go. The seed pops and spirals into itself. I smile, delighted.

"Can I try?" I ask, moving closer.

"Be careful, they'll blow at the slightest touch." He guides my hand toward the seed. "Okay, you do it."

I squeeze and let go. I squeal at the funny feeling of the seed exploding.

"Jewelweed can cure poison ivy," Dan says. "And it often grows nearby."

"Seriously?"

Dan smiles at me. "Seriously." He breaks off a stem of jewel-weed. "The liquid inside the stem staves off the effects of the rash."

"'Staves off'?"

"Prevents. Or at least reduces."

Dan knows something about everything. "How do you know all this stuff?" I ask.

"Which stuff? Words or nature?"

"Um, nature."

"I was an Eagle Scout. And don't say *um*." His tone is impatient, like when he had to remind me of something that he'd already said. "You've seen all of my patches. Nature was one of them. We had to learn about plants and collect their seeds. I learned that if you brush against poison ivy, you could spread some of this on you." He squeezes the stem of the jewelweed until a whitish liquid bubbles out. With his forefinger, he rubs it on my inner arm.

His calloused finger tickles that tender area. After a moment, the whitish liquid becomes clear and sticky on my skin. I rub it off.

"But you would need to know that you rubbed against poison ivy in order to know that you needed the jewelweed," I say.

"True."

There is still no sign of Mom and Emma on the trail behind us. "Geez, where are they?"

Dan turns to look back down the path. "Emma may have needed to stop."

"Emma's so slow. Maybe we should hike back to find them."

"Be patient," he says. "Your sister is still little."

That's true. In September, I will be in fifth grade and Emma won't even be starting kindergarten yet. She is cute and all, but right now I want to keep hiking.

"Do you want to go wading for crayfish? Or looking for sassafras?"

I weigh my options. I love how when you pull sassafras from the ground, the plant smells like root beer, but I am very good at catching crayfish. "Wading," I say.

"I'll hold your clothes."

"Huh?" The creek is only about five inches deep and I have excellent balance. Mom has said so. There's no way I would fall.

Dan sighs. "Don't say *huh*. You have your bathing suit on, yes?"

I nod.

"Take off your shorts and T-shirt in case you get wet."

I know that I won't get wet, but I also know not to argue with Dan. Everything has been so good today. Mom's been happy and I don't want to mess it up.

I wriggle out of my jean shorts and tank top and hand them to Dan.

With care, I step from stone to stone, peering down into the rippling water to spot the crayfish that hide among the rocks. "There's one," I whisper, knowing from experience that a shout will scare it away. I squat and watch the spot where the crayfish hid. With slow, careful movements, I reach into the water with cupped hands.

"Skylar," Dan says in a low voice.

I turn, and Dan snaps a photo on his phone.

"Perfect," he says, still looking at me. "You're a nymph out there in the creek."

A nymph sounds like something mysterious and beautiful from one of Dan's huge novels. But I'm just a skinny kid in an old bathing suit. The crayfish scuttles away.

"We're here!" Emma crashes through the weeds, a four-year-old monster frightening every living thing within a quarter-mile radius. "Look what we found!" She clutches a fistful of wildflowers. "Ooh, can I go in too?" She takes a step toward the water.

"You might slip and fall, Emma," Dan says, grabbing the hand that wasn't holding the flowers.

"Did you catch anything?" Mom asks.

"I spotted a crayfish, but he got away." I stood up.

"I want to find a crayfish too." Emma's lower lip pushes out.

"It's okay, Em," I say, leaping from rock to rock toward the sandy bank. "I'll show you this cool jewelweed that Dan just found."

"Where are your clothes?" Mom asks when I land on the shore.

"Dan thought I might get wet."

Mom wrinkles her brow and then shrugs. "Better to be safe than sorry, I guess."

Dan hands me my things.

"My goodness, I need to get you some new clothes," Mom says as she watches me wriggle back into my shorts. "Those are getting a bit too snug."

Dan glances at me and then at Mom. He walks Emma to the main path. "Ready for our next adventure?" he asks.

"Yes!" Emma says, and they march down the path.

"Don't forget to show Mom the picture," I say, taking my spot behind Dan and Emma. "Dan said I'm a nymph," I add proudly.

4

And What Happens After That

"HOW WAS THE sleepover?" I ask as Emma climbs into Lucy.

"You're late," she snaps at me. "I was the last one picked up."

I wish she'd talk a little quieter, but I deserve this. Even though I never would've done all those shots if it weren't for seeing Dan at the house.

"You're right. I'm sorry." I pull away from the house, paying close attention to the traffic. I'm so hungover that I don't totally trust my driving right now. We pull out of Julia's neighborhood, a sparkly new development called Penn's Manor, full of McMansions on tree-less plots of land that used to be open fields. "But besides me being late, did you have fun?"

"Julia's mom had to be somewhere and I tried to call you, but you didn't pick up." Emma is not going to let me off easy today.

"I'm sorry. I overslept."

A flash of the night before slides into my mind. Ben saying he's tired. Keith passed out on the recliner. Something about strip poker.

"Julia's mom said that she'd only planned for kids to stay through breakfast. Not lunch," she says.

"Julia's mom sounds like a bitch."

Ashton and I sitting on the couch. My stomach churns.

"You're not supposed to talk like that."

"Sorry, but she sounds like she has a stick up her butt. I don't see the big deal."

I dig into the muck to try to remember Ashton leaving. I can't find any memory of what happened. The blanket. Who put the blanket on me? If it was Ben, did I hook up with him? I can't even let my mind go there. Not to mention: missing bra.

"You shouldn't talk about people when you don't even know them," Emma's saying. "Julia's family is so nice."

I imagine that by *nice* Emma means normal. "You're right, I shouldn't. But if Julia's mom was so frustrated, she could've just taken you home."

"That's not how sleepovers work," my sister says to me. "God," she says to the window.

"Did you try to call Mom?" I ask.

Emma shakes her head. I let that sit for a minute before I think of the possible reasons why Emma would rather be embarrassed at her friend's house than call our mother.

"Because you were afraid of getting me in trouble?" I ask.

She nods, and now it's not just my head cracking in half. It's my heart too.

"Other families are there for one another." I can hear the tears clouding her whisper. "Other families are normal. Ours isn't. Ours sucks."

"Oh, Em." She's playing with the zipper on her jacket. I did this. I made her wish that she lived in a different family. "Em, I *am* here for you. This was just a dumb morning where I messed up. Doesn't mean our family totally sucks."

Emma looks down at her lap.

"Think about the fun stuff we do. Painting our rooms?"

She nods, and I hope she's remembering how much fun we had creating the blocks and stripes of color in her room after I'd moved to the basement.

"Dance routines? Makeovers?"

Emma nods and wipes her tears away.

"Movie nights with takeout from Hunan? With chopsticks and tea in tiny Chinese teacups?"

She nods again and I see a smile ghosting the corners of her mouth.

"I was late today and I'm so sorry. But we don't really suck, right?"

"We don't."

"Now tell me, did you have fun?"

"Yes," Emma says grudgingly while staring out the window.

"Well, what did you do?" I poke Emma. I can always get her to smile. Always. "Come on." I poke her again. "Did you raise the dead?"

"Stop," she whines halfheartedly and then smiles. "We baked the world's ugliest cupcakes. They had popcorn in them and sprinkles, which was pretty gross, but also fun."

We drive past strip malls of take-out restaurants, banks, and pharmacies, where storefronts with FOR LEASE signs in the windows sit empty and dark. Our town-house community is wedged just off Pennswood Pike, the main road. "At least we have a pool," Mom often says when something goes wrong. Not that she ever has time to use it. I'm sure she'd prefer a little single home with its own driveway to a town house where things break down—even if it has a pool—but when she left Dad, Mom couldn't afford a regular house. And Dad was no help, all the way in Santa Fe with barely any money.

Our building is at the far end of the community, bordering a wooded area blocking us from the Pike. I wonder if Dan will be at the house. I haven't texted Mom because I'm not sure I want to know.

"We watched *Grease* and sang all the songs. Julia says I'll get a part in the musical, no doubt."

"Of course you will. Tryouts this week, right?"

"Yeah. Oh, and we texted these boys, Thomas and Liam . . ."

I glance at my little sister, eleven going on fifteen, in her multicolored leggings and oversize shirt. A few tiny braids start at her temple, disappearing into the rest of her long hair piled on her head and secured with an elastic. I had long hair like that when I was eleven too. But I'd cut it off and I've kept it short ever since.

"Are you even listening to me?" Emma says as I pull into the parking spot in front of our house.

"Yeah!" I try to push a smile into my tone. "Texting Thomas and his friends to meet you somewhere only you're not there."

The windows of our town house reflect the sun back into my eyes as we get out of the car, hiding what's inside.

"Emma?"

"Yeah?"

"Thanks for not calling Mom."

When we walk in, Mom is curled up on our worn, red couch reading a magazine. She's alone. My shoulders drop in relief. Her long hair is pulled back, and she's wearing a sweatshirt and jeans. At this moment, I'd call her *Whirligig at Rest*. Mom is always moving, and even when sitting, she's usually on her email or going through bills or folding clothes. Seeing her sitting and reading is like witnessing the sun stop its movement across the sky.

"There are my girls!" she says with a big smile. I can't help but smile back. Mom's smile does that to people.

"Hi, Mom." Emma flops on the couch and starts thumbing her phone. Their heads nearly touch, the same dark brown hair as mine, though Mom's color comes from a bottle now.

Mom hugs her. "How was your sleepover, honey?"

Emma eyes me and then looks at Mom. "It was great. Julia was super happy and we all had a lot of fun."

Emma smoothly censors what she's sharing. She's not telling Mom how I let her down by being late and she's not saying how much she loves Julia's family, because she knows it will hurt Mom's feelings. I make a mental note to create something for Emma. Mom squeezes Emma like she's still a little kid, not an almost twelve-year-old girl. I get that, though. I like to think of Emma as little too, even though I can see that she's not.

"Did you have fun with Luisa?" Mom asks me.

"Yeah, I did," I say, suddenly all too aware of my lack of a bra and hungover eyes. "I'm going to take a shower."

"Okay, but I wanted to share something with you girls."

My Spidey-senses start tingling.

Mom takes a deep breath and smiles at both of us. "Whew! This is harder than I expected," she says. She takes another breath. "You know that Dan and I parted ways a while back, but we reconnected, and we have been seeing each other." She pauses to let that settle in.

"You've been seeing each other for how long?" I ask, dread snaking down my spine.

Mom rubs her lips together. "Five months."

The cold shock of betrayal washes over me. "Five *months*? And you haven't said anything?"

Mom worries the magazine between her fingers and then raises her eyes to mine. "I wanted to be sure that we were serious before I told you girls."

"So it's serious then," I say.

"Yes," Mom says. "He was here last night, in fact. We were talking over our next steps together."

So that's why he was here. Worst fears confirmed.

"But you . . ." I glance at Emma, wondering how much she remembers from those days. "You ended it. So long ago."

Mom nods and swallows, like she's expected my statement. "I know five years seems long to you, but it's not that long for us."

She's right, it seems like a very long time to me. Long enough to shut that door for good.

"And like I said, we've been seeing each other."

"When?" I scoff. "At Mac and Judy's annual pig roasts?" I remember the first one after Dan and Mom broke up. He showed up with some skinny woman who smoked and didn't eat anything. Mom wept for days after that. Judy came by with food for us and to rub Mom's back and tell her that everyone was on "Team Beth." Mac took us to school for a couple days when Mom couldn't get out of bed.

"I have a life outside of work and my time with you girls, you know."

I thought back to nights she asked me to watch Emma or afternoons when she said she was going out for a few hours.

"I didn't want him back in your lives until it felt right. And now it does. In fact, he'll be here for dinner this week. He's anxious to see you girls again."

"I'm happy for you!" Emma says.

"Do you even remember Dan?" I say to Emma. My tone cuts in a way that I didn't intend.

"Of course she does," Mom says, but the way she glances at Emma shows me that she's not certain.

"You don't have to speak for me, Mom," Emma chimes in. "Yes, Skye, I remember Dan. I was in first grade when he left. I remember all that fun stuff he would do with us. Those hikes we did and the baseball game and camping." Her tone drifts off.

Hiking, the baseball game, and camping. Three things over the four or so years that Mom and Dan were mostly together. I used to think that way about Dan. How smart he was and how fun too. He always wanted to teach us something new, and he'd do it in his wacky way. But then he fractured that perfect image and I could never see him the same way again.

"I need to take a shower," I say again.

Mom's eyes flick over me. "Good idea."

I head down the steps into the basement, which is pretty much mine. At the bottom of the steps is an open area with a couch and a chair, but most of the space is taken up by my drafting table and art supplies. The washer and dryer are tucked behind folding doors along one wall. Opposite that are my bedroom and my own bathroom. Mac had built it all when I turned thirteen, and it was pretty much the best birthday gift ever.

In my room, each wall painted in different colors and patterns, I sit heavily on my bed. My fingers trail the bookshelf we'd snagged from a curb one day. We'd painted that too, me and Mom. Teal green with purple polka dots. All of this was after Dan was gone. There's nothing of him left in my life. At least that's what I'd assumed. I kick off my boots and head for the bathroom.

After locking the bathroom door, I do my morning stuff— brushing my teeth, taking my birth control, and washing my face. I strip down to step into the shower, and as I let the hot water rush over me, I try to wash off the guilt from not remembering what happened last night and the confusion about Dan returning. Five months she's been seeing him. How could I not have realized it? I've got to get that scholarship to MICA and get out of this place.

5

Another Day in Paradise

"UGH. CONTINUOUS SKETCH for our warm-up?" I say when I slide into my stool across from Ben in art class on Monday morning.

Ben nods. "That's right. Do not lift your drawing implement from your sketch pad—or risk death and dismemberment."

"That's a bit harsh. Even for Mr. M," I say. I stare at the blank page, knowing that as soon as I press the pencil to the paper, I can't start over.

"Creating artists is no joke," Ben says in his best Mr. M voice. He glances at me staring down my blank page. "Just go for it," Ben says, like he always does, in a combination of support with the barest shade of impatience.

No one ever needs to tell Ben to go for it. He sketches like it doesn't matter. Like he has no need to see the whole picture in his mind before he starts. Not like I do. The image must be fully formed before I can begin. Finally, I allow the pencil to touch the sheet of white. I start with the shapes that make up the body, careful not to lift my pencil.

Ben watches me work, which feels more personal than if he watched me do pretty much anything else.

"Eyes on your own paper, Schwartz," I growl at him.

"Emma?" he asks, still watching as I start to give the shapes more definition.

I nod as I work on her leg curled under her body while she leans over her script, focused on memorizing her lines for the audition. She was doing this just last night. I haven't quite captured the way her thigh rests on her calf, but I can't pick up the pencil, so I sigh and keep going.

"You know her so well," Ben says.

"I could draw Emma in my sleep." I smile at the picture taking shape. "I know her better than I know myself."

"I get that," Ben says.

My eyes snap up to look at him. I frown, not in criticism, but in confusion. "You're an only child."

He pauses his pencil, looks at me, and looks back at his sketch. "I mean it's easiest to draw what you're most familiar with, right?"

"Right," I say, but that's easy for Ben to say when he often draws from his imagination. My pencil moves with care around the curve of Emma's back. "So . . ." I say, careful to keep my pencil and my eyes on the paper. I can't look at Ben when I ask him about this. "Saturday night . . ."

"Man, we were all wasted, weren't we?" Ben says as he draws.

My pencil pauses on the paper. "We were," I agree. I continue my drawing. I need to fill in the blanks. Even if I don't want to know what happened. "Um, I'm not sure . . ."

"Just another Saturday night," Ben says, head bent over his drawing. I think he sighs a little bit.

Just another Saturday night. If I read into his words, I have to assume that he and I didn't hook up. Since I wasn't wearing a bra when I woke, that pretty much confirms that I hooked up with Ashton. God, I'm a piece of shit.

"I had fun hanging out with you," I say, to break my internal self-flagellation.

Ben glances at me and then back at his paper. "Yeah, me too."

From my pencil, Emma's head emerges from the oblong shape and I flower it with her hair in long up and down motions. This picture of Emma would be called *Sugar & Spice*. Sometimes I wish I could go back to her age. Before . . . everything.

"Until Ashton showed up," Ben says. "And Keith," he adds as an afterthought.

My hand stops its motion. At least I didn't mess up our friendship. Ben continues his drawing, not looking up. But what does Ben think of me now? My pencil makes a jagged line across Emma's face and I drop it on the table.

Luisa and I enter the crowded cafeteria where Ellen and her Spirit Squad are doing a routine to get everyone superpumped for the upcoming basketball playoffs (their words, not mine). I can't help but notice how perfect Ellen is at Spirit Squad, not just the precision of her moves, but also her leadership. In a moment when other girls would be ignored or laughed at, Ellen's team is actually getting people pumped. I'm not up for admiring the perfection of our former friend, so I make a U-turn.

"Where're you going?" Luisa says.

"I'll be in the art room. You want to hang with me?"

Luisa squishes her lips to the side, like she's thinking. "I sort of want to see Matt. But I could bring you something to eat."

"No, no, I'm good," I say, because I know she's excited about seeing Matt and I don't want to pull her away.

"Okay," Luisa says. Then, like she's reading my mind: "It was just one night."

"I'm fine." Fine. My go-to nothing word.

"Yeah," Luisa says, "nothing sticks to you. You're my Teflon girl."

There's a class going on in the art room during my lunch period. I head to the area in the back of the room where Mr. M has easels reserved for his seniors. I'm working on a pastel portrait of Emma that I'd like to take to MICA, but I can't get her eyes quite right. Mr. M stops by, staring at my piece over his reading glasses in that way he tends to do—right elbow perched on his left arm, his thumb between his teeth. A crease furrows his thick, dark brow.

"Don't overwork it," he says.

"You think it's done?"

He purses his lips. "No, it's not finished. Just don't overwork it."

"Do you have any suggestions that actually make sense?" I can speak to Mr. M this way after three straight years of art classes with him.

He stares at it a moment longer. "Use your instinct," he says and then he walks away.

Which instinct does Mr. M think will help me here? The one that made me drink so much tequila that I have no idea how my bra left my body? After staring at the piece for a while longer, it's time for my next class and my instincts have done nothing to improve my drawing. I put the pastels away and take one last look before I leave the room. Three more periods and then I can come back.

When the last bell finally rings, I return to the art room. I leave the overhead fluorescents off and just look at the portrait through the afternoon sunlight that swims through the big windows. Closing my eyes, I see Emma's open-eyed innocence when something surprises her. I see the determination when she's focused on a challenge. I see her affection when she hugs Mom. And I see her grin when I suggest we do some sister-thing.

I open my eyes and I know what I need to do to bring this piece alive. The white pastel adds a touch of sparkle. Then, with a light touch of the darkest blue and black, I deepen the edges of her eyes. I step back to take in my work and realize that I'm holding Mr. M's critical pose. But it seems to work. I can see that the portrait is finished. Satisfied, I check the clock on my phone and realize that I need to head over to Emma's school. Her tryouts will be over soon.

"Mom is home!" Emma exclaims when we see Mom's car.

"Huh," I say. Mom rarely arrives home before seven, and at least once a week she can't leave the law firm in time for dinner at all.

When we walk into our tiny town house, I remember that Mom said Dan was coming for dinner one night, but I didn't imagine it would be so soon.

"Hello, girls." Dan smiles his crooked-tooth smile from behind our mother. His arms are wrapped around her midsection. She smiles at us too and places her hands over his. It's more than a smile, really. She's glowing. She might even be floating. Dan leans down and kisses her neck.

"Dan!" She squirms away. "The girls."

"Hi, Mom," Emma says. "Hi, Dan," she adds, like she's trying it on. She drops her backpack on the floor.

Dan steps around Mom, smiling. His auburn hair is as wiry as I remember, though dashed with more gray. He still has his trademark goatee, also grayer than before. "I understand that you just had tryouts for the middle school musical."

He always had been interested in our—well, *my* school activities. Emma was so young that she didn't have school stuff back then.

"Yes," Emma says, grinning. *"Beauty and the Beast.* I should know in a couple days which part I got."

"Did you try out for a lead role?"

Emma nods, smiling.

"Very good," he says with approval.

He turns to me. "And Skye, how are you?"

He's not a big man, I realize. He seemed so big then, but he's only a few inches taller than me. Not even as tall as Ben.

I nod in response to his question. "Good."

Dan leans back with both hands wide, as if to take me all in. "It's only been a few years and you're all grown up!"

The statement is one you hear from your parents' friends a hundred million times, but with Dan's eyes on me, my insides squirm. I don't know what to think or feel. I haven't had to dwell on any of the stuff that happened back then in so long.

"And you, Emma." He chuckles. "I remember reading to you before bed. Guess you're too old for that now."

"I can definitely read on my own," she says with a giggle.

"I expect that you brush your own hair now too," he says, grinning. He turns to Mom. "Remember how she was?"

Mom laughs. "How could I forget?"

Emma looks from Dan to Mom as if they are crazy. "I definitely brush my own hair."

"It's nearly as long as Skye's used to be." He turns to me. "Right?"

My eyes follow the river of hair waving down her back and I nod, remembering.

"And now you're in fifth grade?" Dan asks, as if he knows the answer.

"Sixth," Emma and I say at the same time.

"Right. Sixth," Dan says.

Dan stands up and rubs his hands together. He bounces a little on his toes, like he always used to do. He bounced on his toes the time that he announced that we were going to the baseball game. And before the camping trip.

6

BEFORE:
I am eleven. July after fifth grade

"GIRLS, YOU NEED to be ready in five minutes," Mom calls from her bedroom. "We don't want to be late. It's not every day that we get tickets to a ball game!"

I hear the smile in her voice as I finish making my bed, which isn't the easiest thing in the world when you have a bunk bed, but Mom likes the bed made every day, so that's what I do.

"I'm already ready!" Emma calls back and I know what will happen because it is the same thing that happens almost every day.

"Not with that mess," Mom says a moment later. She sighs. "Come on. Let me brush your hair."

"Nooo!" Emma yells. I don't need to be in the hallway to know that she is smashing her little hands to her head to protect her knotty hair from the dreaded brush.

"You can't go in public with your hair like that, Em."

"Can too!"

"Emma!" Dan bellows from downstairs. "Enough. Go to your mother and get your hair combed. We will not have you going to a baseball game looking like a wild animal."

I roll my eyes. Emma drags herself to Mom's room in a death march, as if she doesn't have her hair brushed every single day. I plop on the floor and pull out my sketchbook, drawing the back of Emma as I just saw her: T-shirt tucked in and her blue hand-me-down shorts ballooning around her little legs.

"Skye?" Mom calls. "Are *you* almost ready?"

"Yup." I had already pulled on clean shorts and a tank top and I have my favorite sneakers on. I don't even have any dirt on my knees or on my face. Success. I close my sketchbook and slide it into my bottom drawer, where I can keep it private before going to stand in Mom's doorway. Emma wails like she's being tortured as Mom works the tangles out of her hair, but I can see that Mom is being as careful as possible. I kneel next to Emma and place my hands on her chubby knees.

"It's okay, Em. It's going to be smooth as silk when Mom's finished."

"I don't care if it's smoove as silk," Emma pouts.

That's how she says *smooth*. I love it. "I can braid it if you want, but only if you let Mom get the tangles out first."

Emma hiccups the end of her tears and nods to me. Her blue eyes, a shade lighter than mine, seem to take up her whole tiny face. Her cheeks are red from crying, and snot drips from her nose. I grab a tissue, wipe her nose, and then peck her with a kiss. She rewards me with a giggle.

Mom smiles at me from behind Emma.

"We are going to have so much fun!" I say to Emma. "There will be a ton of people there. And popcorn and cotton candy . . ."

"Don't forget the baseball game," Mom says, laughing. "That's the actual point of this afternoon."

"I just want cotton candy," Emma says.

"Skye," Mom says to me as she works through Emma's tangles, "you might want to pull your hair back too. It'll be hot at the stadium."

"Okay." I return to the room I share with Em where I brush my hair with care and pull it toward the crown of my head. After I smooth out the bumps, I twist the elastic once then twice around and then pull at pieces of hair until it looks the way the older girls at school wear it. I turn from side to side, admiring the look. I could pass for thirteen easy with my hair like this. Except that I don't have any boobs yet, just little buds, as they call them in health class, like we are something planted in someone's garden and not living, breathing girls.

"I'll be downstairs when Em's ready for braids," I call out to Mom.

Dan is in the living room sipping his drink. He frowns and motions me over to him, patting the couch.

"I don't care for this look," he says. He reaches over and pulls the elastic from my hair. "It's common."

"Hey, I just got that perfect!" I protest as my hair tumbles around my shoulders and to the middle of my back. As for looking common, I don't know where Dan thinks we live. It's like he is the king of freaking England sometimes.

"At the nape of your neck," he says, lifting my hair and holding all of it in one fist at the point where my neck curves into my skull. "Make a ponytail here."

Glancing at the amber liquid in his glass, I see that it's almost empty. I try not to test Dan after he's had his drinks, so I pull my hair into a low ponytail.

He sips his drink and looks at me. "Sexy," he says. "And classy."

At the word *sexy,* my stomach feels funny, but I don't understand why. I stand and my reflection in the mirror over the couch shows me an old-fashioned hairstyle. Not like the older girls at the high school. Not cute at all.

"We're ready!" Mom says as she and Emma come down the steps.

"Your hair looks pretty," Mom says to me. She ruffles her own hair. "Too bad mine's too short to wear like that."

Dan looks at his watch. Most people use their phones as their watches, but not Dan. "We're late." He finishes his drink, sets the empty glass on the coffee table, and stands up. "Let's go."

"You're supposed to braid my hair," Emma whines at me.

"No whining, Emma," Dan says sharply.

I turn to Emma with my stupid low ponytail, feeling like a fake version of myself. Emma's lip starts to quiver. I pull the elastic out of my hair.

"I'll do it in the car," I whisper to her and grab her hand. "Come on."

We slide into the backseat and I start to work on Emma's French braid as we drive out of our neighborhood. By the time I finish and then redo it to get rid of the bumps, we are on the highway. Emma leans toward the window, watching for the stadium to appear as we veer off the highway and into traffic.

"Almost there," Mom singsongs.

"'Take me out to the ball game,'" Dan starts singing, and we all chime in. When the song is finished we are finally at the parking lot.

"Highway robbery," Dan mutters after paying for parking. "We should've taken the train, like I said."

"Well, driving is easier with the girls," Mom says as she gathers our bags of water bottles and sandwiches.

"I thought we were buying food in there," I say, trying to keep the whine out of my voice.

Mom smiles. "We'll buy some fun stuff, but the sandwiches are outrageous at the stadium."

"Okay," I say, even though I'd really had my heart set on a cheesesteak.

"Braid yours too," Emma says as she climbs out of the car. I quickly braid my own hair, but I don't have an elastic so I just braid it to the very end and let it snake down my back.

Emma rushes ahead to Mom, who is walking with purpose, the tickets and bags clutched in one hand. Emma latches on to her free hand. Together, they pass the guys hawking soft pretzels and warm water bottles until they reach the turnstiles. Dan tugs the end of my braid and I jump. "I like this even better," he says, tucking a stray hair behind my ear.

I shiver despite the summer heat.

7

One Big Happy Family

"I'M MAKING DINNER tonight," Dan says, like this is on the same level as a baseball game.

Mom makes dinner at least five nights a week and never needs to announce it.

"You two better get started on your homework," Mom says.

Emma and I grab our backpacks. Dan holds up both hands. "Hang on," he says, "I'm not trying to interfere." He smiles at Mom. "But how about if you two set the table first?" He's been back in our lives for approximately five nanoseconds and he's already telling us what to do.

"Sure," I say, because even though he's bossy, he's trying. Plus, I remember from before how he could get if we didn't obey.

"Mom usually likes me to do my homework first," Emma says, because she doesn't remember. She looks to Mom for confirmation and Mom is looking at Dan. I can't tell if there's a whisper of worry on her face or if she's just waiting to see what he says. I'm out of practice.

Dan clears his throat and smiles at Emma, his hazel eyes sharp. "If we complete the table setting quickly, we won't lose time to do our homework, correct?"

The royal *we*. I'd forgotten about that.

"Yeah, Butter Bean," I say to Emma. "We'll just be quick, okay?"

"Ugh! Stop calling me that!" Emma sighs dramatically.

Dan pours two glasses of white wine. His drink used to be Jack Daniel's, three fingers' worth, over ice. But maybe his taste has changed over the years. After we set out the place mats, I return to the kitchen for silverware and napkins.

"*Cloth* napkins, Skye," Mom says.

I frown at her. "I don't even know—"

Mom pushes me out of the kitchen and pulls open a drawer in the dining room hutch. "Right here, you know that," she says, like we use cloth napkins every night. Like we've used them at all since Dan left.

"And don't forget to set out the candles."

The candles. That was always Mom's touch. Candles on our fake wood dining room table. Whatever. Not worth arguing over. "Got it."

An hour later, Emma appears at my bedroom door. "I'm so hungry!" She clutches her stomach and then falls backward on my bed.

"You'll definitely get the part you want with that level of drama. How's it going up there?"

"Not sure."

I go to the kitchen under the guise of getting a glass of water. Dan has taken up every flat surface in the kitchen with his dinner prep.

"Almost ready," he says, wiping sweat from his forehead. "Beth!"

"Yes?"

"A little help?"

Mom appears in the entryway.

"It's getting late," I whisper to Mom.

She surveys the kitchen, quick eyes glancing at the oven clock. "Ten minutes," she whispers back.

Finally, at precisely seven thirty, which Dan declares is the civilized time to eat, Mom lights the candles and Dan announces that dinner is served. We all sit down and the whole thing is totally over the top for a Monday night dinner, starting with the menu that Dan must've pulled from some gourmet website.

There's fish wrapped in paper and these super skinny green beans and some tiny potatoes that are purple and covered in sautéed onions. Dan refuses to tell us the English names of any of the food he's concocted, seeming to think it will taste better if we only know the French names. Emma and I catch each other's eyes. I hate fish and she hates string beans. Too bad we can't combine our plates.

"Can I have the butter?" she asks, pointing.

"Of course, you *can*," Dan says. "The question you should be asking is, *May I* have the butter? Or, even better, Would you please pass the butter?"

Emma seems completely unruffled. "Okay, would you please pass the butter?" she asks, smiling.

"*Mais oui!* But of course," Dan replies in an overly pleased tone, like he's just taught a smart dog a new trick. "What part did you try out for in *Beauty and the Beast*?"

Emma butters her bread and bites off a mouthful. "Mrs. Potts," she manages to say around her hunk of bread.

"Finish chewing before you speak," Dan says.

Emma's eyebrows raise, her cheeks puffed with bread. She glances at me and keeps chewing.

"Dan, this is wonderful," Mom gushes and then sips her wine, as if the potatoes are so dry that she needs some moisture stat.

"Thank you, Beth."

It's weird how they're calling each other by their names so much, but I guess it's better than yelling each other's names like before.

"Skye, what do you think?" Dan asks. "*C'est magnifique, n'est pas?*"

"Yup," I say. He thought our elementary school was excellent because they started us on French in second grade. The language of love, he'd said. Mom didn't know any French, so it was always weird to me that he would speak it in front of her like that.

"I told Dan that you're applying to art schools," Mom says, changing the subject.

And that's fine, because even though I hate talking about college and My Future, I'd rather do that than hear Dan speak French.

"Yeah, that's right."

"Yes," Dan says.

"What?"

"Not *yeah*. You sound common."

Common. All these years and Dan still imagines that we live in Penn's Manor among the other multiple-car families with golden retrievers and vacations in tropical places when really, we live in Miller's Crossing, which is the pimple on the ass that is Pennswood. But this is not worth fighting over with him.

"Yes," I say, enunciating clearly. "I have an interview at MICA, Maryland Institute College of Art, this week. On Thursday. I'm up for a big scholarship."

"You feel that you have something new to bring to the visual arts medium?"

I push my string beans, aka *haricots verts*, around on my plate and then stop before Dan can reprimand me for playing with my food. "I'm interested in studying art if that's what you're asking." I don't say the part about wanting to get out of this crap town.

"So much of what's coming out of art schools today is derivative and trite. I hope that you have an original vision to bring to your studies."

An original vision? I can't even decide on the theme for my senior portfolio.

"I tried out for Mrs. Potts," Emma announces again, like she's just come up for air.

"Don't interrupt your sister," Dan says. "She was going to share her artistic vision."

"Oh, I'm good," I say to Emma.

"Sure?" Emma says. I nod.

"So, I tried out for Mrs. Potts, but we all had to try out for other parts too, as a backup. I really hope I get Mrs. Potts though."

"That's wonderful, honey," Mom says.

"I can help you with your lines, if you like. I have some musical theater background in my past." He smiles at Emma.

"Are you still teaching at Penn?" I ask.

"Good memory, Skye. No, last semester I started teaching at Gratztown University, and it looks very promising. I've got the requisite freshman English sections that all incoming professors must take on, but the course I enjoy teaching the most is a survey of great novels of our time."

He used to say he'd never teach in a state school because the students were all subpar, and I remember how thrilled he was when he landed the position at Penn. "What happened to the old job? I thought you liked it there."

Dan clears his throat. "That position didn't work out. It wasn't tenure track," he adds quickly. "When will you find out about your part, Emma?" he says.

"I think the end of this week? Or maybe next week, and then rehearsals will start."

Dan finishes chewing his undercooked green beans. "Being a part of a musical is an excellent way to build one's education outside of the classroom." He nods at Emma.

"That sort of steals the fun out of it," I mumble to my potatoes.

"What's that?" Dan asks.

"We should get together with Mac and Judy soon," Mom interrupts and sips her wine.

Mac is like the uncle we never had. Judy's cool too, but she's a little out of it sometimes. Mom says she's on enough painkillers to kill a horse. It might seem surprising that Mac still rides his motorcycle even after the accident that put Judy in a wheelchair, unless you know that he moved to Pennsylvania on account of the no helmet law. He has the New Hampshire state motto stitched to his leather riding jacket: live free or die. And he tricked out this van for Judy so that she can still drive because she's just as fierce as he is.

"Yeah," Emma says as she pushes away from the table. "I want to ride the stair lift!"

"Where are you going?" Dan asks.

"I'm finished," she says like *duh.*

Dan glances at Mom and then back to Emma. "Please be seated until *everyone* is finished."

By everyone, he refers to himself, because the rest of us have been finished for a while. After all, we have lives to live. Emma raises her eyebrows toward Mom, but she sits back down. Finally, several years later, Dan dabs his mouth with the cloth napkin and places his fork and knife at four o'clock on the plate.

"You two may start the dishes. And we"—Dan's hand slides beneath the table and he looks at Mom—"are going to relax."

Mom jumps and slaps at Dan's hand playfully, so I know he must have squeezed her thigh under the table. Ew.

Emma and I hit the kitchen to tackle the dishes. And *tackle* is the operative word, because Dan has used every pan in the entire house to make his culinary creation. This sketch would be called *Behind the Curtain*. A little while later Mom and Dan appear in the entryway to the kitchen.

"I bought brownies for you girls," Dan says, sipping his wine and sliding a hand around Mom's waist.

"From Lindsor's?" Emma asks. Lindsor's is one of the good things about our town. Their brownies have you ready to turn over your prized possessions to the baker, just for one more taste.

"Absolutely. Who would buy brownies anywhere else?" Dan's smile crinkles his eyes.

"Yum!" Emma exclaims, untying the string from the white bakery box. "Thanks, Dan!"

"You are welcome," Dan says to Emma. "Maybe we could make this a weekly occurrence," he says to Mom.

I'm not sure how I feel about anticipating a weekly mountain of dishes following an unpronounceable meal.

"And maybe we can do the fun stuff we used to do—like a baseball game?" Emma asks with shyness that isn't her at all.

"'Take me out to the ball game,'" Dan starts to sing.

"'Take me out with the crowd!'" Mom joins in.

They're singing and they're not even drunk. This has got to be a first.

"'Buy me some peanuts and Cracker Jack.'" Dan sweeps Emma into a hug.

"You guys are major dorks," Emma says, but she's grinning at Dan.

Dan reaches out to pull me in with them. His hand grasps my shoulder, and I stiffen.

8

If You Can't Stand the Heat

I ROLL AWAY from Dan's touch and disappear downstairs to my room. I rub my shoulders. I don't like him touching me. I know he means well. At least I'm sure he does. Of course he does. But I pace the small confines of my bedroom and avoid looking at myself in the big mirror that sits over my low dresser. I text Ben that I need him.

Mom is too goo-goo-eyed to run me through an inquisition, so when Ben confirms that he's outside waiting, I leave without incident. My thrift store jacket is little comfort against the chilly evening, but I don't want to tempt fate by going back inside, and anyway, Ben is right there with his car idling.

"Thanks for picking me up," I say as I buckle my seat belt.

"What else are emergency friends for?" Ben peers at me in the harsh glow of the car's dome light. "What is the emergency anyway?"

"Dan's back," I say. I'm relieved when the overhead light goes out and I can be hidden in the cocoon of Ben's car.

"Dan?" he says.

Sometimes I forget that Ben and I haven't been best friends for our whole lives. "My mom's ex-boyfriend. He was . . . they broke up a while ago. But now he's back. And they've been seeing each other for five months."

"And this isn't good news."

"I don't know. I mean, Mom and Emma think he's great . . ."

"But you see it differently." Ben is filling in the blanks when he doesn't even know the sentences, and I love him for that.

"Yeah." I run my fingers through my hair. Too short to pull it into a ponytail, too long to really be short. "But maybe it's fine. Maybe I'm wrong. But he's going to be around a lot. In our house with us. I mean, obviously, right? Only it wasn't obvious to me until just now and I just . . ." I stop. "Forget it. I just want to forget it."

Ben nods. "Okay. We'll forget it."

We drive in silence until we reach the quarry. Ben hands me a joint and a lighter. I light up and take a deep hit. With care, I hand the tiny joint back to Ben. He's in sweats and his hair is a mess, curls poking every which way. I'd barely noticed him when I'd gotten in the car, I'd been so inside my head.

"A baseball cap'd go a long way to hide that mess," I say, trying for Normal.

"Emergencies mean that sometimes you leave the house without a hat."

He's following my lead, but I can't forget the thing that's squatting on my chest. I can only breathe shallowly and pretend it's not there.

"Are you okay, Skye?" His question floats to me, barely above a whisper. My name in his voice is as soft as a caress. And that softness chips at the walls inside me. This is Ben—the friend who shows up at a moment's notice. I can trust him. But what would I even tell him? It was so long ago and it made no sense. Besides, if I let those words into this space, Ben will know just how damaged I am. I can't imagine looking him in the eyes after that.

Staring out the windshield at the bushes bordering the black water, I don't speak. I don't even shake my head yes or no. I want to tell him not to take it personally, but I don't trust my voice right now.

Ben taps my arm. He holds the joint out to me. I don't want it. Not really. What I want is to lean over into Ben's shoulder and bury my head in his chest. I want to feel his hands smoothing my hair and his voice whispering in my ear that everything will be okay. I want to climb inside the pocket of his sweatshirt and be carried like a baby kangaroo. But I can't do any of those things, so I take the joint. Our fingers touch, making me ache deep inside.

"Sorry," he says, and I don't know if he means he's sorry that I'm obviously not okay or if he's sorry that he grazed my fingers with his. He wiggles his fingers. "My manly hands."

That one coaxes a smile from me. I lean my head back and close my eyes. I so needed this. I decide that I can say that out loud. "I so needed this."

"I know," he says, scrolling through the music on his phone.

It's so simple with Ben. When I needed to get out of my house, he was the first person I'd thought of. Was it because I knew he'd have weed or because I wanted him? My feelings are all mixed up. I secretly thrilled at the moment we almost but didn't have the other night and then I ended up wasted with Ashton.

Ben lets out a triumphant noise. "There you are!" he says to his phone. With a tap on the screen, he fills the small space with a single guitar, a bass, and a guy singing in a gravelly voice about losing his way. In the dim dashboard lights, his grin glints at me.

"Better?" he says.

I nod and can't help grinning back. "Yes. Better."

The roach cupped in Ben's hands is no more than a tiny orange ember in the dark car, like he's Prometheus holding his miracle out to me and I accept it like the gift that it is. The drums come in and Ben turns up the volume so the music obliterates us in the tiny car, the notes pounding through my eardrums and escaping through my rib cage. Ben sings and I join in on the chorus, screaming the words and forgetting, for a moment, the thing camped out on my chest, just as Ben had promised. I turn and Ben is looking at me and singing and I wonder if he's singing to me or just with me and either way it's magical because we're together in a way that I've never been with any guy.

Then the chorus is over and I slump back against the seat, my hands twisting together in my lap, because singing with Ben in the safe bubble of his car is just temporary. When the song is finished, Ben wordlessly maneuvers the car back onto the street and toward my house. I already ache with the loss of this moment. Nothing real has changed, but for a little while I escaped.

9

BEFORE:
I am twelve. Late spring of sixth grade

EMMA AND I have exceeded our allotment of marshmallows, so we are just sitting around the campfire while Dan whittles. I tie knots in some string that Dan has given me while the fire licks at the logs, embers throbbing like tiny heartbeats. The forecast hadn't been great, so none of Mom and Dan's friends are with us, even though it's Memorial Day weekend. Dan being an Eagle Scout, he doesn't believe in giving up on camping just because of a few raindrops. It was always fun when Mac and Judy came, but I sort of like it being just us. Dan drains his drink, sets it down, and picks up his knife, paring off more pieces from the chunk of wood.

Mom's flashlight bobs toward us. She plops into her chair and clicks the flashlight off. "I can't believe that wine is gone already!" she says, like she's not the one who drank it.

"I thought you were going to the bathroom," Dan says. "I would've asked for a refill for myself." He peers into his cup.

"Did go to the bathroom," Mom says. When she's had a few glasses of wine, she drops words from her sentences. "And then I got some wine." She raises her plastic cup as proof.

The black trees rustle in the breeze, surrounding us in their papery song. Emma squats before the fire, tossing little pieces of pine needles and bark into the flames. They sizzle and smoke. I wait for Mom to say something to Emma, but Mom's head is tilted way back. I can't tell if her eyes are opened or closed.

"Move away from the fire, Em," I say. "You're getting too close."

"Fine," she says with a huff, which is how six-year-olds seem to say most things, at least this six-year-old. She moves back a few inches.

"And no more pine needles," Dan adds. "They give off too much smoke."

"Okay," Emma says with more huffs. She tosses the pine needles back to the forest floor.

"I can't see a single star tonight," Mom says.

"It's supposed to rain soon," I say. "That's what the Internet said. Do you think we can climb the Whomping Willow tomorrow?"

My favorite part of coming to this park to camp is the Whomping Willow. It isn't really a willow, Dan has said, but I call it that because it reminds me of the tree in Harry Potter. It has these huge, low branches that we can climb, and it doesn't look like any other tree in the whole park. Frogs croak from the nearby pond and the sound seems extra loud in the dark night.

"We'll have to see how the weather is," Mom says.

"How are those knots coming along, Skylar?" Dan asks as his block of wood transforms into a small owl.

I'd learned that square knots were the ones used for macramé bracelets. "Look," I say, holding up my new project over the light of the fire.

"Square knots might be fine for bracelets, but never use them for a critical load such as controlling a sail or rock climbing. Two half hitches are a safer bet."

I wasn't sure when I'd need that information, since I don't sail and I'd never climbed, but sometimes Dan can't turn off the information coming out of his brain. He's like an old-fashioned Google.

Dan continues his whittling and starts humming the good night song that he sings whenever it's time for one of us to head off to bed.

"Nooo!" Emma wails.

"'s time, Butter Bean," Mom says.

"It's *not* time!" Emma takes a handful of pine needles and tosses them in the fire. She looks at Dan and then Mom. My fingers freeze in their knot-tying. Dan stops whittling, giving Emma his full attention.

"That was an inappropriate way to express yourself, Emma," Dan says. "Off to bed with you."

Relieved, I start tying knots again. Dan isn't in one of *those* moods tonight. Belligerent is what Mom called him when he acted that way. I had to look that one up. But tonight, he isn't hostile and aggressive. You never could tell if he would be fun or not fun after he'd had his drinks.

Emma stands up and gestures with both hands. "I can't go to *bed*."

"And why can't you?" Dan says, amusement in his tone. He taps the point of the knife against the unfinished owl.

I hope that this *non*belligerent mood hung on.

"There's no bed!" Emma says, arms wide. "It's only a tent with sleeping bags, so I can't go to *bed*." She shakes her head solemnly, like she's made the world's most logical argument. Emma pushes in a way that I've never dared to do. I do as I'm told and I keep quiet to avoid a scene.

Dan flips the knife closed and slides it into his pocket. "If you don't head off to your *sleeping bag* right now, you're going to experience the consequences." A warning laces Dan's tone.

"Come on, Em," Mom says, standing and swaying a bit. "Let's go."

Emma huffs once again, but she follows Mom without a word.

After they disappear into the dark, Dan flicks his cup so that the melting ice cubes fly into the darkness. He holds the cup out to me. "Skylar, how about you get me a refill?"

It seems like he's already had a lot and I'm not sure it's a good idea to give him more, especially with Mom not here to have a say.

"Mind your elders, Skylar," Dan says, like he can read my mind.

The light of the fire creates a deep black circle around us.

"You can take my flashlight," Dan says, as if the darkness is why I am hesitating. I hold out my hands for the flashlight and the empty cup.

"Three fingers—"

"And some ice. I know," I say.

I open the hatchback where I find his bottle of Jack Daniel's. I pour two fingers instead of three, hoping that he won't see the difference in the dark. Then I add ice cubes from the cooler. As I walk back, I hear Emma and Mom whispering their good nights. A big fat drop plops on my head. I walk two steps and several more land on my shoulders and my forearm. Big fat raindrops usually mean that a big fat rain is coming. About two seconds later, lightning whitens the sky. I start counting Mississippis and turn back toward the car for my raincoat.

Thunder booms. I'd counted ten seconds between, like Dan had taught me. The heart of the storm is still a while away. Maybe it won't even head in our direction. I set Dan's drink down to shrug on my raincoat. As I pass by the tent, I hear Emma whining to Mom.

"Just the gods bowling up there," Mom says to Emma. "That's all thunder is." Mom's words slide out like syrup, slow and heavy.

"'s okay."

"It's not okay! I want to go home."

"Not going home, Emma," Mom says. We'd been camping with Dan enough to know this to be true.

"You have to sleep with me," Emma states, plain as fact.

We had pitched two tents that each slept only two people, so Mom sleeping with Em meant I'd have to sleep in a tent with Dan. We'd done that before, but not for a while. Usually, Emma is happy to sleep with me, but thunder is a deal breaker for her. She'd need Mom.

"Go to sleep, Butter Bean," Mom slurs, sounding like she is half asleep already.

I make my way back to the campfire, careful not to spill any of Dan's drink. If it isn't full, he might ask me to go back and fill it some more. I hand the drink to him.

"Mom is sleeping with Emma because of the thunder."

Dan nods and sips his drink. "She'll grow out of it," he says. "Eventually."

I shift from one foot to the other while the fire sizzles in response to each raindrop. Dan's unfinished owl sits next to him on the log.

"Come here," he says, careful to speak clearly, like he does when he's had a few.

"It's starting to rain," I said.

"Oh, what's a few drops? We're camping!" He pulls me onto his lap, tucking his left arm around my middle, and holding me close. "We're completely safe." Lightning cracks the sky. I jump and some of the amber liquid from Dan's drink spills on my thigh.

"Whoops!" he says cheerfully. "Here, let me." He wipes the bourbon from my leg with his calloused thumb and licks it off. He drops his hand back down on my leg, his hairy fingers spanning my skinny thigh. Thunder booms.

10

Ducks in a Row

THE BELL SIGNALING the end of the school day rang a while ago, but Mr. M and I are still talking over the pieces that I'll take to MICA.

"Don't forget that I'm already admitted," I say.

"The scholarship committee will be looking at different aspects of your art from the admissions committee. I want to be sure that the pieces you're taking represent your full range of talent."

"I have a full range of talent?" I say.

Mr. M eyes me over his glasses. "You know you do. Don't make yourself small. It won't serve you in this process." He walks to the one of Emma that I'd just finished the other day. "This turned out well. You did an excellent job with the eyes, which can be murder for so many portrait artists."

"Thanks, I'm happy with it too."

"Including that one, I think you have a nice selection. Are you happy with these pieces?"

I eye the five pieces that we've selected. There's the portrait of Emma in pastels. A reenvisioning of the *Beauty and the Beast* movie poster in Sharpie with Beauty as a seven-foot-tall cyborg and the Beast as a perfectly average guy. For my landscape, the park where we used to camp with the Whomping Willow still intact. A still life of Emma's discarded hair accessories—bows, headbands, and barrettes—in colored pencils. And a multimedia piece that started as a portrait of Emma and Mom until I was inspired to add pressed flower petals, pieces of fabric, bits of magazine spreads, and hand-printed words, transforming it into a fantastical interpretation of a mother/daughter portrait.

I nod.

These eighty-five minutes are the only minutes during which I haven't thought about Dan moving in on our life or me hooking up with Ashton. When Mr. M releases me, telling me that these are the best pieces and that I'll do great, I swim in that affirmation for about thirty seconds before I allow reality to crash back into my mind. If I don't do great, I can't go to art school.

"Skye." Ben catches me as I'm lugging my portfolio out of the classroom. "You want to come over today?"

"You're still here?" I say.

Ben shrugs. "I was helping stage crew with their mural."

"You're such a paint whore."

He laughs. "You got me. I'll do anything for a paintbrush."

Ben holds the door open for me, and we step into a cold February rain.

"Careful," I say. "People might get the wrong idea." By people, I think I mean me.

"Just helping you and your enormous portfolio out the door. Besides," he says, grinning, "if I wanted to give people the wrong idea, I'd slide my hand into your back pocket."

"Oh, please," I say, wondering what it might feel like to be that way with Ben. "I do not ever want to look like *those* couples."

Ben laughs. "I know, right? But seriously, are you coming over?" He holds his hands up. "No hands in back pockets. I swear."

"I'm working at five," I say, making sure that my portfolio is zipped against the weather.

"You suck," Ben says, pulling up the collar of his jacket. "Call in sick. You don't even need to call in sick. You can just tell Sal that you're stressed about your trip tomorrow and he'll give you off no problem. Besides, it's a Wednesday and it's raining. No one is going out to eat."

I'm sort of in awe of Ben's ability to dance from flirting to treating me like one of the guys. "Sal loves me *because* I don't call out at the last minute," I say. We continue walking through the parking lot. "You seriously hate getting high by yourself, don't you?"

"Who said I wanted to get high?"

I give him a look.

He shrugs. "What can I say? It's more fun with people."

People.

"How about Keith? Or Ashton?"

Ben shoves his hands in his pockets and shakes his head. Raindrops tug at his curls. "Nah."

There's something in his tone that urges me to press him but also holds me back. I'm rebuilding my wall brick by brick and I'm not looking to demolish it again. I almost kissed Ben, but I didn't. And I won't. I unlock Lucy and place my portfolio with care in the back.

Ben squints at me in the rain. "Would you at least drop me at my house?"

"So *that's* why you're stalking me." I jangle the keys in my hand. "Yeah, jump in."

I amp up the Jeep's heat. "Where's your car?" I ask because I don't know what else to say. We'd felt so close the other night after Dan's dinner and this is the first time we've been alone since then.

Ben rubs his hands back and forth like he's trying to create a spark. "You know Freddie doesn't like the rain," Ben says, fiddling with my ancient radio.

"I don't blame him." Ben's old Mercury is notoriously fussy, refusing to start in rain or very cold weather.

"Are you psyched for tomorrow?" Ben asks as we pull out of the parking lot and head toward his neighborhood.

Here's a topic I can talk about. "Beyond psyched," I say, searching for how to communicate the proper level of psychedness, but none of the words are adequate. "What's bigger than psyched? Thrilled? Out of my mind? God, none of these words is enough."

"Bet you could put it in a drawing."

I smile at the windshield dappled with raindrops as I pull into traffic onto Pennswood Pike. "You might be my biggest fan. After Mr. M."

"You're putting me after Mr. M? I'm mortally offended."

"You're going to die of being offended?"

"Meh, guess not," Ben says. I can hear the smile in his voice.

We're quiet for a minute and my thoughts focus on tomorrow's visit to MICA. "I need to get out of here. Going to art school, you know, it was only a dream. But now people might actually give me money to do the thing I love? It's—"

"Hard to believe that *your* dreams could come true?"

I nod. We're in front of Ben's house now and too soon. I put the car in park. "Sort of surreal, you know?"

"I do. That's how I feel when the band gets decent gigs. Like we're not just some high school garage band. We could actually be something."

I get that. To actually *be* something. Something more than my mom got to be. Something beyond this town. "Exactly," I say.

Ben sits there for a beat and then slaps his hands on his thighs. "Okay. Well . . ." He looks at me with dark brown puppy dog eyes. The drive was too short. We were just starting to talk about real stuff.

"You still want me to come in?" I ask.

He nods, those eyes trained on me.

"You are seriously pathetic, you know that?"

Ben's face breaks into that smile. "And you fall for it every time."

Boy, do I.

Moments later, we're in Ben's basement, where I'm wandering the room while Ben packs his bong. In the dish on the table by the door, there are two guitar picks, a single key, a broken seashell with a hole punched through it, and a set of earbuds tangled in its own wiring. I begin to untangle the wire to set the earbuds free.

"You sure?" he says, holding the bong toward me.

So tempting. Ben's right. I could call out on Sal and he wouldn't fire me. He would totally understand that I need to get ready for my trip tomorrow. Except that I wouldn't be getting ready for my trip, I'd be high with Ben.

"Yeah, I'm sure," I say, loosening one part of the wire and feeding the end through the opening. "I'm not calling out on Sal and no way I could juggle plates high. I'm not nearly as talented as you."

He looks at the bong like he is debating and then flicks his lighter. "Okay," he says, "your loss."

When the wire is one long line instead of a bird's nest, I lay the earbuds on the table. "Where's this from?" I ask, holding up the small seashell, its private pink insides turned toward me.

He tilts his head toward the ceiling and blows the smoke out, then glances at the shell in my hand. "Kelsey."

His ex-something from last summer. He never called her his girlfriend, but I think she thought of herself that way. "Was it a necklace?" I ask, peering at Ben through the hole.

"I think so. But it broke."

"You don't talk about her. Is she still around?"

"She lives in Jersey."

"I know." They'd met at a gig at the shore. "Doesn't mean she can't be around."

Ben cocks his head at me and laughs. "Don't you think you'd know if Kelsey was around?"

He has a good point. In fact, I can't think of any girls that Ben's been with since her. "Just making conversation."

"Let's make different conversation. I made you a playlist. For your drive to Baltimore. I'm sharing it right"—Ben presses a button on his phone—"now." He removes his hand from his phone with a flourish. "Also, this." Ben hands me a bowl and a baggie of weed.

"What did I do to deserve you?" I say. I don't get high by myself, but it's sweet that he thought of me, so I slide his gift into my bag. My phone pings. "Got the playlist. You rock. Pun intended." Then I see the time. "And duty calls. I've got to fly. Picking up Lu on my way."

"Hang on," Ben says, standing. "I think I have something of yours." He grabs a plastic grocery bag from behind his chair and hands it to me, not meeting my eyes.

From inside the bag, my neon pink bra glows and I can feel my cheeks turning the same color. "Oh."

"Yeah, found it in the couch." He looks away and scratches a spot below his ear. "So, I should start practicing." He grabs his guitar.

I feel like he's trying hard to change the subject. I shove the bright pink bra into my bag.

"Slay them at MICA," Ben says. "And then text me all about it."

Despite his well wishes, it's shame that follows me out the door when I leave.

I'm quiet when Luisa gets in the car.

"What's up?" she asks, like she has a second sense about me.

I point to the bag and she peers inside. "Why am I looking at your undergarment?"

"Ben found it. After the other night."

"That's awkward," Luisa says.

"Yup," I say, tapping my fingers on the wheel and not meeting Luisa's look. "Let's change the subject. What's up with Matt?"

Luisa sighs and drops her head back against the headrest. "Oh my God, I like him so much. Baseball boys have the best butts, don't they?" Luisa giggles.

"Now, now, no objectifying the opposite sex."

"For real though, I like him for him. The butt is just a nice bonus. He *seems* like he's into me. But I don't know. Maybe he's just being nice. How would I know?"

"He's definitely a nice guy. Does he laugh at your bad jokes? That could be a sign."

"I don't tell bad jokes."

"Maybe you should. And see if he laughs."

"Did anyone ever tell you that you're not that great at relationship advice?"

"Duh," I say, "I've never been in a relationship."

Louisa doesn't have a response to that. I pull in front of the long, low building that includes Sal's Diner. The space next to the diner has been empty for months, and the black window yawns at us. We turn into the alley that connects us to the parking lot around back where all of the staff is supposed to park.

"We should paint that sometime," I say as I put Lucy in park.

"Paint what?"

"The back of Sal's building. It's so ugly. We could make it awesome."

"You're such an art nerd. I've never even noticed that wall."

"You're such a future doctor. You'd only notice it if it were exhibiting odd symptoms."

"How exactly would a concrete wall exhibit odd symptoms?"

"The point is that I'd like to paint it."

"Point taken."

As we start our shift, the rain pouring against the wall of windows matches my mood. With no customers clamoring for service, Sal has us filling ketchup bottles, topping off salt and pepper in the shakers, and wiping down the already gleaming stainless-steel counters in the station. An old-timer grumbles about the busywork, but Lu and I move from table to table, figuring that what we finish now is work we won't need to do at the end of the shift.

"That's why I like you girls," Sal says loud enough for the other servers to hear. "You take initiative. Most young people these days just sit and wait for people to do for them. You need to do for yourself. That's how you get ahead in this country." He smiles broadly at us, thinking he's giving us a compliment, which he is. But Sal doesn't realize—or doesn't care—that he pisses off the other servers when he says that stuff to us.

About an hour in, the bell at the door jangles and Sal guides the customers to a booth in my section. I wipe my hands on my apron and approach the table.

Mom smiles up at me and Emma giggles, like they are in on a joke. I'm stunned for a minute, thinking that I would've been seriously caught if I'd bailed on my shift and hung out getting high with Ben all afternoon.

"We figured you wouldn't have many customers on a night like this and I wasn't up for cooking," Mom says.

"We totally surprised you!" Emma says, pointing at me.

"I'm surprised all right!" I smile as I pull out my pad of paper, unable to shake the feeling of narrowly escaping trouble.

Usually Sal is superstrict about waitresses chatting overlong with customers. But tonight, on account of the bad weather and few customers, he relaxes a bit. And when Emma orders a brownie sundae, he says it's on the house and tells me I can sit with them. I plop next to Emma, once again grateful that I wasn't high and that I'd shown up. Emma and I dig into the sundae.

"Want some, Mom?" Emma holds out a spoonful of ice cream dripping with chocolate sauce and melting whipped cream.

"No thanks, sweetheart." Mom smiles at Emma and then looks to me. "Are you ready for tomorrow?" she asks as she stirs fake sweetener into her decaf coffee. I wonder where Dan is tonight, but I don't ask.

"Yes," I say, licking my spoon. "Mr. M helped me choose the last three pieces today."

"I hope you included that one of Emma."

I smile. Mom had seen an early version of the drawing of Emma. "That one made the cut. It's one of Mr. M's favorite pieces too."

"You're taking one of me?" Emma says, popping the cherry in her mouth.

I lean into her like sisters do. "Definitely! Got to represent, right?"

"Right!" Emma agrees. I dab her nose with whipped cream.

"Oh my god, you are such a pain!" She squeals, wiping the whipped cream off with the back of her hand.

"What time are you leaving tomorrow?" Mom asks, interrupting our fun, like moms do.

"Eightish?" I say. "I have a tour and then I'm sitting in on a class at eleven. I'll have a break after that because the scholarship interview is at two."

"You should leave closer to seven. Rush hour could be terrible, and you'll need to find parking in the city, which won't be easy."

Leave it to Mom to kill the buzz of my big trip.

"I will take your suggestion into consideration," I say with mock seriousness. "And you're okay for getting off early to pick up Em?"

Emma offers up a huge dramatic sigh. "I'm right here, you guys. And I don't need to be taken care of."

Mom smiles indulgently. I probably do too. "I've blocked my calendar," Mom says. "Five thirty, right?"

"Five o'clock," Emma and I say in unison. Emma hates to be the last one picked up, as evidenced by her post-sleepover wrath. Also, the teachers aren't superthrilled with late pickups, as I learned once when I lost track of time in the art room.

"Oh, I'll need to tell my boss that he'll have to let me go a bit earlier." Mom sips her coffee while Emma and I ravage the sundae.

"Do you think you might be able to see Towson University while you're in Baltimore?" Mom says.

Outside the windows, the rain smears the reflection of the diner's neon sign, with the letter *n* dark. I'd have to capture this one with watercolors: *Dreams Washed Away.*

"Towson?" I have no idea why my mother is bringing up a Maryland state school that has exactly no reputation for art.

"Dan knows faculty there," Mom says, looking into her milky coffee. "I'm sure he would put in a good word for you."

Dan vouching for me is pretty much the last thing I want. Maybe not the last thing. The last thing I want is him back in our home. "I think I'm good, but thanks."

"If you don't get the scholarship, you'll need a backup plan. You shouldn't turn away help," Mom says.

As if I don't know that paying for college is tough. As if I'm not hearing all about it constantly—at home, at school, everywhere. Ben is the only person in our friend group who hasn't been stressed, and that's because he's chosen to take himself out of the mix by skipping the dreaded college app process and focusing on his music instead.

"Tyler is my backup plan. We'd pay in-state tuition and Mr. M knows faculty there so . . ." I leave the rest of the sentence unfinished, hoping that I don't need to point out that Mr. M's connections at Tyler are more valuable than Dan's connection in the English department of a Maryland state school. I didn't actually apply to Tyler, but Mom doesn't need to know that. I'm all about MICA. And as long as I do well in the interview, it's a done deal.

Mom cups her hands around the coffee mug, like its feeble warmth is a comfort to her. "As long as you have alternatives," Mom says.

"I am going to art school." My tone is firm.

"Skye." Emma draws out my name, like she's distracting me. "Here, have more sundae." She pushes the dish closer to me, trying to reduce the tension between Mom and me.

"You're a wonderful artist, Skye." Mom pushes her coffee away. "But you need a practical skill, so you can make a living."

She sounds like she's talking about me, but I think she's talking about herself. About ending up divorced with two little kids and no job to support us. But I'm not my mother. I have no intention of ending up stuck here like her.

I push myself from the booth. "Thanks for coming in. I'm going to do my cleanup duties. I'm driving Lu, so I'll see you at home."

"Okay," Mom says quietly.

"Bye, Skye." Emma sounds a little sad.

When I return to the table later, I see that Mom has left me a twenty-dollar bill as a tip. I pocket the money and make a mental note to use only if necessary.

11

When in Rome

BEN'S PLAYLIST ROCKS my ride to Baltimore. My phone pings with good luck messages and a thousand emojis from Luisa. The sun glistens on the river as I speed across the bridge, and I feel like some shiny alternate version of myself, a version who's allowed to dream big. After I've coaxed Lucy into a parking spot, me and my big, black portfolio are standing before the double glass doors of the art school. A real art school. This shiny version of me is giddy.

In the Admissions waiting area, there is just one guy slumped in his chair, as if he's trying to squeeze in a last few minutes of sleep before the tour. His mother looks a little type A. She is studying a pamphlet as if there's going to be a test, while the father thumbs through his phone in that way adults do that takes all the fun out of it.

A girl with a forest green hijab and cherry red lips greets me at the admissions desk with a smile.

"Your name?"

"Skylar Murray," I say. "For a tour? And an interview with the Meyerson committee?" I didn't intend to end my statements like questions. Guess I'm nervous.

She pulls a folder from a stack and explains the schedule before handing it over.

"Be sure to be back here by one fifty for the scholarship interview," she says. "You can't be late."

"Class at eleven. Interview at two. Free lunch. Don't be late. Got it," I say.

I'm barely two sips into the complimentary coffee when the tour guide shows up. It's just me and the sleepy guy, who I now see is very cute with his black hair shaved on one side and falling over his face on the other.

We do the obligatory introductions. The boy is Joon from some area of Baltimore that I've never heard of, but it must be fancy, given the way that he seems embarrassed and his parents proud.

As we walk toward the campus center, Joon asks, "So, what's your medium?"

"Is that how you plan to pick up people when you get here?" I smile at him.

He looks over his shoulder at his parents. "No romance for me. I am here only for the study of art." His eyes are warm as he breaks into a shining smile of perfect white teeth.

"Now, let me guess." He looks me up and down. "Watercolor?"

I wonder if the lame outfit I've chosen makes him think that.

"Nope. And you are most definitely street art."

He holds his hands up and I spot a small tattoo on his inner left wrist. "Guilty as charged."

"Joon, don't miss what the guide is telling us," his mom chastises. She adjusts the straps of her huge purse on her shoulder and pointedly returns her attention to the tour guide. The dad is paying exactly no attention, staring at his phone while walking.

We walk for a few minutes without talking while the tour guide leads us through a library. Joon leans in to speak to me in a low voice. "The parents are still in denial that I'm not attending one of the Ivies followed by business school."

"I get it. My mom is trying to steer me toward graphic design as a 'practical application of my talent'—her words."

"The Internet has killed graphic design as a viable professional choice."

"Yeah, she works in a law firm, so she's unaware."

We enter an academic building and the tour guide tells us about access to professors and individual attention.

"Great street art in Philly," Joon says. "Wish I knew you when I visited Tyler. Would have been way better than hanging out with my aunt."

It occurs to me that Joon is totally hitting on me and he doesn't even know me, so it's not like he has any reason to think he could get something out of it. This is new.

"Next time you're in Philly without your aunt, we'll tour the murals of the City of Brotherly Love," I say, flirting back because flirting is fun.

"Are you applying to Tyler too?" he says.

"I haven't. Philly schools are a little too close to home. Are you?" I don't tell Joon that I'm here for the scholarship interview. Seems like he doesn't need to worry about such things.

"Already did. SCAD and RISD too. I don't want to stay too close to home either."

I nod while the tour guide walks us through a building filled with room after room of studios. Huge windows cast sunlight across easels of semi-complete works while the smell of paint hangs in the air, tempting me to take part. My eyes eat up the studio spaces, placing me in front of those easels. The last stop on the tour is the bookstore. I pick up a MICA sweatshirt and imagine myself in it. I look at the price tag and place the sweatshirt back on the shelf. Instead, I select a T-shirt from a tottering stack. Plain black with white block letters.

Back in the Admissions waiting area, Joon says he'll look for me at lunch. Amber, my escort to class, shows up a few minutes before eleven. With her purple hair and various piercings, she looks like most of the other students here, unlike me. I'd worn what I thought was an artfully draped scarf, but it seems like it's trying too hard. At least my beloved scuffed black boots fit in here.

"Skylar?" she asks.

"Skye," I say.

Amber nods and motions for me to join her. "Coffee," she says. "What?"

"Can't speak till I have coffee. Come on." She guides me to the coffee shop next to the main building where she orders a red-eye, which I learn is a shot of espresso dropped into a large coffee. Amber blows on the coffee for a moment and then takes a long slurp, her eyes closed in apparent bliss.

"Okay," she says, her eyes flickering open. "Sorry about that. Pulled an all-nighter finishing a project. Hope you're cool with all-nighters. If you come here, they'll be a part of life."

"No problem with all-nighters. I relish them." I sound like a complete nerd, but also I'm still a little high from seeing the awesomeness that is MICA—and Joon wasn't too bad either.

"The ceramics professor is very chill. He'll let you make whatever you want—as long as it shows off your personal vision. Oil painting prof is a hardass, totally focused on technique, not fun at all. But you'll learn stuff. Sign up for figure drawing early, everyone tries to get in that class because of the nude models." Amber stops for a moment. "So immature," she says. Then, quieter and with a smile, "But I've got to say, they do get some very hot models." She winks at me, her eyebrow ring winking in unison. I've learned more in ten minutes with Amber than I learned in a whole hour with the skinny-jeans tour guide. Amber glances at her phone. "Oh no! Come on."

I'd thought that art students were all slouch and chill, but not Amber, not now that she's downed her red-eye. "We can't be late. Come on!" she says again, practically breaking into a run.

We arrive breathless at the ceramics room and the moment I step inside, I'm in awe. Pottery wheels sit in a circle in the center of the room, each one with a bucket of water set nearby. Amber grabs two balls of gray clay from a shelf and sidles around the edge of the room to stop at an open wheel next to a tall girl rocking a tank top and a shaved head. By the way that Amber sneaks a glance at the girl, I'm guessing that she's the reason Amber couldn't be late.

The teacher is younger than I expected, and in his jeans, button-down shirt, and fancy leather shoes he looks more like one of the new attorneys at Mom's law firm than what I expect a ceramics teacher to look like. He wraps an apron around his waist and hands me one.

"Grab two balls of clay and take a seat," the professor says to me, gesturing toward an empty wheel.

My eyes must go big because he smiles. "Clay won't bite."

After I sit, he asks the student next to me to school me on the basics. The student has a towel draped over his thigh, and I soon learn why. Throwing clay is messy. Once everyone gets going, the professor circles the room, commenting quietly on each student's progress. I'm surprised by how much I like the soft feel of the wet clay beneath my hands, even though I can't center it. After three wobbly attempts, the professor helps me get the fourth lump of clay centered. I work my hands in and out of the clay until I have a half-decent bowl. All around me students use their two hands and a spinning wheel to transform gray lumps into plates, bowls, and vases. If I were to draw this moment, I'd call it *Life Like New*.

By the time the class is over, Amber has created a series of plates with perfect spirals starting from the center and working out the farthest edge. Meanwhile, my bowl collapsed after I tried to widen it more than it wanted to go. I leave my half bowl, half lump with other failed attempts. Amber shrugs off her creations, like she makes those in her sleep.

"Do you think you'd like throwing clay when you get here?" Amber asks while we wash up.

"Never thought about it before just now, but I might." I do love the idea of making an actual product or using my hands to build something. I wonder if Mom would view that as practical.

"Well, you seemed right at home at the wheel," she says.

"Ha. Right up until my bowl died," I say, even though I love that she said that.

"That happens to everyone," she says, dismissively. "You have your lunch voucher? I've got to run."

"You're not coming?" I try to play off my disappointment.

"Can't. Sorry," Amber says. "I'm helping a friend hang paintings for their upcoming show." She smiles at me, her lip ring glinting in the light. "Good luck."

As I'm looking for the campus map to find the cafeteria, I hear a voice from behind me.

"Ready for lunch?"

I turn and smile when I see Joon waiting for me. "I was going to use my voucher."

Joon shakes his head. "That's not an option. You aren't from Baltimore. It's my civic duty to take you someplace cool."

"I need to be back for an interview at two."

"Okay, you're making it hard on me, but we can still have fun if we go right now. You up for it?" Joon's energy is infectious.

"You're not going to make me eat a Baltimore version of a Philly cheesesteak, are you?" I say, skeptically.

"No, we don't have those here. Not even bad ones. Come on." He takes off and I need to rush to keep up. We walk around the corner and two blocks up where he stops in front of a nondescript place with a walk-up window.

"Stay right here and prepare to be awed," he says and goes up to the counter to order. In a few minutes he returns with a tray holding two packages wrapped in wax paper, two sodas, and some fries.

"Are you ready to be awed?" he asks. "I don't think you're ready to be awed."

I've already been awed. By MICA, by Joon, and by the pottery class. I'm not sure how much more awed I can get. But I answer, "I am ready to be awed."

He gestures for me to pick up one of the sandwiches, which I unwrap with curiosity.

"Go ahead," Joon says. "Take a bite."

A real Maryland crab cake fills my mouth with all the good

things. "Mmm." I moan, unable to say anything more coherent.

"Right?"

I nod.

"You never told me your medium," Joon says.

"Charcoal. I love the way you can smudge it and make a whole new look."

"What? No pastels? No oils? I already know you don't use watercolors."

"I think in pastels and I work with them or colored pencils when I need rich color. But my heart is with charcoal. Oils scare me, and watercolors are too . . . watery. I make things too—mostly for my family—but those are more crafts than art, I guess." I pause. "I just went to a ceramics class and I liked the idea of manipulating things to make art, you know?" I think about my failed bowl. Seems like I'm better at breaking stuff than making it.

"Not me," Joon says, wiping his mouth with a tiny napkin. "All I think about is where else I can tag. What I can do to a huge blank space. I want my art to say something. To make change."

"Be careful. You might end up as successful as your parents," I say, teasing. But Joon's words stay with me. I love to draw and create projects for the people I care about, but I've never considered that my art could create change.

We munch our sandwiches and dust off the crumbs. I pull out my wallet. "What do I owe you?" I know that crab cakes can't be cheap, but it was totally worth it. Maybe this would be a good use of Mom's over-the-top tip.

Joon holds up his hands. "On me," he says.

"Are you sure?" People don't usually offer to pay my way.

"I'm sure."

"Okay, and if you're ever in Philly . . ."

"Cheesesteaks on you." He grins at me, and suddenly I so want to kiss him right on the mouth, but I don't.

"Guess I'd better . . ." He gestures toward the campus.

"Right. Go find the parents. And I need to get ready for my interview."

"I can't tell you to break a leg," Joon says, tapping his finger to his lips. "So, break a stick of charcoal."

I grin after his retreating figure. I can't help it. A nice boy just bought me lunch. I love it here. I can imagine being happy in Baltimore with my art and my crab cakes and a cute street artist.

I take a moment to settle my thoughts. The sun is red through my closed eyelids. My eyes flicker open and I start to walk toward the Admissions office. It's hitting me that moving toward my dream means moving away from my family, and that is a future I can't visualize yet. Mom, Emma, and I have been a tight unit since Dan left. When Mom got the promotion to work for the partner at the firm, more fell on me to make sure Emma got home safe and all. Being Emma's big sister is so much of who I am, but I also want to see who else I could be.

Back at the Admissions building, students sit on the steps and lean against the wall, talking or smoking or staring at their phones. They clutch sketchbooks or lug big, black portfolios like mine. I almost look like I fit in, but I feel like a square peg trying to pass as round. I push that thought down and pull in a deep breath. I'm allowed to be here. It's okay to pursue my dream.

12

BEFORE:
We're still camping.
I'm still just twelve

NO NOISE FLOATS toward us from Emma's tent. Mom must have fallen asleep there. Dan had pulled me onto his lap, and his palm lay on my bare thigh. I'd just turned twelve—too old to be on anyone's lap—and I am practically gagging from the bourbon smell. The fire hisses in response to raindrops. I stay a moment longer until I can't take it.

"I don't want to get wet before bed. I'm brushing my teeth and going to sleep," I say, wriggling up. He pats me on the butt. Another thing I am too old for.

"Good night, Skylar. Sweet dreams, and don't let the bedbugs bite," Dan says, as he always said before Emma and I went to sleep. He slurps at his drink and stares at the fire with an unfocused gaze. The frogs go silent in their pond as thunder booms once more.

I swim out of sleep.

I'd had trouble sleeping beneath splintering lightning and roaring thunder. But the storm must have passed and I must have fallen asleep because I'm waking up and there is no thunder. No lightning. No rain driving into the tent roof. But something has woken me. Something not right. A feeling on my body.

Tickling?

No.

Touching.

I blink my eyes open to the dim night. A dark figure leans over me. Dan. His breathing is heavy and stinks like bourbon. His hands stroke my body. My pajama top is pushed up to my neck. His rough fingers play with my small breasts. Fear nails me to the tent floor. Dan is touching all the parts of me that no one is supposed to touch. His hands are everywhere.

I'm scared. I'm so scared.

I can't speak.

I can't move.

I'm frozen in the tent and I can't move.

He's breathing heavy and his fingers are going to my secret places and I want to cry out, but I can't. His hand slips down, down. He pushes my legs open. His fingers are seeking. They're turning me inside out. I'm so scared. I don't know what's happening. Then he rubs his heavy man-body against me. His thing is hard against my leg. He goes faster. Faster. He grunts. Then the full weight of him crashes onto me. His breathing is wet in my ear. My body starts trembling. My body is telling me to move now. To get out of this tent. A tiny whimper escapes my throat. I push at him and push at him, holding back an animal wail that wants to rip out of me. He groans. Wriggling my body out from under him, I scramble out of the tent.

I fix my pajamas with shaking hands. There's sticky stuff on me. I rub and rub it away. My body shivers like it's freezing, though it's a warm May night. The ground is wet from rain. I suck in the sharp smell of damp dirt, trying to calm my little bird heart. I go to the other tent. I shake Mom's shoulder, careful not to jostle Emma.

"What is it?" she says in a wine-soaked voice.

"Dan," I croak.

"Dan what?" Mom is impatient. She doesn't like her sleep disturbed.

I can't make my mouth form words that I don't understand.

"What?"

"He . . . touched me. Under my clothes. He touched my chest and . . ."

I can't see Mom's expression in the dark, but I can see her head wobble back and forth on the pillow. "He touched you? He probably just hugged you," she mumbles. "He loves you." She breathes out a sleep-filled sigh. "Go back to sleep. It's fine."

The tone of her voice is an iron door slamming shut. I know he loves me, but I know he wasn't hugging me. It's not fine. But I can't say anything more to the iron door.

"I'll sleep with Emma," I say.

"Jus' go to sleep," she says groggily, rolling back over in the sleeping bag.

I back out of the tent and stand, barefoot on the wet dirt, looking from one tent to the other. I can't go back into the tent with Dan. I can't. I climb into the tent with Mom and Emma, squeezing myself into the narrow space and try to find my way back to sleep while the frogs make their noise all around us.

The next morning, Mom rolls over and bumps into me. I was already awake, waiting for her and Emma. I didn't want to go out there alone. Mom blinks a few times. She frowns. "What are you doing here?" Her voice is scratchy, like always after she'd had a lot to drink.

Didn't she remember?

My mouth gapes like a little fish as I try to say it again. "Last night I came to you. Dan . . ."

"Was he snoring again?" she asks. "I'm sorry, sweetie. He always snores when he drinks too much." With a great sigh, she crawls out of the tent without waiting for my reply.

"Wake your sister. We've got to strike these tents," she says.

I wanted to make her understand. But how?

I shake Emma awake and climb out of the tent. Dan is packing up our supplies and loading the car. His tent is already struck, and he'd poured sand over the ashes in the fire pit, assuring that they wouldn't reignite. The morning was gray, and a light drizzle spit on our faces.

"Is there coffee?" Mom asks.

"In the thermos." He points. "But don't be long. I want to get going. Girls, pack your things," he says to me and Emma, only he doesn't look our way.

As we drive out of the campsite, I see my favorite tree, sliced in half with a big burn mark in the middle.

"The Whomping Willow!" I say.

"Oh, how sad. Looks like it was hit by lightning," Mom says.

Dan just grunts. The whole morning, he acted like nothing had happened. He's supposed to be a dad, but dads don't do what he did. And Mom acted like I was wrong. But I'm sore down there. What happened wasn't my imagination. I feel like my favorite tree, ruined in one bad night, and I don't know how to fix the damage.

13

My Heart on the Outside

"HELLO?" I CALL when I walk in the door of our house. The drive home had been long, but nothing could dim my euphoria from the visit to MICA and the interview, which I was sure I nailed.

"Up here." Emma's voice floats down from her upstairs bedroom.

I find her lying on her stomach on her bed, watching *Beauty and the Beast* on her computer.

"I'm researching my role," she says, all serious.

"Research. Got it." I try to keep the amusement out of my tone. "Did you find out about parts today?"

She turns, a huge grin filling her face. In the background, Belle sings about feeling out of place in a little town. Sounds familiar.

"You got a part! Which one?"

Emma jumps up from her bed. "You are looking at the next Mrs. Potts."

"Whoa, she sings the title song."

"That's right." She grins, and her joy makes my heart balloon.

"Way to go, Em!" I offer my fist for a bump.

She fist bumps me. "Well, I *am* pretty awesome," she says with mock seriousness.

"How about we celebrate how awesome you are." I still have Mom's twenty in my pocket and this is for sure a legit way to spend it.

"Wait! How was your interview?"

"They loved my portfolio, especially that portrait of you." I smile at Emma. "And I think I did okay on the questions they asked me. So? Celebration?"

"Froyo?" she asks.

"You got it. After dinner, okay?" I say. "Where's Mom?"

"At work."

"Didn't she bring you home?"

"No, Dan picked me up."

"*Dan* picked you up?"

"Yeah, he said that Mom got held up doing whatever. He didn't even know where to go. They called me up to the office. Can you believe that?" She rolls her eyes.

"That's terrible!" I slump down on her bed.

Emma frowns at me. "It wasn't *that* big of a deal. He just doesn't know the pickup system."

During a quick dinner of leftovers and even as we're driving to get frozen yogurt, I'm distracted by the fact that Mom asked Dan to pick up Emma. I should have been there for Emma, that's my job. But also Mom totally backed out on her promise.

"Do you have any gum?" Emma asks.

"In my bag," I say.

She fishes around in my bag and I remember the bowl that I tossed in there. The weed is in a hidden pocket and I don't know why I didn't tuck the bowl in there too. I clutch the steering wheel. She pulls out the pack of gum and offers me a piece. I relax my hands on the wheel and shake my head no. She tosses my bag in the backseat.

In the Froyo shop, Emma mushes gummy bears into a concoction of four different flavors.

"Did it bother you," I ask, "that Mom had Dan come get you from school?"

"No," Emma says, stirring. "It was totally fine. He let me put on whatever music I wanted. He came in for a little while to make sure I was fine, but I told him that I stay home alone all the time."

I frown. "But you don't."

She shoves a huge spoonful of yogurt into her mouth. "He doesn't know that." She grins at me.

I poke at the yogurt with my spoon, thinking about how quickly Mom is shoving Dan back into our lives.

Emma speaks. "Mom says she and Dan are having a special weekend to celebrate Valentine's Day."

I stir my chocolate/vanilla combo until it's just brown slop.

"How come you're not happy about them?" Emma says, staring at me.

"It's not that I'm not happy." I pause. That's a lie. I'm definitely not happy. "I'm just used to it being us three." That's true at least.

Emma lifts a Froyo-coated gummy bear to her mouth. "Well, *I* think it's perfect. Dan's going to help me get ready for the musical and . . ."

She stops talking, but I can tell she wants to say something else.

"And?"

Emma meets my eye. "I remember how sad Mom was when he left. I want her to be happy again, Skye. Don't you?"

"I'd like everyone to be happy, Butter Bean," I say, looking at my little sister slurping Froyo.

"What a train wreck of a day," Mom says when she gets home around eight. "I'm exhausted. Did you girls eat?" Mom lays her purse on the table by the door and hangs up her coat.

Emma is upstairs watching more videos of Mrs. Potts's performances. I'm sketching our dining room table with its four chairs and two silver candlesticks, each sprouting a candle topped with a blackened wick.

"We heated up leftovers. I think there's still some in the fridge."

"They fed us at work. Just wanted to make sure that you two

had some food." She tugs her hair out of a clip and lets it fall across her shoulders. "Well, how did it go?"

"I *think* it went well. They definitely liked my portfolio. And I was ready for their questions. I won't know for a while, though."

"But you think you made a good impression?" She plops on the couch next to me and tosses her heels on the floor.

I nod. The candles are burgundy, impossible to put down in charcoal. But I can get the shine of the candlesticks, which Mom polishes once a month.

"Fingers crossed," Mom says. "Because if we don't get that scholarship—"

"I'm aware." I can't help but note Mom's use of *we*. I add some shading beneath the chairs. Used to be that no one sat in the chair closest to the sliding glass doors. That way we could see out the window. Not anymore. Now all of our chairs are used. I start working on the sliding glass doors. With the dark night on the other side, the glass is a mirror reflecting our room back to us.

"I guess you didn't visit Towson," she says, rubbing her feet.

"No, Mom, I didn't visit Towson."

Mom gets up, pours herself a glass of wine, and sits back down.

"How come you didn't pick up Emma today?" I ask, careful to keep my voice neutral.

"My boss needed me to work late at the last minute. He was filing a brief."

I know that it's hard for Mom to say no to her boss. If he needs her, she stays.

"But, Mom, you *just* brought Dan back into our lives. It's like you just pushed Emma off on him."

"I'm not pushing your little sister off on anyone." Mom's tone is clipped. "Dan was like a father to her before. To both of you."

I say nothing. He *was* like a father. I had loved him like a father.

"Besides, if he wants to be in our lives again, he'll need to get used to helping me out," Mom says, retrieving her glass from the table and sipping from it again.

Mom had asked him to leave when I was in seventh grade. He'd been drinking a lot more and he'd become so angry. I never knew exactly what happened, but I remembered the tearful nights and long phone calls with Judy. Emma wasn't wrong when she talked about Mom being unhappy after Dan left.

Maybe I've been overreacting. He *was* always great at teaching us new things and taking us places. And it *would* be nice for Emma to have a father-type person.

But then the memory of what happened twists my guts.

"Just seems like we've been happy since he left." But when I say *happy,* I think what I really mean is *safe.*

All of those things that I said to Emma to make her remember how awesome we are—they were all things we've done since Mom and Dan broke up. Having makeovers together. Doing girls' movie nights. Painting our bedrooms. We did all of those things just the three of us—a small family, but a sort of happy one. Mom stares at the blank television screen, not agreeing or disagreeing. At least I'd thought we were happy.

I'm quiet then, unsure if I should press on or not. For as long as I could remember, Mom's whole life had been Emma and me and work. As she tells it, our father had been more interested in other women than in his wife and kids. When he had an affair with her supposed best friend, Mom called it quits and moved back to the Philadelphia area to raise us near family, which meant Nana. Then there was Dan, with his fancy education and his job at the college and his smart way of talking and his manners. And he'd fallen for Mom, even though she just had a high school diploma, not to mention two little girls. Us. And he seemed like he really wanted to be a father. He wanted to do things with us, to teach us things.

Then Nana got sick and Dan was there. Sometimes it seemed that all Mom saw when she looked in the mirror were the burdens: no college education, having two kids at a young age and an ex-husband who cheated all the time. Like she should be lucky that someone like Dan would pay attention to her.

When Mom speaks, her voice is quiet. "I'd never trade you girls in for anything. I love you both so much."

And I know this. I've never doubted that Emma and I are the center of Mom's world.

She continues. "But I want to be in a relationship. With Dan. *That* will make me happy."

On the Saturday after Valentine's Day, Dan comes to the house to pick Mom up for a "romantic night." Mom is all giggly-nervous.

She's been upstairs getting ready, while Emma offered tips for her makeup and hair. When the doorbell rings, I come up the steps from my basement room to find Mom in very high black heels and a crimson dress that clings to her curves She's looking seriously va-va-voom.

Dan stands in the doorway in his trademark look: khakis, a blue button-down shirt, and a dark blue blazer. He's shaven except for the goatee, which he touches when he sees Mom. I imagine the moment as *Little Red and Her Wolf*, mixed media. I'd use bits of fabric and pages from discarded picture books to capture this fractured fairy tale.

"Aren't you a vision?" he says, eyebrows raised.

"You like?" she says, spinning so that the skirt of the dress ruffles softly around her slender legs.

"I like." He hugs my mother and kisses her full on the mouth, as if Emma and I aren't standing right here. "Are you ready?" he says, smiling at her.

Mom nods, her eyes large and shining like those anime figures that boys are always drawing in art class. She turns to us.

"So, you girls will be okay?" Mom asks, but she's not really asking. She's picked up her overnight bag and is walking to the door. I wonder what would happen if I said that we wouldn't be okay—if I suddenly got sick, which doesn't feel completely impossible right this moment when I see Dan eyeing Mom.

I know what would happen: instead of them going out, Dan would be at our house overnight. For a split second, my mind flashes to that night in the tent. He hasn't spent the night at our house since they've been back together.

"Yup, we'll be fine," I quickly say.

"Of course!" Emma seconds.

"Okay, I'll be back tomorrow morning. Don't stay up too late."

"We won't," I say, holding back the eye roll.

"Have fun!" Emma sings out.

What are you doing tonight? Luisa texts me a little later.

Home w Emma. Mom on romantic overnight (ew!) You?

Don't know. Quarry maybe but feel like loser w no bf.

It bugs me that Luisa is so focused on landing a boyfriend, like being one half of a couple is better than being a whole person on your own.

Come here! We'll binge GG. It'll be fun

Love me some Lorelai and Rory, but that sounds like a super-depressing V-Day date. Sorrrrrrry! Are you working tomorrow?

Yeah, lunch shift.

See you there.

Later, I get a text from Ben and I tell him how I'm on Emma duty all night on account of Mom's sleepover. He says he doesn't feel like going to the quarry. With old memories pressing on me, I don't want to be alone with just Emma. And that is how I end up spending Saturday night babysitting with my best guy friend. At first Emma balked at the idea of a boy at our house, but Ben showed up with pizza and sundaes and won Emma over in two minutes flat. We play cards and charades and then Emma gives us both makeovers.

"You look lovely with blue eye shadow," I say to Ben. I haven't had this much fun without substances probably since I was Emma's age.

"I know," he says, batting his eyelashes. "You should see me with purple. It'd knock your socks off." He winks at me, and something flutters deep down.

After Emma goes to bed and Ben and I have both cleaned Emma's work from our faces, we hang out on the couch, eating microwave popcorn and making fun of the romantic comedy marathon that's running on cable.

"Oh, Skylar," he mock-swoons, grabbing my hand in his. "You complete me."

"Oh, Benjamin," I say, leaning close and placing my hand on his cheek. "You had me at *Oh, Skylar.*" I feel the stubble of his jaw under my palm. If I moved my thumb, I could graze his lower lip.

We hold each other's gaze for a beat and neither of us is laughing. I realize I'm pressed against him. I've taken it too far. It would be so easy to numb myself with Ben—and fun too, I bet. Really fun. After all, that's what I do. I hook up.

But hooking up is *not* what I do with Ben. With all of my willpower, I push away from him and laugh it off. "If anyone looked in my windows now, they'd think we were a couple."

Ben sort of coughs. "Yeah."

I retreat to the farthest part of the couch, grabbing the clicker to find something besides romance and kissing on the screen. A war movie maybe. Or a special on parasitic infections. But the energy of the room has shifted. I'm aware of his every movement. He's running his hands down his thighs to his knees. I love those hands. He rubs his jaw where I'd just laid my palm. My body vibrates with the urge to close the distance between us, and I'm not even high. I can only blame the stupid Hallmark holiday that Mom and Dan are celebrating. Seems I can't be trusted tonight.

"You know, it's getting late," I say.

Ben looks surprised, but he stands. I herd him to the door without touching him because who knows where that would lead. After I lock the door behind him, I descend to my room, where I draw and draw and draw, trying to purge myself of these traitor feelings.

I just need to get to the end of the school year without screwing up my friendship with Ben. That's only a few months. I can do this. I can do anything for a few months.

14

No Good Deed

LATE SUNDAY MORNING while Emma and I are eating pancakes, Dan and Mom return home. They both look way too happy. Mom looks shyly at Dan, and he grabs her hand.

"Girls, we have some news," Mom says, breaking into an elated smile.

I frown and stop chewing. News?

"We're getting married!" Mom says.

I look from Mom's grin to Dan's proud smile to Emma's pure joy. The pancakes are dry in my mouth. I have trouble swallowing.

"You're getting married?" Emma asks, a grin splitting her face.

"Yes!" Mom says. "We're getting married," she says again, looking at Dan. She holds out her left hand where a tiny diamond perches.

"Oh my gosh, I have to tell Julia." She starts typing a text. "A wedding! I can *not* believe it. White dress. Veil. Flowers." Emma ticks the necessary items off on her fingers. "Oh! Can we be *in* the wedding?"

Mom laughs. She's beautiful when she laughs. Will this really make her as happy as she hopes? Emma seems to think so.

"I'm not sure about a *white* dress," Mom says, "but I'd love for you to be in the wedding, Butter Bean!"

"Oh my god, Mom. Stop calling me that!" Emma smiles to soften the words and holds Mom's left hand in both of hers, examining the ring.

"We'd love you *both* to be in the wedding," Dan says, looking to me. I don't miss that he is trying to include me. Especially because he rarely talks directly to me. Mom stares down at Emma, the picture of maternal bliss. Standing before them, I feel like an orphan.

"You're getting married?" I finally blurt. My tone doesn't come near matching the joy of Emma's.

Mom's smile falters.

"We know this seems quick," Dan says, then smiles at Mom. "But we know what we want, and there is no sense in waiting."

I was just trying to get used to the idea that Mom was dating Dan again, but I have to remember that they've actually been dating for over five months now. But engaged? Maybe there's something wrong with me that I can't let Mom be happy. I try to force a grin, but it feels like a grimace.

"I need to go to work," I say, scraping the rest of my pancakes into the sink. I turn on the disposal and let it chew up the remains of my breakfast.

During the lull between breakfast and lunch, Luisa is studying for an English test and I'm sketching on a paper napkin. Dan, Mom, and Emma stand together, their bodies touching. I draw myself half off the napkin.

"What's a word for being the odd one out?" I ask.

Luisa looks up from her flash cards. "Third wheel?"

"No, sort of like you don't fit in with the rest." I shade in Dan's goatee, but the pencil tears the napkin a little bit. Behind us, Sal calls to the dishwasher to make sure the glasses are clean before the lunch rush.

"Peculiar? Aberration?" Luisa says.

I scribble *aberration* on the sketch. The sizzle and scrape of the cooks cleaning the griddle is punctuated by their sharp banter while a busboy stacks empty trays in our station. A ping on my phone tells me an e-mail just came in. I have about a million unread messages, but I tap the phone to see what it is.

"Oh my god, oh my god, oh my god." I cradle the phone in both hands, as if the e-mail might disappear if I'm not careful.

"What is it?" Luisa asks.

"An e-mail from the scholarship people at MICA!"

"Read it!" Luisa says.

I hold my phone out to her. "You read it."

Luisa holds up her hands, refusing to take my phone. "I'm not reading an e-mail that could decide your future before you even look at it," Luisa says.

"Then read it out loud to me," I beg. "Please?"

Luisa sighs and shakes her head at me. She tucks her flash cards into her apron pocket and takes the phone from my shaking hands.

Luisa reads:

Dear Skylar Murray,

We are pleased to share with you that you've been awarded the highly competitive Meyerson Scholarship. The scholarship is a full, four-year award designed to cover all tuition, room, board, and added fees during your time at MICA. Please note that the scholarship is contingent on you maintaining a full course load and a grade point average of 3.0 or higher.

The committee was impressed with your portfolio and enjoyed the opportunity to talk with you about your interests and goals related to the study of art at the Maryland Institute College of Art. We believe that you will be an exemplary student and are thrilled to support your education in this way.

Please look for materials to be sent by mail,

which will finalize your acceptance of this scholarship. Best wishes for a strong finish to your academic year.

Sincerely,

Meyerson Scholarship Committee
Maryland Institute College of Art

Luisa screams. I open my eyes and I scream.

"Ladies!" Sal shouts. "No shouting in my restaurant."

We stop screaming, but we grab each other and jump up and down. "You did it! You got the scholarship!"

"And we'll only be a train ride away from each other."

"Or a Bolt Bus. I'll come see you and you can come see me at Temple. Easy."

I grip her arm. "It's real, right? I'm not dreaming?"

"Ladies!" Sal calls to us. "Are your tables spotless? Are the salad dressings refilled?"

Luisa straightens the napkins in our station. "If you were dreaming, would you be hearing Sal boss you around?"

"Probably not." I smile and pull in a deep breath and then let it out. "I got the scholarship. I'm going to MICA!"

"You're going to MICA," Luisa says.

"Ladies?" Sal says.

"Everything is ready for the lunch rush, Sal," Luisa says.

"Yup, everything refilled and wiped down," I add.

"Okay," he grumbles. "I don't pay you to study and draw pictures."

"But we're showing initiative!" Luisa says.

Sal breaks into a broad smile. "You got me. But when you're here, you show initiative for restaurant work, understand?"

We both nod.

On the drive home, I can't wait to tell Mom and Emma about my scholarship. I didn't even text anyone because I want to tell the people who are important to me in person. When I walk into the house, Mom is on the couch staring at her laptop. "How was your shift?"

"Good!" I say and I'm getting ready to announce my big news when Mom speaks again.

"We've set a date."

My mind is on MICA, on my future. I'm so far away that I have no idea what she's talking about. "Set a date?"

"Yes, for the wedding." Mom watches me, like she's gauging my reaction. "Second week of April. We want to do it soon. Emma is excited to be a bridesmaid and obviously, we hope that you—"

"You knew, didn't you?" Something has dawned on me.

"Knew what?" Mom says.

"You knew he was going to propose," I say. "That's why you brought him back into our lives after you'd been seeing him for all those months in secret."

Mom clears her throat. "I knew that things seemed serious, yes. Why bring him back into your lives if it wasn't going anywhere?"

"Don't do it, Mom." The words tumble out of my mouth before I even know what they are. I'm so excited for MICA. I can't wait to get there and start making art. I imagine Mom and Emma visiting me in Baltimore. Me introducing them to crab cakes and showing them the art scene. I don't see Dan in those dreams.

Mom frowns.

"Why do you have to get married? Why can't things just stay like they are?"

"We've been over this, Skye. I've wanted this for a long time. And Dan wants to be more than a boyfriend. And it will be so nice for Emma. You know, to have a father."

Mom misreads my expression. "Oh, honey, I don't want you to feel left out. You'll always be a part of this family."

Mom has deluded herself into believing what she wants to believe.

"I don't want to be your bridesmaid. And for the record, Emma and I have a father."

"Sweetie," she says. "Dan *wants* to be here. With *us*."

I press my lips together and look away. She's made her point. I haven't heard from my father in a long time. Haven't seen him in even longer. He always seems happy to hear from me when I call or text. He usually says he wants to come see us or fly Emma and me to him in Santa Fe, but he never seems to get around to it.

Mom clears her throat. "Could you try to meet us halfway, honey?"

I notice that her hands are shaking when she grabs her wineglass and stands to leave the room.

"You don't have to leave," I say, defeated. She never understands. She won't even try. She never did. "I'm going to my room."

In my room, I pull out my sketch pad again. Usually I like to draw things that I can see in the stark contrast of charcoal on white paper, but right now all I can see is the blur of my emotions. I'd been so happy about getting the scholarship, but Mom brought me back down to the reality of what's happening to our family.

I pull out my soft pastels and scrawl all over the paper until each page is thick with color When I stop, my stack of papers holds the whole of the color wheel: the angry colors and the sad ones. I rip and tear at the paper again and again until the floor of my bedroom is covered in confetti. Poppy Red, Indigo, Coral, Yellow Ochre, Cool Gray, and Caput Mortuum all lie next to one another, a jumbled confusion of color, and that's pretty much what I feel like right now: a jumbled confusion. If Mom hadn't gotten pregnant, she wouldn't have had to marry Dad and put her life on hold, and if Dad hadn't cheated so much, maybe she would never have ended up with Dan. It's easy to feel like I was never intended to exist and it's even easier to feel like I don't belong in this family now.

But I am here. I do exist. I kneel on the floor and gather the torn pieces of color from my rug. I tug my sketchbook from the bed and grab a glue stick from my backpack. Sitting there, I start gluing the torn pieces onto the paper. When I'm finished, I stand back to look at what I've created. I decide to title it *The Fragmented Whole.*

15

If You Don't Have
Something Nice to Say

BEN SLIDES INTO art class just as the bell rings and takes the stool closest to the door. I try to catch his eye, but he's watching Mr. M.

"It's Critique Friday!" Mr. M says. Half the class groans. "Janelle, you're up. And who will be ready to go after Janelle?"

No one raises a hand. Even if we're dying to be critiqued, most of us won't volunteer for it. Ben thinks the critiques are pointless because most of us have already shared our thoughts on one another's work beforehand. But I don't hate them. I make halfhearted eye contact with Mr. M.

"Skye? Will you go after Janelle?"

I shrug. "Sure."

"And then Tristan."

Tristan groans. "Mine's not finished."

"Most of these works are not completely finished. That's the point. You'll receive input on where to go next so that they'll be ready in time for the art show in April."

Janelle clips her pieces to the display bars.

"My theme is hands and what they hold."

Janelle's pieces are each on black paper with hands drawn in darker black charcoal and white pencil. One depicts a hand open, palm upward. A bright orange butterfly is perched on the forefingers. The next piece is a hand holding another hand. Both hands are slender and delicate; they look like female hands. One is mostly black with white highlights and the other is white with black highlights. The last drawing is of two hands cupped around each other. A quiet yellow glow peeks from the seal between fingers, but the viewer can't see inside.

Janelle stands by her work, shifting from one foot to the other. She looks down at her construction boots. Her long, dark-blond hair hangs in front of her face and drapes over the shoulders of her oversize black T-shirt. Bracelets of leather and beads snake up most of her right forearm. Words and doodles cover the back of her left hand.

"Who would like to comment first?" Mr. M says, prompting us.

"I'll start," Shana says. "I love the hands. They are gorgeous. And I like how the butterfly offers a pop of color. I wonder what the hands are holding in the last one. It seems like a firefly, but I don't know and I like the mystery."

"Yeah," someone else adds. "I like that too. Also, the detail on the hands is excellent. They seem so real. The one with two people holding hands is interesting too because they are opposites."

A couple other students share their thoughts, but it's nothing new. After Mr. M says some artspeak things about use of negative space and composition, it's my turn. As Janelle unclips her work, I ask, "What do you think is in the cupped hands?"

Janelle looks at the piece. Her eyes are ringed in black eyeliner. "They're holding a secret."

I think of the second drawing of a white girl's hand holding a black girl's hand. Janelle isn't with anyone that I know of. At least not at our school. Maybe everyone has a secret that they hold deep inside. I wonder how many girls finally tell their secrets and what happens when they do.

I clip up my charcoal drawings. "I don't have a theme yet, but I'm working on it." No one says anything for a while and I start to think that my art probably sucks. Ben stares at my pieces. Not like he's so intent on the art, more like he's intent on *not* looking at me, which is unusual.

Finally, each person raises a hand one by one and comments on my work. So maybe my art doesn't suck after all.

"Ben?" Mr. M says. "Do you have anything to add?"

Ben crosses his arms over his chest. "Nope."

"Ben, you know the deal. Offer Skye something productive that she can use," Mr. M says.

I notice his hands clench and then release. "I don't have anything *important* to share."

I blink at him and frown.

"It's cool," I say, even though it isn't.

As we move on to Tristan's work, Ben does not look up. Across the room, he fiddles with the bracelet on his wrist.

"What the hell?" I say as soon as Ben and I are in the hallway after class.

"What?" he says, like a total asshat.

"Don't *what* me." I poke his chest. "What was that back there? You don't have anything 'important' to share?"

"No, do *you*?" He stares at me, his eyes locking on mine. "Some *big* news, maybe?"

And I realize what's going on. "You're mad that I didn't tell you. About the scholarship."

He just tilts his head to the side, waiting.

"I didn't tell anyone," I say.

"You told Luisa."

"Technically, I didn't *tell* her. I made her read the e-mail to me because I was too nervous to read it."

"It should have been me," he says quietly, looking down.

"What?"

"*We* are the art people. You and me. It should have been *me* reading you that e-mail."

When I realize that he's not angry so much as hurt, I'm flooded with the urge to hug him. I grip my backpack straps instead. "I was at work."

He nods. "But why didn't you text me?"

"I wanted to tell you in person."

"But you didn't."

He has a point, and it's one that I don't know how to answer. I was so excited in the moment. Being given that scholarship is a dream come true, and I never believed in dreams coming true. I thought that was just for Disney movies and rich kids. But then when I got home and Mom told me about the wedding date, I shoved my big news aside when I was faced with this new reality.

"You're right. My mom announced that she's set a date for the wedding and it sucked the joy right out of me."

He shakes his head. "But her marriage isn't going to really affect you, right? You'll be at MICA. On a full ride."

His forehead creases like he's trying to understand, but he doesn't. I can't blame him. I don't even fully understand my reaction.

"I'm sooooo sorry," Luisa says over the phone. "I figured you would have told him about MICA."

"Not your fault," I say. "It's sort of weird that I didn't."

"Totally weird. Sometimes I think you tell him more than you tell me." Luisa doesn't say it like it bothers her. "But he was pissed, huh?"

"Yeah. We've never fought before. I didn't like it."

"You guys will be fine," she says. "Anyway, what time should I pick you up? We've got to celebrate that scholarship!"

As we talk, I walk the small space between my bed and the door to my room. The fluffy rug feels soft on my bare feet, but I'm all angles and edges inside. As I pause, I catch my reflection in the mirror over the low dresser that sits opposite the door. I look like shit. I lean forward, peering at my face. Yanking the clip from the top of my head, I let my hair fall over half my face. Oh, much better.

"Um, nine thirty?"

Mom barges in.

"Knock much?" I say, before registering her angry reflection in the mirror.

"What's this?" she says, ignoring my comment.

I turn to face her. She is holding Ben's bowl. The one that had been in my purse.

"Gotta go," I say to Luisa and set my phone on the dresser.

"If I had to guess," I say to my mother. "I'd say it is a tool used for ingesting smoke."

"Don't play with me, Skylar." Mom's mouth is a thin line.

"What do you want me to say? You know what that is. You have a similar one in that cupboard over the fridge."

Mom's eyes widen, but she gets herself back on track. "This conversation isn't about me. You are a minor and this is a serious infraction." She points the bowl at me to emphasize each word.

"Newsflash, Mom: it's not that serious of an infraction. Weed is basically legal now."

This time I don't derail her at all. In fact, she's gathering steam. "I wasn't aware that you have a condition allowing you access to medicinal marijuana. Where did you get this?" she pushes.

"It's not mine." My reply doesn't answer the question, but technically, it's true. Ben lent it to me.

"Possession is nine-tenths of the law."

Bad idea to argue with a legal secretary who has always wanted to be an attorney.

"Let me switch gears," Mom says. "Do you know how this little item came to be in *my* possession?"

I flash back to Emma rooting around in my bag. No, she wouldn't do that to me. She didn't even call me out when she was miserable the time I was late picking her up from Julia's sleepover.

"I plead the fifth," I say.

"Cut the attitude, Skylar. Your little sister gave this to me. She's concerned for you. What a lovely example you're setting."

Concerned for me? Those sound like Mom's words, not Emma's. "Em probably doesn't even know what that is."

"She knew enough to bring it to me because it was something related to drug use."

Awesome. My little sister is now a narc.

I raise my hands in surrender. "Okay, Mom, what do you want?"

She holds out her hand. "Your phone, please."

"What?"

"Your phone. You are grounded. That means you aren't going anywhere." Like she needs to define *grounded*.

"But my phone too?" I'm no stranger to being grounded, but she's never taken my phone from me. Quick as possible, I try to send off the message to Luisa so she knows I'll be unreachable. But before I finish composing, Mom snatches the phone from my busy fingers.

"Sorry," Mom says, in a singsongy, not-sorry voice. "You've lost this particular privilege."

"I pay for my phone so you shouldn't be allowed to take it away." I cross my arms over my chest.

"I can do what I like while you live under—"

"Your roof. I know. But I need my phone."

"You'll get it back when I'm ready to give it back."

"How about if I do extra chores, but I keep my phone."

"Your eleven-year-old sister found drug paraphernalia in your bag. You don't have a leg to stand on here."

"God, Mom, it's not like it's a needle and a bag of heroin."

"Is she going to find that among your belongings as well?"

"Oh my God! Mom, no. I'm sorry to disappoint you, but I'm not the drug addict you think I am."

"You have no idea what I think you are."

The way she hisses the words out, I don't think I want to know.

She continues. "And maybe you're past caring what I think. But what about your eleven-year-old sister, Skye?"

Mom has a point. I feel like shit that Emma found that bowl and that she knew what I would use it for.

"Skye?" Emma's quiet voice whispers through the door a little while after Mom leaves my room.

I'm lying on my bed, tracing the intricate batik patterns on my comforter with one finger. I hiss out a sigh. "Don't want to talk to you, Em."

"Please?" Her tone says that she knows what she did.

"Go away." Being betrayed by the little sister who I love more than anyone stings. I bury my face in my pillow.

"I got you in trouble, didn't I?"

I turn my head so that she can hear me. "I don't want to talk about it, Em. I'm serious."

"I'm sorry," her tiny voice says through the door. "Please? Can I come in?"

I sigh again, melting at her sad tone. "Okay."

Emma cracks the door and peers in before she slides her skinny frame through and shuts the door behind her.

"That thing, it's why your eyes are red a lot, right?"

"I'm not talking about this with you."

"I'm really sorry," she says.

I roll on my back and tuck the pillow behind my head. "Why didn't you come to me first?"

She picks up the wooden drawing figure from my shelf. Emma moves the figure's arms and legs and then puts it back. She shrugs. "I was mad."

"You were mad at me?"

Emma nods.

I'm starting to wonder who is *not* mad at me. "Why?"

"I heard you with Mom last night. You don't want the wedding to happen and then Mom was crying on the phone with Dan and saying that maybe it's not the right time. She was so sad, Skye. I just can't imagine her like that again."

Emma's talking about how Mom was after they broke up the last time, but I ignore that part for now. "Mom was saying it might not be the right time?" A flutter of hope wakes up deep inside my chest.

"Yeah, but I convinced her that it's the perfect time."

The hope dies before it takes off.

"How did you know about the . . . ?"

Emma rolls her eyes. "We're *always* having school assemblies about this stuff." She says it like she's so over it, which would seem funny if she hadn't gotten me grounded. "I'm sorry I got you in trouble. But please don't stop the wedding."

"I can't promise that, Butter Bean."

She crosses her arms over her chest, a move that imitates the one I just did minutes before. "Don't call me that."

"But—"

"Just tell me why you don't want Mom to marry Dan."

I look at my little sister who seems so young, but who knew what a bowl was, and I choose some words, forcing them to march out one at a time like soldiers. "Just because Mom was sad when Dan left doesn't mean she'll be happy now that he's back."

Emma frowns like that's a non-compute. "I don't remember much from before. But he's so great. He's helping me with my lines and he makes Mom so happy. Not like Dad."

"Well, I remember more than you do."

"Like what?"

My eyes travel to the ceiling, blank like a sketchbook page. The one part of my room that is plain vanilla. I'd wanted to paint it midnight blue with little stars, but Mom said it would be too dark with just the one small basement window. I got to do whatever I wanted on the walls though. All of us painted them. That was before we found the bookcase. We did swirls on one wall, zigzags on another, stripes on a third. Mom said it gave her a headache to look at it, but I love my room. It's my space and mine only.

Should I tell Em what I remember? She's almost the same age I was when it happened. But I don't know how to say those words to her when I've never made sense of it for myself. It was just one night. I can't tell Emma. "Can we change the subject?" I ask instead.

Em shrugs. "I guess."

"Do you think you could do me a favor? Sister to sister?"

She presses her lips together, the picture of skeptical. "What is it?"

"Can you send a text for me?"

"Will you promise to stop messing with the wedding plans?"

I guess we haven't changed the subject. Emma is more strategic than I realized. I shake my head no. "But I'll let you use my sparkly eye shadow," I offer in a cajoling tone. I poke her and smile. "Come on, Em." I wait for the smile that always comes. Only this time it doesn't. Emma won't smile for me.

"Will you stop messing with the wedding?" Emma says again.

"What about my purple top? I'll let you wear it," I say,

remembering the shirt that Emma begged to borrow and I refused to lend her because it was new.

Emma rolls her eyes. "Already borrowed it."

"What? You did? You little bugger!"

"Are you going to stop messing with the wedding?" Emma asks for a third time.

Emma's determined stare impales me. I can't remember when we've ever been on the opposite sides of something. Not something so big anyway. Everything in me wants to give Emma what she wants. The problem is that I don't believe Dan is who she wants him to be. "I can't, Em."

"Then I'm not going to help you." She turns on her heel and heads out the door.

16

YOLO

AFTER EMMA LEAVES my room, I wonder why I would stay in a house where I'm the odd one out. Luisa already thinks she's picking me up at nine thirty, so I go with the plan.

Dressing for Major Mom Disapproval, I'm rocking a ripped T-shirt that shows quite a bit of my assets, a short, very short, kilt and thigh-high tights. My eyes are black as night. As I brush my lashes with mascara, I catch myself wondering what Ben will think when he sees me. Will he think I'm slutted up? Or will he not notice? Neither of those possibilities sits well with me. Even worse is the realization that I'm allowing those questions into my mind.

After I'm satisfied with my look, I turn on some music, shut my bedroom door, and slip out the basement door to meet Luisa. Mom isn't likely to come back down to my room, so I should be in the clear for a few hours. Luisa hands me a ginormous soda cup with a straw. I slurp deeply and almost wash the windshield with it.

"Holy crap, how much Southern Comfort did you put in here?" I say after I choke it down.

Luisa shrugs, laughs. "Enough," she says.

As we leave the suffocation of the suburbs, I tell Luisa about what happened at home and warn her not to text me.

"I can't believe Emma did that. She's as sneaky as you!" Luisa says.

I hadn't seen it that way and it doesn't make me feel any better about the situation. Soon we are on the highway and flying toward the towering buildings of downtown Philadelphia with their all-night lights chasing the dark away. We take the exit for South Street and wind through narrow streets created for horses and buggies and bordered by row houses. As the streets near the single digits, the row houses give way to brew pubs and restaurants and shops. Neon lights beckon with promises of cheesesteaks, gyros, and beer. Murals wash sides of buildings. Joon would love this. Around Tenth Street, one building is plastered in mosaics. It's near there that we find the dive where Ben's band is playing.

"Okay, jacket or no jacket?" Luisa says when she gets out of the car. She's wearing leggings with boots and a loose-fitting shirt.

"No jacket. It'll be hot in there and you look great without it."

"Okay. Is my hair weird in the back?" She turns. "You know I have trouble reaching when I'm straightening it."

"No weird hair. You're good. Do I have lipstick on my teeth?" I bare my teeth at Luisa.

"No, and I love that shade. Is it Vampire Vixen?"

"Black Cherry Bomb. Want some?" I pull it from my bag.

Luisa shakes her head. "Ready?"

The dim room is packed with bodies, and Arthouse Scream Machine has just been introduced. We've arrived in time. The lights cast a blue hue over the audience and the bass beat takes hold of my heart. Ben moves to the mic at the center of the stage. He's wearing the dark red skinny pants that I love and that black T-shirt that hangs just right on him. A leather cuff encircles his right wrist, the hand strumming the guitar. He begins to sing, his gravelly voice filling the room, filling me.

Luisa smiles and starts dancing. I smile back, but my mind is on Ben in a way that I wish it weren't. Watching from the back, I see the audience move as one writhing mass, a being with a single mind and Arthouse Scream Machine feeds their desire.

"Come on," Luisa yells, and pulls me forward by the hand. I can't tell if she's into the band or just looking for other kids from our school, but I follow.

We work our way toward the front by sliding up the side of the room. A group of girls at the edge of the stage puts it all out there, arms in the air, shimmying their shoulders and hips like a bunch of lame groupies. One blonde in particular works her way to the edge of the stage while Ben whales on a guitar solo that I never get tired of hearing. I raise my hand in a little wave, but Ben isn't looking at me. He grins down at the blonde as he sings into the mic.

I roll my eyes in disgust—at the girl, not Ben. He's amazing, completely lost in his jam. I poke Luisa and gesture to the girls. She rolls her eyes and shrugs.

I search the crowd for the suit that is supposed to be here watching Arthouse perform. He's easy to spot: an older guy near the bar who doesn't move to the music at all. Instead, he watches the band the way Mr. M watches us draw, all brow furrowed and arms crossed over chest. He's analyzing them, weighing them against what he's seen before. Of course, I'm biased, but Ben is definitely on fire tonight. I cross my fingers that the suit will think so too.

The blonde is singing along like she knows the band, but she doesn't know how Toby and Marcus worked over the lyrics again and again while Ben worked on the music or how I pointed out a hiccuppy transition that they then fixed. She sure as hell doesn't hear Ben's songs playing in her dreams from listening to them on repeat when the band is working on a new set list. But the way she's dancing and staring at him and the way he's staring back makes me think that maybe this song will be in her dreams tonight after all.

I've lost count of how many shows I've seen Ben perform, but this is the first time I remember feeling jealous of the girls he sings to. After a few songs, I turn toward the exit, and with the music of Ben's guitar following me, I walk out into the chill of the night.

"Are you okay?" Luisa asks when she catches me outside.

I shrug. "Just not feeling it tonight."

"You guys are in a weird place," Luisa says. "It'll work itself out."

I bark a laugh. "You make us sound like a couple."

Luisa makes a face like she's calling it the way she sees it.

I roll my eyes. "Whatever. Want to leave?"

"We just got here!"

Keith, Ashton, and some other jocks cluster in a clumsy circle, passing bottles of Gatorade that anyone who paid any attention would know are not filled with just Gatorade. I spy Ellen with girls from the Spirit Squad, each one looking like the next. I wonder if they measure their hair to ensure that they all have the same exact length. One of them leans in to speak to Ellen. She nods and then separates from the group and glides over to Ashton, who drapes his arm around her slight figure. Luisa starts toward the group, but I hang back. I'm not looking for any drama tonight. Matt catches sight of us and pulls away from the others.

"Hey, Matt." Luisa smiles. "I didn't see you before."

"I didn't see you girls either. How's the show?"

"Good! Hot though." She fans herself.

A baseball player I had a thing with once ambles over too. I remember him being a surprisingly good kisser. Also, he has those blue eyes that make it impossible to look away. Those eyes skip from the low scoop of my tee to the slice of leg between my thigh-highs and short skirt. He shakes his head. "I'm helpless, Skye."

I dressed like this on purpose, but now I guess he's expecting something and I'm not feeling like such a party girl anymore. "We were just heading out," I say.

"No, we're—" Luisa smacks me on the arm at the same time that Matt speaks.

"You are?" Matt says. "Could I get a ride?"

"Sure," Luisa says brightly, pushing her hair behind one shoulder. "Come on."

"You sure you don't want to stay?" the baseball player says to me. "*I* could take you home." I imagine him drawn in Sharpies: *Beware: Boy Next Door* on account of those grinning blue eyes, freckles, and that ginger hair disguising the player that he is. Usually, this sort of attention makes me buzz with pleasure. But right now, I'd rather be invisible.

"I snuck out. Need to get back in the house before my mom realizes."

I slide into the back seat and Luisa turns and whispers *thank you*. I'm feeling like the third wheel while Luisa laughs at Matt's lame jokes up front. But Luisa always has my back, so I definitely owe her this one. As we make our way back to the highway, I fantasize about asking Luisa to jump on I-95 South, take me to Baltimore, and let me start my new life tonight—away from my mother's judgment and her impending wedding. Away from boys who think they know me because they know about me. But I don't say anything. I am quiet in the back until I tell Luisa to drop me off first. When she agrees too quickly, I know that she's hoping something will happen after I'm gone.

I slip back into my house through the basement door. Of course Mom is standing at the door to my room in her bathrobe. She holds a pile of folded laundry in her arms. Her eyes scrape over me and she shakes her head.

"I don't know what to do with you. I really don't."

She looks so defeated. This is exactly the disapproval I was striving for earlier in the night, but now I feel like a girl playing dress up in all the wrong ways.

"Get some sleep," she says, handing me my laundry. She heads for the steps and stops, turning to me. "I just want to keep you safe, you know."

I nod, but the thing my mother can never seem to address is that the danger for me wasn't out there. It was inside. With us. And now she planned to marry it.

I trade in my "slutty" outfit for sweatpants and a T-shirt as I try to figure out what's going on with Ben. He knows me better than most people, but he doesn't know the whole me. I grab my sketch pad and some earbuds and try to drown out my conflicting feelings about wanting to be seen and wanting to be invisible. The drawing that emerges is of me as a kid looking for crayfish. I draw myself as a water nymph, just like Dan had said. I remember feeling proud that he'd seen me that way, as if I was something special. But I wonder if that's the moment that started it all? I remember Dan talking about the plant that helps get rid of poison ivy. Too bad I couldn't use jewelweed to erase the effects of Dan's touch on me.

Late Saturday morning, Mom hands me my phone. "I'm giving this back so that I can reach you. But you are most definitely still grounded. Location services stay on. If I check and you've turned them off, you lose the phone. Got it?"

I nod.

"If I check and you're not home, you lose the phone. Got it?"

I nod again.

"And don't forget about our appointment this afternoon," she says.

The phone's screen is a waterfall of texts and updates from the last fourteen hours.

"What appointment?" I mumble, scrolling through the messages. None of the messages are from Ben.

Mom has said something.

"Huh?"

"Did you hear me?"

"Yes, I heard you," I say. "Keep the phone on or lose it again."

After Mom and Emma leave, the house is dead quiet. I should feel relieved to be left alone, but I feel jumpy, like I want to get out of my own skin. I could call Ben to get high, but I don't.

It's way past time for me to pull my creations into some semblance of a senior portfolio, so that's where I turn my attention. There's an art show at the end of each year, so I need to have something to show. Within minutes, artwork is strewn across my workshop area in the basement. I draw like other people journal, so all this stuff going on with Mom and Dan has given me plenty of inspiration. Sketches hang from clips that I'd installed across the long wall. Two pieces perch on my drafting table. Lesser pieces scatter on the couch next to the table. My eyes rove the pieces, willing them to come together with a coherent theme, which Mr. M requested a while back and which I haven't delivered at all.

"The theme should be something that tells the viewer who you are as a person, what's important to you, what speaks to you," Mr. M said when he described the requirements for the project. He'd said that we couldn't just throw together our best pieces. The whole thing had to hang together with intention.

I'd been stumped then and stumped ever since. Ben's was easy: his theme is the intersection of art and music. He took an old acoustic guitar and used permanent marker to create a scene across the front of it. He built a drum entirely from pencils, twine, and an oil painting canvas and then, as if that wasn't enough, across the top he wrote the lyrics from Tame Impala's "Apocalypse Dreams." And those were just two of his projects.

Looking at the pieces, I have some decent stuff. I examine some of the better ones. I'd transferred the sketch I'd called *Aberration* from the napkin I'd drawn it on to a large piece of black paper. Inspired by Janelle's sketches, I'd drawn Mom, Dan, and Emma full-on in white charcoal and then I'd drawn myself off to the side and half in shadow. Then there's *The Fragmented Whole,* the heart shaped by the little torn pieces of colored paper. And me as a water nymph in *Jewelweed.* Mr. M wants a self-portrait, but I don't think I want to use that one. I'd feel too exposed.

All of the little pieces forming the heart of *The Fragmented Whole* inspire me. I like the idea of the torn pieces coming together to make something bigger. I grab a big stack of Post-it notes that were intended to be used for studying, but which I've been using for doodles. An image blooms in my head. I slide my big headphones over my ears, put on a playlist, and start creating.

I don't know how long I work. When I get hungry, I go upstairs and grab a slice of cold pizza from the fridge and a glass of water. The house is still empty. I return to my basement art space. I haven't been in the zone like this for a long time. It's not a typical self-portrait, but it is me. It's just a version of me split into a lot of Post-it notes that each have their own doodles on them too. I'm nearly finished when I'm aware through the noise of my headphones that someone is calling my name. I pull the headphones off and drop them on the drafting table. I let out a nice clean breath. Working on my art like that is even better than getting high to help keep my mind off of other stuff.

"Skye!" It's Mom calling. And she sounds pissed.

"Down here!" I call, walking to the bottom of the steps. "Come down and see—"

Mom stands at the top of the steps with her hands on her hips. She radiates rage. "Where the hell have you been?"

"Doing art stuff." I gesture with one arm to the area where I've been working on my project. "What's up?"

"You are unbelievable," she scoffs.

"What?" I'm completely baffled.

"Really?" She frowns at me.

"Yeah, really. What's going on?" I try to run through the reasons she could be angry with me. She already knew pretty much everything that has happened lately. She takes the steps down to the basement slowly, talking as she descends.

"You have drug paraphernalia in your bag. I ground you. You sneak out. And now *this*. We had an appointment for dress shopping this afternoon. We just spoke about it this morning."

I sort of remember her saying something, but if I'm honest, I hadn't really been listening. I have nothing to say. "Oh."

She stands on the last stair, looking down at me. "Honestly, Skye."

The way she says *Honestly, Skye* sounds like *You are so damn irresponsible.* It's easy to forget, looking at her right now, that she loves me at all.

"Sorry," I say, and it sounds like *You're such a bitch.*

"You are just doing everything in your power to tip me over the edge, aren't you?"

The irony is that I didn't do any of those things with the express goal of tipping her over the edge. Well, except for sneaking out, I guess.

"I forgot, Mom. Just make another appointment. God, what's the big deal?"

"Go to your room." She points like I don't know where my room is.

I cross my arms over my chest. "Seriously? You're sending me to my room because I didn't go dress shopping with you? I'm seventeen years old."

"While you're under—"

"Your roof? That again, Mom?" I'm a dog backed into a corner and my tone snarls like one.

Then she's in my face, hers ugly with anger. She raises her hand and I straighten to my full height, so we are eye to eye.

"You're going to slap me? Go ahead." I'm acting like a bitch, but it's not like I got high or wrecked my car. I forgot about the appointment and I was doing *schoolwork*. But Mom only sees what will fit into her version of what we all are. I'm the slutty, loser daughter. Emma's the sweet daughter. Dan's the loving father figure. And Mom is the perfect parent.

Instead of hitting me, she lowers her hand. "If you're trying to distance yourself from this family, you're doing a damn good job of it."

17

Two Steps Back

"SKYE?" MOM'S VOICE sounds sorry through my bedroom door.

I could pretend to be asleep, but she'd probably assume I'm high or something. Besides, it's been less than thirty minutes since I disappeared into my room and crumpled on my bed. Her saying that I'm not part of the family was worse than if she had slapped me across the face.

"What?" I say.

"Okay if I come in?"

"We're under your roof."

Mom enters my room and perches on the side of my bed.

"I'm sorry I said that, honey." I turn my face away from her cloying tone. "I'm just under . . ."

". . . a lot of stress?" I finish her sentence into my pillow.

She clears her throat. "I thought that you skipped the dress shopping just to spite me."

"Whatever," I say to my pillow. "I had location services on. You knew I was at home."

Mom's tone changes. "I came here to offer an apology. The least you could do is be civil."

I keep my back to her, hugging my pillow to my chest.

"Look at me," she says. Her tone has shifted, no longer apologetic. I turn toward her. The room feels small and airless with its tiny basement window and my mother filling all the space like a giant in a dollhouse.

"You were inconsiderate to miss the dress fitting, not to mention disrespectful by sneaking out last night. I am sorry that I said something that upset you, but you have a role to play here too."

Mom talks about these little things, but she never addresses the big ones—like how I'm Emma's second mom, picking her up and making sure she gets dinner and keeping her safe.

"I didn't miss the fitting on purpose, and last night was Ben's big show that we've been planning to attend forever. I couldn't miss it."

Mom looks to the ceiling, trying to leech patience from it, I guess. Then she looks back at me. She shakes her head. "You follow my rules while you live under—in this house. If I say you're grounded, that means you stay home. I don't care how important you feel a particular social situation may be."

Mom stands and smoothes out the bedspread, erasing her presence. At my bedroom door, she stops.

"I'm having dinner with Dan this evening. You're responsible for your sister."

"What should we do for dinner?"

"I left some money for you to get takeout."

"Even though I'm grounded?"

"Look, I'm giving you some rope here. Don't hang yourself."

Seems like I'm only grounded until it's inconvenient for her.

I'm still lying on my bed contemplating the suckiness that is my life when Emma calls down that Ben is here. Ben's *here?* I scramble up the steps to find Ben standing in my tiny living room, where he hasn't been since our awkward movie marathon.

"This is unusual," I say. First, he is all hurt that I didn't tell him about MICA and now he's at my house unannounced.

"I need new strings. Thought you might want to come with," Ben says a little too casually. Like he's rehearsed it.

My glance skips from Emma watching TV to Ben standing awkwardly by the door. I wonder if he ended up with that blonde last night and I remind myself that it's none of my business. Speaking of awkward, I'm still in my droopy sweatpants and a paint-stained T-shirt. At least I'm wearing a bra. "Come on down." Ben follows and his boots beat out a rhythm on the steps. *Da-bump. Da-bump.* He makes music through his sheer existence.

"Whoa!" he says at the bottom of the steps. "What is *that?*"

A huge grin spreads across my face at his enthusiasm. "A project I'm working on. What do you think?"

My Post-it project is a huge three-foot-square fractured self-portrait.

He walks closer to examine the piece. "It's amazing! You finally made a self-portrait, but each of these is its own little stand-alone picture too."

"That's the cool part, right? You could take one Post-it and it would be a picture all by itself, then put them all together and you get—me!"

"That's why you got the scholarship." He smiles at me and I feel embarrassed, so I look away.

"You need new strings, huh?" I say, to get the focus off of me. "Is that really why you're here?"

His shoulders slump and he runs a hand through his curls. "It was weird Friday night. You not there."

"Friday was weird."

"I just . . . You're amazing. Look at this project you just created. Your art is such a big part of who you are, and I was bummed that you didn't think to share that huge news with me."

"Yeah, like I said, I didn't really tell anyone."

"I didn't think I was just anyone," he says quietly, fiddling with the bracelet at his wrist.

I don't say anything then because it's true that Ben's not just anyone, but I'm not sure exactly what that means right now.

"I *was* there. At your show," I say, heading for my room.

Ben follows me in, which I don't expect. I figured he'd stay in my workshop area and mess with my art stuff. "You were?" He starts to smile.

"I need to change?" I say.

"Oh, right, sorry. But—" He rubs his neck in that spot below his ear and he grins at me. "You were there?"

I roll my eyes. "Yes, not for the whole show. I saw the suit." I don't mention the blonde. "Have you heard anything yet?"

His smile widens, and mine mirrors his. I can't help it. He's contagious.

"What's going on?" I say.

He takes in a big breath, still smiling.

"Arthouse Scream Machine is getting a recording contract."

"Best news ever!" Before I think, I throw my arms around him and crush him in a hug. His arms wrap around me and lift me from the floor. For a split second, I take in the sheer maleness of him and the fact that we fit so great together. This hug feels like home. I pull away when I realize what I've done and busy myself by looking for a clean shirt in the teetering stack of clothes perched on the chair by my dresser.

"When were you going to tell me?" I ask, not looking at him because I still feel the blush in my cheeks from throwing myself at him.

"I'm telling you now," he says. I can hear a trace of a smile and something else too. "That's why I came over in person. Toby just called to let me know. You're the first person I wanted to tell."

The first person he wanted to tell. I clear my throat and face him, hoping my cheeks don't give me away. "When do you start recording?"

"Next Saturday," he says. "Only thing is—the guys have made me promise to not be messed-up during the recording sessions."

I ruffle my hair, trying to get it to look less slept on. "Man, they're such hardasses," I protest. "They party too."

"Yeah, but I was really high when the guy came to talk to us after the show. It wasn't great. So, they want me to chill until we get the recordings done."

"That's totally harsh. You play great high."

"It's cool. I want this so bad. I can go a few weeks without weed at the sessions if it means I get a record out of it." He bites his bottom lip, and for a flash I see him as a little boy, getting exactly what he wanted for his birthday. He breaks into a grin. "A record. Skye. A *record*! Can you fucking believe it?"

He holds both arms open, like he's expecting me to jump into them again, which is a bad idea for obvious reasons. I don't make the leap.

I smile at him, but I'm afraid to hold his gaze. "Never doubted it for a minute!"

He picks up the wooden figure model that Emma had played with and bends its arms and legs in different directions. "Just think, I'll have a record and you'll be in art school!"

He sets the figure down. It's frozen with arms and legs spread wide, like a cheerleader caught midcheer. Like me when I jumped into Ben's arms. I run my hands through my hair again, this time because I don't know what else to do with them.

"The sessions start *next* Saturday?" I say, trying to change the topic. "*After* the concert, right?"

Ben had scored Tame Impala tickets through a music connection and he'd been counting the days until he was able to see Kevin Parker live.

He grins. "Yup. Concert's Friday."

"Good. We'll have fun that night."

"Yeah, and I'll start the straight life the next day."

"Speaking of which, I'm not sure what I'm going to tell my mom. After being grounded, I doubt she's going to let me out for a concert. Turn around."

Obediently, Ben turns his back to me. "You'll think of something. You always do."

"Very true," I say. Dropping my sweats in a puddle, I slide on a pair of leggings. I yank my ratty T-shirt up and over my head and toss it on the floor. "Who all is going?" I snag my new MICA T-shirt from the end of the bed, but I've probably worn it too many days in a row by now, so I drop it and reach for a clean sweatshirt instead.

"What?" Ben says as he's turning around.

"Ah!" I yell, covering my lacy bra and the cleavage blooming out of it.

Ben's eyes go wide, but he turns back around quickly. "Sorry! I thought you were done."

"I'm not done until I say turn around!"

"Okay. Um, what did you say before?"

"Who is going with us to the concert?" I pull the sweatshirt over my head. "And you can turn around now."

Ben faces me, and his expression is one I've never seen before. At least not since that night we sort of almost did but didn't. That night that I've written off as a result of too many substances. He doesn't look hungry like Ashton or other guys. He looks like someone just gave him another gift. His expression almost makes me wish that I left the sweatshirt off.

"Sorry again," he says. He smiles a half smile and scratches his neck.

"That's okay." I shrug. "I'm sure it's nothing new."

"It's definitely new." His voice is low, inviting.

At his tone, every particle in the room kindles and all of those charged particles bounce from Ben's body to mine. My queen-size bed suddenly looms large in this tiny room. I shove my hands in my sweatshirt pocket to keep them in check.

Similarly, Ben's hands are jammed in the pockets of his jeans, making me wonder if he's hiding his reaction to seeing me in my Victoria's Secret special. My bras are always getting me in trouble. He looks at me through those curls, from below his dark eyebrows.

After a heartbeat or two, which I am sure he can see pounding right through my sweatshirt, I make a choice in favor of our friendship.

"So, the tickets?" I ask.

"Tickets. Right. Shelby didn't have the cash and Matt said he couldn't go."

"Luisa bailed too. Sal wouldn't let her off, so who's left?"

"Keith," Ben says. "And Ashton."

Ashton's name is like cold water on a fire, which maybe is a good thing.

"Come on," I say, opening the door to my room. "Let's get out of here."

"Out of where?" Emma's voice surprises me. "Sorry, I was just coming to see what's going on."

She looks past me at Ben and then back to me, narrowing her eyes. "You're not supposed to have boys in your room." She crosses her arms over her chest. I'm so not used to having Emma pissed at me, and it pretty much sucks. I wonder if she's going to use this against me like she did the bowl.

"You say *boys* like it's not *me*," Ben says, in mock hurt, jabbing a finger into his chest. He moves past me out of my room, charming Emma like he does all the girls. "How could you dismiss me that way?" Ben acts like he's been mortally wounded and falls onto the couch.

I quirk my mouth to one side, trying not to smile, but I can't help it. Maybe we've moved past that moment in my room, like we moved past our other weird interactions recently.

"You're more of a drama queen than I am," Emma says, eyeing Ben draped over the couch arm.

"Yeah, too much Shakespeare for him lately," I say, also eyeing Ben.

"Where are you guys going?" Emma asks, pulling my attention back to her.

"Ben needs new guitar strings. Want to come?"

Ben pushes up from the couch and raises his eyebrows at me but doesn't argue. I shrug a little bit and wince. He stands up and offers a small smile. "Yeah, you want to come?" Ben says to Em.

"Uh, duh?" she says. I can tell that she's excited by how fast she slips on her shoes. "You're supposed to watch me, remember?" Emma says, stopping to put air quotes around *watch me.*

Ben points at me. *You owe me,* he mouths. I smile not just because I'm grateful, but also because this feels normal. Even though he just saw me half-naked, it feels like how Skye and Ben usually feel—uncomplicated. We pile into Freddie and head to the music store.

"Mom's going to be gone for dinner," Emma says. "Can we do something besides just the music store?"

I turn in my seat to look at her. "What do you have in mind?" If I can keep her happy, then maybe she won't blackmail me again.

"I don't know. What do you guys usually do?"

Ben looks sidelong at me. Neither of us is about to tell Emma what we usually do.

"How about bowling?" he suggests.

Emma and I are sitting on the molded plastic chairs, watching to see how badly Ben is going to beat us. He launches a ball down the lane with a precision that I didn't know he possessed. Who knew stoner boys could focus? Also, from this angle, I can appreciate how good he's looking in those jeans. Even if I'm making a conscious decision not to give in to my urges, I can still appreciate the jeans.

"I'm thirsty," Emma says.

It takes a moment to pull away from my daydream.

"Here," I say, pulling a ten-dollar bill from my pocket. "How about a pitcher of soda? Your choice." Emma snags the money and she's gone.

"You can totally sneak out for a quick hit," I say to Ben.

"What about you?" he asks.

I shake my head. "Not ever when I'm watching Emma. By the way, she found the bowl you gave me and gave it to my mom."

Ben raises an eyebrow.

"That's the reason I'm sort of grounded right now."

"I don't need to get high."

"Are you sure?" I've never known Ben to give up a chance to smoke.

He keeps his eyes on mine for a beat longer than necessary. "Yeah. It'll be practice for not getting high while recording." He grins at me and I smile back.

Emma walks toward us with careful steps, holding a full pitcher in her two hands. She seems small and big all at the same time, and I realize that I was just a little older than she is the first time I ever got high. My heart splinters.

18

AFTER: I am still twelve.
One week later

"I SWEAR IF Ashton makes one more joke about my dad being a landscaper, I'll punch him," Luisa says. "My dad works in an office, which is more than Ashton can say about *his* dad."

It's a Friday afternoon and we are walking to my house from the bus stop. It's a blue-sky day of flowers blooming and trees bursting, but it feels gray to me. Every day this week has felt muddled and overcast.

"Yeah, you should," I say.

Luisa pokes me in the arm. "I don't think you're listening to me."

"Sorry."

"Are you okay?" Luisa asks. She clutches the straps of her backpack and squints at me against the afternoon sun. Her long hair is pulled back in a ponytail. I wonder, if Dan is at the house would he notice her hair? I push the thought away.

"Yeah, of course," I say. "Let's go."

I start to walk faster, thinking that maybe if I pick up my pace I'll snap out of this mood.

"Sheesh, slow down!" Luisa says. "You don't need to speed walk, dork. Just don't flake out on me."

I slow my pace to match Luisa's and try to focus on her words so that I'll stay in the moment. Grass pokes between cracks in the sidewalk. I'd never noticed all the cracks and how in some areas, the sidewalk is uneven, like something beneath has pushed up and broken the squares of concrete.

As I let us into my empty house, Luisa thumbs through alerts on her phone and sighs. "Everyone is doing cooler stuff than us. If *we* were cooler—or more popular—Ashton would totally stop teasing me."

"I don't know. I think that's just Ashton."

"He doesn't tease Ellen about being Korean. No one does."

Luisa has a point. No one teases Ellen about anything. She has a perfect life. I slump into one of the kitchen chairs. It wobbles on uneven feet.

"Are you okay?" Luisa asks.

The truth of what happened in the tent last weekend bubbles up. I want to tell someone, but it is so confusing. Dan loves me. I know he does. Like a father. And I love him, but then he did that to me and Mom didn't believe me. But I *knew* it was wrong. In my body. Then again, Mom is Mom and she loves me too and . . . no, I didn't want to talk about it. Better to just change the subject.

"Want to see something?" I ask.

Luisa looks up, sensing something in my tone. "Like what?"

"Something that I'll bet *Ellen* has never tried."

Emma is in afterschool care until Mom picks her up, which means that we have a couple of hours alone. I motion for Luisa to follow me to the kitchen and tell her to wait while I pull a chair over to the fridge. Stepping up, I can reach the small cabinet over the fridge. I open it and pull out a little glass pipe and a zippered pouch.

Luisa's brow is furrowed. She's confused about where this is going. My hands shake a little bit as I unzip the pouch and show her the marijuana inside. We'd learned about drugs in school last year.

"Want to try it?" I say. I push those words out in front of the ones that would tell her what happened to me. I'm not sure I really want to try it, but I want to get my mind off of Dan and that tent and Mom and the confusion.

Luisa's eyes light up. "Yeah!"

We take some matches, the pipe, and a little bit of marijuana out to the woods, but we have no idea what we're doing.

"My granddad smokes a pipe, so I think we do this." Luisa pinches some of the marijuana into the bowl part of the pipe.

"Then he lights the match and breathes in." She hands the bowl to me. "You try."

I light the marijuana and breathe in. All of a sudden smoke pours into my mouth. I cough like crazy. Luisa tries and she coughs too, but less than me. Then we both start laughing, which makes us cough some more. Worried that we're going to get caught, we run back to the house and return the stuff to the cabinet over the fridge.

Standing there in the kitchen, we look at each other.

"Do you feel anything?" she asks me.

"I don't think so." Luisa's hair looks so pretty, thick and almost black. I want to touch it.

"Let's go back outside. Into the woods," she says.

We follow the path that leads to the stream.

"Can you hear that?" I say, full of wonder. "It's so beautiful the way the water sounds over the rocks."

"Hey, do this!" Luisa says. She's spinning with her arms out and her face lifted to the sky. I join her. The trees blur and merge, becoming a green sky with a blue spot dotted with puffy clouds in the middle. It's amazing. We fall on the ground, laughing.

I lie there, staring up at the sky, the trees no longer spinning. Instead, they rise up high into the sky. Clouds float into the space between the trees.

"Look! An elephant," I say, pointing.

"With a crown on his head! And look there—a dragon!" Luisa adds.

"I see it! And a face."

"Where?"

I point to the face.

"Does it have its mouth wide open like this?" Luisa opens her mouth as wide as possible. I laugh so hard that I almost pee myself.

"Yes! Yes! Yes!" I roll around on the ground giggling. I love this feeling.

"Oh my gosh. I feel so funny," Luisa says, touching her face. "My nose feels rubbery. Does it always feel like this? Does yours?"

"I don't know!" I touch my finger to the tip of my nose. "Not really," I say.

"No, like this," Luisa says. She leans over and takes my nose between her thumb and forefinger and wiggles it. "It *is* rubbery!"

We couldn't have stopped laughing—not even if someone threatened to take away our phones unless we stopped laughing.

"I'm hungry. Are you hungry?" I say.

"So hungry. Oh my god, now that you say it, I need to eat right this minute."

I push myself off of the dirt path and up to a standing position and then lean down to give Luisa a hand up. I skip back to the house. Luisa's thumbs fly over her phone.

"Who are you texting?"

"Shelby and Ellen. They're going to be so jealous."

All of a sudden, I feel sad. "I don't want anyone to feel jealous."

"Oh." Luisa's smile falters. "Me either."

"Tell them . . . tell them that they can come next time!" I jump up and down because I'd come up with a good idea to keep everyone happy.

"Okay. Next time. Good." Luisa finishes texting by the time we get to the house.

"Get the chips and whatever else you want," I say as I peer into the fridge. I find some dip and lemonade. Luisa and I dig into our snacks like we've never eaten before.

"Why doesn't everyone do this all the time?" Luisa asks and crunches a chip.

"I don't know!" I shove a handful of chips in my mouth.

Luisa's phone chirps. She studies it and starts laughing.

"What?" I ask.

"Shelby says she can't wait for next time and, look"—Luisa holds out her phone for me to see a stream of funny emojis that Shelby has sent. Then a text from Ellen comes through.

"Oooh, look, Ellen is not happy with us."

Luisa reads the text. "Ugh, she's so judgy." Luisa looks at me. "I guess we won't invite *her* next time." We both start laughing, but I don't like the feeling that Ellen thinks we're doing something wrong.

"What made you want to get high anyway?" Luisa asks, her mouth full of chocolate chip cookie.

At her question, the memory surges again. The tent. Dan. Telling Mom. But this time the memory feels trapped behind cellophane. Like I know it's there, but it can't really touch me. "Something happened," I say as I dip a chip. My voice sounds far away, like it's not me talking.

"What?" she presses.

"Something bad. With Dan." The crunching of the chip is like thunder.

"What happened with Dan?"

The memory presses again, this time starting to break through. I shake my head.

"I don't want to talk about it."

"Are you sure——?" Luisa starts to say.

"I'm sure." I interrupt her. "Anyway, what you were saying before? About Ashton? He's a jerk," I say. "Who cares what he thinks?"

Luisa sighs. "I'm just sick of people thinking they know everything about me when they only know one thing."

I know what she means because I sort of feel the same way. If people knew what happened, they'd see that one thing, not the whole me. I crunch another chip and wonder how soon I can dip back into Mom's stash without her realizing it.

19

All Dressed Up

TUESDAY AFTER SCHOOL, I can't get out of dress shopping the second time around. Mom drives us to this fancy schmancy place full of obnoxiously expensive dresses. The shop lady doesn't seem to believe that we're serious about buying dresses. She leads us over to the sale section of bridesmaid dresses and then mostly she stands to the side, watching us like we're going to steal something. As if we could fit one of these ginormous dresses under our clothes and waddle out without suspicion. As if we'd want to.

My eyes eat up the rich shades of color, even if the pastels are a little overrepresented. I fall hard for one dress in deep plum taffeta with a seriously plunging neckline, but Mom says no. She wants us in mauve, which makes me puke a little bit in my mouth. She pulls out a few for Emma and me to try on.

Emma and I model our dresses while Mom alternately analyzes

our look and wipes tears from her eyes over her girls growing up so fast. After the third dress, which it turns out isn't completely horrible, Emma says, "What about you, Mom? We need to find a dress for you too!"

Mom looks longingly at the gowns and then shakes her head. "This is a bit out of my price range. I'll borrow something from someone. Don't worry about me." She forces a smile and flutters her hands at us. "Try on more dresses. I can't believe how beautiful my girls are. Oh, how Nana would have loved to see you both."

Maybe it's seeing Mom so emotional about us growing up and about Nana not being here. Or maybe it's because I'm still euphoric that I got my scholarship and Ben is getting a record deal. Or maybe it's some weird female hormone reaction to all of this taffeta and tulle, but I feel sad for Mom. She never buys anything for herself. Nothing beautiful, anyway. She has five billion sensible suits, but on the weekends, it's always beat-up jeans and old sweatshirts. And she never had the traditional wedding that she'd wanted. When she found out she was pregnant with me, she and my dad went to a Justice of the Peace. I set down my dresses in a whisper of silk and say, "We are finding you a dress, even if it's just to try on for fun."

"Yeah!" Emma drops her dresses in a pile and we both grab Mom's hands and pull her over to the wedding dresses.

"I'm sorry," the attendant says. "But you need an appointment to try those on."

"Oh, that's fine," Mom says, ready to sit back down.

I look around at the empty room. "You don't look superbusy.

How about we make an appointment for now?"

The attendant chews the inside of her cheek for a moment. "I guess that's okay." She pastes on a fake smile and guides us to the dresses. "If you show me the ones that you want to try on, I'll pull them out for you."

Emma chooses the fluffiest, sparkliest dress with yards of tulle and way too many sequins and fake pearls for any dress that's not intended for Vegas. I choose an ivory dress with a slender silhouette, dotted with crystals here and there. Mom chooses a couple as well, beaming as the woman follows her into the dressing room in a rustle of rich fabric.

"Thanks," Emma whispers, like I'm doing her a favor.

Mom comes out in each dress to our oohs and aaahs. It's amazing to me how beautiful she looks when she smiles and puts on something that fits her decently. Emma, predictably, loves her choice the best. Mom and I share a look that conveys how much we both hate it, and I'm reminded of how close we used to be. Mom disappears and then emerges one last time in the dress that I chose.

"Oh," she says, looking at her reflection in the triple mirror. The salesperson pulls the dress in across Mom's torso, showing off her figure. "We would order you a smaller size that would fit better here and here," the attendant says, gesturing across Mom's stomach and chest.

"Wow," Emma says.

"That's The One," I say. The ivory complements her skin, and the cut of the dress is made for her curves. She shines in that dress, and when she smiles, she's years younger.

"You've always had such a good eye, Skye," Mom says, looking at me gratefully through the mirror.

"Will you wear your hair up or down?" Emma asks. "I think it should be up."

"I hadn't thought about it," Mom says. She pulls her long hair back at the nape of her neck and turns from side to side, examining her reflection.

"Maybe like this. Dan always did want me to grow my hair long. He'll love it."

It's like lightning crashes into the small dressing room. I remember Dan commenting on my hair when I was young, and I suddenly feel ill. I'd always known that what he did was wrong—no matter what Mom's response was that night—but now, with Mom holding her hair in just the same way that Dan had wanted me to wear mine, I'm shaken. I look from Mom's gorgeous face to Emma's hopeful one. This beautiful moment is wrecked by memories.

"Too bad that dress is so expensive," I say, and I turn from the mirror so I don't have to see their faces fall.

"Hello, ladies," Dan says, "I thought I'd make dinner for you all again."

It grates on me that he says *you all* and *again*. Like he wants to be sure he gets credit.

"Did you know we were dress shopping?" Emma says to him.

"I may have heard something to that effect," Dan says as he

sprinkles a handful of perfect carrot coins across some greens in a salad bowl. Next, he starts slicing a cucumber with exact precision.

"We tried on so many beautiful dresses *and* we found the perfect one for Mom." She plucks a carrot from the salad.

"If you'd like a carrot, just tell me and I'll cut up some for you," Dan says, moving his salad bowl away from Emma, as if she's a toddler with snot-covered fingers.

"I'd like a carrot," Emma says in her eye-roll tone. She pops the stolen carrot into her mouth and crunches.

"The perfect dress, eh?" Dan says, his tone is amused. "Was it *The One?*"

Mom sighs. "It was. But it's too expensive."

"Don't worry about it," Dan says.

"You think we can find the money?" Mom asks, hope lighting her eyes.

"I meant don't worry about the perfect dress. It's just a few hours, right? Wear something you already own or borrow something. Let's not turn our wedding into a circus. You know it's just a ritual designed by society to mark the beginning of what's real: the actual marriage." He points the knife at her. "Let's not lose sight of that, shall we?"

Mom's eyes drop to the floor. I don't know what she's thinking, but if I had to guess it would be that Dan just stuck a pin in her hopes of dressing in a wedding gown and looking beautiful on a special day. A drawing of this moment would be called *The Dissolution of Dreams.*

"Oh my God, are you kidding me right now?" Emma says, hands on her hips. "Obviously, Mom needs a wedding dress. Hello? She's a bride. You are such a *guy*," she says, like the word is gross in her mouth.

I smile to myself that Emma is not subdued by Dan's superiority. The dinner isn't as awful as the first time, but Mom is quiet. I am too. The scholarship means that in approximately 176 days—give or take—I won't be sitting at this table listening to Emma share every detail of play rehearsal or hear Mom talk about the stress of work. But I also won't receive Mom's daily good-bye kisses or witness Emma standing up to Dan.

When dinner is over, I clear the table while Emma starts the dishes. She's still talking about play rehearsal. The warm orange flame of the dinner candles flicker in response to my movements around the table. I blow out the flame; the smoke drifts across the table and disappears. As I'm wiping down the table, Dan calls Emma over to him.

"Let's talk about your part," he says. "Come here." He pats his thigh.

Emma hesitates and then slides onto Dan's lap. Her long legs nearly hit the floor. He rests his palm on her thigh, just like he did to me all those years ago. A shiver runs down my spine. He brushes a lock of her hair behind her ear. I've been so focused on avoiding Dan, that I haven't even considered that it might happen again—to Emma.

20

What Goes Up

"WHAT'D YOU END up telling your mom anyway?" Ben asks after blowing out a stream of smoke.

"Sleepover with me!" Shelby says as she cracks open a beer.

We are at Shelby's house, pregaming before the concert because her parents are away. It's perfect, really. I've parked Lucy here and I can crash with Shelby after the concert so we can keep the party going all night long.

"So you're not grounded anymore?" Ben asks.

"Mom wanted to spend the night with Dan, and Emma was invited for a sleepover, so Mom thought it would be better for me to stay with Shelby than be left alone to my own devices." I tip a beer to my lips and take a deep drink. "I sort of left out the part where Shelby's parents are out of town."

"Ah, good thinking," Ben says.

"This show gonna be any good?" Keith says to Ben.

It's finally Friday night. The night of the Tame Impala show, and I'm trying to be the happy party girl that everyone loves. But I keep thinking of Dan's hand on Emma's thigh.

"If you like Tame Impala, it'll be epic."

"At least it'll be a chance to party," Ashton says.

"Yeah, his last chance." Keith gestures to Ben.

Ben uses a razor blade to cut short, thin lines of cocaine onto a mirror sitting on the table. "Temporarily," Ben says.

I've never tried coke and I wonder how it will make me feel. I'm sort of hoping it'll help me not feel.

Keith shakes his head and takes the bong from Ben. "Selling your soul to the man."

"Come on, man. Our band is getting a recording contract. I just need to chill on the partying starting tomorrow and until the recording sessions are over. No big deal." Ben snorts a line and rubs his nose.

"I thought the whole point of being in a band was that you could party and no one would give you a hard time," Keith says.

"Maybe not the *whole* point," I say as I follow Ben's lead and lower the straw to the coffee table to pull in a line. The powder burns my nose and I squeal.

"Rub it," Ben says, laughing.

"You all are forgetting about unlimited access to females," Ashton says, grinning.

Shelby rolls her eyes. "One-track mind."

"Not one-track," Ashton says. "Two-track. I think about football too."

We each do one more line and drink more beer while we wait for the car to arrive. I expect the burning feeling next time. There's also a weird sort of gross drip down the back of my throat. But I also feel amazing. Within minutes, the worry that was gnawing at me has dissolved. I am me, but better.

"Car's here," Ben says, putting the drugs away.

"You know I could have driven," Ashton says.

"But we have a promise not to drive when we're messed up," I say, looking at Ben.

"It's not my promise," Ashton says.

"Go ahead and drive. Lose your scholarship. I don't give a shit." Ben smiles and shrugs.

Ashton grunts in return.

"Hope it's an awesome show," Shelby says.

"I wish you were coming with!" I say.

"It's okay. We'll be mad partying when you all get back."

We squeeze into the car and head to the concert. My brain is electric. There's so much to say and I can't get my thoughts out fast enough.

"What's Ellen doing tonight?" I ask to change the subject. "Not that I care. I mean, it's not like I hate her or anything. But she probably hates me. Anyway, you don't have to answer. I was just trying to . . . I don't know . . . fill the space, I guess. Never mind. I'm totally babbling." I turn to Ben. "Where are our seats again? They're way up high, right? That's okay. It would have been fun to be on the floor, but it'll be fun anyway. Don't you think so? Keith, do you think so?"

"No more lines for you, girl," Keith says to me, but he's laughing. We're all laughing. The world is sharp as glass, the sky as clear as water. I'd like to paint it. I could paint it perfectly right this very moment. Maybe I'll paint it when I get home. The idea of home reminds me of Dan's hand on Emma's thigh.

"Please, just a tiny bit more?" I ask when we are out of the car and Keith pulls out the stash. I need to banish the idea of home.

We finish the little bit of coke that's left by snorting quick bumps off Ben's key. Then it's the long walk across the lot to the concert venue, so we have to stop a couple of times for sips from a water bottle that Keith has filled with vodka and Kool-Aid, and finally we arrive.

"We're here!" I shout, throwing my arms in the air. I hug Ben, but it's totally cool because it's just about the excitement of making it to the concert and the fact that I could get away from my mother and Emma had a sleepover. "Everything worked out exactly right."

Ben laughs, hugs me back, lets me go. We find our seats, but who cares about seats when you can dance dance dance? Every song is better than the one before. And when I start to think about Emma again, I just dance harder. I'm sweating, but it doesn't matter. Ben hands me a water bottle that he produces like magic. Ben is magic. I slug it back, push my damp hair out of my face, and keep dancing. What will happen when I'm gone, and Dan is living in the house?

I close my eyes and dance. I can't wait to leave for college. I need to leave for college. I dance.

The music fills the whole arena, reaching us all the way up in our section, spinning us around before it dips and sways in a new direction. What will happen to Emma? I lean toward Ben, singing the lyrics, both of us right there in that moment of that song and it's as if we'll never stop, we'll never change, we'll freeze in a perfect moment of a perfect song.

Ashton moves behind me, his hands on my hips. He moves with me. Ben looks at us, unsure of where he fits in, and I remember that I'm not that girl anymore. I'm a better me. I push Ashton away. I'm a girl on my own, flying through the bright night carried by the music. My arms are wings, and if I dance hard enough, fast enough, maybe I'll take off toward the black roof and watch everyone from the rafters, floating on the invisible current of music. I laugh, and Ben asks what's funny, but I can't make the words come out right. I can't make it clear for him, so I keep dancing. Then the concert is over, but it's not over because there's an encore and I think maybe they'll play forever. Maybe the music will never stop.

But the awful bright lights come back on and then we're filing out like ants, only we aren't sad. We aren't depressed. We won't allow it. Because it's still the miraculous night and we don't need to stop our laughter and dancing and partying. We wind our way back to the parking lot through the millions of cars parked there.

"Are you okay?" Ben asks.

I pause and then once again, push the thoughts away. "I'm

amazing!" I yell to the sky. Sky. Skye. I laugh. "Oh, my heart's beating so fast!"

"Let's take it easy, okay?"

I push at Ben playfully. "Sure, Dad."

I stumble and Ben rights me. I lean into him and he smells so good and feels so right. This is an easy way to stop thinking about Dan. I tip my head up a little bit and kiss him on the neck. Finally, I can give in. I snake my arms around him and press against him. He puts one arm around me. I lick his earlobe. "Let's have some fun," I whisper into his ear.

Ben pulls away. I step closer, my grin feels sharp. Ashton and Keith have stopped at the corner, waiting for us.

Ben puts his arm up, stopping me. "No," he says, his voice low. "Not like this."

Not like this. What does he mean?

I turn away from him and march toward Ashton and Keith where they wait for the ride service to take us home. When the car arrives, Ben and I are wedged together in the back, but I make myself small and don't allow any part of my body to touch his. I turn my face to the window where I can see the reflection of my face, jaw grinding back and forth.

I'm pressed against a wall. Kisses miss my lips and land half on my cheek. Hands fumble with the button on my jeans. I remember kissing Ben's neck and I remember leaving the concert. Something is poking me in the back. He pulls me closer though we both almost fall over because we're so wasted. I respond automatically, pressing my body into his, the way I know makes boys crazy. But . . . wait. Ben pushed me away. I was pissed so how did we end up closeted in the back room of Shelby's basement, trying to keep quiet? Muffled party sounds squeeze through the slit at the bottom of the door. I wrap my arms around his neck, tangling my fingers in his hair to pull him closer. But it's not right. This hair isn't curly. I feel twists beneath my fingers.

The kisses are sloppy, not the stuff of my fantasies. I want to wipe the saliva off my neck. He slips his hand under my shirt to fondle my breast and I freeze.

Dan. In the tent. Touching me.

"Stop . . ."

"What?" His voice is thick with alcohol and coke and a dagger of impatience. And it's not Ben's voice. He pulls back. I focus my eyes. Ashton. Twists. Of course, but how could . . . ? I peer around the back room. I'm dizzy.

"Damn, you're even more fucked-up than last time, Skye."

"Get off," I say. My words come out fuzzy.

"I thought you wanted to." Ashton doesn't move, his boozy breath suffocating me. "Just one more time?"

This is what happened that night at Ben's. I was drunk, and he put his hands on me. This is what happened all those years ago with Dan. He was drunk, and he put his hands on me. But then, I didn't have the power to do anything about it.

"Get off!" I yell. I push him again and he backs up, hands in surrender.

"Chill!" Ashton adjusts himself and whispers, "What a psycho." He grabs two beers from the fridge and opens the door.

I'm shaking from that memory, so I curl into myself and stay in the back room. This is where I belong after coming out of a black-out to realize that I was hooking up with Ashton . . . again. Keith's booming voice slips in through the sliver of light coming from the open door.

"Finally," he says to Ashton. "Thought you'd gotten lost in there. Ellen is looking for you."

"Ellen's *here?*" Ashton's tone holds the same shock that I'm feeling.

I cradle my head in my hands. I wonder if Keith knows I'm in here. If he's talking about Ashton getting lost in me, if he was covering for his best friend. I squint at the light like a dark-dwelling creature and peer into the next room. Everyone is partying in Shelby's basement. Ben's on the couch, arms behind his head, eyes closed. Ashton cracks open a beer as he makes his way to the corner of the room where Ellen sits with a friend.

I hear Ellen say, "I was hoping to surprise you."

"I'm surprised all right," Ashton says and takes a long drink from his can.

I've got to get out of here. I slink out of the back room and move toward the stairs.

"How 'bout a round of Quarters, Chicken Little?" Keith yells.

I was hoping not to be noticed. Impossible in this basement party space.

"No, I'm good." The words mush together, come out *No . . . mmmmgood.*

"Skye." Ben's voice is not a yell and yet it reaches my ears amid all the noise. I ignore his insistent tone and reach for the handrail to guide me up the stairs and out of here. "Where are you going?" he says, a little louder.

"I'm leaving," I say. *Mmleafing.* I wrestle with the laces of my boots until I unravel the key tied there. I can't shake that memory, and I can't stay here.

"You shouldn't drive," he says. He's suddenly next to me. How'd he do that? "And I'm way too messed up to drive you."

"I don't need you," I say, dangling the keys for him to see. "Got it off on the first try and retied my boot too." The last part is a total lie. My laces flop on the ground, untied. I try to smile, but the muscles of my face feel weird. He doesn't try to smile back.

"You're wasted," he insists in my ear. "You can't drive."

I want to go home. I want to be away from Ashton and his hands and from Ben and his judgment. My stomach feels jumpy. Not like I'm going to throw up, but like I'm freaking out on the inside.

"I need to leave," I say. I see two of Ben and then they merge into one. My breath starts to hitch.

He holds his hand cupped toward me. "Give me your keys."

I shake my head and then shake it again harder. "I can't stay here. I can't. I can't." I start to cry. I'm as shocked as Ben is by the way my shoulders start shaking and the tears run down my face.

"Come on, come on," he says in a quiet voice. He guides me away from the stairs and toward the sliding glass doors that empty into the dark backyard. "What are you talking about?"

I can hear the care in his voice, but I'm still shaking and the tears keep coming. Ben rubs my back and I shrug away. I can't be touched.

"How about you give me your keys while you tell me what's going on?"

"No!" I scream at him. "No, you're not taking my keys!" I can't explain why this feels so important. But he can't take them from me. No one else can take anything from me unless I want to give it. I shove the keys in my bra, which is not comfortable, but I know Ben won't go for them there.

"Skye, I'm begging you, we have a promise not to drive if we're messed up," he says.

"Stop!" I put my finger up to show I mean business. I wipe tears and snot away with the other hand.

He holds up his hands. "Okay. We'll just talk. What's going on?"

"I've got to get out of here. I can't stay." The tears start all over again. I see Dan's hand on Emma's thigh and all I can think is how badly I need to get out of this town, how I'll suffocate if I stay. My hands start shaking again and I press them to my skull. I want to scrub away Ashton's touch and all the memories that precede that touch too. What will make it all go away? What can I do?

"Is there any more coke?" I ask, my voice tiny and pathetic.

He shakes his head. "You don't need that." He motions to me. "Come here." He holds his arms open.

I'm confused. I tried to kiss him before and he pushed me away. I blink and blink again, trying to make sense. He just didn't want me in front of the other guys. That's what he meant when he said "Not like this."

"Oh," I say, putting it together. "You want to fuck me too? But in secret like Ashton."

"What did you say?" Ben frowns.

I start to take off my jacket. Might as well be what they all want me to be. Can't escape it. I stumble a bit and toss the jacket on the ground.

"This is all I'm good for, right?" I start to unbutton my shirt.

"No! Skye, no. That's not . . . button your shirt, Skye. I just wanted to help, that's all."

I unbutton my jeans.

"Just . . . stop, Skye."

"So . . . you don't want me?"

"No, I don't want you." His voice is so low I almost don't catch what he says.

Ben doesn't want me. The thing I think I'm good for isn't good enough for him. I button my shirt, but it's all wrong.

"Good-bye, Ben."

"Skye—"

"I'm leaving!"

"We had a promise." His voice is resigned. I notice that he said it in the past tense, like he's already given up on me. Everything about him is hard: a clenched jaw, arms over his chest. I'd draw him in charcoal: *Study of a Boy in Granite.*

"Our promise?" I say. "Means nothing." Spittle flies from my mouth.

21

AFTER: I am twelve and a half. Winter of seventh grade

AFTER DINNER, I start doing the dishes right away because Luisa, Ellen, and I are sleeping over at Shelby's and I don't want to miss one minute. Mom is giving Emma a bath. I can't wait until Emma's old enough to help. Six-year-olds are definitely not any good when it comes to cleaning up dishes.

Dan walks into the narrow kitchen. After adding ice cubes to his glass, he reaches into the cabinet over the fridge for his Jack Daniel's.

"What are you wearing?" Dan says. "It's freezing outside."

It wasn't really a question. I could tell by his tone. "What do you mean?" I ask.

I scrape food off of a blue dinner plate into the sink. Mom had gotten the plates as a gift from Nana. They're all different colors and this one's my favorite, a blue so dark that it looked like a deep moon-lit night. I always take this one for myself.

"I *mean* do you intend to go out in public dressed like that?"

I'm wearing black leggings with a big T-shirt that slides off one shoulder. The T-shirt has a giant cartoon cat on the front. It's ironic. I'm dressed pretty much the way all the girls at my school dress every day.

"I'm just going to Shelby's for a sleepover. I don't know if that counts as public. I doubt it'll be freezing inside her house."

I pivot to slide the plate into the dishwasher. Dan's hand swipes toward me. The plate flies from my hand, shattering on the floor.

"You do *not* speak to me in that tone," Dan hisses in my face. His is red with anger. I freeze. Mom said work was giving him trouble and that's why he was having a hard time. He wasn't bouncing on his toes like he used to. He wasn't suggesting family game night. He wasn't very happy.

He stays bent over me, breathing heavily. His breath stinks like bourbon, same as the night of the tent. It has been months and nothing has happened since, but my body's been changing in dramatic ways that I'm trying to get used to. Would he try to do that stuff to me again? Mom never said anything about what I'd told her that night about Dan touching me. I avoided being alone with Dan and I locked my bedroom door when I went to sleep.

Dan reaches out and clutches my bare shoulder, where my shirt had slid off. My entire body tenses, every part of me remembering. He pulls my shirt up to cover my shoulder and then straightens up to standing. Staring at the shards of plate scattered across the floor, he runs a hand over his mouth and clears his throat.

"Clean this up," he says. At least he isn't so close to me anymore.

"And change those clothes. I don't want you going out looking like a harlot."

After he leaves the kitchen, I think about going upstairs to tell Mom, but I'm not sure telling her will help anything. Besides, I'll have to walk past him in the living room to get to the steps. Instead, I kneel to sweep the broken bits of plate into a dustpan. Just before dumping the plate's remains into the trash, I snatch one triangular shard from the pile, the only physical evidence of any of the things Dan has done. I cup the piece of broken blue plate in my palm and drop the rest in the trash.

In my room, I pull a pair of baggy sweatpants over my leggings and trade my top for a similarly baggy sweatshirt.

"Mom, I'm ready," I call.

"Dan, can you take Skye to her friend's house? I'm with Emma," Mom yells down the steps.

Alone in a car with Dan? No way. "Mom! You said that *you* would take me."

"Dan?" Mom says, ignoring me.

Do I exist? Do I speak out loud? Sometimes I wonder. My hand finds the piece of broken plate in the pocket of my sweatshirt. I rub my thumb along the ragged edge and press my finger into the point until it hurts.

"Your daughter wants you to take her, Beth," Dan announces. He sips his drink.

Mom stomps down the steps. "Dan, you are a big help, as always." The sarcasm in her voice is heavy. "And why do *you* have to be so difficult?" she says to me. I want to tell her that it's because of what happened in the tent. She holds up her hand. "I know. It's the age. Do you have your bag?"

I nod and we head out to the car. "God, I need a drink," she says under her breath.

"What's a harlot?" I ask.

"A prostitute. Why do you ask?"

I wonder if that's what Dan thought of me, if that's why he did what he did to me.

"No reason."

"Do you guys still want to try getting drunk?" I say, after I set my bag on the floor at Shelby's.

"Yes!" Luisa says.

"I don't know," Ellen says.

"Come on. Let's do it!" Shelby chimes in. Her parents are out for the night, which Mom doesn't know, of course. And Shelby's sister is supposed to be watching us, but she's out with friends. Luisa and Shelby had suggested trying alcohol, but Ellen and I hadn't been sure. For me, it seems like when Dan was drunk, that's when all the bad stuff happened. Ellen is more about following rules.

Tonight I'm thinking that if Mom needs a drink to deal with Dan, then maybe I do too.

"What should we drink?" Shelby asks, eyeing the bottles lined up on the bar.

"Everything!" Luisa says. She turns the music up loud and starts dancing around the room.

"If you say so," Shelby says. She pours a little bit from several bottles of clear and amber liquid.

"Are you all sure about this?" Ellen asks, arms crossed over her skinny chest.

"Live a little, Ellen," Shelby says.

I wonder how the liquor will make me feel. Mom always seems less stressed after she has a couple glasses of wine. Things don't bother her as much.

"This smells *dis-gus-ting,*" Shelby announces, holding the glass of liquid to the light.

"Do you have any juice? Maybe we can make it taste better," I say. Mom usually drinks wine, but sometimes she drinks vodka with orange juice. Dan only ever drinks Jack Daniel's on the rocks. I'd licked my finger once after stirring his drink and I thought it tasted like cough syrup without the berry flavoring, only way worse.

We pile into the kitchen. "Here!" Luisa says, brandishing a bottle of orange juice. She pours some into each of the four glasses, turning the drink a sickly orange-brown. We each grab a glass and a straw and slurp.

"Ew!" Luisa exclaims. But she slurps it anyway.

"Oh, man," Shelby says, making a face. "I don't know."

"No way," Ellen says. She pushes her drink aside.

I toss the straw and finish mine in one long gulp. Then Luisa and I finish off Ellen's drink while Shelby takes little sips of hers, grimacing after every one. Ellen tries some wine. We're feeling no pain, as I've heard my mom say. I squeal when I hear the beginning of the next song.

"This is our song, you guys!" I jump up and start dancing.

"Since when?" Shelby says, but she starts dancing too.

"Since now! Every time we hear this, we will think of this night."

"This is the most fun you've been in forever!" Luisa says. We've stripped to our bras and undies and we're prancing around like supermodels.

"I don't know what you're talking about," I say in a terrible British accent, sucking my cheeks in and flipping my hair up with my hands. "I'm always fun, darling."

"Not always," Luisa says. "Not since—" Luisa seems to think twice about what she was going to say, and she stops talking.

"Tonight's all that counts!" I say.

Shelby grabs Ellen's hand and spins her around. I grab Luisa's and spin her. Then I start shimmying and we all shimmy.

"Selfies!" Luisa yells, holding her phone out for a photo.

"No way! We're in our undies!" I say, moving as far away from the camera eye as possible. Ellen hides with me. We look at each other and giggle.

"I don't care!" Luisa says, pursing her lips for the camera. She lifts her hair from her neck and takes another photo.

"Me too!" Shelby says. They squish together.

"Should we get our boobs in this one?" Luisa says.

"What boobs?" Shelby says, and we all laugh.

Watching them, I sense the memory of the tent pushing at me. "I need another drink!" I announce.

"Skye needs another drink!" Luisa shouts.

"Drinks all around!" Shelby shouts.

After the second drink, I understand Mom's saying about feeling no pain. Nothing can bother me. I don't remember anything either. Except throwing up in the trash can. Ellen had held back my hair. I remember her asking why I'd want to get so drunk that I got sick. I didn't have any answer except that the feeling of being free seemed totally worth the price.

22

Must Come Down

THE VIBRATION OF the phone pulls me from sleep. I peer at the screen. Luisa.

"Oh my god, oh my god, oh my god!" Her voice sounds loud. I hold the phone away from my hungover ears. "Are you okay?" she asks.

My body is still clothed, though my shirt is buttoned weird, and I appear to have all my parts intact.

"Yes," I say, cautiously.

I probe my throbbing, hungover brain for information on how I got home, but no memory emerges.

"Where are you?"

I look around. I'm on top of the covers of my bed. "Home."

I can't believe I would have driven drunk, but here I am in my room.

"I just wanted to make sure you were okay after everything that happened last night."

"Everything that happened?" I repeat.

I can't remember much. I threw myself at Ben, but he pushed me away. Then it was Ashton. And then a fight with Ben? But Luisa can't be talking about that. She wasn't there. At least I don't remember seeing her there.

"Wait. You don't know?" she asks.

I sigh. "I guess I don't."

"Oh my gosh. Okay. Well—"

I cradle my splitting forehead in one hand and close my eyes to listen.

"Sometime around one-thirty in the morning, the cops showed up—"

"The cops?" I have no recollection of cops.

"Yeah! A neighbor called. Apparently, it was mayhem with everyone trying to get out of there. But the cops stopped Ben."

"Was he busted?"

"Probably!"

I let the news settle in.

"They took him away. At least that's what Shelby said."

"*Busted.*" I can't believe I missed all of that.

"I thought the cops took you in too. Shelby said to text you because you'd been really wasted and she didn't know what happened to you. She's obviously in a shit-ton of trouble right now with her mom."

"Man, you think Ben was really arrested?"

"So he hasn't been in touch with you?"

"No."

Ben had never been arrested before. None of us had. I wanted to know what happened, but I wasn't ready to call him. I couldn't remember last night entirely, except for the part where he said he didn't want me. Shame creeps up my neck.

"Pick me up? My mom has the car today," Luisa says.

"Sure. I need to clean up a little and then I'll be there."

As I am walking to the bathroom, something falls from beneath my shirt. My keys. I lean down to pick them up, frowning. I have a vague memory of sticking them in my bra. The mirror reflects back bloodshot eyes and wrecked hair. I brush my teeth twice to get the gross taste out, mash a beanie over my hair, and decide I'm good enough to go to the diner. I feel like shit, but at least I made it home safe. Somehow, I narrowly averted disaster, but Ben didn't?

Upstairs, no one is home. I wasn't supposed to be home. I lock the door behind me and walk to the parking lot.

No car.

I walk farther down to see if maybe I parked it in another lot and stumbled home from there. It's nowhere in our town house lot.

I call Luisa.

"I can't find my car."

"You what?" Luisa's surprise acknowledges that this is a new low for me.

"You heard me."

"What is the last thing you remember?"

"I wanted to leave." I'm working it out as I talk. "And Ben wanted my keys, so I put them in my bra where I knew he wouldn't try to grab them."

"I bet he wanted to though." Luisa's tone is playful.

I think about Ben's dismissal of me. "It wasn't like that," I say. "Anyway, I found my keys this morning, but no car."

"And you don't remember how you got home?"

A new wave of shame washes over me, reminding me of what a stinking pile of shit I am. "Nope, not a shred of memory."

"Hang on, I'm texting Shelby."

I squat on the curb, the bright winter sun shining on me like an accusation.

"She said that some cars got towed because her mom was so pissed."

"Does she think mine got towed?" I ask.

"She doesn't know for sure, but probably. You know who you're going to have to call, don't you?"

"Ugh. Talk to you later, okay?"

Keith's dad has the biggest towing business in our little town. If my car was towed, it would likely be in his lot, and if not, he could probably find out where it ended up. Bracing myself for the abuse I'm sure to receive after last night, I press his number on the phone.

"Yo, Chicken Little! What a surprise."

I grit my teeth at the nickname and register that despite his greeting, Keith doesn't seem at all surprised to hear from me. I forge ahead. "Keith? Wondering if you could help me with something?"

"Skye, whoa. You were flying high last night. Man."

"Keith . . ."

"You need a little something to take the edge off that hangover? Sorry, I don't give away free pot. Don't know where you're going to get it, now that your boy is gone."

"I'm not calling—wait, what are you talking about?"

"You don't know, do you?" He barks out a big laugh.

I bite back the insult that springs to mind because it would just be fuel to his fire. "Keith, look, I'm calling about my car."

"Where'd you end up?" he continues. He's toying with me. "It was *out of control* last night. Ashton and I were lucky to get out through the basement door."

Talking to Keith when I don't know what I did the night before is like walking in a minefield. "I don't know where my car is."

"Why don't you ask your *boyfriend*?"

Keith is on a roll today.

"Can you help or not?" I ask.

"Oh, right," Keith continues, as if I hadn't spoken. "You can't, since he's gone. For twenty-eight days."

Twenty-eight days.

I know what that means. All of us do, like we know that possession of a small amount of weed isn't a big deal, but a big bag could be trouble. And that it's better to be charged with a hit-and-run than drunk driving. Even knowing all of that, I laugh. The idea of Ben going to rehab is ridiculous.

"I *knew* you didn't know. But don't worry, only a month until you can get your free supply back."

"Are you serious right now?"

"Serious as a heart attack. My pops heard the whole thing go down last night because he was towing cars. The cops were there and Ben's father was yelling and his mom was crying. It was a whole thing."

Obviously, Keith and his father are both 100 percent clueless because there's no way that Ben would head off for a month without calling me first. Or at least texting. I was the first person he told about his recording contract. He would call me. Then again . . . I see him pushing me away when I tried to kiss him, telling me he doesn't want me, and I see the hard line of his mouth when I said our promise meant nothing to me.

"If you and Ashton got out, why didn't you grab Ben? What happened to that whole *no man left behind* credo?" I ask.

"Man, people were flying in all directions. Ben was in the middle of it. We had to get out while we could. We've got *scholarships* to protect."

My patience with Keith is running thin. "Look, can you help me find out if your dad towed Lucy?"

"What's the license plate?"

I tell him and wait while he checks in his father's system.

"Yeah, it's at my dad's lot. You want to come deal with it?"

I know that I need to retrieve my car and get it back to my house before my mother realizes that I misplaced it. It would be a very bad idea to let her know just how fucked-up her daughter is. But Luisa doesn't have wheels and Ben is . . . MIA. I won't believe Keith until I confirm for myself that he's gone for a month of clean-living, twelve-step brainwashing. Especially on the very day that he was supposed to start recording.

"Actually . . ."

"Oh my god, you need me to give you a ride, don't you? You are pathetic, Murray!"

I know Keith is teasing, but it's true. I'm beyond pathetic. "Please?"

"Fine. We'll be there in twenty. Sound good?"

"Pick me up at Luisa's." I can walk there in twenty minutes and I don't want my mother to return home and find me car-less.

When Keith had said *we,* for some reason I thought he meant him and his father, since his father runs the impound/salvage yard. But I should have guessed that it would be Keith and Ashton. Luisa and I climb into the back of Ashton's SUV. Keith greets us, but Ashton barely grunts. Screw him; I don't need his attention anyway.

"Why'd my car get towed anyway?" I ask as Ashton drives us to the lot. "It wasn't parked illegally."

"Shelby's mom was pissed that Shelby had a party while she was gone. So she claimed that there were trespassers on her private property," Keith says, turning his head to talk to us over the seat. "Not that my dad was complaining about getting the business, though."

We pull into the lot and I see Lucy right away. "Oh, thank God!" I say.

I climb out of the truck and start to walk toward her.

"Where you going?" Keith asks.

I hold up my keys. "Getting Lucy out of here," I say.

He shakes his head. "We've got to process it."

We go into the trailer that serves as an office. Keith's father is in there, a fatter, older version of Keith.

"Hey, Pops," he says. "This is the girl I told you about. Can you hook us up?"

"Hi, Mr. Williams, I'm Skye." I hold out my hand to shake his.

Mr. Williams eyes me over his reading glasses and doesn't move to shake my hand. "License plate?" he says, not smiling.

I recite Lucy's license plate with a growing sense of worry. He taps into his ancient desktop computer and stares at the screen.

"The 1988 Jeep Cherokee?" he asks.

"Yes," I say.

"Don't see too many of them anymore," he says.

"No," I agree.

"Three hundred twenty-six dollars," he says, again eyeing me over those glasses.

Luisa gasps. She knows what that money means to me. Between the amount of money and my hangover, I almost puke all over his desk.

"I'm sorry?"

"Those are the fees."

"I don't have that."

"How much do you have?"

"Come on, Pops, she's a friend," Keith says, and I'm surprised first by his submissive tone and second by the fact that Keith considers me a friend.

Calculating how much of my measly savings I can spare, I say, "Not enough."

"I wish I could help," Luisa says.

"I wouldn't let you," I say over my shoulder. Luisa and I need every dollar we earn.

"How much?" Mr. Williams asks again.

"Half?"

"Half." He leans back in his chair and looks from me to Keith. "You'll need to work the rest off," he says.

"Pops, please. Shelby's mom freaked and had those cars towed."

Mr. Williams holds his hands up as if in surrender. "If I'm told that the vehicle is blocking a driveway on a residential property, I tow it. It's not for me to judge why the person calls it in."

He looks from me to his son.

"But you're a friend of my boy, so I'll offer you a deal. You pay me one hundred dollars and plan to work here a few hours and we'll call it even. Now, that's less than one-third of the income that I should be receiving. I hope that you both understand what I'm giving up here."

"We do, Pops," Keith says, and I hear relief in his voice.

"And I can take my car today?"

Mr. Williams looks at me over those glasses like I'm not in full command of the English language. "You can take it after you pay me and work off the hours."

I cast my eyes down. "Sir, I get that you are helping me out, but I need my car to get to work. Is there any chance that I can take it after I pay you the money?"

"I can vouch for her," Keith says.

"After you pay me and work off the hours," Mr. Williams repeats. "You kids need to learn consequences for your behavior." He types something into his computer.

"Thank you, sir," I say, because there is no way I can pay the full amount, and I don't want to lose this deal. "When do you want me to work off the hours?"

"I'll look at the schedule and have my son get in touch with you."

"I can drive you to Sal's until you get Lucy back," Luisa says from behind me.

"Thanks, Lu, that would be a huge help," I say.

"We good?" Keith says to me. I nod. "Then let's go."

Ashton looks up like he's just seen us. Through all of this, he's been leaning against the wall, thumbing through his phone. He pushes off the wall and pulls his keys from his pocket. He doesn't look at me. I half remember making out with him and then freaking out. I wonder if he's always like this when he doesn't get what he wants. If so, I actually feel a little sorry for Ellen.

"How'd you get home anyway?" Keith says as we're walking back to Ashton's truck.

I shrug, embarrassed to say out loud that I do not know.

"She walked," Ashton says.

"You saw me?" I ask.

He nods.

"And you didn't give her a ride?" Luisa says. "What a gentleman." She lays the sarcasm on thick.

Ashton shrugs. "Sometimes it's good to walk it off."

As soon as I'm back at my house and know that my car is safe, I call Ben's house. He hasn't answered any texts or calls to his cell phone, and I can't deal with Keith knowing more than me.

"Mrs. Schwartz?" I say. "It's Skye."

"Hello, Skye. How are you?" Mrs. Schwartz sounds like there's a chain around her throat.

"Okay, I guess," I say. "Is Ben home? He's not answering his cell. And I'm worried."

Mrs. Schwartz is quiet.

"Mrs. Schwartz?"

"He's gone away, Skye."

Even hearing his mother's statement, I'm still not ready to believe it. "Away?"

"To straighten out."

"Oh." So, Keith had it right.

"The call from the police was the final straw," Mrs. Schwartz says.

Final straw? Ben always acted like his parents didn't care that he partied so much.

"Well, how can I reach him while he's . . . straightening out?"

She's quiet again and I don't know if I'm supposed to speak, but if she expects me to agree that Ben needs straightening out, she's going to be waiting a long time.

"I think that Ben needs a . . . different influence right now."

I wonder if Mrs. Schwartz has given the same talk to Keith and Ashton or if it's just me that everyone agrees is the bad influence. I pick at the Arthouse Scream Machine sticker on my mirror and press it back again. I'd helped Ben design the logo. We'd chosen an art deco outline font in small caps that had a retro feel, but also had curves that suggested movement (since a scream machine is basically a roller coaster). We'd stacked the words and right justified them. I figured that once the band got a record deal, a pro would create a more polished logo. But for now, it was perfect.

"So, you don't want me to call anymore?" I ask.

"His father was going to force him to leave the band," she says, like it's an explanation. And then with apology lacing her voice, "He needs this."

By *this* I don't know if she means the band or the rehab, but either way it doesn't matter, because her message is the same. According to Mrs. Schwartz the one thing Ben *doesn't* need is me.

As if she's reading my thoughts, Mrs. Schwartz says, "Skye, I'm sorry. But you know how it is. The band means so much to him."

"Right," I say, and we hang up.

I hate that Mrs. Schwartz thinks I'm a bad influence. It's not as if I'm the one who introduced Ben to weed or coke. But I know how much Arthouse Scream Machine means to Ben. Obviously. I can see him agreeing if they made rehab a condition for staying in the band. Toby and Marcus wanted him clean anyway, so they're probably fine with it. But it's killing me that Ben will be gone for four whole weeks and our last night together ended with insults and tears. And I don't even know if he believes that I broke our promise.

23

Role Reversal

THAT NIGHT LUISA begs me to go out. "Please? I missed out last night. I need you as my wing woman tonight."

"I just got off being grounded," I say. "Need to be on best behavior."

"That's not why you're staying in," she says.

"Tomorrow's Emma's birthday," I say to Luisa. "I want to make sure I don't screw up again."

"Suit yourself," Luisa says. "But you never know what I might do without you."

"I'd say don't do anything I wouldn't do, but that list seems pretty short these days."

She snorts. "I'll let you know what's up with Matt."

"Yeah, do. And be careful." I still can't believe the party got raided last night and Ben got caught.

"Where's the fun in that? As you would say," Luisa answers with a laugh.

I'm in my workshop, messing around with other ideas for the Post-it notes when Mom clomps down the stairs dressed to go out. She holds a brown leather purse that matches her shoes.

"I'm going out with Judy tonight. Not sure what time I'll be home." Mom speaks in that clipped way that tells me I shouldn't screw with her. "Tomorrow's your sister's birthday, so don't sleep all day."

My eyes roll reflexively before I can stop them. "Obviously, I wouldn't sleep in on Emma's birthday. Did you get all the stuff?"

When she smiles knowingly at me, her whole face transforms. I can't help but smile back. "What stuff?" she says with mock ignorance.

Ever since I turned thirteen, we've had the birthday fairy tradition. When you wake up on your birthday, every room is decorated, and your presents are hidden throughout the house. It feels like everything magically appeared overnight, like a fairy did it. Even though I was kind of old when she did it the first time, I loved it then and have ever since. It's funny, in most ways Mom seems so practical and sort of serious. I wish this fun side came out more often.

"Over the fridge," she whispers, even though Emma is nowhere nearby. Then louder she says, "Make sure Emma doesn't stay up too late."

"I'll try." I should ask her why she's not going out with Dan, but that would be hypocritical because I'm actually relieved.

Mom kisses me on the head before she leaves.

For the rest of the night, Emma and I watch *Grease* together and sing all the songs. After she goes to bed, I head downstairs to create some fairy lanterns that I saw online. I'd been collecting pieces to make them for the past few weeks, and now I set about putting them together. With the help of a YouTube tutorial, I re-create the fairy lantern as best I can with real moss and a little battery-operated tealight and a cutout silhouette of a fairy. And glitter. While I'm working I think about Ben and how it's only been two weeks since the Saturday night when he was here. So much has changed so fast.

When I'm finished, I turn off the lights in the basement to see how the lanterns look in the dark. They are magic. I stare at them for a while, wishing that I could fix my life as simply as I make projects. I wonder what Ben's thinking tonight locked in that rehab. Is he thinking about missing his recording session? Chilling in his basement? Me? I wonder how long I'll have to wait to find out.

I'm cleaning up my project area when, at 1:42 a.m., my phone buzzes with a text from Judy: Need some help with your mom. We r outside.

I groan and shove my phone into the back pocket of my jeans.

There is only one reason why Judy would need help with Mom. In the parking lot, Judy's souped-up van is chugging exhaust into the cool night. She rolls down her window.

"Sorry, kiddo. You know I'd help if I could."

Of course Judy can't help because she's paralyzed from the waist down, but the fact that she brought my mother home at all in this condition is a testament to the fact that Judy and Mac have no children. Or a testament to what she thinks I can handle, I guess. But come late August, I won't be here to help in this way. I hope all the adults get their shit together before then because nothing is keeping me from MICA.

"I know you would," I say. Mom slumps against the passenger window. "Can you roll down her window?"

I walk to that side where the open window is reviving Mom somewhat.

"Mom?" I say, leaning into her window.

Mom looks blearily at me. "Skye," she slurs. "What're you doing here?"

"I'm here to help get you inside." I open the car door, and Mom spills onto the ground. "Come on, Mom. You've got to get up."

I grab her under one arm and wish, not for the first time, that I was taller, stronger, bigger. But I manage to get Mom to her feet. I hope none of the nosy neighbors are peering at us through their blinds to see the latest episode in the Murray House Drama. And I hope that Emma's not looking either. I glance at her window and breathe a sigh of relief that it's dark.

"Now I just need to get her up the steps and we'll be good," I say to Judy.

"Can't you just leave her on the couch?" Judy asks in a way that says she's trying, but she knows she's helpless here.

"Yeah, nothing says *Happy Birthday* to a middle school girl like her mother passed out on the couch still in her clothes from the night before."

"Emma's birthday. Right," Judy says.

"What happened?" I ask as I struggle to balance Mom's weight against my body. Mom gets really drunk sometimes, but she hasn't been this bad since the time she found out that Dan was seeing someone new. And the time she went out with Judy and some others for her birthday. Emma had Julia sleeping over that night and Mom fell over the coffee table.

"Margaritas," Judy answers.

That doesn't seem to tell the whole story, but Judy doesn't say more.

"Ahgottapeee," Mom mumbles.

"Okay, I've got it. You can go," I say to Judy.

"Okay, hon. If you have trouble, I'll send Mac over," Judy says, and then she leaves me with my sloppy mother.

But it's fine. I don't want someone around while I deal with Mom when she's like this. Somehow, I manage to get Mom upstairs and on the toilet. While I'm in her room, turning down the bed, I hear a thump and run to the bathroom. She's fallen off the seat. I shut the door so that we don't wake Emma and I wrestle my mother from where she'd wedged herself in the narrow space between the toilet and the wall.

"Did you go?" It feels weird to ask my mother this question.

She bobbles her head in a yes. In her room, I can't deal with undressing my own mother, so I take off her shoes and tuck her into bed. I'm turning to leave when I hear her speak.

"He doesn't want to be with me after all." Her words merge and sigh together.

So, it *is* about Dan, but this is not the time to engage Mom in a real conversation. "It's okay, Mom. It'll all look better in the morning," I say automatically.

She starts crying in that messy drunk way. "*He* says I drink too much." She hisses. "Can you believe that?"

Cannoobeeleefdat? Then she starts wailing.

Quickly, I kneel by the bed. "Shhh," I say in a soothing voice, brushing her hair from her face. "Shhhh." I want to yell at her to shut up and get herself together, but again, I know where that will lead and all I want in this moment is to keep Emma from waking up and seeing Mom messed up. I grab two tissues from the box on her bedside table. She blots her eyes and then bunches them against her mouth and moans into them.

"Go to sleep, Mom," I whisper. "We'll talk in the morning. It'll all be better in the morning," I say again.

She nods and rolls to her side, the tissues falling from her hand to the floor. I pick them up and watch her, squeezing the used tissues into a smaller and smaller shape. By the time Mom's breathing becomes regular and I'm fairly sure that she won't fall out of bed, I toss the balled-up tissues in the trash and leave, shutting Mom's door whisper quiet. At Emma's room, I stop and press my ear to her door. Certain that I hear nothing, I creep away, letting out a lungful of air.

The gifts for hiding, as Mom had hinted, are in the cabinet above the fridge. Her favorite hiding spot. In addition to the little gifts for Emma's birthday there are a couple bottles of booze. Mom's baggie of weed and bowl are gone, I notice with surprise. Maybe she realized I was poaching a little bit from her now and then. Or maybe after Emma narc'd on me, she figured she'd better get rid of her own "paraphernalia."

The decorating supplies are in the little closet on the other side of my bathroom in the basement: swaths of tulle in different colors, twinkle lights, fairy balls that have seen better days, and long strands of fake flowers. I start with the tulle, draping it over the sliding glass doors, weaving it through the chandelier and winding it around the stairway banister. I work the twinkle lights around the tulle. Two fairy balls dangle from the chandelier. Next, I tuck the small items Mom bought in the brightly colored glitter boxes she's saved over the years and hide them all around the house. When the living room/ dining room looks sufficiently "fairy'd," I creep up the stairs.

Holding the last of the decorations, I open Emma's door as quiet as a mouse and hope that she doesn't wake. In sleep, she's curled into herself like a larger version of the stuffed animals that line her windowsill. Even though she's replaced some little kid stuff on the walls with band posters and photos of her friends, the stuffed animals have stayed. I allow the door to click shut behind me and she doesn't move.

I get to work.

"Skye . . . Skye."

My name is a whisper weaving into my mind.

Then a jostle of my shoulder and "Skye," a bit louder this time.

I fight against the tendrils of sleep binding me in place.

"Skye," the impatient voice says. "Wake up!"

My eyes flutter open to find Emma about six inches from my face, a huge smile spreading across hers. "You slept with me!"

I rub my eyes and stretch. "Happy birthday, Em," I mumble. Emma was brokenhearted when I wanted my own room. So brokenhearted that I almost changed my mind. But I was thirteen and didn't want to be in a little girl's room anymore. I've had my own space ever since Mom got Mac to build it for me.

"And the birthday fairy came," Emma says in a singsong voice that tells me that she knows it's not real, but she wants to pretend anyway.

I squint at my handiwork and smile. "You're right!" I say.

Tulle is festooned across her headboard and footboard. The fairy lanterns line the space from her bedroom door to her bed. They barely glow in the daylight, but they still look pretty. The fake flowers are wound along with twinkle lights through the tulle. A fairy headband sits on one bedpost, dark green, purple, and blue silk ribbons streaming from a woven crown of flowers.

"Put on your crown, Birthday Fairy Princess," I say.

Emma places the crown on her head. "Do you think Mom's up?"

"I'll check," I say. "The birthday princess should stay right here." I want to make sure Mom is coherent enough to remember that it's Emma's birthday.

"I heard you guys last night," she says, as if she's read my mind.

"You did?"

"Yeah, all that banging and then . . . crying."

"Mom wasn't feeling well," I say quickly. "She must have eaten bad shrimp at the restaurant." No idea where I got the shrimp idea from, but I hope Emma buys it.

"Mmm," Emma says noncommittally and I wonder how much she realizes.

"Give me a quick minute. I'm sure she's fine."

I tap on Mom's door and then enter. It stinks like a hangover. "Mom," I whisper. "Wake up."

Mom rolls over and squints at me.

"Here." I hand her a glass of water and two aspirin. "It's Emma's birthday."

"Right," she croaks. "I know." She pushes the covers off and looks down at herself, still fully dressed. I see a question forming in her mind. "Here," I say, this time handing her something comfy to put on. "I'll leave so you can change."

In the hallway, I pull my phone from my back pocket. Luisa has sent a bunch of texts telling me what a party I missed last night, but all I can think about is Ben spending his first weekend in rehab and how happy I am that Emma has at least one un-hungover person to celebrate her today. I peek in on Emma and ask her to wait two minutes. Then I rush to the kitchen to start coffee for Mom and hot chocolate for Emma. By the time I return upstairs to hand Em her hot chocolate, complete with whipped cream and chocolate shavings, Mom is curled on Emma's bed. She's brushing Em's hair from her face like she's six and not just-turned-twelve. But I get it. Even I want to keep Emma young.

As we head down to the kitchen, Emma loops one of my fairy lanterns over her arm as she takes each step with care, running her hand along the tulle woven with flowers and peering over the banister to see the living room. I pour a cup of Mom's black sludge and hand it to her. Emma on the couch, with the ribbons of the fairy crown flowing into her own long hair, could be an actual fairy. I'd call this sketch *The Fey Princess Before Her Wings Came In*.

"Ready to start looking for what the birthday fairy hid?" I ask Emma with a smile.

"Yes!" Emma says, handing Mom the lantern.

Mom holds up the lantern, examining it. I realize that I was too light with the glitter on one side.

"This is beautiful!" she says. Then she looks up at me with her red-rimmed eyes and mouths, *Thank you.*

I like that something I created can make the people I love happy and I like that I'm feeling closer to my family than I have in a long time. But it doesn't escape me that I feel this way in part because Dan is not here.

24

How Do You Fill an Abyss?

ON MONDAY AT school, despite fourteen hundred students milling around, the halls feel empty. There are murmurs about Ellen and Ashton fighting. Again.

Sunday night, we'd had a fun little birthday dinner for Emma. Dan wasn't there. Mom didn't seem to remember what she'd said to me about Dan on Saturday night. She made an excuse about him grading papers and I didn't push for more. I did notice that she didn't drink any wine.

After dinner, we'd all tucked up on the couch to watch *Beauty and the Beast*. Again. For Emma's research. I have to admit that it was fun, though. It reminded me of how we used to spend Saturday nights, after Dan and Mom broke up but before I started going out every weekend with friends. We'd watch musicals together, like *Grease* and *Hairspray,* and then we'd download the soundtracks and listen to them over and over until we could sing every song by heart, even though we only really liked the fast songs.

But now, at school the thing looming in my brain is the lack of Ben. Ben not in the hall. Ben not in the nook where our group hangs out. Ben not in art class. My day is a Ben-shaped hole, and by the afternoon, I sorely need a distraction.

"Want to come over?" Luisa asks as we're heading to last period. "Miguel's got therapy, so he won't be home till late. Shelby and some others are coming too."

Emma won't be home until five thirty. "Sure."

We sit around listening to music. Not Ben's and my music, just pop music. They're all sharing a joint, but I'm trying to honor Ben. If he can't party, maybe I shouldn't either. Besides, I don't need Emma commenting on my red eyes. I laugh at all the right times and act like the girl hanging with her besties, but the hole inside me is still there. I need something else. My phone chimes a text and I pull it from my pocket to look.

Ashton: Keith says you can pick up your car.

Why wouldn't Keith text me? I was expecting to hear from him about working off my bill. Not to mention that I owe his dad money.

Skye: okay . . .

Ashton: I can come get you

Skye: okay . . .

Ashton: where are you?

Skye: Hangin' with the girls at Luisa's

Ashton: r u all making out w each other?

Luisa is telling Shelby all about Matt. How dreamy he is. How he laughs at all her jokes. Vi and Lex are surfing their phones for funny vids.

Skye: um, no. you wish

Ashton: I do. Haha

It's weird for Ashton to be texting and even weirder for him to be so . . . nice. If that's what you call this.

Ashton: I'll be there in 10 mins

Lex announces she's got a good one. Everyone crowds around her phone to look. Luisa squeals in delight while Shelby rolls her eyes.

Ashton: 10 mins. Okay?

These are my girls, so I don't know why I feel so alone despite being with a bunch of people—it's just like the night I went to that party after seeing Dan at my house. That night, Ben gave me an out. Ben's not an option today. All I've got is Ashton. But at least I'd be getting my car back.

Skye: Fine.

"I've got to head out," I say after a few minutes. "Ashton says he can take me to pick up Lucy."

Luisa raises her eyebrows in skepticism. "Ashton?"

"Weird, right?" I say to her.

She nods. "Text me later."

Ashton's SUV cruises to a stop in front of Luisa's house as I'm walking out. No Keith. I climb in and Ashton flashes me his Hollywood smile before pulling back into traffic. It takes me a few turns to realize that we aren't going to the impound lot.

"What's the deal, Ashton?" I say.

He pulls into the parking lot that borders the quarry, puts the SUV in park, and shrugs. "I was bored. Thought we could have a little fun. Pick up where we left off on Saturday." He offers me another grin. Those hazel eyes grab me. We're not drunk or high, so he's not trying to hook up with me because one or both of us is wasted. The unfamiliar thought that he actually likes being with me for me creeps in. My eyes drop to his lips and I force them back to his eyes.

"This is a booty call?"

He reaches out and traces the seam of my skinny jeans from my knee up to my hip where he rests his hand. My body wakes up at his touch. I can't help it. Ashton leans in, kisses my neck with those lips and whispers, "All I know is that I need you today."

Ashton needs me. And I need an escape. And he's sort of asking permission. Sort of. Sure, Ashton's a jerk, but he's the devil I know and I'm clear-eyed today. Maybe what I need right now is a little bit of devil.

He leans toward me to kiss me. I kiss him back, but I can't relax. He starts to undo my bra and I stiffen.

"Aw, come on." His voice is husky. "I fantasized about this all day." His hands rove my bare stomach beneath my shirt, his touch raising goose bumps in their wake. Is this really what I want?

"No," I say, with a firmness that surprises both of us.

"You don't mean that, do you?" he says.

Usually I don't think much about what I'm doing with boys. If some guy thinks I'm hot, it makes me feel special, like they see me. The way they can't resist me makes me feel like I have power. Sometimes what we do makes me feel good too. But usually, I'm messed up and not thinking much at all. Today is not like that.

"Ashton, what is this?" I ask as he leans in to pepper me with more kisses.

"What we do now." There's a chuckle behind his words. He guides my hand to where he wants it. But the thing is, this is not what *we* do. It's what *he* does. The last two times we hooked up,

I was wasted. Who knows? Maybe I came on to him, but it seems like a decent guy would have made sure I didn't do something that I might regret. And this time, he lied to get me to make out with him. That's not asking permission, no matter how I try to spin it.

"I don't want to do this with you anymore." I pull my hand away.

"Cool," he whispers, like he's cajoling me. "We'll stop after today. Promise." He grabs my hand again.

"Where's Ellen?" I ask, snatching my hand back once more.

"Buzzkill," he says, with a warning tone.

"This is wrong on so many levels. You *lied* to me to get me to go with you. *And* you have a girlfriend."

"I'll take you home. I promise," he whispers into my hair. "Just blow me first."

I lean away from him, from those hands. "Blow yourself."

"You know I'll give back," he says in a low voice. His hands have found me again, are working at the button of my skinny jeans.

I push his hands away and wedge myself as far away from him as I can be in the front of his SUV. "If you don't take me home, I'll walk."

"You're going to walk five miles?"

I button my jeans. "You've let me walk home before. Besides, don't you have a girlfriend to do this stuff with?"

"She's all pissed at me for some shit," he says. "Besides, you're so much fun." He starts to lean toward me again.

My body likes that he says that. My body thinks it has power over him, but my not-wasted brain can see he's manipulating me and he has been manipulating me every time. I place a hand on his chest, keeping him at a distance. "You mean, you like what I let you do."

"No, I mean it's not all heavy like consent and we'll only go this far today and rules and shit."

"And this?" I ask, gesturing between us.

"A way to kill time. Not a big deal. Besides, don't pretend like you don't have fun."

I don't love that I'm just a way to kill time, even though I know I was hoping for a distraction too. But that doesn't mean I owe him anything. "Put the truck in gear. You're taking me home."

Ashton lets out a long sigh and then reverts to the Ashton I saw after the concert, after the other time I didn't give him what he wanted. "Fine," he says, unsmiling. He doesn't speak to me for the entire five miles to my house. He pulls the truck to a stop and won't even look at me.

"You're a dick when you don't get what you want. You know that, right?"

Ashton shrugs. "Whatever, Skye. You getting out or what?"

"Enjoy your cold shower," I say and slam the truck door shut.

"Where's your car?" Mom asks as we're getting dinner on the table. "I didn't see it outside."

She doesn't sound accusatory, just curious.

"It needed a part. My friend Keith is working on it for me." The lie rolls off my tongue with ease and I feel a little bad for not telling the truth, but Mom can't know what really happened.

"How much is that going to cost?" Mom asks.

I hadn't expected that question, but I give her the truth. "One hundred dollars. It was going to be a lot more, but he's giving me a deal."

"You have the money, right?"

"Technically, yes, but I was trying to save it for college."

"If you need help, just tell me."

"Thanks," I say. There's no way I'm taking money from my mother to get my car out of the impound lot, but I appreciate her offering to help when I know that things are always tight financially for us. Our conversation reminds me to text Keith for an update. After what Ashton pulled, I want to be sure I'm getting my information from the source.

> Skye: I need Lucy back. When should I come to work my time off?

> > Keith: Pops says this weekend works
> > How's Sunday?

I sigh at my phone. Being without a car this whole week will be annoying, but I remind myself of the deal that Mr. Williams gave me.

> Skye: Tell your dad thanks. Needs to be in the afternoon. Working a.m.

Keith texts back a thumbs-up emoji and I slide my phone into my back pocket.

"Where's Dan?" Emma says. "He promised to help me with my lines for the play."

Mom is bent over her laptop, trying to catch up on work. She's always trying to catch up.

"I can help you," I say.

"Yeah, but Dan has experience with theater. That's what he said. I wanted *him* to help me."

"Was he supposed to be here tonight?" I ask.

Emma nods. "Yes, he'd said we'd practice after dinner tonight. He said that last week. But he didn't even come over for my birthday dinner. Mom, what's going on?"

Mom finally looks up from her laptop. She takes off her glasses. "I'm not sure, Em. I'm sorry that you feel disappointed. Dan and I are just trying to work out a few things."

I'd thought they'd worked out all the things during the five months they'd been seeing each other in secret and that's why they were getting married. Life's too short and all that. But then again, I remember what Mom said that night when she was drunk.

"Are you still getting married?" Emma asks now.

Mom squeezed her eyes shut. "I don't know. I truly don't," she says. The sadness in her voice is almost enough to stop me from feeling relieved that the wedding might be off. Almost.

25

Just Like Her

ON TUESDAY, AS I'm coming out of the bathroom stall, I find Ellen leaning against the sink. A few other girls are there, checking their makeup or fixing their hair. "I knew you were a slut," Ellen says in a loud voice. "I mean, who doesn't know that?"

I glance at the girls, who are pretending not to hear. Ellen's statement is probably nothing new to them.

"But now you've dropped to a whole new level."

Oh, shit.

She shoves her phone in my face. I have to back up a little bit to understand the photo displayed there. When it resolves, I see that it's me and Ashton in his SUV. At least all we did was kiss. And we're not even kissing in this photo. Thank God.

"You need to stay away from my boyfriend," Ellen hisses at me. Her curtain of shining black hair falls forward, obscuring half of her face. I can't help thinking that if I drew her, I'd need some white or even a shade of blue to capture the way that the light catches on her hair. I'd call the drawing *The Other Side of the Wall.*

I want to pull out my phone to show her the text exchange—that he sought *me* out. But that wouldn't explain why I agreed when I knew he was Ellen's.

"That was nothing," I say.

It's true that nothing really happened. Nothing huge, anyway, but Ellen doesn't need to know more. I've stopped the madness with Ashton. I think about our text exchange and I realize he covered his ass. Our texts were about my car. I go with his lie.

"He was taking me to deal with my car."

"Then why are you parked at the quarry?" She stares at me, both of us knowing that the only reason anyone goes to the quarry is to party or to hook up.

I take a breath and look Ellen in the eye. I feel guilty for the stuff that's happened with Ashton. I never planned to hook up with someone else's boyfriend. And Ellen and I used to be friends. I think about Ashton lying to me to get me to hook up with him.

"Why don't you ask him? He was the one driving."

Ellen flips her hair out of her face. "Be straight with me. Were you or were you not hooking up with my boyfriend?"

"Okay, Ellen, I'll be straight with you. How's this? You could do so much better than Ashton."

Ellen sighs impatiently. "He's the quarterback and I'm captain of the Spirit Squad," Ellen says, like she has no choice in the matter.

"Just because it *sounds* perfect, doesn't mean it *is* perfect. You've got spies watching him and reporting back. How is that an ideal relationship?"

"I don't have spies," she says, looking away. "That person just happened to see Ash's truck."

I cross my arms over my chest. "Really, Ellen?"

Ellen angles her head, evaluating me. She pulls in a deep breath through her nostrils and lets it out again. She looks away and then back at me. "Just stay away from people's boyfriends, Skye."

I want to tell her to make sure her boyfriend stays away from me, but I keep my face neutral and she leaves.

Toward the end of the day, I call the rehab where they sent Ben. Hanging with the girls didn't help. Being with Ashton definitely didn't help. There's only one thing to fill a Ben-shaped hole and that's Ben. I need to hear his voice.

"Good afternoon, Blue Valley Treatment Center, where we help you become the best version of you. How can I help?"

"I'm trying to reach a . . . patient."

"We are not a hospital," the pleasant female voice intones. "Our *client*s are here to better themselves."

"Right. I'm trying to reach a *client*. Ben Schwartz."

"And you would be?"

"A friend."

"As per our confidentiality regulations, we cannot confirm or deny that such a client is staying here, but you can feel free to leave a message, and if that individual is staying with us, we will be sure that he receives your message."

What kind of bullshit is this? "Okaaaay. *If* Ben Schwartz is there . . . bettering himself, can you tell him that Skye Murray called? And that she's thinking about him?" Okay, that last part sounded pathetic. But it's true. I'm thinking of the absence of Ben every single moment of each day.

The unfailingly pleasant voice responds, "I will give the client the message, should he be here."

"Ms. Murray!" a voice booms behind me.

"Uh . . . thanks."

I click off the call just as Vice Principal Kincaid waddles up to me with his hand out. "You know the rules, Ms. Murray."

No cell phone use during the school day. Period. I could claim that it's some kind of emergency, but knowing Kincaid, he'd want to call to confirm. It's not worth a fight.

"My phone is password protected, so don't try scrolling through all my selfies, Mr. K," I say as I drop the phone into Mr. Kincaid's sweaty palm.

"Watch it, Ms. Murray, or you'll be serving detention alongside your phone."

I hold my hands up in surrender.

"You can retrieve this at the end of the day."

I nod and wait for a minute to see if he wants to give me one of his canned lectures on missing class, breaking rules, and generally being a fuckup at Pennswood High. But all he says is, "Now get to class."

Once I was a girl who read lots of books and did well in school and was chosen by teachers for all the teacher's pet things. Once I was the girl who inspired principals to smile and say words like *proud, award, accomplishment.* Then I became the girl who looked for the easiest way to chase away bad memories.

I turn toward the unending row of lockers heading toward the science classes. When I am sure that I'm out of Kincaid's line of vision, I sneak into the studio, hoping the artsy overachievers won't be working on their next scintillating episode of *This Week at Pennswood High.* Luckily, the studio is pitch-black. I slump into one of the chairs used by the interviewers and try to imagine the next four weeks without Ben . . . or his weed.

I wake up when the last bell rings and rush out the door. I'm disoriented from falling asleep in that dark room during the school day. I'm hitting all kinds of lows lately. Today is Emma's short day— no rehearsal—and I'm supposed to meet her at home. Not that she thinks I need to. With no car and Ben gone, I sprint to make the bus.

When I get home, the house is empty. I go to pull my phone from my pocket and remember that Kincaid took it and I was sup-posed to pick it up at the end of school. I stalk through the house, as if I'll find Emma behind a door or in the shower. I think about things she's told me lately about her friends—weren't she and her friends texting boys at Julia's sleepover? I think about what I used to do when I was her age. I look toward the woods. Would she?

It takes me about ten minutes to find them. A group of six kids—boys and girls—sitting in a circle on the carpet of pine needles. Emma and another boy are kneeling and kissing. From the looks of it, this isn't Emma's first kiss. My stomach tumbles.

I clear my throat and four sets of eyes look guilty. Emma and the boy take a moment to register the noise and pull apart, a bit of saliva connecting them for a fraction of a second.

Her eyes go wide when she sees me standing nearby. She covers her mouth with her hand, as if she can erase what just happened. Slowly, she rises from her knees and walks over to me like the accused walking the plank. I want to be the cool older sister. I want to, but I can't. Worry has choked the cool right out of me.

"You weren't home," I say and recognize my mother's accusatory tone coming from my mouth.

"I texted you." She looks surprised.

"I don't have my phone."

She bites her lip and frowns. "And that's my fault?"

"Get your stuff." I can't seem to bite back the Mom-edge from my voice. "You need to go home."

She glares at me. "I'm hanging out with my friends."

"You're kissing boys in the woods!" I hiss at her. "You were supposed to come home after school."

She looks over her shoulder toward the group of kids. The boy she'd been kissing, the tall boy with dark hair, says something, and they all laugh. Must be Thomas. I remember her mentioning him after the sleepover at Julia's. Fear tugs at me from the inside, freaking me out about Emma growing up so fast in this way.

"What's the deal with him?" I tilt my chin toward the boy.

"Thomas? Nothing. We're just playing a game." She giggles and then covers her mouth.

I think of Ashton and how much *fun* he thinks I am. And I think of Ellen confronting me in the girls' bathroom. Is this the cycle that we've created? Dan did what he did. I made my own bad choices and now Emma.

"Come on," I say. "Let's go."

"Skye," Emma hisses. "You're embarrassing me. I'll be home soon. I promise."

There's trust in her eyes and I hate myself a little when I say, "No, get your bag. We're leaving now."

"God, you're just like Mom."

After she says that, I hate myself even more. Emma and I used to be allies, and it rips at my gut to have her compare me to Mom. I don't back down even though I want Emma to think I'm the cool sister. Being cool is just surface shit compared to keeping her safe and making sure she doesn't make the same bad choices that I did. As we walk back, Emma fuming and muttering under her breath, I have a teeny sense of what it must be like to be Mom—except Mom didn't keep me safe when I needed her to. I won't fail Emma in the same way.

26

AFTER: I am fourteen. Summer before ninth grade

TWILIGHT ON THE boardwalk seems magical, like anything can happen. During the day, the boardwalk is just a wooden sidewalk with lots of stores and food. But at night, it's a carnival where groups of kids wander like packs of wolves. Lights blink and music pounds from inside the arcade. The night is coming on purple and blue, and Luisa and I are looking for a party.

"That's Joey's friend," Luisa says, pointing to a guy coming out of Franzoni's. "He's the guy I told you about who knows where all the parties are."

"Tall," I say as I lick my soft serve. It is melting a little bit in the heavy salt air.

Luisa wrinkles her nose. "Yeah, but too skinny." Then she calls, "Derek! Over here."

He veers toward Luisa's voice and she waves. He bounces a little on his toes when he walks. He *is* super skinny, but I like his longish hair and the scruff on his cheeks. Boys my age don't have that.

"You're Shelby's friend, right?" he says to Luisa.

"Yeah, Luisa." Luisa points to herself. "And this is Skye." Luisa points to me.

"What's up?" Derek says in my direction.

I lick my ice cream and nod at him. His eyes hover. Does he like me?

"So, where's the party tonight?" Luisa asks.

"How old did you two say you are?" Derek says, eyes skipping from one of us to the other.

Luisa and I don't even look at each other. Shelby had been very clear about the fact that we could not let these guys know that we were only starting ninth grade in a few weeks.

"Sixteen," Luisa says.

I look at Derek and take the entire top of the cone in my mouth, sucking the sweetness. I'd seen a girl do that in a movie, and I wondered if it would get this boy's attention. He blinks and looks back at Luisa, but his eyes skip over to me again. I lick all the way around the cone, letting my tongue twirl around.

"Yeah, okay," he says. "It's not far from here. I'll text you where to go. Unless you want to meet here when I get off and we could go over together." His eyes linger on me and my ice-cream cone.

So he *does* like me. I try to act cool by licking my lips and tossing the cone in a nearby trash can. "Let's meet. What time do you get off?"

It hits me that maybe my words sound dirty. I feel my face turning red, but I play it off like I meant it and smile at Derek.

He blinks again and clears his throat. "Ten thirty. I'll meet you here."

"Okay, see you then." Luisa and I turn to head down the boardwalk. I wonder if he's checking out my butt in my cutoff shorts.

"Hey, Shelby's friend," I hear him call to Luisa.

She walks back to him and then jogs to catch up with me.

"What was that about?" I ask.

Luisa laughs. "He can't remember our names, but he said he likes the way you eat ice cream."

The heat of a blush creeps up my neck to my cheeks again. I giggle. At home, boys didn't pay attention to me and I wasn't sure why. I'd been told I was pretty, and I had the curves boys seemed to like. It was as if they knew I was damaged in some way. But here, I could be someone else.

Luisa leans against me. "Gonna be a fun night."

"You know it," I say, trying on my new persona.

Derek walks us from the boardwalk to the party, which is on the beach. An enormous bonfire sends flames licking at the stars. Somehow, there's a keg on the beach and music pours through an unseen speaker. I'm not dressed right. I don't know what to do with my hands. I'm sure that the older girls will see that Luisa, Shelby, and I are all too young. And then Derek will be disgusted that he was hanging with a girl who had just turned fourteen at the beginning of the summer.

Derek places a big red plastic cup of beer in my hand and I gulp at it, hoping to show that I'm not some little kid. Luisa and I haven't gotten drunk a ton since that first time, but we aren't total newbies. She'd made sure to eat bread before going out tonight, but I'd wanted to get drunk as fast as possible, so I hadn't eaten anything since the ice-cream cone.

He refills my cup for me. One time? Two times? Dancing barefoot in the sand with the sound of the waves crashing on the shore is like no other party I've ever been to. I twirl to the music and fall down, splashing beer everywhere. I laugh when Derek pulls me up and I wrap my arms around him.

Then we're dancing and he makes sure I have beer at all times. I feel like one of the popular girls at school. So, when he asks if I'll take a walk with him, I nod. After those huge cups of beer, he needs to sort of guide me over the bumpy sand. I giggle and lean against him.

"Here," Derek says, pulling his shirt over his head and setting it on the sand. "So you don't get sandy."

He's so nice to me. I didn't know boys could be this nice. I sit on the holey T-shirt, even though it's not going to keep sand off me. It's sweet and I don't want to hurt his feelings. He thumps down next to me and slides his arm around my waist.

Then we're kissing. He whispers in my ear about how he'd been thinking all night about me and the way I licked my ice cream and he could barely concentrate on making pizzas. I like knowing that I've been on a boy's mind for hours. No boy has ever said anything like that to me before and it feels good. I touch my mouth and giggle again. I feel so funny. Sort of numb, but so alive too.

Derek's hands skim over my skin like fire. Soon the straps of my tank are down around my shoulders and he's touching my breasts. At his touch, the memory of Dan and the tent looms. I freeze, and Derek whispers in my ear, asking if I'm okay. If I kiss Derek harder, then maybe I'll push the memory of Dan out.

The world sways as Derek leans me back, the stars dancing and bouncing in the clear black sky. I close my eyes, but the whole world rocks like I'm out at sea, not on the beach. I open them again and try to focus on the stars while Derek touches me.

After a little while, Derek's fingers are sliding into my jean shorts and a minute later inside me. It feels sort of good, but I know I shouldn't be letting him do that. But I also want to replace my memories with a real boy, a boy who is maybe not my boyfriend, but at least close to my age. Derek guides my hand to him. I don't know what to do.

He keeps whispering nice things in my ear about how I feel and how it makes him feel. He asks if it's okay, what we're doing, but my tongue feels thick, like it doesn't know how to make words anymore. If he wants to do this stuff to me, I guess it's okay to let him. Even if it doesn't feel right. Maybe Luisa and Shelby are doing this too. I push at Derek a little bit, but he doesn't seem to notice. Somehow my shorts aren't on anymore and I don't remember them coming off.

Derek asks if it's okay and something about protection and the stars keep dancing overhead.

Then he pushes himself inside and pushes and pushes. I cry out, but he doesn't stop moving. It seems to make him push harder. I don't know how long this goes on. All I can see are the stars. Then he grunts and his weight comes down on me. Just like Dan.

This time, I can't push the memory of Dan back out. Then I'm crying and Derek seems worried.

"This isn't your first . . . ? Did you ever . . . ? Oh my god, why didn't you say anything? I thought . . ."

I curl onto my side, shaking. That night from before smothering me. Derek pulls his pants up and leans toward me, but now he seems afraid to touch me. His hands hover around my face and shoulders.

"Are you okay? God . . . Look, I had no idea. I thought you were into it. Let me just . . . I'll take you back. I'll get you a beer or something."

"I'm fine," I say. My automatic answer. "You go ahead. I'll be there in a minute."

Derek leaves without his shirt. I didn't expect him to actually leave me. But why wouldn't he? I'm not special, like he'd said. I'm just a girl, split apart.

When I return to the party holding Derek's shirt, he's talking to some guys at the far side of the bonfire. Luisa and Shelby grab me and pull me over to the side. I glance back at Derek, but he isn't looking at me. One of Derek's friends peers around him and his eyes catch on me. I turn my back on them like I don't care.

"Oh my god, you are covered in sand," Luisa says, brushing the back of my tank top. "Obviously, you didn't just take a walk. Tell us everything."

"Yeah, you're the only one getting any attention here," Shelby adds.

They hadn't been off with other boys doing what I'd been doing. They'd been here, drinking beer and doing what we always did.

"Was he a good kisser? What was it like?" Luisa asks.

"Is he like seventeen? Do you think he knew how old you were?" Shelby asks.

It's so dark outside of the bonfire that they probably can't see that I've been crying. And if they don't know I'm upset, I can pretend I'm not.

"Get me a beer and I'll tell you all about it," I say. I let them think I am wild and daring. I won't tell them about my tears or my memories.

27

What's a Synonym for Weird?

THE NEXT MORNING, I stop by the office to claim my phone. Mr. Kincaid hands it to me with a look that warns me not to test him. Aside from all of the texts, there's a voicemail from Ben's house phone. It's been five days since he disappeared to rehab. I duck into the girl's bathroom to listen to the voicemail. No way I can wait until the end of the day to listen to a message if Ben is home. For a split second, I think it's weird that he'd call me from his house phone, but maybe his parents took away his cell.

But the message isn't from Ben, which I should have guessed. Rehab is twenty-eight days, not five. The message is from Ben's mom, telling me that the rehab—only she doesn't say rehab—told her that I'd called, and she wanted to remind me of our conversation over the weekend. I delete the message and shove the phone in my bag. Ben's mom is right. I should leave Ben alone. If he wanted to be in touch with me, he'd find a way. So, obviously, he doesn't.

I slip into my chair in art just before the late bell rings, but I can't draw anything. I can't even feel happy that maybe Mom's wedding is off. I lay my head on my arms and close my eyes. A loud rap on the desk makes me jump and my eyes fly open. Mr. M taps his finger on my closed sketchbook. "Ms. Murray, please come see me during your next free period."

"Sure thing, Mr. M." A good talk with Mr. M is exactly what I need. It's weird that he called me by my last name instead of my first, but Mr. M can be like that. I wallow my way through my other classes until my free period. Mr. M's got to know about Ben, even if he doesn't know about my home drama, so he'll get why I couldn't draw today. Or during the last art class, the first day without Ben. He knows that I can catch up. He'll help me. When the bell finally rings, I hustle to the art room.

I drop my bag on the floor and slump into the comfy chair without even saying hello. Most teachers just have the basic desks and chairs, but Mr. M has brought in real furniture that makes his office like a cozy room.

Mr. M doesn't say anything either, which is odd. Usually he greets me when I come to his office. I wait while he types something into the computer. Mr. M types like he expects the keyboard to bite. I settle back and wait to hear him sympathize with me about Ben, tell me about my options if I just applied myself, make a plan for overcoming my latest hurdle.

But Mr. M says none of those things.

"When do you plan to give me the theme for your portfolio?" he asks after he's pushed the keyboard away from his fingers.

"Um, I had a setback."

He looks at me over his reading glasses. "You need twenty original works with a theme that ties them together. Your theme idea is already overdue."

"But the final project is not due until, like, April or something, right?"

"First week of April. Prior to the art show opening the following Thursday. The pieces from your portfolio will make up your entries for the show."

"Right. That's forever away. You know I'll have everything by then."

"It's less than five weeks away. I need a theme now, Ms. Murray. Your final grade is based on you hitting *all* of your deadlines. That includes providing me with a theme and a plan for meeting the project goals. I'd expected yours months ago and you've failed to inform me of it."

"Look, I'm sorry, Mr. M. I really am." I give him my most apologetic look; the sad eyes are easy because I *am* sad.

"And?"

I don't know what to say next. I thought the *sorry* was good enough. I try again. "It wasn't my fault. I had a good start, but—"

Mr. M holds a hand up. "Seems like there's always an excuse with you, Ms. Murray. I need your theme."

He's being so formal. "Seriously, Mr. M?"

"You've known about the deadline since we returned from winter break."

"But you know about Ben. And my mom—"

Mr. M shakes his head again. Where is the pep talk, the acknowledgment that Ben isn't here and my world is rocked? I wait for the words of encouragement, for the plan on how we will tackle this giant obstacle together. Instead, Mr. M peers at me over his reading glasses and I feel like he can see inside me to the dark, gnarled parts, the ugly me that squats behind these eyes.

"MICA could withdraw your acceptance if you don't fulfill this requirement."

Mr. M is serious. He's not messing around. Panic fills me. "Aberration," I blurt. "Aberration is my theme."

"Aberration?" Mr. M frowns.

"Yes," I say, improvising. "You know, like things that are weird or unexpected. Off-kilter, not normal." Like how I am on the inside versus the outside. Like how my family is. Like how I feel ever since Ben left. Like what happened with Dan.

"Interesting choice," Mr. M says. "Go on."

I rush headlong into the abyss. "And I'm working on my specific plans now for, you know, how everything will be pulled together. And relate to Aberration."

"Very well." Mr. M writes a note in his book. "I'll see you on Monday with more details for your plan."

Days pass by and early March can only be drawn with pastels of gray and umber. Ben has now been gone a full week and has not tried to contact me. Not by phone, not by e-mail, not by messenger drone, if there were such a thing—which there should be just so that Ben and I could send each other drawings to show how we're getting through this time. I find myself thinking that I'm supposed to be somewhere or that I'm waiting for someone and I realize that it's the absence of Ben that I'm reacting to, which, to be honest, seems slightly on the pathetic side. Meanwhile apparently the wedding is back on.

At some point, Mom and Dan reconciled their differences and now he's filling up the house. He has a big presence for a small man.

"That's it," Dan says to Emma. "You're getting it!"

Emma beams. "Give me the next line."

Dan sets down the script. "I will, but when you're delivering your lines, you want to speak from here." His hand spans her belly. "Like this." Dan does an exaggerated intake of breath. "Now your turn." He keeps one hand on her shoulder and the other on her belly as she breathes in deeply and then lets it out.

"Exactly. Do you feel that?"

Emma nods.

"If you speak from there, you'll project in the way that the teacher is asking of you."

His hand remains on her shoulder and her belly as she practices the lines they've been going over and over and over. I watch his hands on my sister's body and my gut clenches.

"Girls, Dan thought we could do a game night tonight." Mom

has just walked in from the kitchen, drying her hands with a dish towel. As usual, she appears oblivious.

Dan releases Emma and turns to Mom. He bounces on his toes. "Yes! What would you all like to play?" He rubs his hands together. "Do you still have Scrabble? Or what about Settlers?" He turns to me. "Skye, what would you prefer?"

His eyes on me make me realize that he hardly ever directs his questions and comments to me since he returned. Most of the time, it's as if I don't exist as a member of this new family. Now, with Dan's eyes on me, I wish I had a turtle shell to climb into.

"Don't plan around me. I'm not sure I'll be home tonight," I say.

He nods his understanding and I can't tell if he's disappointed or relieved.

"You can't stay in tonight?" Mom asks hopefully.

"Either way, I want to play Scrabble," Emma says.

I escape to my room, where I grab my charcoal and start a sketch, but I feel agitated. I toss the sketch pad on my bed and root around in my drawers for a little something to take away the discomfort that's boiling up from the inside, ready to take over. Matches. Cigarettes. No weed. No pills. I pull everything out and dump it on the floor. All I've got are two bracelets like the one I made for Ben last summer, a concert stub from the last time we went to a show, a peace sign earring. And the dark blue shard of broken plate from that time in the kitchen right before Dan and Mom broke up. I rub my thumb across the smooth, painted surface of the fragment of plate. A thought sneaks into my mind uninvited: it's probably sharp enough to cut. I push the unwelcome thought away. I refuse to allow these feelings to lead me to hurt myself like that.

Upstairs, Dan and Mom and Emma play happy family. I think about the broken heart I'd created with pieces of colored paper. And my Post-it project. The firefly spark of inspiration flits through my brain. I cup the shard in the palm of my hand and imagine pieces that might fit around that one and others that might fit around those.

Leaning back on my pillows, I grab my sketchbook and start to flesh out the idea. By the time I stop, pages of false starts litter the floor around my bed, but I have something. I definitely have something.

"I need backup," I say to Luisa on the phone. Funny, it was Luisa I called on the first night that Dan showed up in our lives again. Four weeks ago, since I learned that Mom and Dan had been back together for months. Between Dan's return and Ben's disappearance, time moves like a prison sentence.

"What's up?"

"Dan stuff."

Luisa doesn't ask what that means. "I'll be there in a few minutes."

"Thanks," I say, relieved and jumpy all at the same time.

After I hang up I stare at my reflection in the mirror, but it's just the same old me staring back.

"We're playing Scrabble?" Luisa side-mouths to me when she walks in. "On a Saturday night?"

Mom looks up from organizing the parts of the game. "Luisa, what a nice surprise! How's your mom?"

"Good, thanks, Ms. Murray. She says hi."

"Oh, say hello to her from me when you go home, okay?"

"Sure!" Luisa smiles at Mom.

I pull her down to my room and shut the door.

"What is going on?"

"I need a second opinion. I need you to watch Dan and tell me if he's weird with Emma."

"Weird how?"

I think of his hands on my body. I think of his hands on her body. "Just . . . weird. Not like a father."

Luisa nods. "Whatever you need."

I open the door and start to walk out. "And act normal!" I whisper.

"I *am* normal. You're the one not being normal."

"You girls want to play?" Mom asks, and she sounds as shocked as Luisa looked.

"We'll be a team," I say.

"That's not fair! You'll know two times as many words!" Emma says.

"We could be a team too," Dan says.

"Awesome. Suck it, Skye, I have an English professor on my team."

"Language!" Dan says.

"Sorry," Emma says, but she doesn't sound sorry. "Wait. What about Mom? She can't be by herself."

"I'm making popcorn. You all go ahead. I'll join in on the next game."

I pretend to be interested in our letter tiles while I steal glances at Emma and Dan to see how he's being with her. Dan moves the tiles around and points at some of them. Emma nods. His hands are above the table the whole time.

"Oh, we've got a good one," Emma says, smiling at her Scrabble tiles and then at Luisa and me. "You all better watch out!"

"Don't be so sure," I say. "We've got some good possibilities over here."

"What tiles are you looking at?" Luisa says to me. "We have four *E*'s and two *I*'s."

I nudge her arm. "Where's your poker face?"

"Should we go for it?" Dan says to Emma, his eyes twinkling. He glances at me then, the smile still lighting his eyes. For a moment I remember how he used to teach me new things and how he supported my interest in art and how he and Mom would always take us everywhere, even though a lot of parents would leave their kids home with a babysitter. I remember him taking us on hikes and teaching me to whittle. Why do I always focus on the bad stuff? Then his eyes skip away from me and he returns his gaze to the Scrabble board.

"Let's slaughter them," Emma says to Dan, grinning.

We play a whole game, and as promised, Luisa and I do get slaughtered. Dan doesn't do anything creepy. I decline a second game and I think I hear Luisa sigh in relief as we head downstairs to my room.

"Nothing weird, right?" I say to Luisa in my room.

Luisa flops on my bed. "He's definitely bossy and sort of annoying, but I didn't notice anything weird. Maybe if you told me—"

"No, you're right. There was nothing weird." I don't want what happened to me all those years ago to happen again, but it seems that I'm seeing things that aren't there. "You want to get out of here?" I ask.

"Yeah, okay." She pulls out her phone. "Where do you want to go? Jeremy's? Or maybe the quarry?"

"I want to go somewhere different. Will you be my wing-woman?"

"Always." Luisa slides her phone into her pocket.

I'm wearing black leggings and I grab a black hoodie. My hair is already dark, so I don't bother covering it.

"Are we robbing a bank?" Luisa asks.

"No," I say, but not in a convincing way.

"I can't get arrested."

"I don't think you will," I say. "You can stay in the car."

"Oh, shit. Then you better lend me some dark clothes."

I gather all my Post-its and some markers and heavy-duty tape because the Post-its might not stick. I shove everything into a backpack and sling it across my back. Then I place a step stool outside the back door.

"I admit that you've got my attention," Luisa says.

I smile at her and gesture for us to go.

"Mom, we're going out for a little bit," I say when we emerge from the basement.

They've put away Scrabble and they're setting up Settlers of Catan.

"But I like the random board," Emma says.

"This time we'll use the one in the rulebook. We can try a random board next time," Dan says, placing the pieces according to a diagram he holds in one hand.

"Where are you going?" Mom asks.

"Over to Sal's."

Luisa side-eyes me, but she says nothing.

"Be back by midnight."

Dan looks up from his orchestration. "Still not dressing appropriately for the weather, I see," he says, and I remember that night with the broken plate.

I zip my hoodie to my neck. "Nope, guess not."

After I retrieve the step stool and we get into Luisa's car, I tell her to drive toward Sal's.

"You know that Sal's is closed now, right?" Luisa says.

"We're not going *to* Sal's. Just head *toward* Sal's."

We park behind the long low building where we always park for our diner shifts.

"Are you going to paint that wall like you said?"

I look at the bland concrete wall. "No, that's way too big of a job for now. I have something more . . . temporary in mind. Also, we're doing it out front."

"I don't want to stay in the car," Luisa says.

"I *could* use your help," I say. "And I guess we'll just run if we have to." I hope that I'm kidding, but I've never done this before.

Around the front of the building, the lights of Sal's diner are out except for the broken neon sign. The shops and restaurants of our town are asleep. Cars rush by on the main street that the strip mall faces. They pay no attention to two girls in dark clothes, one carrying a step stool and the other a large bag. I stop in front of the storefront next to Sal's that's been empty for months. I stare at it for a moment until the image emerges for me.

"Start a bottom row. Here." I hand Luisa a stack of yellow Post-it notes.

"I'm not an artist!" she protests.

"You know how to stick Post-it notes, don't you?"

She stares at the huge window. "I guess?"

"Stick them in a nice straight line. That's all you need to do."

I choose the electric blue notes and start working on the concept I'm holding in my mind. When Luisa is finished with the bottom, I start her on the sides. It's a good thing we brought the step stool, but a ladder would have been even better. We'll only be able to reach so high. I keep working, stepping back from time to time to check how it's coming together.

"This is so calming," Luisa says, pressing yellow square after yellow square. "Except for the fact that I'm nervous we're going to get caught."

"Yeah, it's a combo of conflicting feelings," I say as I adjust some

Post-its to achieve the effect I'm imagining and then continue to work, slowly covering the broad sheet of glass.

"Skye, I love it!" Luisa exclaims when she sees the picture emerging.

Covering an entire storefront window takes more time than I'd expected. And a ton of Post-it notes. When the glass is covered as far as we can reach, I step back one last time to see how it's come along. I've never created something so big or so public. Luisa was right, pressing the Post-its had a calming effect, quieting the worry and confusion in my mind. But knowing we could get caught had gotten my adrenaline pumping in a way that I liked even better than that coke before the concert. The best thing, though, is seeing the mural we'd created huge and bright against the dark night, shouting to anyone who takes a moment to glance this way.

28

The Singer or the Song?

THE NEXT MORNING, when Luisa and I wake up, I decide to make pancakes before our morning shift.

"This makes zero sense," Luisa says, "when we're going to be delivering pancakes to strangers for the next several hours."

I pull out the griddle and turn the burners on. "We don't get to eat those pancakes. Besides, ours are going to be way more awesome. Can you get the eggs and milk from the fridge?"

The happy feeling after our adventure last night has lingered into the morning, and I sort of want to get to work early to see if our creation has stayed up or if someone took it down.

I'm pulling the pancake mix from the pantry just as Emma walks into the kitchen, still in her pj's.

"Can I help?"

"Sure. Measure me a cup of milk. Luisa's going to crack the eggs."

"I'm really good at cracking eggs though," Emma says. "Are you good at it?" she asks Luisa.

Luisa pushes the eggs toward Emma. "Crack away!"

Emma cracks an egg into the bowl and then fishes out the shell that fell in.

"Thought you said you were good at that," Luisa says, watching Emma.

"I am. A little bit of shell always falls in," she says with authority.

"If you say so," Luisa says. She measures the milk.

"I'm working on a collage for Mom for the wedding after this. Want to help?" Emma asks me.

Normally I wouldn't mind hanging with Emma for a change, and cutting and pasting photos together sounds relaxing, but I'm surprised she hasn't accepted that the last thing I want is to do anything for Mom's wedding to Dan.

"Can't," I say, "Lu and I are headed to work, and then I'm going to the junkyard."

We combine our ingredients together in a big bowl and I stir them until their individual aspects disappear to form the batter. Butter sizzles on the flat surface of the griddle, sliding to the sides and pooling in the corners.

"Junkyard?" Emma repeats, like I'm crazy. "Why?"

"To get Lucy."

"Oh."

She's quiet and I can hear the disappointment behind the silence—that we aren't spending time together, that I'm not helping with the wedding. So much has changed between us recently and it's too easy to trace it all back to Dan's return. I pour three even circles of pancake batter on the griddle.

"Maybe we can do something later?" I say.

"Maybe," she says, but her voice doesn't hold much hope.

"Thanks for spending the night," I say after Lu and I have stopped at her house so she could change into her uniform.

"No prob. I'm here for you." Lu glances over at me and then returns her attention to the road.

"I know," I say.

When we'd returned from our episode of guerrilla artfare, Dan was still at the house. It was late, so game night was over and Emma was in bed, but Mom and Dan sat on the couch, talking. I wasn't sure if Mom was letting Dan stay overnight. He hadn't stayed yet, but I knew it had to happen at some point. And it made me feel sort of squirmy. I'd locked the memories of him into a corner of my mind and refused to examine them for years, but now that he was back, it was as if they'd quadrupled in size and could no longer fit in that tiny corner of my then-twelve-year-old mind.

I'd asked Luisa to stay and she said yes, even though I knew that her mom would probably be angry that she was asking so late at night. Lu had even asked if I wanted to talk, but I'd told her I didn't and she didn't push, which let me breathe a little bit. I'm sure that some mental health expert somewhere would recommend that I talk everything out, but I just couldn't. Not yet. We watched a couple episodes of *Gilmore Girls*—season three, our favorite—and fell asleep. Now, we're uniformed and ready for our shift, but we both know that the quiet buzz in the car has nothing to do with the fact that we will be waiting on tables for the next few hours.

"I can't wait to see," she says now, sort of conspiratorially.

"Me neither!"

When we pull up, I can't stop the huge grin from spreading across my face. Our creation is still plastered on the empty storefront connected to Sal's building. A Post-it mural of a giant blue broken heart on a yellow background.

"It looks even better in daylight," Lu says.

"It sort of glows, doesn't it?"

"Look." Luisa points. "Looks like someone wrote something."

My stomach drops. I wonder if we're being called out for vandalism or maybe even delinquency. We walk up to get a closer look. Not only one Post-it is written on. Several are. One says *Broken hearts are hard to heal.* Another: *My bf dumped me via text.* A third: *I've loved her for years, but she doesn't know I exist.* And a fourth: *The only way out is through.*

Luisa and I smile at each other, but we try to be all low-key on account of the fact that no one is supposed to know that we did that Post-it mural.

"People are responding to what you created!" Luisa whisper-screams at me as we walk in the back door of Sal's and clock in.

"I know!" I whisper-scream back. "And you created it too!"

In the diner, people are talking about the Post-it mural. Not everyone, but some people. I try really hard not to smile like a huge goofball. I wish Ben were here to see it.

"Who is vandalizing my property?" Sal grumbles as people leave to write on the mural and return for their meals.

"That empty store is yours?" I say.

"Unfortunately for me, yes."

"But . . . it's not vandalism if it doesn't cause permanent damage, is it?" I say. I don't want to think of myself as a vandal.

"No, I suppose not. But still. This person did not ask my permission." He grumbles some more. Then he says, "Oh, please tell your mother we can speak tomorrow."

"My mother?" I don't know what Sal means or what he thinks he means.

"Yes—" The door chimes ring. "Customers. Back to your station!"

Halfway through my shift, Ellen walks in with three of her Spirit Squad. I pray that Sal will put them in someone else's section and groan inwardly when he seats them in one of my booths, telling me that they requested me especially. Oh, joy.

"What can I get you?" I ask, pen poised over my pad.

"Just a Diet Coke for me," Ellen says.

I don't know the Spirit Squad girls. One has her blond hair in two long braids. She's examining the tip of one. It reminds me of a paintbrush. Another keeps sliding the charm on her necklace back and forth along the chain. The third stares at her phone. This drawing would be called *A Jury of My Peers*.

"Okay, a Diet Coke. And you all?" I say to the other three girls.

"Diet Coke," says braids.

"Diet Coke," says necklace.

"Just water," says phone, without looking up.

"Three Diet Cokes and a water. What else?"

"Oh, that's it. We're having a Spirit Squad meeting, so we'll be here awhile. Just keep those drinks filled, okay?" Ellen says.

There is no way I'm going to put up with Ellen and her minions and not at least run a decent tab. I glance at Sal. "Sorry. The owner won't let you stay here if you're not ordering food." That's a basic lie.

"Oh." Ellen looks back at Sal as if she's considering whether to check what I've said or not. She must decide it's not worth it. "I'll have a side salad."

I grit my teeth. Ellen's family is one of the wealthiest in our town. She can afford more than a side salad.

"What else?" I say.

"That's all," Ellen says. Her smile is fake, and I wonder what happened to her. Was she always this way and I didn't see it when we were friends in middle school?

"Sorry," I say again, matching my tone to her fake smile. "Everyone needs to order something." I'm really pushing it now.

"I told you that we should have just gone to the coffee shop. They don't make you order anything there," says Necklace Girl. She shifts in her seat and the vinyl whines in response.

"You did say that," Ellen says, still smiling at the girl. "I just really wanted to come to Sal's." I'm sort of impressed that Ellen can sound friendly while putting the minion in her place.

"Fine," Necklace Girl says. "I'll have a hot fudge sundae with vanilla and whipped cream."

"That'll go great with your Diet Coke," I say, smiling. She doesn't get my snipe.

"And I'll have a slice of blueberry pie," says Braided Girl.

"We're out of blueberry. Cherry okay?"

She wiggles one braid in the air like she's thinking and then nods.

"Ice cream on the side?"

She nods again.

"And you?" I say to Phone Girl.

"Cheese fries."

"Great. Coming right up." It sounds so cliché, but I can't help myself.

I'm putting their order in when Ellen approaches me at the server station. I grit my teeth in anticipation of whatever torture she's about to dish out in my place of employment. After all, the customer is always right.

"Can we talk?" she whispers to me.

I gesture to my awful uniform and the general space around me. "Sort of working here?"

"It's important."

That's a surprise. I look around. "Lu!" I whisper. Lu stops

adding croutons to a salad and looks up. "Cover for me?" Lu looks from me to Ellen, narrows her eyes, and nods.

I motion for Ellen to follow me into the women's room. After I check that all of the stalls are empty, I lock the door and lean against the counter to find out what Ellen could possibly want to say to me that's so important.

"Ash and I are over."

I nod, but I'm careful not to show any expression. They break up more often than I go through charcoal.

"For real this time. He cheated." She holds my gaze, and I'm the first to look away. "Again. I know that there were other times. With you and Ash. Before the photo in his truck."

"Look . . ."

Ellen holds up her hand. "Wait. I need to say this. I wasn't there. Ashton says that you—and the others—were all over him."

I take in a deep breath. I don't know if I was all over him or not because I don't remember the two times before the truck all that well.

"But from what *I* heard, you were really wasted." She looks away. "And so was this other girl."

I wonder where Ellen is getting her information and I also wonder who this other girl is. But the details don't matter because whoever told Ellen I was wasted was right and Ashton *is* a player. He always has been.

"Seems like my asshole *ex*-boyfriend decided to get action off girls who couldn't even give consent." She examines her face in the mirror and fixes her perfect hair.

Girls that couldn't give consent. I let that phrase roll around in my head for a moment. Is that who I was?

"Nobody forced tequila down my throat." I know that I'm not winning myself any points by saying this, but it feels like it needs to be said. "I'm honestly not even sure what went down that night."

Ellen eyes me through the reflection in the mirror. "Look, what happened, happened. All I know is that I am not going to stand by any guy who thinks it's okay to hook up with a girl who is so drunk she can't remember what happened to her."

I don't say anything. I've attended all the same school assemblies that Ellen has attended—about consent and safe sex and the dangers of drugs and alcohol. But I've always still assumed that what happens to me is my fault. Now Ellen, who doesn't even like me, is sort of telling me that it wasn't my fault.

"Why are you telling me this?"

"You got me thinking. That day in the bathroom. About Ash." Ellen pushes her hair behind her shoulder and shrugs. "Consider it a public service announcement."

"Okay," I say. "Thanks?"

Ellen leaves first to return to her booth, but only Necklace Girl is there. The others have gone out to write on my Post-it mural. I hold in a smile. When I arrive moments later to set the cold drinks down, Necklace Girl complains about the order taking so long. Ellen and I catch a glance, but she doesn't say anything.

"Sorry, there was some drama in the women's room," I say. "But your order will be right up."

Back at the server stand, I'm still chewing over the idea that what happened with Ashton wasn't my fault. I think I should feel relieved or absolved or something, but really, I can't shake feeling ashamed. The cook dings the bell indicating that the order is ready. I gather the plates and return to Ellen's table.

True to what she'd said in the beginning, they are having a Spirit Squad meeting—talking about the next game and a pep rally and how to get everyone pumped full of school spirit. I set the plates before the four girls and leave the check. As I walk away, I'm feeling a bit of admiration for Ellen's ability to break up with her long-term boyfriend, lay some deep shit on me, and then go back to conducting business as usual.

Toward the end of the shift when Luisa and I are cleaning up our areas, she asks me what's up.

"Hypothetically speaking, do you think when a girl gets really messed up, it's then wrong for a guy to hook up with her?" I ask.

"Absolutely."

"But what if the girl is into it or throwing herself at the guy or whatever?"

Luisa studies me and pulls in a deep breath. "Skye, Ashton should not have been with you if you were wasted."

"But it's not like he roofied me. I *chose* to get that fucked up. And"—I lean in and whisper—"knowing me, I *did* come on to him."

"But he should not have done what he did."

He should not have done what he did.

An electric buzz runs from the crown of my head down my spine and out through my fingertips. I'm not thinking of Ashton anymore. I'm thinking of Dan. I was a little girl who trusted that she could sleep in a tent with the man who acted like her father. He was a grown man who should not have done what he did. For all these years, no one has said that to me. No one has acknowledged that Dan should not have touched me in that way.

"Are you okay?" Luisa asks.

The world is rocking around me. Parts of me might come spinning apart and fly in different directions. Luisa tells me to sit in one of the booths in the back. She brings me a Coke, which I slurp gratefully.

"I know that this is about more than Ashton," she says. "But whatever it is, you'll be okay. You're my Teflon girl."

I try to smile and believe her, but Luisa's words have cracked my Teflon coating, allowing all that I've kept hidden deep inside out into the light.

29

Another Man's Treasure

AFTER MY SHIFT is over, I stand next to my Post-it mural and wait for Keith to show up. I tuck my hands into the center pocket of my sweatshirt and curl into myself against the early March chill. Squinting into the sun brings the burn of tears to my eyes. Keith's truck pulls up and he beeps the horn as if I'm not sitting right there. I blink away the fake tears and stroll over to the truck.

"Whoa! What is *that*?" He gestures with his chin to the mural.

"Post-it mural?" I say.

He side-eyes me. "Do you know who put up that Post-it mural?"

"Maybe?"

"Damn. That's bold. I like it." He grins at me.

I hold up my hands. "I didn't say it was me."

"Uh-huh." He's totally on to me.

He exits the parking lot and heads north. Twenty minutes later, we pull into his dad's junkyard. Keith parks near the trailer that serves as the office.

I hand Mr. Williams the cash toward my car.

"Okay, young lady, now you'll work the rest off. There is a pile of new items that need to be carted to the appropriate location. And I also need you to find a blabbity-blabbity for a 1990 Honda Accord." Keith's dad doesn't actually say *blabbity-blabbity*, but he might as well have because I have no idea what he's talking about.

"Pops, she doesn't know that stuff!"

Mr. Williams looks over his reading glasses at Keith.

"Great. So, *she's* supposedly working off the fee for her car, but it's really me working it off?" Keith says.

"I guess so. And the sooner you get started, the sooner you're finished."

Keith and I leave the small, cramped trailer. "Look, you paid your money and you have no idea what my dad wants. You can go."

"No way! If it weren't for you, I'd be paying the full amount. Direct me toward what I need to do."

"Okay then," Keith says with skepticism. He shows me what to look out for, and together we work on moving a pile of random car parts into the bed of Keith's pickup.

"So, I had a superweird conversation with Ellen today."

I pile pieces into a wheelbarrow and wheel them to the truck while Keith carries bigger pieces himself.

"Oh, yeah, they broke up again. Ashton's not worried. He says she'll be back."

Ellen seemed pretty firm when she'd talked about Ashton in the diner. I stack side mirrors and hubcaps in the back of the truck and I say nothing.

"What'd she say?" Keith asks.

"She just seems pretty serious this time. That's all." I'm not about to share the full details of my talk with Ellen.

"We'll see," Keith says, tossing tires onto the pile. "Girls aren't usually done with Ashton until he decides they're done."

All around us, carcasses of old cars lie abandoned. Other cars, like mine, wait for their owners to pay up for the right to take them home.

"*I'm* done with him." It's the first time I've said it out loud. I'd been thinking that I was done with Ashton ever since the stunt he pulled that day in the truck. And even though I'm not sure I agree with Ellen that maybe I wasn't at fault for what happened before, our conversation makes me feel even more sure that I don't want it to happen again.

"You girls forming a club or something?"

I laugh. "Yeah, me and Ellen. It's the Anti-Ashton Club."

"There'd be more than you and Ellen." Keith says this almost under his breath.

It's the first time I've heard him say anything remotely negative about his friend, so it surprises me, but I don't call attention to it. He throws one last tire in. We drive the pile to another part of the junkyard and start to unload.

"If you've got this, I'll go look for the part my dad was talking about."

"Yeah, I'm good," I say.

I unload the side mirrors onto an already existing pile made up of chrome door handles, hubcaps, and other mirrors. I love the way that this pile of cast-off parts glints and shines in the sunlight. A drawing starts to form in my mind: *Another Man's Treasure.*

One of the side mirrors has broken in transport—or maybe it was hit by the tires Keith had tossed in. As I pull the pieces out of the back of the truck bed, I watch slices of sky captured on the broken mirror. I imagine this bit of mirror on a wall somewhere, capturing bits of people walking, of birds flying, of clouds passing all day, every day. There's something cool about creating art, like the Post-it mural, that can be here and gone like a sunny day. But what if I wanted to make more of a mark? What if I wanted to do something that couldn't disappear so easily, that couldn't be denied? I think about Joon, so bold in creating public art that could effect change.

I fish through the cast-off items, pulling out pieces that catch my eye—even as I have no idea what I'm going to make with them. When I return to the truck with my arms full, Keith laughs.

"Told you salvage yards were gold mines," he says.

"You weren't wrong. Did you find a thingie?"

He holds up an object that looks like a large cylinder with a small cylinder attached. "Yep. What's all that crap for anyway?"

"I'm not sure yet."

After a few hours of collecting, we arrive back at Mr. Williams's trailer, where he surveys my selection.

"You didn't want to pay the full amount for your car, but you'll buy all of this?" Mr. Williams says.

"It's for my art."

"Well, it appears that I get some money either way." He smiles at me and it's the first smile I've seen on his face.

He charges me what seems a ridiculously low amount for my bounty.

"So, we're cool?" I say to Mr. Williams.

"We're cool."

"Thank you. Really."

He nods and turns back to his work.

As Keith is helping me load my treasure into the back of Lucy, he says, "Hey, I know you can take your Jeep and head out, but do you need to get back right away?"

I'm surprised that Keith wants to spend more time with me. "Depends, what do you have in mind?"

He wiggles his eyebrows up and down. I hope he's not expecting something from me. "Just messing with you," he says. Everyone else seems to think that they can get with me, why wouldn't Keith?

"Seriously," Keith says when we're finished loading Lucy. "Do you trust me?"

"Not at all." I grin.

"Hah!" he barks. "Let's go."

The truck engine rumbles to life and we bump our way out of the junkyard where he turns the wrong way for home. Thinking about Ashton hijacking me makes me wonder if I should start worrying about being alone in trucks with boys. He continues maneuvering his truck through back roads in a way that shows that he knows where he's going, even if I don't.

After driving for about ten minutes, he pulls into the parking lot of a little elementary school, only today it's been transformed into a miracle of artistic opportunity. It's a flea market. I jump from the truck and shut the door behind me.

"How'd you know about this place?"

"Are you kidding? My grandma goes apeshit over flea markets. She should be on that show where people are drowning in their crap. She scouts them out every week, and this is one of her favorites. I bring her here on account of the truck. Mom's told me that I can't take her to any more flea markets because we don't have space for any more shit, but I'd be a total dick to say no to Grams, right?"

"Can't say no to Grams," I agree. "That's probably a commandment somewhere." I can't imagine Nana at flea markets, but I remember her collection of china. There's no way I could've said no if she asked me to take her to buy a new piece.

Keith and I pass tables that nearly bend under the weight of excess. What some people believe they can sell, my mom would throw in the trash without a blink. And it's not like we're rich. One table is all boxed foodstuff. I spy Brown Sugar Pop-Tarts, my fave. They're past their expiration date, but not by a lot, so I treat myself to a box of delicate toaster pastries with fake brown sugar filling. Working at the salvage yard gave me an appetite.

Another table is piled with men's dress socks and women's panty hose. Farther down, a litter of little boys clusters around a display of obsolete handheld game devices. We wind our way around countless tables until Keith finds what he wanted to show me. Tables upon tables showcase mismatched plates, bent silverware, and chipped glasses.

"It's the Land of Misbegotten Kitchenware," I breathe out.

"What?"

"Nothing, but seriously, this is awesome."

I pick through the pieces, pulling out colors that grab my eye.

Keith pulls out a plate here or a glass there, holding them up for inspection. "For Grams?" he asks.

I approve a burnt orange plate, but dismiss a chipped bowl. "How come you're never this nice when we're with the guys?" I ask.

"And allow my reputation as badass linebacker to go all to shit? I can't have that. That's why *you're* here helping me choose things for my Grams, and not them."

We move on to a table of tile from a home renovation gone wrong. I gather from the woman sitting at the table that a divorce halted the renovation and they had to cut their losses. Her loss is my gain because the tile is beautiful. And cheap. It's not until I've paid that I realize how heavy tile is. Keith rolls his eyes at me and hauls the box up onto his meaty shoulder.

"Good to know the muscles are good for something besides battering the opposing team," I say.

"Oh, they're good for more than that."

Now it's my turn to roll my eyes.

When we arrive back at the junkyard, Keith lets me out to get Lucy and then loads all of my finds into the back. I walk with him to his truck.

"Thanks, Keith. For everything."

"You say that now, but if Grams hates these plates, I'm blaming it on you." Then he smiles at me and gives me a little salute. "Be good, Murray."

"If I can't be good, I'll be careful."

Keith grins. "You got that right."

I follow Keith out of the lot, and when I return home, I stand at the back of Lucy to survey the makings of a new project. I feel pieces coming together. If I give the idea some space to expand, I might be able to give new life to these damaged items.

30

One Man's Trash

"WILL YOU GO to thrift stores with me today?" I ask Emma as we pull away from her school.

"Why?" I hear snark in Emma's tone, and I don't know if it's because of the wedding tension or the fact that I took her from her friends the other day. Either way feels like someone is pinching my heart and twisting.

"Just for fun. You can find supercool stuff in thrift stores." My tone tries too hard as we idle at a stoplight. The truth is that visiting the flea market with Keith sparked an obsession with old stuff—the items that people get rid of—and finding a way to make art out of it.

"That sounds cool," she says. I can hear the rejection in her voice. "But I have homework."

The light turns green and I head toward home.

"You don't want to do it after?" I ask anyway.

"Um, Julia and I are meeting at the park later."

I give her credit for being honest with me. I pull into our town-house parking lot. "Will Thomas be there?" I ask.

"I don't know." She fiddles with the miniature figures hanging from her backpack. "Maybe." She glances at me. "Probably."

I shift Lucy into park in front of our house.

"It's weird for me that you're hanging out with boys in the woods. Mom would freak out."

"I'm twelve. I'm not a baby."

"You were kissing him!"

"Oh my god, it's so not a big deal. Didn't you ever play spin the bottle?"

"Not when I was twelve," I say honestly, but maybe what I was doing was worse.

"So, are you coming in?" she asks, hand on the car door handle.

I look out the windshield. Dan's not here, so maybe it's okay leaving her alone for a bit.

"What time are you meeting Julia?"

"Five."

"Okay, if I'm not home, text me when you leave to meet her."

"Fine," she says in an eye-roll sort of tone. "Bye." She enters the house without looking back. It used to be me rolling my eyes and begging her to stay home so Lu, Shelby, and I could flirt with boys without an annoying shadow. My sister is changing in ways that I'm not prepared for. She's no longer the little girl in the portrait that I took with me to MICA. Maybe she hasn't been that girl for a while and I just haven't been looking closely enough.

While I'm out prowling through thrift stores to rescue cast-off houseware items, Mom texts me that Mac and Judy want to drop by with a late birthday gift for Emma. Dan is coming over too. She asks if I can pick up Chinese for everyone. I wonder why she or Dan can't stop for Chinese, but I agree and then text Emma, so she knows what's up.

"Where's Emma?" Mom says when I walk in, laden with brown bags full of take-out containers from Hunan Garden.

"She didn't go with me. I was already out when you'd texted. She isn't here?"

"No, I already went upstairs to change. She's not in her room. I thought she would be with you."

"I only went out for an hour to run some errands. Hang on."

I set the bags on the dining room table and pull out my phone. In between leaving the thrift store and calling Hunan, I'd composed the text, but somehow hadn't sent it. Of course, I know where she is, but I am not going to get her into trouble.

Mom pours herself a glass of wine. "I'm so sorry, you all," she says to Mac and Judy.

Dan comes over. "Should we be worried?" he says in a low voice. "Does she have location services on? Can we find her that way?"

"I don't think we need to do that," I say. "I'm sure she'll be home soon."

"Will all due respect, Skylar, I think the adults should handle this," Dan says to me. He turns to Mom. "Beth, let's see where she is."

Dan has no clue what I've been handling since he's been gone. I shoot off another quick text to Emma, this one warning her about the urgency of getting home as soon as humanly possible.

"It's loading," Mom says, staring at her phone. "Oh, and Emma just texted me. She's at a friend's house. She says she's sorry and she'll be home soon. Oh, thank God."

Mom sets her phone on the table. "Can I get anyone a drink? I may need another one." She laughs a little bit and takes a gulp of her wine.

"I'm glad she's okay. How great that you can use the phone that way," Judy says.

"Since we know Emma's okay, can we eat? I'm starving," I say.

"She's not where she said she was in her text," Dan says, holding Mom's phone.

"What?" Mom says.

My stomach flips, and not in a good way. Dan holds the phone out to Mom and the screen plainly shows that Emma's phone is in the middle of the woods, not at a friend's house. Oh, shit.

"Maybe she's walking home from her friend's house," I say, trying to cover.

Mom frowns, as though she'd like to believe that, but it doesn't quite compute. There aren't houses on the opposite side of the woods where we live.

"We'll see what she says when she gets home," Dan says.

"Oh, maybe we should leave," Judy says to Mac. "This is a family matter."

Mac nods and starts to get up.

"No, no, we got all this great food. Please stay," Mom says. She hands Judy a wine spritzer and Mac a beer.

"I've got it all set up. Let's dive in. Emma says she'll be here any minute," I say.

"Where are the forks?" Dan asks, surveying the table.

"We use chopsticks," I say.

"Get some cutlery, please," Dan says.

"No problem," I say, to keep Dan appeased, even though I need to wait until he's finished pouring himself a drink because he's standing directly in front of the cutlery drawer. I place forks and spoons next to the chopsticks on the table, and everyone digs in.

We're all starting to shovel food into our mouths when Emma bursts in, flushed. I don't know if it's from the cold air or from kissing Thomas. Dan sets his fork down and stands.

"Where have you been?" His voice booms.

Emma is all innocent eyes. "With Julia."

"At Julia's house?" Dan asks.

Emma must sense that she's being baited because her eyes flick to me. I widen mine to warn her.

"No, Julia's house is too far to walk." She starts off with honesty. That's good. "We were at . . . Tonya's house." If the phone hadn't busted her, the hesitancy would have.

"No, I don't believe you were," Dan says, arms crossed over his chest.

"What?" Emma's face shows that she knows she's been caught, but she's not yet sure how bad it is. I've been in her shoes a million times, though I know this is a first for her.

Dan holds up Mom's phone, like he did just a little bit ago. "The GPS put you in the woods. Why are you lying?"

Emma's eyes widen. "I . . . I . . ." She looks at me and then at the floor. "I don't know," she says honestly.

"Who were you with?"

"Some friends."

"Then why the lying?" Dan presses.

Emma clears her throat. "There were . . . boys there."

At this, Mom's eyes snap up. "What boys?"

Dan says, "What are you doing with boys at your age?"

"Some boys from my class," she says to Mom. "We were talking and hanging out," she adds to Dan. "Nothing bad or whatever." She looks at her shoes.

"Come here," Dan says.

My stomach was flipping before, but now it's threatening to come up through my throat. Emma walks slowly toward Dan as if she's walking the plank.

"Young lady, you need to learn respect and honesty and I intend to teach it to you. The next time you think about going off without letting your mother know or lying about where you are, I want you to remember this."

I remember how Dan disciplines.

"This is for your own good," he says.

I push from the table.

Dan grips Emma's shoulder.

I jump up and my seat clatters to the floor. "Don't!" I say.

Five sets of eyes swivel toward me.

"Don't what?" Dan asks, irritated. He's holding the phone close to Emma. I thought that he was going to hit her. I was sure of it.

"Oh." I back off a bit.

He turns to Emma. "Your mother pays a lot of money for you girls to have these nice phones. In return, you leave location services on so that we know you're safe. If you think you're smarter than us and you figure you'll just turn off location services next time you want to go somewhere without permission, you lose the phone. Got it?"

I watch the interplay, relieved that Dan didn't hit Emma, embarrassed that I made a scene, and irritated that he's shunted Mom to the side and created rules of his own making.

Emma nods.

Dan sets the phone back on the table. "We understand each other?"

Emma nods again.

"I can't hear a nod," Dan says.

"I understand," Emma says in a quiet voice.

Dan nods at Emma and I sort of wish she'd tell him that she can't hear a nod either. But she doesn't. Dan turns to everyone and rubs his hands together. "Let's continue our dinner, shall we?"

Emma sits next to me and I squeeze her hand under the table. She squeezes back. Everyone is pretty quiet through the rest of dinner. Judy says she loves how spicy the pork dish is, and Mac says that spicy food is great with beer. It seems as if they are trying to fill the silence. Dan nods as he forks some fried rice into his mouth.

Mom, Emma, and I use chopsticks. It took a while to teach Emma, but she was determined to be able to use chopsticks right alongside us.

"I suppose this is fair for Americanized Chinese food," Dan says.

Hunan Garden is our favorite—Mom's and Emma's and mine. We love the pan-fried dumplings and the hot and sour soup and the Kung Pao Chicken. When Mom got a raise, we ordered from Hunan. And when Emma "graduated" from fifth grade and when I got my acceptance to MICA too.

"We forgot tea!" Mom says. She gets up to make the tea that she always makes when we order Chinese. I get up to help her, and Emma follows. Mom leans down to hug Emma.

"Don't lie, Butter Bean, okay?"

Emma nods into Mom's chest and then says, "But don't call me Butter Bean." We all laugh.

"Also, you're grounded."

I cheer on the inside, not because Emma is grounded, but because Mom is still the boss of us.

"What?" Emma has the nerve to sound offended.

"You lied about where you were, you were with boys, and you were late. You're grounded."

"Fine."

When the water boils, Mom pours the hot water over the tea bags in the delicate midnight-blue teapot. I carry the small matching cups, and Emma grabs some sugar.

"Is the teaching going well?" Judy is asking Dan when we return.

"I could teach these Freshman Comp sections in my sleep," he says. "But I've put together a proposal for a Russian Lit class, and I'm hopeful that they'll let me teach that next semester."

"Russian Lit?" Mac says. "I'd rather shoot myself with a nail gun."

Dan laughs a little too loudly. "It's important to introduce students to Tolstoy and Dostoyevsky. Not to mention Nabokov."

He keeps talking about Nabokov, even though no one seems interested. Mom sets cups before everyone, but only she, Emma, and I drink the tea from the tiny cups. After a while, empty take-out boxes litter the dining room table.

"We have something for you, Emma," Judy says. "Mac, could you grab it?"

Mac gets up and lumbers to the table by the front door to pick up a bag that I hadn't noticed.

"We know we're late for your birthday, sweetheart, but we didn't want you to think we'd forgotten you." Judy hands Emma the package.

"Thanks, Judy," Emma says in that shy voice that means you

know you're still on thin ice. She unwraps the paper and smiles at Judy and Mac. "An origami kit. Thank you!" She looks at the box and turns to Judy again. "I love it."

Emma looks at Dan. "May I be dismissed?" I'm impressed by how quickly she's learning. He nods to her, and she disappears upstairs with the origami kit.

"Beth, how are the wedding plans coming along?" Judy asks after Emma leaves.

I start to collect the take-out containers.

Mom gulps her wine. "Well, our last location fell through."

If the wedding is off again, this is the first I've heard of it. Mom sets her wineglass down. I put away the few leftovers and shove the empty boxes into the trash.

"What happened?" Judy is saying. "You were so excited about that venue."

"You're right, I was"—Mom pauses—"but it turned out to be too expensive. I had to let it go."

I return to take the plates away.

"Thanks, honey," Mom says, and I smile at her.

"It wasn't the money," Dan says, dismissing Mom's statement. "That place was too bland."

"Judy," Mac says, "why don't we let them have the wedding in the barn?"

Everyone seems to be inspired by ideas for this wedding all of a sudden. I start to wash off the plates, but I can still hear the adults talking around the dinner table.

"The barn would be great!" Dan says. "Rustic. None of those sanitized spaces lacking soul. And we will write our own vows."

"Well . . ." Mom starts to speak.

"Beth, I haven't asked for anything in terms of this wedding ceremony," Dan says. Even though he certainly has. "But I'm asking now. I want to have the wedding in the barn."

"We can't."

"What do you mean we can't?" Dan says.

"I put a deposit down somewhere else today. Nonrefundable. It's not antiseptic or whatever you called the last place and it was available on the date and we can't wait any longer, so it's a done deal."

"Where did you put this deposit down?" Dan asks. He doesn't sound very excited.

"Sal's."

I stop rinsing the dishes. She's having her wedding at the diner where I work? I cannot get away from this fucking wedding.

"Sal's Diner?" Dan's eyebrows fly to the top of his forehead.

"They have that outdoor space out back with those cute string lights and nice big wooden tables. And Sal said that he'll get heaters brought out because it might still be chilly at that time next month. Plus, Sal's food is great. You said you didn't want boring food, and no one does Greek like Sal. It'll be my little, tiny Greek wedding." Mom's joke falls flat.

"Well, I guess that's that. No rustic wedding for us, but thanks, Mac." Dan tips his drink to his lips and doesn't say another word.

I finish the dishes and make sure the table is cleared. Having her wedding reception in the back of a diner on Pennswood Pike can't be what Mom really wants. She feels pushed to have the reception there because she has so few options available, which seems to be the story of Mom's life. I feel a little sad for her, but it's not like someone is forcing her to marry Dan. She's made that bad choice on her own. It occurs to me that the servers will be people I know. I grimace and count the days until I'm out of this town.

31

Odd One Out

BEN HAS BEEN gone for two weeks. I'm sitting on the couch, sketching him from memory and thinking that I'd call it *Reward If Found,* when Mom says my name.

"Yeah?" I say, not looking away from my work.

"I've been telling myself not to ask, but I can't help it. Have you heard anything about the scholarship?"

My hand pauses on the sketch. I'm at Ben's jaw and trying to get it just right. It's been three weeks since I heard and somehow I haven't told Mom and Emma. I remember Mom saying that I didn't seem to want to be a part of this family. I sigh.

"Oh, I'm sorry. I didn't mean—"

"I got it," I say, with no dramatic lead-in. "I got the scholarship." I meet my mother's eyes and she looks confused.

"You got it?"

I nod.

"So, you're going."

"Looks that way."

"Honey, that's . . . great," Mom says. "But you don't look all that happy."

My hand is moving again, adding shading the way that Mr. M always tells me to do, the way that Ben seems to do effortlessly.

"Hello?"

I look up.

Mom is smiling that smile. Her whole face transforms and she's ten years younger and happy.

"I know that we've had some . . . tension . . . but I'm so excited for you, sweetheart. You've worked so hard and now you will be able to follow your dreams."

I smile back. All she's ever wanted was for me not to end up like her—divorced at a young age with little kids and little money. That's one thing we agree on.

"Even if you think that my dreams are impractical."

"I never said impractical," Mom says. "I just said that it could be hard to find a job."

I give Mom a look, and she holds her hands up in surrender. "It doesn't matter because you're going. Do we need to pay the deposit or what?"

I flip the page and start a new sketch, also from memory. Mom wonders why I don't seem happy and I wonder how I can leave when she's marrying Dan.

"Mom, what if Dan did something that was really bad?"

Mom's smile fades like the sun behind storm clouds.

"What do you mean?"

From the charcoal in my fingers, Dan's face emerges on the page.

"Like what would you do if you found out he did something terrible?"

"I guess I'd talk to him and try to work it out."

"What if it was so bad that you couldn't work it out?"

In my sketch, Dan's face takes up the page and he stares out of it dead-on. Like a mug shot.

"What are you talking about, Skye?"

"Before, you know, he . . ." God, this is so hard. I told her before and she didn't believe me. What makes me think she'll believe me this time?

"Everything will be okay this time." Her eyes plead with me.

"But what if it's not?" I say.

"We'll deal with it."

This is the first time that Mom seems to be willing to circle around to how it was before. I think that maybe I could meet her halfway, but she's not even a quarter of the way to me.

"Okay," I say. My voice sounds small. "I'll find out about the deposit to MICA."

I scrawl *Deviant* on the bottom of the sketch and close my pad.

"It's time, Skye. Your mother will know to find us there," Dan says.

It's Wednesday night and Emma's show starts in thirty minutes. I stare at the clock on my phone. Then I peer out the window, trying to will my mother to show up or time to move backward. I'd dropped Emma off early, armed with her costume and more make-up than any middle schooler should have, as per her instructions. I imagine her now waiting in the wings for the performance to begin.

Dan showed up twenty minutes ago, dressed in a sport coat and khakis, like he was going to some country club dinner. Neither of us has heard from Mom.

"Maybe I'll wait for Mom and you can go ahead. Or maybe I'll go ahead and you stay and wait for Mom." Either way I'm hoping to avoid being alone with Dan for much longer.

"That's what you said ten minutes ago. Your sister worked too hard for this. Come on. I'll drive."

Dan and I agree on one thing—Emma needs to have someone in the audience for her big night. I follow him to his car, angry on Emma's behalf that Mom has blown this and pissed on my own behalf that I have to escort Dan to the show. I haven't been in a car alone with Dan for a long time. It's not the same car that he used to have. Not the old car that he drove when he took us on that camping trip. This one is smaller, but newer.

The tiny space smells like Dan. I don't know what to do with myself. My leg jiggles and I place my hand on it to stop. I stare at my phone, pretending to text so that he won't talk to me. He fiddles with the radio. NPR is broadcasting an interview with the victim of a women's sports scandal. I want to change the station, but it's not Mom's car.

"Whoever designed this school did not plan well for parking," he mutters, turning down the volume on the radio.

"You figure every parent with a kid in the show is here, plus all the grandparents who live close enough to come out," I say.

I wish that Nana were still around to see Emma. If Nana were still around, a major component of Mom's support system, I wonder if Mom would've agreed to marry Dan.

"Do you mind if I get out here?" I ask when Dan slows down in front of the school. "I'll find seats and text you."

"Very well," Dan says.

When I'm out of the tiny confines of Dan's car, I breathe. Inside the auditorium, I drape my jacket across three seats that I find on an end of a row toward the back. Not a great view, but you've got to take what you can get. After I text the location of the seats, I sneak backstage to find Emma. She's all decked out in her costume, looking like the cutest teapot anyone has ever seen.

"Look at you!" I say, lifting her teapot lid hat.

She grabs the hat from me and places it back on her head. Her eyes dart around. "You shouldn't be here!"

"It's okay, Em. I know Ms. Bender. It'll be cool. Where are your friends?"

"Julia's the lead, so she's over there. And Anna is in dance corps, so she's back there. Is Mom here? Do you think she's okay?"

"Don't worry about Mom," I say.

"She made it?" Emma bounces on her toes, and I'm not sure

if it's her excitement that Mom is here or preshow nerves.

"Mom is super proud of you. She knows you're going to do great." Not a lie, really. Those statements are true; it's just that Mom isn't actually here to say them.

Emma tries to peer around the curtain to find Mom.

"You won't be able to see her because of the lights. I'd better go. Break a leg, Butter Bean!"

Emma scowls. "Don't call me that!" She looks around, like she's making sure that no one heard.

"You'll do great," I say.

She offers a nervous smile. I see her as *Little Girl with Big Dreams,* drawn in soft pastels. "Thanks."

When I return to the seats I'd reserved, Dan sits one seat in from the end. My jacket lies across his lap. No Mom. I start to sink into the seat on the end when he leans in to me.

"Let's save that one for your mother."

He moves his legs to the side so that I can squeeze by him to sit on his other side. Moments later, the lights go down. I'm so close to Dan that our knees nearly touch. The urge to bolt zips through me, and I need to hold the seat of my chair to keep myself in place. I glance down at our knees. I was so small back then, but I'm not small anymore. This realization helps me relax a little. Does he even remember that night? I've always wondered.

After the principal welcomes everyone, and reminds us to silence our phones, the curtain rises and the show begins. Emma is amazing, but I can't concentrate. My head swivels from the stage to the doors to my phone and then starts all over again. The kids are doing a fantastic job of bringing the story to life and I think about how much Mom would eat it up: she'd believe the message that love can transform an abusive jerk into a kindhearted prince. In the beginning of the final act, Mom finally sneaks through the doors and slides into the seat that Dan saved. But she's missed most of Emma's lines.

Dan squeezes her leg. I hear her whisper something about a flower vendor and a dead phone.

At the end of the show, Emma finds us. "What a wonderful show!" Mom gushes, squeezing Emma close.

"You saw? You made it?" The hope in her eyes could light a city.

"I'm here, aren't I?" Mom's dodge of the question pisses me off, but not enough to break Emma's heart by dragging out the truth.

"Well done, Emma," Dan says. "Apparently, our work on your song paid off." He smiles at her like the father he thinks he is.

"Thanks!" Emma beams. "I think I really projected, like you said to do," Emma says, like the perfect daughter.

"Everyone loved when you came onstage with the cart and the little kid as a teacup," I'm saying, but Julia has come to grab Emma. She whispers something in Em's ear, and Em laughs.

"Cast party! Got to go!" Emma says, and she's snatched away.

I stand next to Mom while she leans into Dan and they watch Emma disappear into the crowd. Dan smiles at Mom and rubs her back. I put my hands in my pockets. I check my phone. I wonder where I belong in this tableau.

32

The Lady Doth Protest

"YOU'RE ONE HUNDRED percent sure?" I say to Luisa. It's the day after Emma's play and we are standing in the crowded hallway as students work their way to class or try to kill time before they're forced to sit for the next eighty-minute block.

"Yes. He's been giving me all the signals."

"It's just that it's not even April."

"I told you—I don't care that it's early. I don't want to wait. When he says yes, then we can start to be a couple."

"Okay." I hand Luisa the sign that we made. I'm a little worried for her. I mean, she's totally badass for throwing convention out the window and asking Matt to the prom instead of waiting for him to ask her. But, still. It's a risk.

I move away so that I can watch and support her from down the hall. She stands next to the entrance of their shared class, AP Philosophy, and she holds up the sign, which says YOU KANT LIE: MATT, WOULDN'T YOU LOVE TO GO TO PROM WITH ME? As students file into the room, she gets a mix of thumbs-up and laughter.

Matt appears down the hall. He sees the sign and he slows down. He's not smiling when he stops in front of Luisa. Placing his hand on her shoulder, he leans down to say something in her ear. She looks at him and says something. He shakes his head. She covers her mouth with one hand and crushes the poster against her body so that the words are covered. She turns and runs down the hallway toward the girls' room. Matt watches her with a pained expression and I take off after my friend.

I find Luisa in a stall weeping.

"Lu, I'm so sorry," I say, pressing my hands to the door, as if I can send my care through it.

"I need to be alone," she says through tears.

"Lu, come on. Let me in. It's me."

"No, Skye. Just leave me alone. I don't want to talk right now."

I stand there for a while longer, my palms still pressed to the cold pink metal.

"Please," Luisa says.

I don't want to leave my friend, but I do want to respect her words. I slide down to sit on the floor with my back to the door. I hear her weeping, but she doesn't speak. When the bell rings, I move to leave. Tapping the door gently, I say, "Text me, okay? No matter what time."

Luisa calls out for her shift that night. The next day, when she doesn't come to school, I decide it's time for an intervention. As soon as the last bell rings, I jump in Lucy and ride straight to Luisa's house. Lu answers her door wrapped in a blanket and looks like she hasn't showered very recently. She turns away and heads back for her couch, and I follow.

"Where's Miguel?" I ask.

"Therapy." Luisa flops on the couch and stares at the TV.

I try a smile as I sit down next to her, but she doesn't return it. "We're on a *Gilmore Girls* binge fest, I see."

"Well, of course. What else would I watch after I humiliated myself in front of the entire school when it turned out that I was reading the signals all wrong?"

"*GG* is definitely the way to go," I say. "But you didn't humiliate yourself in front of the *whole* school."

She gives me a look. "There are probably memes of me at this point."

"I'm sorry, Lu."

She sighs. "I thought that if Matt and I became a couple, everything would be perfect."

Luisa's comment makes me think about Emma all those weeks ago saying that she wanted Mom to marry Dan because then we'd be a perfect family.

"There's no such thing as perfect, Lu," I say softly. "Because we're all a little fucked-up." I poke her in the arm and she looks at me, unsmiling. "That's what makes us interesting."

Luisa rolls her eyes. "Are you creating inspirational posters now?"

I ignore the snark. "Look at me, I'm the class slut, but at least I'm not boring!"

I try to laugh, but Lu doesn't laugh with me.

"Does it ever bother you?" Luisa asks, just as softly. "The way people talk?"

I'd come here to cheer her up, but instead I'm now the one in the limelight.

"I've got *you*. You've always had my back—even when I made questionable choices. And I guess I'm used to the talk. I know how those guys think of me. And girls too."

"And you don't care?" She turns and looks me in the eye. Like this is our own private Truth or Dare.

"Do I care?"

I rest my head on the back of the couch and consider her question with more thought than I've ever considered that question. I have to admit that I crave the attention from boys, especially when I'm partying. Getting a guy to want me feels like a victory, like their desire makes me worthy of taking up space in this world. But some mornings after, when I look in the mirror, the person reflected back at me doesn't match the person I *feel* like I am. Lately, I think that maybe I've just been letting stuff happen to me rather than choosing what I really want, because I've never been sure that I'm allowed to have what I want. Seems weird to say all that to Luisa, though. Even if she is my best friend. I press my hands into my belly to squelch the uncomfortable feelings burbling there.

"I cared when you and Ben seemed judgy," I say. Ben's name in my mouth reminds me that on this day next week, he'll be back.

"I didn't mean to be judgy. I think I was a little worried."

We're both quiet for a bit, watching the classic Rory-Dean-Jess love triangle play out.

"Have you tried talking to your mom?" Luisa says after a while. "About Dan?"

Luisa and I only talk around Dan. She still doesn't know what happened, though maybe she's getting closer to the truth, and I'm still not ready to tell her.

I bark out a laugh that holds no joy. "Brick wall there. All she wants is to be married."

"I'm sorry," Luisa says, and I feel like I'm sinking in quicksand with no one to throw me a rope.

On the television, Lorelai is trying to give Rory advice about the boy situation. I'm jealous of their close, open relationship. Lorelai would have believed Rory all those years ago. But my mom is not Lorelai. Also, Lorelai is not real.

"You know what we need to do?" I say.

Luisa looks at me with trepidation.

I lean over to her and whisper, "We need to make some art."

Finally, I get a grin from my best friend.

Late that night, I return to pick up Luisa. This time I have a ladder in addition to a stepladder and even more Post-it notes.

"Where do you get all these Post-its?" she asks as she looks through my bag.

"The first ones were supposed to be study aids. I just bought these today, and you know what? They aren't cheap!" We pass the high school, which means we're getting close to Sal's.

"What are we making tonight?" Luisa asks.

"Your call. We're cheering you up."

"We already did a broken heart."

"Yeah, and a broken heart won't cheer you up. It'll keep you sad. What would cheer you up?"

"Oh! I think I know!"

"Lay it on me."

As we start to lay out Luisa's idea, I keep thinking about Sal calling me a vandal, even if he didn't know it was me he was calling a vandal. I sketch something that I'd seen online, and Luisa nods. We work for hours on our project and we laugh—a lot. At one point I'm sure we'll get caught just because we're laughing so hard. That buzzy feeling from getting away with something returns, and just like before, the methodical pressing of Post-it notes to the window has a calming effect.

When we're finished, we get in the car and drive across the street to experience the full effect of our work. We've created a round bomb in gray Post-its. It has a black fuse protruding from the top with a red spark at the end. In the middle of the bomb is a giant yellow letter *F*.

"We created an *F*-bomb," Luisa says.

"We did."

Our new Post-it mural stays up for only a day. When I go in for my shift that Sunday, I hear Sal talking about how he needs to catch the delinquent who is defacing his property. He says something about it being a family restaurant. Apparently, this mural inspired people to spell out what the *F* stood for in the *F*-bomb. Several times and with specific thoughts attached as to who or what should receive the *F*-bomb. It surprises me how people react to different art in different ways. This wasn't what we were going for and I feel guilty that we created a springboard for such negative messages. But only a little guilty.

On Monday afternoon, my mind trips to Ben's arrival this week. Keith and I are pulling together a welcome back party, and I'm trying to imagine what it will be like to see Ben again.

"Mac is here!" Emma says as I pull in to park. Sure enough, that's Mac's work truck. Dan's car is there too. At first, I think maybe Dan is doing another ridiculous dinner and Mac is keeping him company. But they aren't on the first floor. Their male voices reverberate from the basement. I wonder what they're doing down there. The idea of Dan in my space, among my things, makes me bristle all over. Emma flies down the steps, but I take them slowly.

"Whoa!" Emma says.

I get to the landing at the bottom of the steps and I stop there.

Mac and Dan are holding a tape measure across the room. Mac's work belt hangs from his waist, laden with every tool imaginable.

"Ten foot, six inches," Mac says.

Dan releases the tape measure and pulls a pencil from behind his ear to scratch out something on a pad of paper. "Hello, girls," he says, glancing up and then returning to whatever they're working on, as if he has every right to do what he's doing.

My drafting table is pushed into a corner. All of my supplies have been piled up beneath it. The art that hung from the clips I'd installed is removed and stacked on my table. They've basically eliminated my art space.

"What are you doing?" I blurt.

"Dan built your Mom some shelves," Mac says, pointing to newly installed shelves above the washer and dryer.

I've never known Dan to be much of a handyman.

"But what's going on here?" I ask, gesturing to my stuff all shoved to the corner.

Dan tosses his pad and pencil on the table. "I think it'll fit!" he says, as if he just solved the biggest problem of this century.

Mac places each of his tools into his toolbox one by one and then clamps it shut. "If you say so. You're the brains, I'm just the brawn."

"What will fit?" I say.

Mac drains the last of his beer and tosses it in the trash. "I've got to get home," he says, as if I'm not there. "I'll let you all deal with the pool table question."

Pool table?

"Thanks for the lesson," Dan says.

"Sure."

After Mac has disappeared up the steps, Emma turns to Dan. "Mom would hate a pool table," she says with certainty.

"Are you sure about that?" Dan says. "We've been talking about reconfiguring this space into an entertainment room with a big-screen TV and a pool table."

"You're making my art workshop into a *man cave*?" My voice quavers a little. All of the pieces of my creative life are shunted to the side and no one asked me if it was okay.

"We want a space where Emma and her friends can hang out," he says. "The house is only so big." He says this like it's an obvious fact that I should understand.

"You think Emma and her friends want a *pool table*?" My voice is rising. "And who is *we* anyway? Does Mom want this? Or is it just you?"

I've never spoken to Dan in this tone. My heart is pounding in my chest and my hands are shaking.

Dan frowns at me. "Isn't our response a bit outsized for the situation?" he asks with maddening calm.

"No! It's not. This is *my* space." I hate that I sound like a child. I want to say more, but my throat is tight and I feel tears coming. I will not cry in front of Dan.

"You'll be off to college in a few months," Dan says in his logical manner.

His words slam into me and hold me under water. Either I'll be here in this house with him or I'll be gone and there will be no one looking out for Emma.

"I'm still here now!" I yell. I want to go to my room and slam the door, but Dan would still be down here, just on the other side. Instead, I march back up the steps, fighting tears the whole way. He pushed away my stuff without asking. He assumed he could just do what he wanted with no one to stop him. Like he always has.

When I arrive at the front door, I realize that if I leave, I'll be leaving Emma alone with him. My hand drops from the door handle. As long as he's here with my sister, I need to be here too.

33

Best Laid Plans

"YOU LET HIM wreck my art space!" I say as soon as Mom comes in the door.

"Give me a minute to get into my house," Mom says. She drops her bag by the front door and slips off her heels. Every time I start to talk, she holds up her pointer finger. She pours herself a glass of wine, takes a sip, and then says, "Now what's this all about?"

"Dan obliterated my work area downstairs."

"Obliterated? That sounds dramatic. Let's take a look."

Mom descends the steps to the basement where Dan is still there, taking measurements or sharpening his wolf teeth or doing whatever Dan does.

"Hello," Dan says to Mom and walks over to kiss her.

"Hello." She smiles and hands him her glass, but he shakes his head and shows her that he has a drink already.

Mom surveys the area. "He didn't wreck it, Skye."

"He pushed all my stuff into a little corner like I don't exist!" I point to where all of my art stuff is smooshed into the corner.

"Skye, please, he was just measuring the space. Everything is still there, right?"

"Excuse me," Dan says as he leaves the basement to head upstairs. "I'll get dinner started."

"Thanks, honey," Mom says.

"Mom! He didn't ask permission to touch my stuff. It's not okay!"

The fact that Mom isn't even a little bit on my side makes me even angrier.

"Skye. Enough. I'll speak to him about moving your things, okay?"

"Fine," I say, but it's not fine. I just don't have anything else I can say or do.

Sometime around 11:00 p.m. Dan leaves and I leave soon after. The ladder and stepladder are still in the back of Lucy because it's only been a few days since Luisa and I created our *F*-bomb. I need to create another mural. It's that or return to my old habits, and I don't want to be in a situation where I might end up with Ashton again.

I visualize my idea, inspired by my mother's seemingly willful ignorance. But the empty storefront alone isn't enough and soon I'm working Post-its onto the actual windows of Sal's diner. I hadn't planned to use the diner windows, but this concept is big, and I'm alone. I've completed *Hear No Evil* and *See No Evil* and I'm halfway through *Speak No Evil* when I hear someone yelling.

"No! Stop! No more!" I turn and see Sal coming at me with a raised bat. "I'm calling the police!"

I drop my Post-its and hold my hands up. "Please don't hit me!"

Sal lets the bat drop by his side. "Skylar?"

I look up and pull my hood down. "Yes?"

"Why are you doing this to my property?" He gestures to his windows, plastered in Post-it notes. He looks so sad that I'm suddenly not sure how I convinced myself that it was okay to do this.

I shake my head. I don't have a good answer. "I just . . . had to create art."

"This is art?" He leans his bat against the building and examines my Post-it art with his hands on his hips. Now that he's closer, I see that he's thrown a coat over his pajamas and he's wearing slippers. His thinning hair is poking this way and that, and the bald part on top shines in the streetlight.

"To me it is."

He turns to me. "But why on my windows?"

"At first, I just wanted to cover that empty storefront window. It always seems so depressing to me."

"True, it is depressing and it's losing me money," he says. He steps toward me, holding his hands together like a prayer. "But, Skylar, you can't just cover another person's property like this." He sighs deeply.

In the diner, he's the big, booming boss—stern, but fair—ensuring that each of us does our job well so that people return to his restaurant. But out here, in his pajamas and slippers, I see that he's much older than I'd realized.

I nod at Sal in the dark night. "You're right."

"You could have asked for my permission." His tone is gentle.

Of all the things that Sal has said, this is the one that hits home. I didn't ask permission. This is exactly why I was angry at Dan tonight—because he didn't ask permission. I remember what Ellen said about Ashton and consent and what Luisa said about how he shouldn't have done that to me, and even though she was talking about Ashton, in a way she was also talking about Dan.

I hang my head. "I'm really sorry, Sal. I should have asked permission."

"Well, I wouldn't have given permission, but yes, you should have asked."

"Now what do we do?" I ask.

"What do we do indeed," Sal says.

Wielding a hammer is more of a rush than I'd expected. For as long as I can remember, Mom made it seem like the world was falling out of orbit if we broke something. Even though she seems to break things when she's drunk. But we don't talk about that. And besides, these aren't her things. They're mine. I paid for them with my own money and I've given myself permission to break the glasses, the plates and the tiles. It's beyond permission. It's a mandate. I *must* break these things. When I'm finished breaking a stack of tile, I gather some of the pieces into the palm of my hand like so many broken-winged birds and imagine what they will become.

Sal and I had talked late into Monday night, and he told me that he wouldn't call the police as long as I was willing to do two things. First, I had to remove all of the Post-its that I'd pasted on his windows. Second, he wanted—as he said—for me to use my talent for good. I immediately thought of beautifying the drab concrete wall facing the parking lot. He had a nature scene in mind that he thought would look nice behind the outdoor seating he'd set up there. So, of course, I agreed. I can't have charges pressed against me. Plus, now I have a project where I could use all of the pieces I'd been collecting. I told Sal that I would do the mural, but not in paint. I told him that I wanted to make a mosaic. It would take time, but I would have all summer.

I thought I might be in way over my head, so the next morning, I checked in with Mr. M about what I'd need. He was obviously more than a little excited by my project because he gave me a long list of exactly what materials I should and should not use as well as strict instructions on what bonding mortar I'd need to adhere the pieces to the wall. He also helped me calculate how much I would have to gather to fill a space of that size. So, basically, Mr. M confirmed that I was in way over my head, but now at least I had a list to help guide me.

Juggling my regular shifts and creating a huge project on my own is a lot. Luisa says to look on the bright side—at least after I'm finished working my shift at the diner, I'm already at the project site. Silver linings, I guess?

I don't love the direction that Sal has given me for this mural. Bland trees next to a bland pond surrounded by dirt and a few flowers. There's even a deer drinking at the pond. Blech. But I'm avoiding arrest and I'm getting paid, so I start the bland project. Before I know it, Friday rolls around, and as I spend the afternoon creating the dirt floor of the mural, I think how much Ben would hate this image. Then I think that soon he'll be able to despise it for himself because he's returning home sometime around now.

"Tonight is the party for Ben?" Mom says when I get home to change my clothes.

"Yes." I draw the word out because I know she's building toward a request, and I don't want to accidentally agree to anything. There's already a case of bottled beer hidden under some blankets in the back of Lucy just for the big occasion.

"I'm going to work on some wedding stuff with Judy," Mom says.

"Is Emma going with you?"

"No, we are doing seating arrangements. Emma's not interested. Now that she's twelve, she's asked to be left alone. We're going to try it out tonight. So, I'm not asking you to stay home. I just wanted to let you know."

Mom's reading my mind in that way that she's able to do about some things. Not the important ones.

"That makes sense. I was babysitting other people's kids at her age."

"Yeah, it's time. Besides, she won't be alone for very long because Dan is coming over in a little while. I think they're planning a movie night or something. Isn't that cute?"

Mom's not asking me to change my plan to see Ben for the first time in four weeks. She's asking me to let Emma stay home alone with Dan, which she thinks is cute.

In a daze, I return to my room to pace and text Luisa. Mom wants to let Dan watch Em. I think I should be here.

WTF???

For Emma.

You told me I had to go! And it's for Ben.
You CAN'T bail.

As I hold the phone in my hand, a new text appears. Not from Luisa. From the one person I've wondered if I'm going to hear from ever again.

Will I see you tonight?

Ben writes like there hasn't been a deafening silence from him for twenty-eight days.

Who is this? I type, maybe just to mess with him, maybe to be sure.

Srsly? Rhymes with hen. Will you be there?
Need to talk to you.

Ben has reached out to me from the black hole of cyberspace. And he needs to talk. Obviously, staying home is not an option. I look up at the ceiling, as if I can see my sister in her room. Leaving her with Dan for a movie night is not an option either. I don't have a choice here, I tell myself again as I march up to Emma's room, where I find her folding colored paper into flowers for the wedding.

"Mom has to go do wedding stuff," I say.

"Yeah, she told me." Emma is focused on her fingers folding paper.

"Em?"

She looks up at me and then back to her work. "You going out?" she asks, her fingers absently folding, turning, folding, turning, folding. A piece of lemon-yellow paper becomes a rose.

"Yeah. Tonight is Ben's welcome home party."

"I know."

My sister sits on her bed, back against a pillow, ankles crossed. Her toenails are painted lime green. A purple bra strap peeks from the edge of her T-shirt. She's so different from me at that age. She grabs a new piece of paper, this one sky blue, and begins folding.

"Do you want to go?" I ask.

Emma's fingers stop their folding. One part paper, one part flower. She looks at me guardedly. "Why?"

No doubt she is replaying every time she's begged to come with me and I've said no.

"Don't you want to see Ben?"

"Yeah," she says, like *duh*.

"Don't ask questions then, get dressed."

"But what about Mom? And I think Dan is on his way over."

I pull out my phone, message them both that plans have changed and Emma and I are going to a late movie with Ben and Luisa. "Done," I say.

I text Luisa this new development and get a !!! in response. At least I'll be there, I text her. Meanwhile, Emma has wasted no time trying to find the perfect outfit, and of course doesn't think that any of her clothes are right. Somehow, even though I tell her a million times that there's no way anyone is coming within ten feet of her, she manages to talk me into letting her wear the purple sparkly shirt. Then, just when I think we're nearly out the door, she decides that she needs some makeup. Of course, Mom would have a fit if she knew that Emma was going to this party, let alone wearing any makeup at all. I agree to some lip gloss and mascara.

"Okay, let's go," I say, checking my phone for the time and updating Luisa on our slow progress.

"I haven't done my hair yet."

"Are you kidding me right now? Your hair looks fine. Besides, it's raining. Your hair will get messed up anyway."

She stands before her mirror and starts flat-ironing her long hair. "It'll only be a minute," she says.

"That's what you said forty-five minutes ago. I feel like I'm with Luisa right now." I fall back on her bed.

"I wish Luisa *were* here right now. She might be able to help me with my hair."

I sit straight up. "I can help with hair. Are you already forgetting our marathon braiding sessions?"

"That was a long time ago."

Might seem long to her. Doesn't seem long to me.

"Do you remember how you'd scream when Mom would brush your hair?" I ask as her reflection runs the flat iron through section after section of her long brown hair.

"Shut up," Emma says, like she's tired of that memory. I laugh.

"How come you don't wear yours long anymore?" she asks, eyeing me critically. "Yours hasn't been long since you were in middle school. Remember when you cut it all off? Mom was like 'what did you do?' And Dan said you looked like a boy."

I remember all of that. I'd done it right after the camping trip. Now, standing before the mirror, I turn my head from side to side. My dark hair is cut super short on the sides and back with long pieces in the front. I push them out of my eyes. "I think short hair suits my badass-ness."

"I guess, but you'd be so pretty with your hair long."

From my experience, the better I look, the more trouble I seem to get into. "Meh," I say. "Beauty shmeauty. Ready?"

"Whoa! A little piece of Skye," Keith says when I walk in with Emma and Luisa. He guffaws, clearly thinking he's the next *Late Night* host. I glance at my sister shaking the rain out of her long hair. Dressed in my top and with a touch of makeup aging her up a bit,

Emma resembles me more than I'd realized. I wonder if Dan's seen it too. I'm glad I brought her with me. She'll be safe here. As long as none of these guys gets near her.

Luisa hugs herself and looks around the room at the small group gathered.

"You okay?" I whisper to her.

She nods. "It's good for me, right?"

I bump her shoulder with mine. "Act like nothing happened."

I turn back to Keith. "Not a drink," I say, pointing at him and then at Emma. "Not a toke."

"I got it! I know she's your sister."

"She's just a kid." I'm a dog with a bone right now.

"Hey!" Emma protests.

Keith leans toward me. "Just a kid?" He raises his eyebrows.

"She's *twelve*." I say it slow so that he can let it sink in.

Keith pulls away from me. "Twelve! What are you thinking? I don't want any trouble."

It's none of Keith's business what I'm thinking. "There won't *be* trouble because nothing is going to happen to *cause* trouble."

I tuck my keys back in my pocket and lead Emma away.

"I'm not a baby," Emma huffs as we walk away from Keith.

"Of course not! But you need to learn the lay of the land," Luisa says conspiratorially to Emma. "You need us to tell you who is okay and who's not."

"Okay," Emma concedes. "Who was that guy then?"

"Keith. You could take him in a fight in a heartbeat."

Emma laughs. "I doubt that."

"You just need to know his weakness. See, Keith is super ticklish on his inner arm. You get him there, and you'll win."

Emma laughs again, and I relax a little. She'll be safe with us, and Luisa seems okay.

We find a table where someone has left cards to play Asshole. Usually we play this while drinking, but tonight we play it straight. Well, Emma and I do. Luisa is pretending to sip a cup of water, but I know better. She's just been through heartbreak, so I don't say anything.

I check my phone for more texts from Ben. Nothing. I keep checking every few minutes and start feeling pathetic. *Finally,* maybe an hour later, Ben walks in to cheers from the dozen or so people hanging out in Keith's basement. He seems taller, though he shouldn't, because his hair is cut short and his curls are gone. I mourn for the curls, but now his face is no longer hidden. He brushes raindrops from his head. His dark eyes catch mine and won't let go. Something about not looking directly into the sun passes through my mind. My stomach quivers like a Jell-O shot, and my hands don't know what to do. Ben quirks one side of his mouth up. My fingers itch for some charcoal to capture him: *Making Smiles Jealous.* Then the smile disappears like he's just remembered something. He ambles over to us.

"Welcome back from the dead," Luisa says.

"Good to be back," Ben says, smiling at Luisa and then those eyes are on me again. His smile is the same, but his eyes are different.

They're clear, but a little haunted. It hits me then what he must have gone through in rehab and I want to hug him, but I'm not sure if it's okay.

"Hi, Ben," Emma says a little loudly.

"Emma!" Ben says. "How are you?" Ben looks at me with raised eyebrows and I shrug, offering him a half smile in return.

"I'm good," Emma says, grinning. "Skye said I could come to your welcome back party, but she and Luisa are making it totally boring for me. No one is allowed to talk to me."

"They're just looking out for you." He doesn't laugh.

Watching them talk, it's weird that after all of this time my little sister is the one to talk to him first. But also, it's sort of perfect. Like he never left, like nothing has changed. Keith offers Ben a red cup sloshing with beer. Ben holds up a pristine water bottle and shakes his head. Someone else holds out a packed bong to him. I cringe and hope Emma didn't see it as Ben clutches his water bottle and shakes his head again. So much for nothing changing.

"Jell-O!" Emma exclaims as someone passes the tray of cherry Jell-O shots.

"No, Em. Not for you," Luisa says, and slurps one down. I want one so bad that my mouth waters. But I can't. I won't.

People orbit around Ben and he greets everyone who's shown up for him, but something seems off. He seems to back up when people approach him, not meet them like he used to. He holds his water bottle like a shield. Emma, Luisa, and I keep playing Asshole, though my eyes can't seem to stay on my cards. They drift toward Ben again and again. A couple of guys come by to join in our game, but we send them away. Then Ben is back.

He leans down toward me and speaks in a low voice that was once familiar to me. "I need to talk to you."

34

Careful What You Wish For

"OKAY," I SAY to Ben, like it's no big deal. Like we've spoken many times since the night that I tried to hook up with him and he got sent away.

"Somewhere quiet," he says.

If my stomach didn't plummet before, it takes a nosedive toward my toes now. "I don't want to be too far from Em."

"Luisa's here," Ben says.

"Okay with you?" I ask Luisa. I don't want to pressure her when I know this party is already difficult for her.

She nods to me and then taps her phone. "You've got thirty minutes."

"Cool?" I ask Emma.

She shrugs and then nods. "You'll be back in thirty minutes?"

I nod. That seems like more than enough time. As Ben and I

walk toward the door, I stop to check in with Keith. "All good?"

"Of course. It'd be better if Mr. Clean there would have a beer though." Keith gestures with his chin to Ben.

"I'm good for now," Ben says.

"Speaking of which, that case is still in my car," I say.

"Save it for when this guy decides to have a little fun."

Ben looks down, doesn't say anything.

"We'll be right back," I say.

"Suit yourself, Chicken Little," Keith says.

"No Chicken Little tonight."

"What? He's not drinking, so you don't either? You two make me puke."

"Emma's here, that's all."

As Ben and I walk toward the door leading upstairs, Ben asks, "So what's with you and Keith? Thought he drove you nuts."

"He's just a teddy bear, once you get to know him."

"I know that. I just didn't think you did." I hear a smile in his tone.

"He helped get my car back when it was towed and helped me find a ton of art stuff that I'm using for a new project."

"What happened to Lucy and what project?"

It hits me how much has happened in these four weeks. "You've been gone awhile."

He rubs the back of his newly bare neck and nods, his lips an unsmiling line. "Yeah, I have."

"I'm making a mosaic mural on the side of the diner."

"Whoa, bold."

"I sort of have to. Long story." I want to tell him how it all went down, but there's this huge gulf between us, made up of twenty-eight days of silence and I'm not sure where I'd begin. Outside, Ben drops to sit on the front steps of Keith's house. I hesitate before doing the same, and when I do, I'm careful not to let my knee touch his. I hug mine close, in case they get any ideas of their own.

"So . . . you're back," I say.

"I'm back."

"Did it suck?" I ask.

He's quiet for a moment. "It was rough. How about you?"

"I'm okay."

"Your mom still getting married?" he asks.

I remember that night in his car with the music and the joint and the feeling that I didn't need anything else in the world. I wish we were back in that moment right now. "That's still the plan. Only a couple weeks away now."

We drop into silence. Cars slide by on the rain-soaked street; streetlamps cast light one way and shadow the other. The music throbs through the windows with bubbles of laughter and still we say nothing. This is not the comfortable silence from before. This one is crowding us with words unsaid.

"Listen—" I say.

"So—" he says.

"You go," I say.

"No, you."

"The last time I saw you . . ." I start. "At the party, you know, after the concert."

"That was one totally fucked-up night, right?"

"Yeah, it was," I say. I push on. "I . . . I mean we . . . had that fight."

"We fought?"

"You don't remember?"

Ben searches the stars. "I've had ample time to consider that night. I remember partying hard. You wanted to leave." He turns to me in the dark. "But you were breaking our promise."

I clutch my knees closer. "What else do you remember?"

I hold my breath while I wait for him to answer.

"Not long after that, I ended up turning out my pockets for two police officers."

I breathe again. He doesn't mention me practically stripping in front of him—or him rejecting me. "Shit. Seriously?" I say.

"Yeah. Then everything moved so fast. Luckily, I only had a little weed on me. Thank God we'd finished that coke. The cops made me call my parents, which was, you know, not awesome."

"Better than getting arrested though. We'd all thought you'd been busted."

"I guess it was better than that. My mom took my phone when they sent me away. I was completely cut off from everyone."

Not just me.

"I tried to reach you," I say.

"You did?" He turns toward me in the dark and I hear his genuine surprise.

"Yeah, I called your phone a few times and then I called your house."

"No way," Ben says, as if he knows what happened next.

"Yeah, your mom told me that I'm a bad influence."

"Mom and Dad wanted to basically nuke my old life down to the cockroaches."

"I tried to call you at the rehab too," I confess.

"You did?" I hear a smile in his voice.

I laugh. "Yeah, that was funny because the receptionist gave me this whole runaround about 'neither confirming nor denying' your presence and then your mom called me back and reminded me that I wasn't supposed to be in contact with you." It didn't seem funny to me at the time, when I was desperate to hear Ben's voice, but I don't share that part.

"That place was an alternate universe. I went from one hundred percent freedom to not being allowed to pee by myself."

"Where does your mom think you are now?"

"With people from the program."

He says *program* like it's in air quotes.

"From the rehab, you mean?" I ask.

He barks a laugh. "Yeah, she thinks I'm with some of the people who graduated before me."

Graduated gets air quotes too.

"Were there *any* cool people?"

He shrugs for a third time. "I guess some were all right. But most of them are seriously messed up. Oxy and meth. Shit we've never tried. And Skye, they're fried." He shakes his head. "You wouldn't believe some of what I heard in our group sessions. There are people our age—and even younger—dealing with hardcore stuff. And you know, I'm all like—hey, I just party. I'm not trying to avoid massive issues or anything, but then in the one-on-one sessions, all this stuff comes up about how I feel about my dad not, you know, really getting behind me with the music and everything? And I know what I want, but I also sort of feel like a failure because I'm not choosing what he wants and . . ."

Ben's voice drifts off. I have the impression that he's said more than he intended. I knew that it was mostly Ben's mom who supported his music, but as close as Ben and I were I didn't know that he felt all this pressure from his dad.

"That was heavy. I'm sorry," Ben says.

My hand aches to touch him, but I keep it pressed against my knee. "No need to be sorry. I just didn't know."

"Partying always meant I didn't have to think about it."

I never considered that maybe I like to party so much because I can't talk about what happened to me. I don't know if that fully explains it, but now that the idea is in my head, I can't not think about it.

"What's going on with the band?" I ask.

"I have some news about that," he says. "I was a model 'inmate' at the rehab and my parents seem satisfied that I've learned my lesson, or some lessons anyway."

He tries for his old sarcastic tone, but it lacks bite.

"Yeah?" I say because I'm pretty sure he hasn't gotten to the news yet. He rubs his hands on his jeans and then takes a deep breath.

"The guys agreed to wait on the recording sessions until I got out, even though we lost some money. I wrote a ton of new music while I was away, so if there's one good thing, that's it." He rubs the back of his neck. "We're going to be recording for the next few weeks and then we go on the road starting the day after graduation."

The words surround me like a fog. I thought I had him back. I thought that we might be who we were before he left, before I unbuttoned my shirt in front of him. Before he told me that he didn't want me in that way. But he's not really back. It's more like a stopover.

"Oh." That's all I'm able to say.

"We start recording tomorrow, actually." He moves to stand up. "So, I'm going to head out."

I look up at his silhouette, confused. "You're leaving? But this whole party is for you."

"Yeah, thanks, but . . ." He shakes his water bottle. "Not really my scene tonight."

Wow. Apparently, this new Ben chewed up the old Ben and spit him out in the trash. I stand up too. "You're taking this rehab stuff seriously."

He barks out a small laugh, but there's no joy in it. "It's definitely in my head. Plus, staying clean is still part of the recording deal, so . . ."

"Yeah, totally," I say as if I understand. "Good luck, I guess."

"Maybe you could come?" he says. "You know, and watch us record?"

He sounds sincere, but I'm sure that it's an automatic invite, left over from before. Whether he remembers how I acted that night or not, things are different now. I miss him, but I miss the old him. I'm not 100 percent sure what I have in common with this haunted, close-cropped version of my former best friend.

"That's cool," I say. "I've got the mosaic and it's a ton of work."

"Right," he says, playing with his keys. "See you around then?"

"Sure, see you . . . around."

Ben starts to walk away and then turns back. "I know this is a weird question, but do you . . . are you planning to be at the art show?"

"We're required to show up, so yeah."

Ben's silhouette nods and then he leaves.

After Ben disappears into the dark, I sit on the step a while longer. My feelings are pieces of mismatched pottery. Relief that I've actually spoken to him, but also confusion. And the more I think, the more it sucks.

The whole party was meant for Ben and all he did was come in for a few minutes to basically tell me he was leaving again, like I was something to check off of his list. And if he only wanted to tell me he was going to start recording, why'd he bother to come? Why not come to my house or meet somewhere? Unless he doesn't want to hang with me alone anymore. Which he obviously doesn't.

I guess I know what that means. No more being best friends

with the class slut. He's moving up. He's going on tour. My mind is all jumbled up by the time I push myself off of the steps and head back into the party. I'm not sure how long I've been sitting there. When I go inside, the house is packed with more people. I see Matt disappear down the stairs. Keith must have invited him because I didn't.

"There she is," Keith says, pulling a new tray of Jell-O shots from the fridge. "Where's Mr. Clean?"

Ben's words ghost through my head. But the idea that people party to erase their painful past sounds like psychobabble bullshit, and besides, Ben doesn't seem any happier now that he's not partying. In fact, he seems pretty miserable. I grab two shots and toss them back. "He went home," I say.

35

FML

PEOPLE KEEP COMING up to me, asking about Ben. The shots are warm in my belly. Maybe a little bit of beer wouldn't hurt. Just a little. I sip my beer and make excuses for Ben. The beer is empty, but I hadn't really filled it up all the way, so I return to the keg for just a splash more.

Keith watches me and laughs. "What happened to being the DD for your sister?"

I drop the cup. Emma. How could I forget Emma? I don't even know how long I've been upstairs. I check my phone. I've been gone over an hour. It takes some time to navigate the steps down to the basement among all the people clogging the hallways. We didn't invite half these people, but word of the party must have spread. Finally, I push my way to the corner.

The table where Em and Luisa had been playing cards has been taken over by a bunch of lax bros pounding beers and laughing too loudly. I scan the room. I don't see Emma anywhere. Or Luisa.

"Where's my sister?" I ask the guys at the table.

They shrug and return to their partying.

I lean down and pound the table. "Seriously, guys. Did you see a girl here? With Luisa?"

"Chill!" one guy says, catching his beer before it topples.

"There was a girl sitting here when we got here. She kind of freaked. Luisa wasn't here though."

"She freaked? What did you do to her?" I'm in the guy's face now.

He holds his hands up. "We were just partying. She freaked and took off."

"Which way?"

Two of them point down the hall where a line of girls snakes toward the bathroom. I push my way to the front of the line while several girls make inappropriate comments about what I should do to myself. I tap on the door.

"You have to wait like everyone else," a girl says. "Some girl has been in there a while."

I tap on the door again. "Em? Are you in there? It's Skye."

"Skye?"

"Yeah, Em. Can you let me in?"

Emma cracks open the door so that all I can see is her tear-stained face. I press the door open a little more so that I can get in.

"That's not fair!" the girl says in irritation. "I'm about to pee my pants."

I ignore the protests and shut the door behind me. Emma has sunk down on the toilet seat. Her mascara is streaking down her cheeks.

"Emma!" I kneel next to her. "Are you okay?"

"No! I'm not okay. Those guys were doing drugs, Skye! They were smashing these little pills and then breathing them up through their noses. They were acting super weird. I want to go home. Please take me home!"

"Where's Luisa?"

"She got upset. She said she'd be right back and then these other guys showed up and said they needed the table."

"Luisa was upset?"

Emma nods, still sniffling. "You said thirty minutes. And I believed you." Emma wipes a tear from her eye. "Please take me home."

"Okay, let's go."

Emma looks up at me from the toilet. "Are you sure you're okay to drive?"

I pause for a minute. The only other person in the world who ever asks me that is Ben. We had a promise.

"Probably not."

"Who can you call for a ride?"

I start to call Ben. He's obviously sober enough to drive. But he made it pretty clear that he was finished with me. Everyone else at the party is in a way worse state than I am, which I'm assuming includes Luisa, even though I have no idea where she is. I check my phone, but there aren't any ride service options available. I'm not even wasted, but I can't take a chance with my little sister. I pull in a deep breath and do the last possible thing that I want to do. I call my mother to come get us from the party.

Mom is thin-lipped and silent on the ride home. As soon as we're in the door she follows Emma up to her room. I drink some water and try to look as sober as possible. Mom is up there for a while.

"Explain yourself," Mom says when she returns to the living room.

"I took Emma to Ben's welcome back party," I say. It's pointless to lie. She picked us up there.

"Where there were high school students drinking."

I nod. Again, pointless to lie.

"And drugs."

"No—"

Mom holds up a hand. "Don't bother. Emma just told me what she saw. What you allowed her to see because you abandoned your little sister at a party."

I'm silent.

"I *told* you that it was okay for you to go to the party," Mom says. The anger is barely in check.

"I know."

"I told you Dan was coming over and it would be okay."

Just because she thought it would be okay didn't mean it would be okay. "I know what you told me."

"What the hell were you thinking? Taking your eleven-year-old sister to a high school party?"

"She's twelve," I say, like correcting my mom makes sense right now.

"I don't care if she's twelve!" The anger unfurls itself like huge black wings whipping the air between us. On black paper with white charcoal: *Metamorphosis by Rage.* "She's a *little girl.* What's the matter with you?"

I wonder where my mother's worry was when I was a little girl. I was thinking that between Luisa and me, Emma would be safe. "She wanted to see Ben . . ."

"Then you take her to lunch with Ben. To the bowling alley. To the movies, which is what you told Dan you were doing, *if* you recall." With every suggestion, the wings whip harder and harder. "You *lied* to me and put your sister in danger. Is there no end to your poor judgment?"

"I just . . ."

"You just what, Skye?" Mom's anger sprouts talons and slices at me. "You just thought it was high time that she followed in your footsteps?"

And I slice back. "Actually, Mom, I was trying to make sure that she *doesn't* follow in my footsteps."

"What?" Mom's tone is condescending now. She'll never hear what I have to say.

"Forget it." I look away, shaking my head.

"Don't tell me to *forget it.*"

I meet Mom's eyes full of fire. "I wanted to keep her safe."

"*Safe?*" Mom's tone is full of the derision that comes from clue-lessness.

"It's more than you ever did." The words careen out of my mouth and hit their mark.

"How dare you?" she hisses. "Everything I've done, I've done for you girls."

"How can you pretend it never happened?"

"What are you talking about?"

"What happened with Dan."

"What does this have to do with Dan?"

"It has everything to do with Dan!" I scream.

She holds her hand up. "Dan was rough with me two times. But I ended it after the second time and all of that is in the past. It has nothing to do with the present."

I'd always wondered if he'd hit her. He'd gotten more and more rageful until it seemed that they fought all the time, and then one day, he was gone and she was wrecked. I'd always assumed that he'd left her. But none of that is what I'm trying to tell her. "Mom." I try one more time.

"Leave," Mom says, disgust coloring her tone. She turns away from me. I feel like I don't exist. She can't hear me. She won't see me. I might as well not be here.

I walk for hours through the nothing time of night in the suburbs when all of the house lights are dark and streetlamps create bubbles of light between patches of black. By the time I make it down Keith's long driveway, the party is dead and I'm no longer buzzed.

I drive Lucy to the quarry. It's nearly morning. The trees are shadows before me and the water is as black as oil. I pop the hatch and pull out the fancy case of bottled beer that I'd bought for Ben. I lift one green bottle and hold it in my hand for a moment before I hurtle it toward the nearest tree, where it crashes in a disappointing explosion of glass and amber liquid. The contents spray against the tree; the broken bottle fragments land muted on the pine needle floor. One by one, I throw every bottle, feeling a spark of satisfaction at each burst, each splintering of glass, each splatter of beer down the trunk of the tree.

After every bottle is obliterated, I go to the tree, pick up one lethal-looking shard, and I carve an image into the trunk. Two eyes wide open. One little slash of a nose. An *X* for a mouth. My fingers are bleeding a bit from the effort, but I don't care. I keep the shard and return to my car. Dawn is gray across the quarry. I head home, not because I want to, but because I have nowhere else to go.

36

The Art of Breaking Things

ON SATURDAY, I'M not sure what will greet me when I finally emerge from my room just before noon. Mom has installed herself at the kitchen table. An abandoned cup of coffee sits near her right hand alongside a plate with a mostly eaten piece of raisin toast. She's looking over a handwritten list that sits next to a folder thick with paper. Wedding planning.

She says nothing as she eyes me over her reading glasses. I fill a glass with water, drain it down and refill it, but still she says nothing.

"Listen," Mom says, and I'm ready for a serious talk about what happened and our fight. "I'm completely overwhelmed with the wedding happening in three weeks. Obviously, you're grounded. And I need your help."

Obviously, you're grounded. That's it?

I frown. "Should we talk—?"

Mom stands up, slipping her list into her folder. "I'm off. I've got to meet the caterer and then run a few other errands. Please check on your sister. I'm giving you this chance to prove yourself, Skye. Don't disappoint me."

"Okay, but Mom, last night—" I start.

She cuts me off midsentence. "I'll be back later."

Evidently, there will be no discussion of last night. I don't know why that should surprise me. After all, she was clear about no more ugliness. Is it possible that she thinks that the whole reason I'm against her marriage to Dan is because he hit her? I didn't even know about that when it happened. We are such a small family with enormous things unsaid. I've tried to talk to her so many times. I don't know how else to make her see. I nibble on Mom's cold toast, and it tastes like cardboard. I stare at the ceiling, imagining Emma on the other side of that six or so inches of wood and drywall and I know I need to face her, but I'm dreading it. I take each step one at a time, like a man heading for the electric chair. I tap on her door.

"Yeah?" I hear her voice float toward me.

"It's me. Can I come in?"

"Oh." Disappointment oozes through the door. "Yeah, I guess."

I push the door open. Emma is propped on her bed, staring at her laptop.

"Thought you were Mom." Emma does not look up. Nor does she remove her headphones.

"She went out. Wedding stuff."

"Oh." Emma still won't look at me.

"Can we talk?"

Emma slides her headphones off as though it's a major inconvenience.

"I'm so, so sorry, Em. You can't know how sorry I am."

Emma looks up from the computer and out the window.

"Em, please. Don't freeze me out."

When she finally meets my eyes, anger lights hers. "We were supposed to have fun, but instead you ignored me all night and people were doing drugs. Like real drugs. And you said you weren't going to drink. But you did."

I have many times felt small and broken, not deserving of the space I take up in the world, not deserving of the air I breathe. But never with Emma. I've never felt ashamed standing before my little sister. I don't try to make excuses; I deserve her disgust, and there are no words that will change what I did and make it right.

"Is there anything I can do for you?" I've reverted to waitress mode.

She shakes her head and I turn to leave.

"Skye?" Her voice is hard.

"Yeah?" I turn back to her.

"Do you hate me and Mom?"

"Of course not!" The burn of emotion snakes up my neck. "I love you more than anything. Why would you even say that?"

"You don't act like you love us."

Her comment reminds me of Mom saying that I don't seem to want to be a part of this family. I think they are both wrong, but if they both see it that way, maybe I'm the one who is wrong. I chew the inside of my cheek and then reach for the doorknob.

"Shut the door when you leave." Emma slides her headphones back on, shutting me out completely.

I'm surprised by a knock on the door. I know it can't be Ben. It's Luisa.

"Hey," she says, frowning. "How are you? I texted you last night, but radio silence. Thought I'd come by to make sure you were okay."

"Fucking awesome." I know that it's not Luisa's fault that I left Emma alone and drank when I was supposed to protect her, but Luisa is here and the arrow of my anger shoots toward her.

"What's that supposed to mean?"

"Emma freaked last night and I had to get my mom to come get us."

"Oh, shit," she says.

"You left," I say.

"You said thirty minutes. Was I supposed to babysit Emma all night?"

She's right, of course. "Why didn't you come get me?"

She looks down.

"I saw Matt," she says. "And I lost it. I had to run out of there.

When I went back, Em wasn't at the table anymore. I figured you'd gotten her. Come on, let me in."

I step back and hold the door open for Luisa.

"Emma's home." I cast my eyes toward the second floor, still stinging from the pain of our interaction. "Let's go to my room."

"What's going on down here?" she says, looking at my art supplies cowering into a corner.

"Dan." I spit his name out.

When we are in my room with the door closed, Luisa tells me to sit on the bed, so she can say what she needs to say. "I've been your friend forever," she says. "And I've stood by you. But you're like imploding or something. I'm worried."

"What do you mean?"

"You thought Em would be safer partying with us than home alone with Dan? Skye, whatever is going on with him, you've got to make your mother understand. For real. And this Ben thing. This is *crazy*. You *drank* over him with your little sister at the party, but you insist there's nothing there? Open your eyes."

Luisa's words slam into me. She's right. It was crazy to take Em with me. I already knew that. But the thing about Ben—I hadn't seen it that way. I'd promised myself that I wouldn't drink with Emma there. The whole point of taking Emma was to keep her safe. But one bad interaction with Ben and I dropped shots without a second thought for me or for my sister.

I shake my head.

"Why are you shaking your head at me?"

I shake my head again. "Fuck," I say softly.

I can't continue to be as blind as my mother. If she's serious about marrying Dan, I can't leave. There's no other choice.

Luisa sits next to me. "Talk to me."

I look at her. "I have to turn down MICA."

As soon as the words erupt from my mouth, I feel the awful reality plow into my heart.

"Skye, no. That's too much. Let's talk this through."

"Okay, let's. My mother won't believe what Dan did to me. She's going to marry him. There's no way to keep Emma safe if I leave. I have to give up a full ride to the school of my dreams in order to stay here and keep my little sister safe who, by the way, hates my guts." I bury my face in my hands. "Everything is shit, Lu."

"You tried to talk to your mom?" she says.

I nod. "I tried last night. She won't even listen."

"And I guess the talk with Ben on Friday night didn't go well."

"It was so awkward, Lu!"

Luisa purses her lips. "And what's this about Emma?"

I tell her about how it upset Emma to see people doing drugs and how angry she is at me. I've shattered everything that matters to me. Luisa plumps the pillows on my bed and retrieves her iPad from her bag.

"*Gilmore Girls?*"

I nod.

We watch Lorelai sneak through a window to have sex with Rory's dad and I feel a little better about myself, but not much. I let my head rest on Luisa's shoulder. We don't speak through the whole show. I wonder how to unwant something. I know that I can't leave my sister here with Dan in my house, but I also don't know how to not want the dream I've had for so long. Will I be like Dean, happy to stay in the same town for all my life? I doubt it. I think I'll be more like Jess, all pissed off and bitter at the world. When the episode is over, Lu looks at her watch.

"I've got to get home," she says. She pulls a joint out of her pocket and leaves it sitting on my bed. "Even Teflon girls need a little help sometimes."

By Sunday, the upcoming wedding holds our small house hostage. Strands of lights and white candles in all sizes occupy the dining room table. Metal bins for the beer and wine stand by the front door. Yards of sheer white fabric smother the couch. If Mom has her way, it's going to be like our fairy birthday mornings, but more. If only she were marrying someone else, I could help her make it the most beautiful night ever. We'd work together, all three of us, like we did when we painted Emma's room. We'd laugh and tease one another, and it would be us again—the Murray girls. But that version of us splintered as soon as Dan came back, after I messed up with Emma. All of the wedding decorations are thorns pressing into my flesh, reminding me of what I'm giving up.

All day, I try to compose an e-mail to MICA, but every time I start to type, I begin to cry. I'm aware of Luisa's joint in my bag, but

I've never gotten high alone before. I've only ever partied with other people.

I let it sit there all weekend, but on Monday, with Mom and Emma still not speaking to me and the wedding crap staring at me, I give in. On the way to school, I pull over and take a few hits. It feels pathetic, to be honest. I stub it, but by the time I arrive in first period art, I am pretty stoned. Ben is sitting on the same stool as always. It's weird to see him in class after all this time, and I'm sorry now that I got stoned. He pulls a stool out with his foot and returns to drawing.

"Thanks, Mr. Clean." I lean my head on my hand. So heavy, head, so heavy. I smile. I think I smile, anyway. I can't remember what smiles feel like. The buzz is like cotton stuffing the big aching spaces inside me for a little while.

"The name's Ben," he says. Then looks at me closer. "You okay?" he asks.

I nod. My brains bobble inside my head.

"Your brains what?"

"Oh, I said that out loud?" A laugh squeaks out.

"Wake and bake this morning? Not generally your style."

I think about how I just needed to get out of the house that morning. How Emma ignored me and Mom didn't put out break-fast like she usually does. I left without our customary peck on the cheek, and as much as I usually grimace when she does that, I felt invisible when she didn't.

"People change."

"So I've been told." He studies me for a moment. "You drawing today or just daydreaming?"

I sigh. "I don't know. Maybe just daydreaming."

"I'm all for the daydream," Ben says. "But he's watching." Ben inclines his chin toward the back of the room.

"Who? Mr. M? Nah." I crane my neck to see Mr. M. He *does* seem to be looking my way. And so intense too. But maybe I'm paranoid. They say weed does that to a person. I snicker. "You had a recording session on Saturday?" I say.

Ben nods. "Went really well. You should hear the new stuff."

"I'd like that," I say, before I remember how much has changed.

I watch my hand reach for the pencil and pad, lift the cover of the pad, find a new page. My hand is miraculous. My hands make art and they make crafts and they even make food for Emma. I'll sketch my hand, that's what I'll do. "I'm going to sketch my hand."

"Go for it."

I start sketching. My hands also shove drugs and beer into my body. "I messed things up with Emma," spills out of my mouth.

"She'll forgive you," Ben says. I don't know how he knows what I'm talking about. I steal a glance at him. He's still sketching, but one hand shields the drawing paper so that I can't see what emerges from his pen. The curls that used to spring this way and that are gone, drawing my eyes to his face. He has that look he gets when he's trying to get the image just right. Top teeth biting his full lower lip, slight crease between his eyes. I imagine *Artist Unmasked,* graphite pencil. Then I remember that I don't draw Ben anymore. He starts to look up and I study my hand.

A tear creeps from my eye, slides down my cheek, and plops on my sketch pad, blurring the first and second fingers of my drawing. I smudge at the wet spot and keep drawing. By the time Mr. M comes around, I have a decent sketch of at least three fingers of my left hand. "Nice, Skye. Don't forget the shading, that's what makes it come alive."

"That's what you always say. Don't you have anything new to teach us?"

As soon as the words are out of my mouth, I know that I'm out of line. Mr. M frowns, but he doesn't miss a beat.

"Learn the lessons I've taught and maybe I'll gift you with new ones," he says. "Ben, let's see yours."

Ben looks over his pad at Mr. M and then me. "Sure." He hands the pad to Mr. M and twirls his pen between his fingers.

Mr. M evaluates Ben's drawing. "Clever." He glances at me and hands the pad back. "Interesting work, Ben."

Mr. M walks to the next table.

"Obviously, my work wasn't at the same caliber as your *clever, interesting* work." I reach my hand out. "Let's see what was so amazing." Ben closes his pad.

"Nah. Not that good."

He moves behind me to look at my work and then he leans over my shoulder and points to the thumb of my drawing. "You've got some nice detail there." He smells safe. I want to breathe him in like oxygen. But he's clean now and I'm shit.

I close my sketch pad. "I think we're done for today." I start to put my charcoal away.

Ben steps back and runs a hand over his short hair. "Come on, Skye," he says.

I shove my pad into my pack and look at him. "What?" My tone has a whip at the end, but it doesn't seem to cut him.

"It doesn't have to be like this." His words are quiet, just for me.

"You sure about that?"

"People," Mr. M booms to the class. "The art show is in less than three weeks. You have this class time to fine-tune the pieces you plan to contribute. I hope that I don't see anyone creating new pieces at this point. It's time to make the ones that you have the best that they can be."

"Skye—" Ben starts.

I toss my pack over my shoulder and stride toward the door. I'd like to think I'm striding, anyway. But my foot catches on a stool and I nearly fall on my face. I recover and head to the door once more.

"Going somewhere, Skye?" Mr. M calls from across the room.

"Lady issues, Mr. M."

Glancing back, I see that Ben stands exactly where I leave him, one hand on the top of his head.

"All right," Mr. M says.

As I leave the room, I wonder how Mr. M can pack so much disappointment into two words.

The wake and bake this morning was good for a little while, but then the high wore off and the ugly feelings returned even bigger and badder than before. I drive to Sal's to work on the mosaic. I just stare at the wall, partially covered in shades of brown. In my head I play over the last few days. Emma's statement that I don't act like I love her repeats inside my head like a death knell, insistent and unceasing. All I've ever wanted was to keep her safe. I'm failing.

I don't know what I was thinking, trying to make a piece of art from a million broken things. I get in my car and head back out without adding one single piece to the mosaic.

The next day is no different. After school, I drive around and before I fully know where I'm going, I find myself on Ben's street. Of course Lucy would bring me here. I slow down as we near his house. Freddie is parked in the driveway. Toby's van is there too. I roll down the window to hear the drums and bass of Arthouse Scream Machine leaking from the basement. Lucy starts to pull over to the curb, like she knows where she is, but I pull her back onto the street and continue on.

I pass the empty storefronts on Pennswood Pike and pull into Sal's parking lot, passing the neon sign with its still dark *n*. My half-assed mosaic mocks me. What's the point in finishing? I won't be going to MICA. Might as well let Sal file a complaint against me. The roach from yesterday morning sits in the little pouch where I'd hid it. I dig it out and look at it. I figure getting high by myself will be easier the second time. I hold it in one hand and flick the lighter on and off with the other while I stare at the broken brown pieces of glass and tile attached to the wall. In just a few weeks, my mother will be celebrating her wedding beneath that barely begun mural.

I set the roach and the lighter down and pop the back of Lucy open and I pull out my supplies. Using the edge of the trowel, I try to pry the pieces off of the wall, but all I end up doing is bending the trowel. I grab a hammer and wedge the claw against the wall, but the pieces still won't come undone. I dig at the pieces with my fingers until two of my fingernails break. I've done too good of a job.

I return to the back of Lucy and drag a pile of tile out, letting it drop onto the asphalt. Satisfied by the thunderous crack, I drop another stack and watch the pieces break apart. I grab the hammer and, remembering how Mr. M cautioned me to just tap the tile gently, I raise the hammer way over my head and bring it crashing down. Pieces of tile splinter apart. I bring the hammer down again and again. When those tiles are little more than powder, I pull more cast-off items out of Lucy and I obliterate them too. I smash a glass, and a tiny shard jumps and lands in the meat of my palm. I drop the hammer and watch the blood drip from my hand onto the ruined tile.

I pluck out the shard and press the wound to my black T-shirt. Chest heaving, I stare at the bits of mosaic mural that refuse to be removed. My mother will have her wedding here, the mosaic is permanent, and there's nothing I can do about any of it. I lean against Lucy, still staring at the gaping concrete wall that remains to be filled. It's true that the wedding will be here—everyone will see the mosaic—and I don't have any control over that. Everyone will see it—whether I want them to or not. I push myself away from Lucy and step toward the broad expanse of wall. I stare at the unfilled space. My mother will see it and Dan too.

The image is barely formed. My eyes scan the surface, evaluating what's there and what isn't. The plan could change. It's the one area where I have a little bit of control. After wrapping my bleeding hand in a rag, I rummage in my bag for my sketchbook. Luisa had said that I needed to find a way for my mother to see the truth. This will be my way. I drop to the ground and start sketching. A vision erupts from my mind, and it's all I can do to get it on paper. None of my sketches work. I rip them off and toss them aside. I keep sketching, the charcoal mixing with the blood and dust from my hands darkening the pages. It's not until I start to lose daylight and cars begin to fill Sal's parking lot that I stop. I climb back into Lucy, exhausted. I text Luisa, asking if she'd be willing to help. Then I turn Lucy back the way I came.

37

Something Borrowed, Something Blue

BACK AT SCHOOL, even though it's dark, I'm able to get in, thanks to some swimmers heading in for practice. There are no guarantees that Mr. M will still be here, but a girl can hope.

"What happened to you?" he asks when I materialize in his office, covered in dust with one hand wrapped in a bloody rag.

"Long story, but I'm glad you're still here." I stand in the doorway hoping to be allowed in.

He stands. "Are you okay? Let's get you cleaned up."

Mr. M walks me to the sink, where he pulls a first aid kit from a cabinet overhead. After I wash the cut, which isn't all that bad, he dabs it with antiseptic, which makes me hiss in pain, and then bandages me up.

"All set?"

"Thanks," I say. "But I actually came here for a different kind of help."

"What do you need?"

"Artistic knowledge."

"I thought I didn't have anything new to teach you."

"Yeah, sorry about that," I say. "Can we sit?"

We walk back to his office and Mr. M gestures to the comfy chair.

"You know that mosaic?"

"At the diner? Of course. How is it coming along?"

"Well, that's the thing . . ."

"Go on." Mr. M leans back in his chair, steepling his fingers.

"I've decided to change the concept, and I need help."

"Do you have sketches?"

I pull my sketchbook from my bag. "I'm trying to figure out how to use what I already began and re-create it as something new. I want to add some ideas and I'm not sure how to pull it off."

Mr. M leans forward to look at the sketches. "What is this?" he asks.

"Jewelweed. It's a plant that can halt the effects of poison ivy."

He nods. "Small orange flowers?"

"Yes, sometimes they're yellow, but I'm going with orange. And that's poison ivy too." I point to the three-leaf plant I drew.

"And this?"

"My favorite tree."

"You have a favorite tree?" He pauses in examining my sketches to examine me. I'd rather he examine the sketches.

"I did. My family used to camp a lot at the same place. I loved this one tree and would always climb it. I called it the Whomping Willow? After Harry Potter?"

He nods.

"But it was hit by lightning and split down the middle."

Mr. M's silence makes me feel self-conscious, but I don't take the sketches away and I don't make excuses. I know what I need to do. The desire to create something permanent was not enough by itself. What happened to me was—is—permanent, and using my art might be the only way to communicate my truth.

"It's not ideal to begin a new plan at this stage." Mr. M finally speaks. "But this is going to be powerful. You have great instincts for conveying emotion through image."

"I don't know," I say, wrapping my arms around my shoulders. I sit there, clutching myself together, as if I'll fall to pieces like my broken tile if I let go.

"But you need to at least try, right?"

"It's scary," I say. "To start a huge project and not know if I can make it happen."

"Like flying."

"More like falling."

"Then let yourself fall, Skye."

I look away, because I don't know how to be okay with falling. Not this kind of falling. Why on earth would Mr. M think that I have good instincts? My instincts do nothing but fuck up everything in my entire life. My instincts caused me to seek myself in random guys, to screw up my friendship with Ben, to get wasted when I was supposed to be protecting Emma. And then a small voice whispers in the back of my mind that it wasn't my *instincts* that caused all of those things.

Mr. M offers some tips for how to translate my sketches into mosaic images and then he says, "A mosaic of this size and detail will take time to create."

"How much time?" I ask.

He looks at the sketches again. "Depending on how much time you can devote, it'll take weeks. Maybe even a month or more."

"I have less than three weeks."

"Then you're going to need help."

I've defined myself by my independence for so long. Even when I would complain about picking Emma up or making dinner for us, I also felt pride that I took care of my little sister. Every time Luisa would refer to me as her Teflon girl, it made me more determined to let things roll off my back. But I kept the secret of what happened all to myself too. And it was starting to seem that keeping secrets like this one doesn't make you strong. This sort of secret makes you ashamed and it makes you lonely. It was time to start asking for help.

"Well, do you have any plans for the next few weeks?"

Mr. M laughed. "Are you asking me to help you make public art?"

"I think I'm going to be asking everyone to help me make public art."

After Mr. M and I hash out a plan, I pack up my stuff and head to Sal's Diner and the wall where my partial mosaic waits for me.

Luisa is already there, so I update her on what's going on, then I run inside to share my plan with Sal and hope he agrees. Although he's reluctant to give up his original idea, he gives me the go-ahead. Before long, Janelle, Tristan, and some others from art class show up. A few minutes after that, Mr. M's little sports car pulls in right behind Keith's truck.

"You called Keith?" Luisa says.

"You called our teacher?" Janelle says.

"I need all the help I can get. I'm borrowing Keith's ladders, and Mr. M knows how to make big projects."

Just as I'm explaining the changes to the mural and showing everyone the supplies, the unmistakable sound of Freddie chugs into the narrow alley. I look at Luisa.

She shrugs. "You said you needed all the help you could get."

I can't ignore the way that my heart stutters and then beats double-time when I see Ben's lanky frame emerge from his car, but I also can't deal with the confusion of my feelings for him and the ways that we've changed. Not now.

"Where do you want these ladders?" Keith asks.

"Over there." I gesture to the side of the building.

Keith walks up, looking at the project and everyone assembled. "Hey, uh, you good?"

"Why, are you offering to help?"

"This is the stuff you got at the salvage yard and that flea market, right?"

I nod.

"Well, I'm invested then, aren't I?"

"If you say so. As long as it won't tarnish your rep and all."

He laughs. "Nah, we're good."

"All right, cool."

One after another, we press the broken pieces into the wall. Luisa works on the bark of the massive tree. Keith works on the dirt path. I give Ben the jewelweed blossoms; the other art students also get detailed work. I climb a ladder and work down from the sky. Pretty soon, I realize that I will never have enough blacks to fill the entire night sky. After descending the ladder, I stand back from the mosaic to consider the whole image.

"You look just like Mr. M," Janelle says.

I hadn't realized that I had adopted Mr. M's signature pose.

"Do I do that?" Mr. M says.

"Every time," Tristan says.

Everyone laughs except me as I continue to take in the shape of the new concept and the pieces we have to work with.

"What are you thinking?" Ben stands beside me and we both take in the open space of the wall.

"Maybe this girl isn't moving through a night sky. Maybe she's moving from dark into a new day."

He nods. "That would work, and it would bring more color into the whole image."

I draw new lines to show my helpers the latest change. "I want this section to feel like she's moving toward a transformed landscape."

"You want movement and texture," Mr. M says.

"I want swirls and circles."

Ben and I catch each other's eyes and laugh. Mr. M shakes his head and moves to gather new pieces of different colors. Ben doesn't move. I can't tell if he's waiting for something or if I am.

"Thanks," I say. "For coming. For helping me. I know how busy you must be."

"No, this is good. Keeps my hands busy. Keeps me from doing what I'd usually be doing this time of night."

I know that he means getting high, and even though I'm not sure I totally understand the decision that he's made to stay clean, I'm glad that by helping me he feels like I'm helping him too. I gather the pieces that I want and begin pressing pieces into the sky, slowly transitioning it from dead of night to a brilliant sunrise. I speckle the dark sky with pieces of mirror to convey stars, and as we work down, the dark, shining night gives way to purples that lead to dark reds and deep oranges and finally bright yellows. The colors swirl and ripple across the sky, not like how a sunrise looks, but like how a sunrise might actually feel to someone seeing it for the first time.

"We need tunes!" Keith says. Minutes later, music blares from his truck's speakers. The noise brings out Sal, who gestures for me to come over.

"So this is the project you needed to create?" he says.

"Yes." I had cleared it with him, but seeing it up close is a whole other thing. I wait while he takes in the mural.

He nods. "Keep it down out here. I have customers."

"I will."

"What was that about?" Luisa asks after Sal returns to the restaurant.

I gesture to the mosaic. "This isn't exactly what Sal originally wanted on the side of his restaurant."

"What did he want?"

"A nature scene."

"There's nature here."

I burst out laughing. It's the biggest laugh I've let out in so long, and it feels really good.

"You're the best, Lu."

"You're right. I am."

We work like that for the next two weeks. Not everyone comes to help every evening, but at least a couple people come most nights. I work on the mosaic most of every day. Between senior privileges and Mr. M pulling some strings for me, I barely need to show up to school at all. When I stop at home for a shower or a quick meal and Emma asks where I've been, I tell her that I'm working on a big project. In the moments when I'm not hammering plates and pushing tile into the wall, I spend a lot of time imagining what will happen when Mom sees the mosaic. She'll arrive to drop off the materials for her wedding reception and she will be looking directly into my past. Will she recognize it? Will she understand? I have a handful of days before I find out.

On the Wednesday before the art show, the Wednesday before the wedding, when there is nothing left to complete on the mosaic except for the girl's body, I tell everyone that they can go. I need to complete the girl by myself. I'd known that all along. Mr. M and most of the art kids hadn't come, because they were setting up for the art show. Keith offers Luisa a ride home, leaving Ben and me alone.

"This is going to be wow," Ben says.

"That means a lot from you." We've worked side by side for much of the last two weeks. I've been hyperaware of his presence and the way that we gravitate toward each other and then spin away, unsure about our relationship now. We haven't had any big deep conversations, but it has felt right to be creating art with him nearby again.

"She's fierce," Ben says, looking at the empty space where the girl needs to be brought to life.

"Not yet, she's not."

"She is. She's fierce." He's looking at me now.

"It almost seems like you're not talking about the mosaic anymore." I try for a light tone.

"I know what a big deal this is." He gestures to the mural. "Your art was always great, but it was always . . ."

"Small," I finish for him.

"Contained," he says. "This is bold."

"Same goes for you," I say.

"What do you mean?"

"Going on tour. That's bold."

"Yeah, or stupid." He laughs. "Seriously, though. I just couldn't wait anymore."

I look at my beat-up boots and I nod. "Well, I guess I'd better finish."

He rubs a hand over his head. "Right." He gathers his things. "But you'll be there tomorrow night? At the art show?"

This mosaic and my struggle to communicate with my mother have been front and center these last two weeks, but I won't miss the art show. Especially after half the class spent their free time helping me create this mosaic mural.

"Yeah, yeah, I'll be there."

After Ben drives off, I sit cross-legged for a good long time, staring at the mural. I pull in a deep breath and whisper it out slowly. The girl reaches toward something. I don't share her sense of hope, but maybe by finishing this mosaic, I'll be doing some reaching too.

Delicately, I place each piece into the girl's body. Beiges and pinks make up her skin, one arm extended before her toward the sparkling sunrise. Piece by piece, the empty space starts becoming a girl, so that hours later, she is nearly complete. Three spaces remain open in the entire mosaic. In the inner pocket of my backpack, I pull out the bit of jagged blue plate. It's the only physical proof I have of anything Dan's done. With a careful tap of a hammer, the chunk breaks into three pieces. I dab the back with glue, and then with a shaking hand, I press them where they belong, as the girl's eyes and one tiny piece in the center of her heart. Except for the grout, it's finished. Every space is filled with a piece of something shattered. A girl had been broken. I put her back together.

38

What It Looks Like

ON THURSDAY, AFTER finishing the first round of grout on the mosaic, I rush into the art show late. Spotlights and easels have created an art gallery out of our school's gym. The buzz of people chatting fills the air. At the entrance, the charcoal sketches are installed together. Some of my pieces are there—Mr. M's handiwork, no doubt—and Janelle's images of the hands are there. Then, as I'm walking, a series of drawings in vibrant colored pencil stops me in my tracks because they are so good, because they are unmistakably Ben's work, and because three of them feature me. One is me dressed like a warrior, Emma peeking from behind me. He captured her perfectly, even though he doesn't live with her day in and day out like I do. Another is me in charcoal bent over my sketch pad while a spectrum of color flows from my pencil, surrounding me in a rippling aura.

Ben appears beside me and I'm trapped in plain view. "I didn't think you were coming," he says. He rubs his scalp and looks away and then back at me again.

"I told you I was." I point to his sketches. "When did you do these?"

"Mostly at rehab," he says. "But that one"—he points at the one where I'm working on a drawing—"I did that day you were stoned."

"Oh," is all I can squeeze out. So I occupied his thoughts as much as he occupied mine. But that's so opposite of what I thought was going on between us. I peek at him and he's looking at me, the actual me, not the sketches.

"They're good. The shading," I say. I shake my head. I never could nail the shading like Ben could. But that's not why I'm shaking my head. I feel so confused.

"Glad you like." Ben smiles at me.

"They are definitely an interesting interpretation of reality." I'm not smiling.

The last drawing is of me sleeping on a bed of leaves in a forest. Trees rise up around me, protecting me, and the sky teems with butterflies in impossible colors. A vibrant blue one perches on my shoulder.

"They are . . . how I see you," he says in a halting voice, absent his usual confidence and wit.

I strangle the paper art show program in my hand. How can he do this? Come in and pretend that we're normal, that we're the same, when he's changed so much, when he's just biding his time until he leaves again.

"Then I guess you're not looking clearly," I say, and my tone is sharp enough to cut.

"I'm looking," he says. "I've never stopped looking."

His words and his voice are low and intimate and I know we aren't talking about sketches anymore. Before, my body would have responded the way it has to so many boys. My body would want to press against him. My lips would want to kiss his neck. My arms would want to pull Ben so close that there would be no end of me, no beginning of him. That was when I craved the feeling of losing myself in someone else.

But I'm finished with defining myself by who wants me or by how I look. I thought Ben saw me, the real me. Not just the parts that the other boys see. I turn to Ben and open my mouth to try to make words in the shape of my feelings. He looks at me, waiting.

"That's not me." I'm surprised by how much my voice is shaking. "I'm not a fantasy girl in armor or a girl living in a fairy realm. I'm a real person. This isn't real." I gesture with my arm to the sketches.

Ben looks like I've stabbed him in the gut. "That's not—"

"Skye!" Mr. M calls me from across the room.

"Got to go," I say, walking away before I can stop myself.

Mr. M introduces me to Ms. Grugan, a friend of his who runs a nonprofit or something. I'm not really listening because I'm confused and conflicted about Ben's drawings.

". . . so, I showed her photos of your mosaic," Mr. M is saying.

"What?"

"Your mural. I took photos and shared them with her. Her

group mostly creates murals with paint, but she loved your work."

"You create murals?" I push my thoughts away and focus on the conversation. I hadn't expected to get so much out of creating public art, and I'm excited to talk to someone who does it for a living.

Ms. Grugan smiles at me like she's happy I decided to engage in the conversation. A halo of blond curls springs from her head. Blue eyes are framed by cat-eye glasses. "My nonprofit works to beautify neighborhoods. We recruit local kids to help. Keeps them out of trouble and allows us to create art."

"Well, you'd have plenty to do in our town," I mumble. I wonder if Ms. Grugan realizes that she's talking to one of the kids who gets herself into trouble. Then I think about how I've felt creating the Post-it murals and then the mosaic mural and how I didn't need to get high or drunk to feel good.

"It seems that you already made a start," Ms. Grugan says.

"I don't know if it's beautification though."

"Well, it's better than a blank wall, and your art has something to say."

"You think my art has something to say?"

She widens her eyes. "You doubt that?"

"No, I mean, I know what *I* wanted to say, but it's hard to figure out if other people get it."

Ms. Grugan nods. "That's always true. There's the art we create and the experience of the art through the viewer's eyes. At some point you need to let go and allow your art to speak to those who choose to pay attention."

That sounds like a big idea that I'm not ready to digest, but I'm definitely interested in her work, so I ask more questions. I eat up all that she shares with me.

After a while, I say, "I've hogged so much of your time."

"It was a pleasure to meet you," she says. "I hope that you'll get my contact information from Christopher if you'd like to talk more."

I nod, even though it's very weird to hear Mr. M called by his first name. Ms. Grugan walks away and when Ben starts toward me, I make an early exit, like the coward that I am.

I can't deal with Ben and his fantasies of me right now.

When I arrive home, Mom is nowhere to be found. I hear voices upstairs, so I go up to look for Emma.

"Like this," Dan is saying. He stands behind Emma, both of them facing the full-length mirror in Mom's bedroom. Emma is wearing the rose dress that she and Mom selected for the wedding. Dan is leaning down and looks over Emma's shoulder at her reflection in the mirror. He holds Emma's hair at the nape of her neck. "You'll look beautiful if you wear it like this."

Time slips back six years. Dan is holding my long hair at the nape of my neck. He tells me that it will be sexy if I wear it like that. Fear zips from my scalp down my spine and out my fingers.

"Get away from her."

They both turn toward me. A smile is sliding from Emma's face and confusion takes its place. Dan looks caught.

"I thought you had an art show tonight," Dan says.

"Yeah, what are you doing here?" Emma is still angry with me.

"Where's Mom?"

"At the store. She just left."

"What are you doing?" I say.

"Trying on my dress for the wedding," Emma says in a *duh* tone. "What does it look like?"

"Not you," I say to Emma. "Dan, what are you doing?"

"Emma wanted to try on her dress. I was just—"

"You told me to try on the dress!" Emma interrupts Dan. "You said that you wanted to see it before the wedding."

My entire body is shaking. "Move away from my little sister."

"Skylar, I don't appreciate the tone you're taking right now. It's disrespectful and—"

"I want you to leave."

Dan pulls himself to his full height, which isn't all that tall, and crosses his arms over his chest. "Excuse me?"

"I want you to leave my house."

"Young lady, you are being inappropriate and I—"

"I'm being inappropriate? Get out of my house or we're leaving."

"Skye?" Emma says.

"Emma." I catch her eye and plead. "Please."

Emma looks from me to Dan. Maybe it's my pleading tone or maybe our sister bond is able to break through her anger at me. She takes a step toward me.

Dan takes in a deep breath. "Skye, this isn't—"

"Em, we need to leave now."

Emma looks scared now. "Have you been drinking?"

"No! Emma, no. I haven't been drinking. Please, please just come with me."

The memories from before with Dan are closing in around me. I back out of the room. I can't be in the bedroom anymore. I know I'm not wrong about what happened. I've never been wrong.

"Skye, are you okay?" Emma asks.

"No, I'm not okay and I need you to come with me."

Emma and I leave Mom's bedroom. Dan does not follow. We start down the steps. My heart thumps. I'm afraid he'll stop me. I remember the tent. His hands on me. His weight on me.

"Skye?"

"Come on!"

"I don't have shoes!"

I grab a pair of Uggs sitting by the door and yank the door open. I look to the stairs, waiting for Dan to come, but he does not appear. We rush to Lucy. I open the passenger door for Emma. I look back to the house. No Dan. I climb into the driver's seat and lock the doors. I'm shaking all over. I don't know if I can drive. Emma is sitting in the passenger seat, staring at me. She's shivering. I pull off my hoodie and hand it to her. I crank up the heat.

We pull out of the parking space and Dan still has not emerged from the house.

"Where are we going?"

"Not sure yet."

I drive around our neighborhood until my heart returns almost to its normal rhythm.

"Are you okay?" I say.

"Yeah," Emma says. "Are you?"

"I mean, did Dan . . . do anything? To you?" I ask.

"No! Skye, what are you talking about?"

"I'm just . . . I'll explain. I need a minute, okay?"

I drive some more. I think about Ben asking me to come to the art show. He wanted me to see those drawings. He wanted his art to tell me something, even if I didn't like what it told me. I think about Ms. Grugan telling me that my art has something to say. I created the whole mosaic to say something to my mother that I hadn't known how to tell her. Now I know. I pull over to the side of the road and send a text.

"Where are we going now?" Emma asks.

"Sal's."

"Why did you ask me that about Dan?"

My words work to break down the wall that's been up for so many years. "Dan . . . he's not . . . safe."

Emma is silent. We pull into the parking lot.

"Is that the important project?" Emma asks as we pass by the mosaic.

I nod.

We park Lucy and I rest my head on the steering wheel. Emma touches my arm. A few minutes later, Mom's car pulls in and she parks next to me. We both get out of our cars.

"What's going on? Are you two okay?" Mom asks. Her brows wrinkle in concern.

"Mom, I need to show you something," I say.

I lean into the car. "Emma, you should probably come too."

I don't know if what I'm about to do is the right thing. All I know is that I need to do it. I've tried to use words and they failed. We walk to the mural. I feel the cut glass of my mosaic churning in my stomach, as if I'd swallowed the shards.

"This is what I've been working on," I say.

"It's big," Mom says.

"I didn't do it alone. I've had a lot of help."

I watch Mom and Emma stare at the image of the girl moving toward a new dawn. Leaves of poison ivy litter the path of her past. Jewelweed perches before her.

Mom steps toward the mosaic. "Is that our Whomping Willow?"

I nod.

"When it was struck by lightning?"

I nod again.

"Why did you put that in your mosaic?"

The world shifts and slants beneath my feet. I'm twelve again, trying to find the words. I press a hand to my stomach.

Emma turns from the mosaic to me.

I pull in air to speak. I look at Emma, who is still studying me. She might hate me more after these words explode her version of the perfect family. A car pulls in, and we need to step aside so that they can drive by. This isn't the ideal time or place. But I tried getting

Mom to talk about it when we were alone and she wouldn't. The wedding is in two days. We are out of time.

"I know you've never believed what I told you, but it was true."

"What didn't I believe?"

Mom looks like she has no idea what I'm talking about.

"What happened to me. That time we were camping."

Emma grabs my hand.

Mom's brow furrows. "Something happened at the campground?" I hear doubt in my mother's tone. The cut glass grinds harder. I've been trying to protect Emma from the truth, but maybe the way to protect my little sister is to make sure she knows what happened to me—what could happen to her.

"I told you. That night. But you didn't believe me."

Mom crosses her arms over her chest. She lets out a sigh. "I don't know what—" Mom starts to say. I can see her building her wall.

"Mom," Emma says. "Let Skye speak."

Mom quiets and looks to me.

"When I was Emma's age," I begin. My mother's eyes are on me, unwavering. Emma is by my side. "When I was Emma's age," I say again. I try to say more, but I can't.

I try to pull in air. My breath comes in ragged gasps. I can't get enough air into my lungs. I sound like a trapped animal. Tears flood my cheeks.

Mom reaches out to put her arm around my shoulders, but I shake my head and step back. I need to get these words out and my mother's hug will only make it more difficult.

"What is it?" Mom says, peering into my eyes.

I brush the tears away and work to control my breathing so that I can speak.

"That one time we went camping around my birthday. When I'd just turned twelve?"

Mom nods.

"It was just us four. Mac and Judy didn't come," I say.

"There was a thunderstorm," Mom adds. "And that tree was hit by lightning."

"Emma wanted you to sleep with her," I say. "Because of the storm."

"Yes," Mom says, but I'm not sure she really remembers that part.

"That night. In the tent with Dan." I stop. I close my eyes. I steady my breathing. "Mom, he touched me."

I open my eyes. Mom's concerned eyes are still on me. "Touched you? What do you mean?"

"He touched me . . . under my pj's. All over." My shame forces these words into a whisper.

Emma squeezes my hand. I hadn't realized we were still holding hands. Mom rears back from me. Her hand goes to her mouth. She grimaces, looking at the gravel road and then back at me. "But I was there," she says, like what I'm saying is impossible.

"You were asleep."

Mom stares beyond me at the mosaic, seeking confirmation of my past in tiny broken pieces of plates and tile and glass.

"You never told me."

"I tried. After it happened. I came into the tent with you and Emma, but . . ."

"Go on."

I glance at Emma and breathe. "I told you, but you . . . didn't believe me. You told me he was hugging me and said to go back to sleep."

Mom doesn't say anything for a long moment. Her face is at war with itself. She looks like she's been ripped apart from the inside. "I don't remember that."

"You don't remember me telling you?"

Mom bites her lip, trying not to cry, and shakes her head.

All this time, I thought that she remembered and denied that it happened. But she didn't. She didn't remember any of it. Maybe not remembering is better than not believing. Except the result is still the same—I've carried the fact of what happened along with the shame for all these years.

Mom covers her eyes with one hand, holding her other arm across her stomach like I was just doing moments ago. "I can't . . . I don't understand."

"I've tried to talk to you again recently," I say. "But you wouldn't listen."

Mom shakes her head, as if to clear it. "I can't . . . I've got to go."

My stomach clenches like I've been punched. She can't do this again. "Mom, I'm telling the truth. You can't—"

"Not here, Skye." She starts walking and then turns. "Emma, come on."

Emma grabs my hand again. "No, I'm staying with Skye."

39

What Was Lost

WHEN EMMA AND I walk in the door, Mom is already sitting at the kitchen table with a glass of wine that is still mostly full.

"Is Dan still here?" I ask, pausing by the front door. If Dan is here, Emma and I won't be.

Mom shakes her head. "I told him to leave."

I shut the door behind me and lock it, and then I lock the dead bolt too.

"Em, I need to talk to your sister alone, okay?" Mom says.

Emma looks at me and I nod. After Emma has gone up to her bedroom, Mom leaves her wine on the table and sits on the couch.

"Back there, it was shocking to hear that."

I look at her without saying anything. I'd tried to tell her in a private place and she hadn't listened.

"All this time, I thought you knew and that you didn't believe me."

"Can we start from the beginning?" she asks.

I nod.

"Do you want to sit?"

I curl myself into the corner of the couch, opposite her. I pull my knees to my chest and wrap my arms around them. Before an hour ago, I hadn't said these words out loud since I was twelve years old. Now I need to say them for the second time. I tell her again about the camping and the rain and the thunder and the tent. And Dan.

After a long while, Mom rises from the couch. She paces, twists the ring that remains on her left finger. She looks at me and away.

"And I told you he was hugging you?"

I nod.

"But he wasn't."

I can see that she wishes that Dan was hugging me that night and that I was just confused, but she needs to understand that he molested me.

"Mom," I say. It's so hard, but I make myself say the words. "His hands were under my pajama top and down my pants. He laid on top of me . . . until he was finished."

She pulls in a sharp intake of air. "Did he . . . ? He didn't . . . ?"

"No, no. He just laid on top of me."

"And that night, when I told you that he was hugging you, I'd been drinking."

"You were very drunk." I don't say it like I'm making an excuse for her. I say it like the fact that it is.

Then I tell her other things, things that don't seem too bad or wrong by themselves, but when you place each fragment together, a picture emerges.

"These other things that Dan did that made you feel uncomfortable." She says it like a statement. She's confirming what I've already told her.

"I remember that I would feel weird, but I knew he loved us and I hadn't really had a dad around, so I wasn't sure that what he was doing was wrong," I say in a small voice. "Until the tent."

"He told you how to wear your hair?" she says. "Why did that feel weird to you?"

"He told me how to wear it so that I would look sexy."

"When you were only in fifth grade." She pauses. "Is that why you cut it?"

I nod. "And that's why tonight . . . I needed to get Emma away from him and I needed to find a way to show you because you wouldn't listen when I tried to talk. He was doing the same exact thing with Emma when I walked in. He asked her to try on her dress and was telling her how to wear her hair. It's not right, Mom."

Mom looks away from me, wounded. Part of me wishes I had never opened my mouth because wrenching this truth out of my heart and wedging it into the space between us is hard. It hurts. But the other part of me knows that the truth was already wedged between us, living in our shadows. It had to come out into the light.

Mom looks at me, tears shining in her eyes. She shrugs in a helpless way. "I keep trying to remember you coming to me. But I don't." She shakes her head and says it again. "I don't remember."

She stands there, her hands covering her face, so different from my supercompetent mother. She steps toward me and kneels on the floor next to the couch where I remain curled. She reaches out her arms and stops, checking with her eyes to be sure it's okay. I lean toward her and she folds me into her body.

We weep as the truth tumbles over both of us and roars into the still air of the living room. And in the end, she touches my face and brushes my hair from my eyes.

"My beautiful, beautiful Skye," she says, and I hear in her voice that after all these years, after all the times I tried, she has finally heard me. She knows what's been stolen.

What happened cannot be undone—neither what Dan did nor how Mom dismissed it—but I've finally been heard. I don't know what I expected from letting the words out. My Teflon coating has been peeled off; I'm all tender skin and raw emotion. I'm the girl in my mosaic, emerging into the light after so long in the dark.

The next afternoon, I find Emma folding origami flowers on her bed. She glances at me and then back to her fingers folding paper. In colored pencils, she'd be *My Heart Whole*.

"I know the wedding's off, but I like making these flowers."

I climb onto the other end of her twin bed. I pick up a piece of paper and start folding, but my flower ends up being an airplane. "Thanks for last night, Em. For sticking by me."

After a long silence, Emma speaks. "Why didn't you ever tell me?"

I stop folding. I've asked myself a similar question for so long. "I hadn't told anyone. Ever. I didn't totally understand it when it happened. Dan acted like a father. Then he did this thing to me. And acted like it never happened. Maybe he didn't even remember that it happened. I don't know. But I didn't know how to handle it. So, I just didn't. I kept it deep inside. I guess I was ashamed."

"I wish you would've told me."

"I wish I would've too."

"Just so you know, I know about that stuff. I know not to let anyone touch me."

"I thought that too," I say. The school teaches you about stranger danger, but not about the danger that could be in your own house or how scary it is when someone who you trust does things that you don't understand. And how easy it is to think that you caused it somehow.

"I'm glad you know what happened." I fold another corner and then another.

We keep folding; the only sound in the room is the soft noise of fingers folding paper into flowers.

"I'm still a little mad at you for what happened at the party."

I stare at the lopsided rose emerging from my flat piece of paper and I nod. "I know."

"I mean, I get why you took me there. Especially now. But you still left me alone and went off and drank."

My eyes meet hers. "Definitely suboptimal sister behavior."

We fold in silence for a while. She's made three flowers in the time it's taken me to make one.

"I love you, Skye. Even when you're suboptimal."

"Love you too, Emma." I think to call her Butter Bean, but she's not a little kid anymore.

"Froyo later?" I ask, sailing my airplane toward her.

"If you're lucky."

"I'm feeling lucky." I get up to head toward the door.

"Wait," she says. "Come here."

She tucks the rose into my hair before I leave.

I touch the paper rose. "You know, my birthday is coming up. I wonder if the fairies might leave me some paper flowers?"

She smiles at me. "You never know."

40

AFTER: I am thirteen.
Late May of seventh grade

ON MY FIRST birthday after Dan is gone, on the day I turn thirteen, I wake to a fairyland. My brand-new basement bedroom, which Mac had built as my early birthday present from Mom, is decorated with silk flowers, tiny lights, and little globes. A trail of flower petals leads from my room, up the steps and into the living room, which is no longer a living room. Flowers and butterflies perch on photographs, the television, the couch. Streams of garland weave through the banisters and crisscross the ceiling. Tiny jeweled boxes sit on the coffee table. Mom smiles at me from the red couch. It's the first time I've seen her smile in a while. Emma curls next to her, sleepy.

"Happy birthday, sweetheart."

"Happy birthday, Skye!" Emma adds.

"What is all this?" I ask in wonder.

Mom shakes her head, as if she's wondering too. "I guess the birthday fairies came to decorate for you this year."

"Momma, why do you think they came this year?" Emma says.

"Because they knew we needed some joy, Butter Bean." Mom squeezes Emma and holds out her other arm for me. Even though I am officially a teenager, I plop on the couch and lean into her body, feeling her familiar shape, her comforting warmth pressing back into me. She places a wreath of flowers with streaming silk ribbons in blues, greens, and purples on my head.

"I love you girls," she says. "More than anything."

"Love you too," Emma and I respond.

Dan's been gone a few months and it's been just us three again. It has been a full year since the tent, and Mom has never brought up what I'd told her that night. But ever since Dan had left, I've felt safer. And now that some time has passed, Mom seems a little less sad.

"What do you want for your birthday dinner tonight?" Mom asks.

"Hunan Garden," I say.

"Great, I'll make the special tea," Mom says.

"In the tiny cups," Emma says.

"Exactly," I say. "You know what we should do today?"

"What?" they both say.

"We should paint my room."

"That's what you want to do on your birthday?" Mom asks.

"Yeah, but not just regular paint. I want to do designs and stuff."

"I can paint too?" Emma asks.

"Of course!"

"Let me make the pancakes first and then we'll tackle painting."

"With chocolate chips!" I say.

"And M&M's," Emma says.

"Ew," Mom says. "But okay. For the birthday girl." She kisses me and Emma on our heads before she rises from the couch. "My beautiful girls," she says and smiles.

41

Cards on the Table

ON SATURDAY MORNING, I text Luisa and ask if I can pick her up early for our shift so that we can talk. Of course she says yes because she's the kick-assiest of kick-ass friends. But before I leave, I need to make one more call.

I stare at my phone for a long time before I call Ben. "Can we talk?"

"That's what friends are for." His voice is gravelly with sleep.

I consider the feelings that I thought would go away but seem to keep growing. Ben has definitely confused me with what feels like a push-pull, but Luisa is right. It's time to come clean about how I feel—no matter what—and he's given me the perfect opening.

"Is that what we are?" I ask. "Just friends?"

He's quiet. "I don't know."

"Could we get together?" I ask. "There's some stuff I need to say."

"Want to go to the quarry?" he asks.

A zing of anticipation quickens my heartbeat. "You're kidding, right?"

"I'm not. It's actually really nice during the day."

I think about the many nights we've been at the quarry drunk and high. Me with some guy and him with some girl. I'm not sure that's where I want to go to talk with Ben.

"I'll pick you up. We'll go for a ride." His voice is low and tempting, like the old Ben, and I think for a moment that maybe we'll get high, maybe he's his old self again. "Or a walk," he says in that new shiny voice of his. "We could go for a walk."

We are definitely not getting high. "A walk? Seriously?"

"No, probably not," he concedes.

Neither of us speaks for a moment. Ben starts humming a song that's playing in the background, like he's got all day for me to answer him. His voice in my ear is air in my lungs. I'm not sure what him being clean means for a friendship that revolved around bongs and tequila bottles. I close my eyes and let my lungs fill with air and then empty again.

"I have to work," I say. "Four o'clock at Sal's?"

"I'll be there."

After I pick up Luisa, we drive to Sal's but stay in Lucy so that I can explain to her what happened to me, all while facing the mosaic that she helped me create and that allowed me to finally speak my truth. She nods a lot and squeezes my hand during the hard parts and when I'm finished, she pulls me to her in the tightest hug ever.

"Lu, need . . . oxygen," I croak.

Luisa loosens her grip, and I can see that her eyes are wet with tears.

"I knew something happened. I knew it way back then. That there was something weird," she says, wiping her eyes. "But I didn't know how to talk to you about it or how to get you to talk about it."

"We were kids. That wasn't our job," I say, because that's what I'm learning—that I wasn't at fault for what happened that night or for what happened after. "You were always there for me though."

"And you for me."

"Love you, Lu." I smile at her and offer a balled-up Kleenex that I find in my bag.

"Always." She looks at the Kleenex. "Ew," she says, and tosses it on the floor.

"Hey!" I say. "Respect Lucy."

Lu holds out her pinkie, and I lock mine with hers. We rest our foreheads together, looking into each other's eyes.

"Ready to sling some pancakes?" I ask.

"I'm ready to collect some tips," she says. "College parties aren't going to pay for themselves."

When my shift is over, I change in the women's room and wait outside for Ben. I offer a small smile as I get into Freddie, but I can't be happy. Not yet. I need to say what I need to say and see how he takes it. So, I'm quiet on the drive to the quarry. Ben plays music and glances at me from time to time. I don't feel up to small talk when this giant thing is sitting in the car with us. I rest my head against the window and watch the scenery roll by. He parks in an unfamiliar spot.

"I haven't been here before," I say.

"Yeah, places. I had to find some new ones."

He lowers the volume on the tunes and turns toward me. I'm struck by how different this is from the night I'd called him to come get me after Dan came back into our lives—and yet how similar too.

"So, those sketches," I say.

"Yeah." His face is serious, no doubt from the blow I dealt him last night. "I didn't mean for you to take them the way that you did."

"But there are feelings?"

He looks at me, and I see hope in his eyes. "There are."

"Since when?"

He looks up at the ceiling of the car. "Art Three?"

"Two years ago?" I feel like an idiot that I didn't see this sooner.

He nods. "Remember that picture we drew together on the first day?"

"The Disco Elephant? How could I forget? She'd accidentally trampled her dance partner." I laugh at the memory.

He laughs too. "Our acclaimed collaboration on Disco Elephant was the moment." He fiddles with the bracelet that he still wears. "What about you?" he asks without looking at me.

It's time to stop hiding from the reality that I've been fighting. "There are feelings."

"Since when?"

"Remember that night at your house when you pulled me down onto you?"

He nods, frowning a little bit. No doubt he's remembering what I did later that night.

"That was the first night I almost gave in. But the feelings started way before that. I remember feeling jealous of Kelsey last summer. That was a surprise."

He rests his hand between us, palm upturned. I let my fingers be enfolded in his and squeeze. He squeezes back. "After Kelsey was when I decided to stop messing around. Remember I asked you to make me this bracelet?" He holds his wrist up.

I frown and nod.

"That was like a promise I was making to myself. I knew I wanted to be with you and if I wasn't with you, I'd be alone. But then when I went to rehab, I couldn't talk to you or see you. I told myself that after I got out, I'd stop dicking around. I knew you were scared, but I was going to show you how I felt—not just hint and wait for you to figure it out."

My mouth wants to spread into a grin at the realization that Ben wanted me for all that time as a girlfriend, not a hookup. Then I think of Ashton and all of the others. "But I didn't make it easy."

"I guess neither of us did."

"And now you're clean," I say.

He meets my eyes, and I feel the same way as the night that we were both wasted—like no boy has ever looked at me in this way before—but this time our eyes are clear.

"Is that the worst thing?"

My heart somersaults in my rib cage not only from knowing how much he feels for me, but also because I imagine how hard it was for him to see me hook up with random guys. I let go of his hand.

"That night that you got arrested," I say. "There's something you should know."

Ben keeps his eyes on me while I try to pull up the courage to tell him the truth. He might decide not to see me anymore, but I've got to come clean. I'm starting to think that secrets are poison.

"So, a long time ago, way before I met you, when I was just a kid, Dan . . . we were camping and he . . . I woke up and he was . . . touching me. In a way he shouldn't." My fingers twist in my lap and I stare at them so that I don't look in Ben's eyes. "I told my mom, but she didn't believe me or couldn't believe me. Either way, I didn't know how to handle it, so I just pushed it way down and tried not to think about it. Ever."

Ben doesn't say a word. I'm certain that I grossed him out and that he doesn't want such damaged goods. Then he reaches over and rests his hand on my wrist. His beautiful hand with its long fingers that pull magic from a guitar. I stop my hands from fidgeting. He twines his fingers in mine.

"Thanks for trusting me," he whispers.

I nod because I'm not capable of much more. He squeezes my hand.

I take a breath. "There's one more thing."

"Okay," he says.

I look at him this time. "The night of the concert? When we were at Shelby's house?"

He nods at me.

"I was very wasted," I say. "And I sort of threw myself at you?"

Ben looks down. "It was a rough night."

I disentangle my hand from his and turn to face him more fully in the small confines of the car.

"Then I told you that our promise meant nothing." I wait to gauge his reaction.

"Like I said—rough night."

"I spent the next four weeks assuming that you were disgusted by me and that our friendship was over."

"Not disgusted."

I rub my hands on my thighs.

He touches me on the shoulder. "Skye."

I look at Ben.

"Not ever disgusted." His eyes are earnest.

Mine jump away, unable to hold his gaze.

"And also, you didn't break our promise."

"Wait, how do you know that?" I turn back to look at him and catch a smile forming on his lips.

"You don't remember what you said after that."

I frown a question at him.

"You put your jacket back on, stomped your feet, and said something along the lines of 'Fine, I'll keep our stupid fucking promise.' And then you walked off."

I smile back and then my eyes drop to my lap. "At your welcome back party, you acted like you didn't remember."

"I wasn't sure you were ready to go there."

"But you seemed like you didn't want to have anything to do with me."

"I was freaked. I'd been in rehab for four weeks. Not talking to you—or anyone—and then I show up and there's a keg and Jell-O shots and weed and . . . I couldn't stay. It wasn't you."

"But it was. I planned most of that party. I thought you'd want all those things."

"I get that you thought that. Things are just a little different now. But I'm still me."

He's still Ben, but he's not. Then again, I'm still Skye, but I'm not. Telling my mom, making sure she believed me after all this time, has changed me. Like maybe I don't need that Teflon coating anymore. But it's not like everything is perfect now just because I spoke the truth.

"I can't be your fantasy girl."

"I'm not looking for a fantasy."

"I still have a lot to figure out," I say.

"Me too," he says.

When I get back, Mom and I talk again. She needs to speak to Dan and wonders if I want to say anything to him. Speaking my truth to Mom was what I needed, so I tell her no, I don't want to see him again. When she returns, she looks tired, but she's not crying.

"Did you talk to him?" I ask.

She nods.

"What did he say?"

She looks at me and there is sadness in her eyes. "He denied everything."

"But—"

Mom hugs me to her. "I believe you, Skye," she says, "and it was good that we met in a public place because I'm not sure what I would have done to him if we were in private."

I want to say I'm sorry, but finally I don't have anything to be sorry for. This happened to me. I didn't cause it. Even though it's so many years later, it feels good to hear Mom stand up for me. That's what I needed all along.

"We'll get through it," I say.

"We will because the Murray girls are strong."

"Yeah, we are."

I hug Mom one more time and then I let go.

On Monday, we're all back in school. With everything that's happened, I feel like my whole world is different, but for everyone else, it's just another Monday after another weekend. The main difference is that this time when Ben and I walk into school together, we're holding hands. Somehow, it doesn't cause the earthquake that I expect. Except for Luisa. She starts cheering by the lockers.

That afternoon, I stop in to see Mr. M. "Do you have a minute?"

"Sure." Mr. M gestures for me to come into his office.

"That lady you introduced me to the other night? She runs a nonprofit?"

"Yes, the Mural Arts Initiative."

"I think I might want to volunteer."

"Oh?"

I nod. "I'm thinking of taking a gap year and working at a non-profit doing public art."

"That's a big decision. Have you talked it over with your family?"

I tell Mr. M that I have. The three of us spent the whole weekend together. Emma tried to cheer up Mom and me by playing old movies and singing the soundtracks as loud as she could. Mom and I did our best, but she was devastated over what happened and I was still raw from the telling.

Mom helped me put my art workspace back together and she'd asked again about the deposit. I'd told her that as much as I wanted to go to MICA, I thought I needed to be home a little longer. It was Mom who mentioned the idea that I look into deferring. I'd e-mailed MICA in the morning to ask about deferral and what would happen with my scholarship. They'd let me know to still put down the deposit and that deferral was definitely an option, as long as I could show that I was doing something that would offer significant impact to me and/or to the world around me. If I could show that, they'd keep my scholarship intact. I'd thought of the mural arts program right away.

Mr. M says that he'll call Ms. Grugan on my behalf and let me know what happens. When I leave Mr. M's office, I feel lighter than I have in months.

42

Falling Is Sort of Like Flying

A MONTH AFTER the wedding that wasn't, I call Ben. It's a blue-sky Saturday and I want to spend it with him. I want to spend most days with Ben, and ever since the drive and our talk, that's what we do. He's finished recording, but he's decided to stay clean. A day at a time, he says. I'm still not so sure if that's the right path for me, but Mom is keeping me on a short leash. What happened with Dan doesn't excuse taking Emma to a party and being unable to drive her home.

I never imagined that I could have fun with Ben and not be high or drunk, but maybe that's because we'd never tried. Now, we're taking things slowly. If he's been impatient with me for not jumping in with the physical stuff, he's never let on. We hold hands a lot and he puts his arm around me sometimes. But never in my back pocket. Ben picks up on the second ring.

"Ready?" I ask.

"I will be," he says. "Lu coming?"

"She's already in the car."

"Cool. See you soon."

I pick up Ben and we all drive to my new project. Well, it's not *mine* exactly, but it feels like mine. Ms. Grugan was enthusiastic about me volunteering with her organization, and after talking through our ideas, we both figured we might as well get started sooner rather than later. She especially liked that I came with a built-in team. We are working on the wall of a building not far from Sal's on Pennswood Pike. This time, we're working mostly with paint, which I've found is much less likely to cut me than mosaic pieces. On the other hand, most of my clothes are paint-colored now. Not long after we arrive, Keith joins us. I can't tell if he's found a sudden love of art or if he's crushing on Luisa, but it's great to have extra hands.

Lu and I thought of the design for this one, and Ms. Grugan was on board all the way. She liked the idea of merging media. We'd finished transferring the design to the wall last night and I can't wait to add color and bring the whole idea to life. I pull supplies from the back of Lucy while Keith sets up ladders. Luisa and I stand back to check the drawing I've made before we start painting.

"It's going to be spectabulous," Lu says.

I look at the images of girls and women, each one different from the next, holding hands and encircling a huge mosaic mirror. Beneath the mirror, painted on a tile are the words *I AM*, and surrounding those two words are pieces of an old school chalkboard where people can fill in what they are that day: amazing, sad, ambitious, loved, beautiful, broken, passionate, worried, hopeful, and so on forever.

"Spectabulous for sure."

Hours later when we're all tired, we start to pack up. Keith offers Luisa a ride home, so she and I hug good-bye while Ben loads Lucy with our supplies.

"Quarry?" I say to Ben when we are buckled into Lucy.

"Of course," he says, but there's no way that he knows what I have planned. I've been thinking about it for a while now.

I drive to our new spot, the one that doesn't hold old memories for either of us. He pulls a blanket and a picnic basket from the back of Lucy. We walk down a bit and Ben stops, but I keep walking.

"Farther?" Ben asks.

"I want to be completely private."

He follows me down a neglected path until I duck beneath willow branches into a secluded area near the water.

"This place is like a secret," Ben says.

"Our secret," I say.

"I made dinner," Ben says as he starts pulling items from a bag.

I laugh when I see the array of store-bought foods. Sour Cream & Onion potato chips. Brown Sugar Pop-Tarts. A few clementines. And two root beers.

"Okay, you know all my favorite things. But the root beers?"

He twists the top off one and hands it to me. "If you can't have the real thing . . ."

"Got it."

After we finish the gourmet meal, Ben pulls his guitar from the case and starts strumming.

"You have your sketchbook?" he says, like he knows the answer.

"Always."

He smiles at me. "Want to play?"

"I do," I say, pulling out my pastels. I already have an idea.

"No charcoal today?"

"It's time for a change."

Ben starts strumming.

"Is that new?" I ask as my hand moves across the page, grabbing one color and then the next to put on paper what I want to convey.

"Yeah," he says, still playing. "Something I was messing around with in rehab."

"It's beautiful. I like that chord change."

"You do?"

I hear the smile in his voice even though I'm not looking at him. Sitting there on an itchy blanket with the sun winking through green leaves, I think back to Mr. M telling me to follow my instincts. I'd thought that they'd always gotten me into trouble, but I see that was just fear pushing me toward whatever would numb me.

Now, even though I feel nervous, I also feel ready. I finish my sketch and hand it to Ben without speaking.

"I kept your curls in this one," I say eventually. "I miss them."

He holds the sketch like he's inhaling it, and I feel my face warming. I wait, watching Ben.

"You miss my curls, huh?" He grins and lets the paper float to the ground. He grabs my fingers in his and runs his thumb across my palm, sending a current up my wrist and to every nerve in my entire body. I squeeze his fingers in response.

"So . . . this is happening?"

"This is happening," I whisper.

"In that case, I need both hands."

I can't help but giggle even though the butterflies in my belly are doing nosedives. Ben sets his guitar down and then he's on both knees facing me. We are so close that I see the flecks of gold in his smiling eyes. His hands hover around my face, like he's not sure if it's okay to touch me. His eyes drop to my mouth and then up to my eyes again.

"I won't break," I say.

I'm choosing this. Being with Ben is a step toward believing that I'm allowed to take up space in this world, not for the pleasure of others, but for myself. It's a step toward believing that maybe, just maybe, I can turn the damaged parts of me into something new.

I press his hand to my cheek and then turn my face to kiss his palm. Then I bite it, just to let him know that I'm still me.

"Ow!" he says, snatching his hand away. "I'll get you for that."

He tackles me and we tumble down to the blanket, both of us laughing. I place both hands on his cheeks.

"I knew this would be fun with you," I say.

"You thought about this?"

"You know I did."

"I just like to hear you admit it."

My eyes seek out his for a fraction of eternity before we lean in. Our lips brush against each other feather soft. Then they melt together. Gently at first and then with more urgency. He takes my lower lip between both of his. I lick his upper lip. I imagine how I'd sketch us: *The World's First Kiss* because that's how it feels to me, like I've never kissed another boy ever. Not like this.

We adjust so that we are lying on the blanket facing each other. He brushes my hair from my face and his lips wander from my temple to the corner of my mouth. His hand skims down my shoulder and then back up, cupping my face. I slide my hand beneath his shirt and delight in the feel of his skin on my palm.

"Can you take this off?" I ask, tugging at his T-shirt.

He sits up and pulls it over his head, tossing it to the side. He lies on his back, one arm behind his head, watching me as my hands explore the planes of his body.

"I can't tell if you want to kiss me or draw me," he says.

I giggle. "Both?" I lean down and kiss his chest while my fingers walk toward his belly button, where I trace circles. He groans.

"Skye . . ."

"What?" I say, leaving a path of kisses up his neck and landing on his lips. I'm not doing this to avoid my feelings or because I think that's all I'm good for. This is me connecting with Ben in a way that I truly want.

"I'm trying to act cool, but I'm pretty much dying right now."

"Do you want me to stop?"

"No, but . . ."

I lean over him and look him in the eyes.

"I want this," I say. "Do you want this?"

"Yes."

"Good." I kiss him on the mouth and his arms pull me closer. His hand finds its way beneath my tank top and his fingers raise goose bumps as they move up my back until he reaches my bra clasp. His hand stills.

"Are you sure?" he asks.

"I'm sure." Those words seem to give him the permission he needs. He unclasps my bra, not like it's a sport, but like he's opening a gift. He explores my body like I explored his until I'm the one dying. I help him put on a condom and then I lie back, looking up at him bracing himself over me.

"I hope no one wanders down here just now." He grins.

"No one will find us here."

I close my eyes as he slides in, and it's electric blueredyellowsilver fireworks in a star-studded sky and it's the feeling of finding your way home after a long, black night.

Later, Ben looks at me like he's just discovered something remarkable. He's been looking at me like that a lot lately. I hope that I get used to it. He kisses me at the corner of my mouth.

"I've wanted to kiss you there for about twenty-seven months." His eyes crinkle with a smile. "Since the time we drew Disco

Elephant. The first time I noticed your dimple."

I smile back and kiss his neck, just below his ear. "You've waited a long time."

"I have. And to make up for lost time, I'd like to kiss your dimple often, with your permission, of course."

"You have my permission." I tuck myself into him and close my eyes.

I wake a little while later to someone rubbing my back. I freeze and then I remind myself that the hands on me are Ben's hands. I hug him closer, relishing the full length of his body so close to mine. My mind whispers warnings that I'm still a little broken and that no guy—not even Ben—can fix me. It's an inside job. I sense myself falling and tumbling. But this time I'm not ripping down the world with me. This time I'm falling because that's the only way to test my wings.

ACKNOWLEDGMENTS

This is the book of my heart, a story that I was reluctant to write because it would make me feel too vulnerable and yet that demanded to be written. While the book is a work of fiction, it is inspired by truth. The man who mistreated me has been dead for many years. For me, it was after his death that I was able to face head-on what happened and start the hard, but important work of healing. I wrote this book, in part, to give a voice to what happened to me, but also to offer a story to girls who don't yet have a voice, so that they might have hope.

My road to publishing has been a long one and this particular book would not be in your hands if it weren't for the encouragement, support, and work of many people. Roughly in order of how it happened, I extend my deepest thanks and gratitude to the people who contributed in making this particular dream come true:

First and foremost, my husband Tom who has always believed in me. He encouraged me to pursue my dream of writing early on, buying me my first laptop when I wasn't even sure that I had a story to tell. The way that he tackles life inspires me every single day.

My first writing group, the Wonder Women Writers: Carolyn Kuehn, Kath Hubbard, Laura Brennan, Laura Kuhn, and Angela Small for helping me start a regular writing practice. Your critiques and book suggestions, not to mention your wit, kept me motivated. Extra thanks to Kath Hubbard, my very first writing teacher and the person who wrote my recommendation to VCFA. Also, a special thanks to Angela Small who read this book and helped me in my revision.

Vermont College of Fine Arts where I found my people and where I learned how to revise so that when I received my first editorial letter, I was fully prepared. Specifically, I'd like to thank my advisors during my time there: Sharon Darrow, Susan Fletcher, Amanda Jenkins, and Martine Leavitt. My class, the Secret Gardeners, is full of generous, compassionate writers who made my time at VCFA even more spectacular than it would have been.

I'm especially lucky that several Secret Gardeners have become trusted beta readers and loyal friends. My sincere gratitude to Cordelia Jensen for urging me to continue writing this story after I shared an early scene with her. Laurie Morrison Fabius for inspiring me to return to the story when I'd become discouraged. Linda Washington for daily emails in which we cheer each other on and provide support during the difficult bits. Nicole Valentine and Mary Winn Heider for great story talks during road trips to writing retreats.

Lisa Graff not only for beta-reading and encouraging me through the entire process, but for being a reliable "co-worker" in coffee shops in and around Philadelphia. Your advice as I navigated this experience has helped to smooth the process.

My former colleagues in Swarthmore College's Office of Career Services for their friendship and support. A special thanks goes to

Lisa Maginnis, who gave me the permission to write that I didn't know I needed and to Nancy Burkett who has read every one of my manuscripts and supported my decision to attend VCFA, even though it meant leaving our wonderful team.

My mother, Kathy Yeager, who provided a model for being a strong working woman in the world, who built the foundation that allowed me to pursue my dreams, and who loves me no matter what.

My Harley-riding stepfather, Jeff Yeager, for always believing. My sister, Harlan McNew, whom I love to the moon and back and who is always the sunshine in every room she enters.

Over the years as I continued to write, my sons Mitch and Zach grew from grade school boys to whom I read books into college-aged young men with whom I can talk story structure and character development. For this book, Mitch was especially patient with my music-related questions. (His friend Cole Frieman is credited with Ben's music taste and Eli Eisenstein is credited for naming Ben's band.) Both Zach and Mitch continue to be a source of inspiration to me as I watch them move through their lives with determination and courage. I can't wait to see how their stories turn out.

Leda Sportolari for helping me work through my conflicting feelings about writing this book and for helping me process what happened to me.

Roddy von Seldeneck for gamely fielding random questions about rehab and recovery. Kevin Raphael for generously sharing his time to answer legal questions about what happens in Pennsylvania to a teen who gets caught with drugs. Any errors are mine alone.

Brianne Johnson for seeing promise in my manuscript and for

being a fierce advocate for my work and also for answering last-minute questions about throwing clay and creating mosaics. (Yeah, my agent is multi-talented.)

Leila Sales for championing this book early on and for identifying Maggie Rosenthal as the right editor for this book. And, of course, unending gratitude to Maggie for falling in love with Skye's story, helping me make the story deeper and more compelling and for guiding me through my first publishing experience with dedication and compassion.

Thanks to Marinda Valenti for her eagle-eye copyediting, to Dana Li and Agata Wierzbicka for a stunning and perfect cover, Jim Hoover for making the inside match the outside, Tessa Meischeid for helping me get my book into readers' hands, and the whole team at Viking Children's, who took a piece of my heart and molded it into a real book.

RESOURCE FOR SURVIVORS

If you have experienced sexual assault or abuse, you might be unsure how to handle your feelings. Healing won't happen overnight, but you do not need to go through it alone. Reaching out for support can help. If you don't have a person you trust to talk to or if you aren't ready to share what has happened with someone face-to-face, you can contact RAINN for a confidential call or online chat with a trained staff member.

Visit RAINN rainn.org or 1-800-656-HOPE (4673).